BADD WIVES

BADD WIVES

A NOVEL

Zee. W

www.zbookpublishing.com

ZBook Publishing, LLC
P.O. Box 2085
Stone Mountain, GA 30087
www.zbookpublishing.com

ISBN: 1941689000
ISBN 13: 9781941689004
Library of Congress Control Number: 2017910588
Zbook Publishing: **Stone Mountain, Georgia**

Book Cover Design by Marion Designs
www.mariondesigns.com

Dedication

This book is dedicated to my beautiful, talented, loving daughter, Abrianah 'Abri'. You mean the world to me and are my number one inspiration. I did to this to pave the road for you and your talent and to prove that your *gifts will make room for you.* You're a wonderful writer. Keep striving and writing. Pretty soon, you'll be here too, even bigger and stronger than I am. I can't wait for your first novel to drop (smiles). Mommy loves you with all her heart.

— Zee. W

Acknowledgements

would like to thank EVERYONE who encouraged me to stop sitting on all my manuscripts and take matters into my own hands.

A very special, with all my heart, thank you to the most loving, positive, beautiful woman I know: my mother, Emah, Chris Ann. You've been my number one supporter since I was five years old. You read all my stories then and you read them now. Without your constant support, I don't think I'd be here. You truly are the best mother a girl could ask for.

Thanks to my Abah (Father), aka 'Clock-man.' Rest in peace, Abah. Words can't describe how much I miss you. You were excited about my talent and stayed on me to stick with it. You held my first manuscript in your hands like it was gold. I'll never forget how proud you were of me.

Thanks Grandma! You hold such a close place in my heart, I tear up just thinking about how great you are. There really is no one in the world like you and I'm so proud to be your granddaughter. You ruled over my education with an iron fist and a leather belt (smiles). If it weren't for you sacrificing hours of your time and making my education your first priority, I wouldn't have the knowledge and ability to be where I am now.

Thanks to my siblings: Chyah, Hahnah, Beulah Yah'memah, Deborah 'Doie', and Matthew Zadok. You guys were my first fans. You made me feel so special, fighting over the draft of my first manuscript years ago, inspiring me to write more. You discussed my characters with one another like I was already a New York Times bestselling author. Chyah, you cried at the end of *Georgia Red* and those tears still inspire me. Hahnah, you were the first person to encourage me to turn my short stories into novels and the very first person to read my first novel. Memah, you fell madly in love with one of my male characters and still remember him to this day. Deborah, you brag about my books all the time and even shared my makeshift manuscripts with your co-workers. Zadok, you looked over my shoulder when I was writing once and instantly got intrigued by a character. Even after six years, you still remember her name as if she is real. I love you all so much its crazy.

Thanks to Katura Tucker, my first paying customer. She gave me $20 for a sneak peek copy of the Badd Wives manuscript and made me feel on top of the world that day. You have no idea how much your enthusiasm inspires me. And, my old co-worker, Betty Celestian who always ask about my books. I hope you know how much I truly love you. And, Krystal Vance my longest friendship. Thanks for all the love and support; plus the back and forth texting (smiles).

Thank you to my favorite little cousin, Ryco Clark and my teenage nieces, Jyah Nicole and Kaylah Kennedy and my daughter, Abrianah who is always looking over my shoulder as I type.

Thank you to my baby nieces and nephews who are the cutest freaking kids on the universe: Elezar Zadok, Alijah, Roniyah, Maliyah Zeporah, Levi Judah and Tolu. I love you guys!

To all my future fans, thanks for giving me a try! I hope to gain your respect and more ZBooks are on the way!

If I forgot anybody, know that it wasn't intentional and that I love you!

— Zee. W

Prologue

The Day of the Wedding...

"Bobby's dead!"

I thought I heard Taffy scream but wasn't sure. I could have been dreaming. Actually, I had to be dreaming because she couldn't be saying what I thought she was saying. Bobby Badd dead? Yeah right. Not my Bobby. That was unimaginable. Badds didn't get killed and Bobby always told me that he was invincible.

Thunder cracked and the wind gushed. A storm was in the works.

I flipped from one side of the bed to the other and buried my face deep into a pillow. I was in the guest room at my sister-in-law, Taffy's, house. I tossed and turned all night just like I'd been doing every night for the past week whenever I tried to sleep. It was hard to sleep when you were watching your back every second. Bobby had gone back to the city and wasn't here to protect me anymore but he told me not to worry because even if he was a thousand miles away, his fist could still strike a mighty blow. I guess that was supposed to make me feel better and it did but after everything that happened recently, I still was nervous as hell.

I've been staying with Taffy at her mansion on the Badd ranch, the private fifty acre development owned by my husband and his family, while Taffy and my other sister-in-law, Mona, planned my second wedding. Bobby and I got married a few weeks ago but he thought it was best that we keep everything secret until he got other things cleared away. Loving

Bobby should have been easy but it wasn't. Being with him wasn't just about us but the entire Badd family. But, I loved Bobby so much I didn't care. I just wanted to be his wife and, if that meant enduring the other Badd wives for a few more days and his two crazy ass brothers Brock and Brip, then so be it.

When I *publically* married Bobby, then I would officially be part of the Badd family. Bobby was going to inherit a lot of money and his very own stake and mansion on the ranch. But, I wanted nothing to do with any of it. I couldn't imagine living on this ranch. It was going to be like luxurious prison, a fucking loony bin! Lucky for me, after the wedding Bobby decided that we were going to flee the scene just like his brother, Billy and his wife Dalla had done.

I never got to meet Billy or Dalla. They left a year before I met Bobby. After living this life for nine months, I understand why they went MIA. After Bobby brought out the Badd family skeletons, I knew the reason they fled was because they were in danger. The same danger that I felt like me and Bobby were in. Bobby still told me not to worry. Nothing scared Bobby. I was different.

A few weeks ago, Bobby and I had the 'just in case of my death' conversation. He made it seem like it was just a formality but I knew better. He had instructions for me to follow if he died. Where to go. Who to talk to. Who not to talk to and a bunch of other stuff I tried not to think about. I couldn't stand to talk about him dying. If he died, I was just as good as dead. Before he proposed, Bobby asked me if I was sure I wanted to be his wife knowing everything it involved and I said, yes. Literally, a few hours after that, the trials started to come in one after another. And, they hadn't stopped, not even for my second wedding day.

The sound of thunder cracked loudly and I jumped up. It started to rain hard. Not the perfect weather for a wedding. I guess the weather was one thing Mona and Brock couldn't control about this day. I rubbed the sleep out of my eyes and saw Taffy's petite silhouette standing over my bed. What was she doing in my room so early? I guess I hadn't been dreaming when I heard her say something to me. She was probably trying to wake me up for one of her crazy, early morning workouts. Well, I wasn't feeling it today.

Lying back down, I put a pillow on top of my head, hinting for her to leave me the hell alone. It was too damn early and I needed my beauty rest before I had to entertain the crowd of strangers at my big circus wedding that was just a few hours away.

Taffy poked me in the shoulder with her finger. I sighed heavily and propped myself up again, wiping the heavy haze of narcotic induced sleep away from my eyes. She had given me a pill the night before to help me sleep and I took it, not knowing or caring how strong it was. I looked up but it was so dark I could barely see her. I felt her looking at me. She kept wiping her face. If I wasn't mistaken, she was crying.

Naturally, I assumed she was reacting to some sort of fight between her and her husband, Brip who was Bobby's youngest brother. They'd been at each other's throats for weeks. But, I wasn't in the mood to talk. Today was my special day and, just like Bobby said, it needed to be over as quickly as possible.

"Taffy, what's going on? It's too early for this," I sighed.

I managed to swing my feet over the mattress and stumble towards the light. Taffy still didn't say anything. I flicked on the light. Taffy looked horrified and her eyes were bloodshot. Her cheeks glistened with tears. When her cell phone vibrated, she jumped like she'd been stung by a bee. I took the phone out of her hand. It was Mona, the eldest Badd wife. That's when I started to get worried. Mona and Brock was the very people I was watching my back for.

"Why is Mona calling?" I asked nervously

After taking a few deep breaths, Taffy looked at me and sniffed so hard it was like she sucked up all the air from the room. I started to feel like I couldn't breathe. Something was wrong.

She cleared her throat and through a cracked voice blurted out, "Bobby's dead!"

This time I knew I wasn't dreaming. I felt like I got punched in the stomach. I gasped. I was so stunned, I couldn't move. I felt my knees get weak. They started to buckle and my body leaned forward. I was falling. I tried to remember the last time I saw Bobby but I couldn't. I couldn't remember anything. I felt stuck in time. My heart pounded and my stomach tightened. Did she just tell me my husband was dead?

I'd just talked to Bobby on the phone yesterday evening. What was the last thing Bobby said to me? I couldn't remember. Then, I remembered something. It was from the 'just in case of my death' conversation. The conversation I refused to have with him. My head started to swarm and felt light on my neck. As my face got closer and closer to the floor, I felt like I was falling in slow motion. Taffy screamed my name. She was standing right next to me, yet her voice sounded like it was thousands of miles away. Bobby had told me to run if he died! But it was too late now. I wasn't running but falling.

I passed out.

Nine Months Earlier...

The sun came out so suddenly it was as if it had never been raining at all. I was sitting in my office at the L-Peters club, balancing the books. I got up from behind my cluttered spread of paperwork to look out the window. That's when I noticed a black Hummer parked outside, right next to my BMW.

The club wasn't opening until the evening. I didn't know who the black Hummer belonged to but before I could start to guess, there was a loud tap on my office door. It startled me. I had made sure all the entrance doors to the club were locked, just like I always did when I was alone. Who could have gotten inside? I was the only one with the key.

Another tap followed the first one. I didn't know what to do. I could have run but where would I have gone? In my closet? That wouldn't get me far and the window wasn't big enough for me to climb out. There was another tap. This time louder and more aggressive than the first two. Then, the door knob started to turn. Luckily, it was locked. At least I thought I was lucky. I heard keys jingling before the locked clicked and the door slowly creaked open. I couldn't move. When the door opened wide enough, I couldn't believe who was walking through it. wondered if I was dreaming.

He walked through the door with stride, holding a single key in his hand, looking directly at me. It had been a year since I had last seen him at the L-Bar and, that time, he barely looked at me. I had just moved to

Memphis from Detroit and was working as a waitress when he and a group of his flunkies came in the club and held down the VIP section all night. I did everything to try and get his attention but still, he insisted on treating me like I was invisible. I had never been the type of girl that turned flips just to get a man to notice me. I didn't have too. My perfect hourglass figure and bedroom eyes were enough, but not for Bobby.

There was something about him that intrigued me. I was completely infatuated with him by the end of the night. Maybe it was the way he moved. So subtle and cool. He had swag for days and it wasn't that phony ass swag most male imposters tried to perpetrate after watching gangster movies or rap videos. It was natural. He didn't talk much that night. He just slowly sipped his Grey Goose and ginger ale and searched every corner of the club with a watchful eye. At the end of the night, he tipped me with a hundred dollar bill. Instead of taking the money, I wrote my name and number on top of it and scooted it back into his hand. He looked at me like I was crazy and put the money back in his pocket. He never called. I waited for him to call every day for a year up until now. And, the nights I couldn't sleep, I fantasized about him touching me in places that aroused me until I put myself to sleep. Now he was here in my office.

Bobby kept his eyes fixed in my direction but he wasn't giving me a flattering look. He was about business. My heart raced, trying to juggle the mixed emotions of fear and excitement. I was happy to see him again but didn't know what he wanted or how it involved me. If he wanted a date, this was a weird way to ask me.

Shying away from his gaze, I nervously tossed my locks from one side of my shoulder to the other while looking down at the floor like it harbored an emergency exit. Thankfully, I looked good sporting my short, form-fitting white strapless dress and basket colored stiletto heels.

After what felt like hours of intimidating stares, Bobby finally spoke. I literally trembled inside at the echo of his deep voice. It was the first time I had heard him speak. When I served him as a waitress, he only whispered what he wanted to one of his flunky friends and they placed his order for him.

I had spent so many nights wondering what his voice sounded like. Now I knew.

"What's up, Lera Way?" He said my name like he knew me. "I'm glad to see you done moved up in life," Bobby raised his chin in my direction. "From flipping drinks to flipping bills, huh?"

"I guess you can say that," I replied, trying to keep a straight face. "So, Lenny gave you a key to my office?"

Lenny Peters was the club owner I worked for. He owned half the nightclubs in Memphis and I had convinced him to let me do promotions for his club. It quickly turned into a management position and, just recently, some sort of partnership that allowed me to take a certain percentage from the door.

The tension in Bobby's face relaxed as he laughed at my theory like it was ludicrous. "Nah…he didn't need to give me this key."

"Really…." I said sarcastically, "So, you some kind of key making magician?"

"Something like that," Bobby said seriously "I got a key to every building in this city," He shrugged. "That way, I'm never locked out. You know what I mean?"

I shrugged my shoulders. "Not really but I guess you're not here to tell me. What's up, Bobby?" I said to him, purposely letting him know I knew his name. The night I served him, I heard one of his friends say his name and I made mental note of it.

His eyes widened a bit, but he didn't seem too impressed. "You know that song from Cheers, *sometimes you want to go where everybody knows you name*, well…that's me all day, all states….everybody knows my name."

"How can I help you, Bobby?"

Bobby smiled at me again. This time it was more natural. He spread his thick lips wide, revealing his masculine, pearly white teeth. When he smiled, a large dimple appeared in the center of his chin, lighting up his face. His sexiness was killing me and I didn't know how much more of him I could take with a straight face and dry panties.

He walked over to my desk and took a seat on the corner. He analyzed me from head to toe. If he liked what he was seeing, I couldn't tell. He kept a straight face. "It ain't so much you I got business wit. It's your man," he said.

I assumed he was referring to Lenny.

"My man?" I think you mean my business partner who just so happens to be a man, right?"

Bobby shrugged his shoulders like it didn't make any difference to him one way or the other. "Whatever…whoever…let's just call him that nigga who got my money. I gave him enough time and Lenny knows I say what I mean and that I only say it once."

He gave me a look that was so intense, I shook. That still didn't stop him from being sexy. Hell, it even added to it all in a kinky kind of way.

I stared back at him curious about what type of shit Lenny had gotten himself into. But still, it had nothing to do with me. I didn't care to deal with any of Lenny's debt collectors.

"Look, Bobby," I softened my voice. I walked around my desk to give him a better look. I watched his eyes lead quickly from my legs, then back up to my eyes. It was a short look, but I took what I could get. "I'm sorry Lenny did bad business with you, but that don't have a thing to do with me. I can give you his number so you can call him directly."

"Word around town is that you handle his money."

"Dealing with you is just like dealing with Lenny. Besides, I'm just here for you to give him a message, that's all."

I watched Bobby curiously with my right eyebrow raised.

"Tell Lenny that when I gave him that money, I meant what I said and I'm only gone say it once."

I shook my head. "You got a better way to translate your parable?"

"Nope" Bobby got up and walked in my direction. The closer he got to me, the fainter I felt. Leaning in close to my ear he whispered, "he know the deal."

Bobby turned around and walked out the door without giving me a second look.

I watched him walking through the parking lot from my office window. He walked like he owned it. He pulled a piece of gum out of his pocket and pushed it in his mouth before discarding the wrapper over his shoulder. When he got close enough to his Hummer, a tall, heavy set dude hopped out the driver's seat and opened the back door for him. Before Bobby got in the car, he looked around the parking lot and then back at my window. I almost bumped my head on the window sill trying to duck so he couldn't see me. I heard the tires screech and, when I looked back up, they were gone.

enny wasn't answering his phone. I must have called him a dozen times and left him messages. That wasn't like Lenny. Bobby wasn't the only person Lenny owed money to. I loaned him the ten thousand dollars I got from my mother's life insurance policy after she died. That money bought my way into the flakey partnership we have and got Lenny out of trouble with the IRS. He promised me a hundred percent rate of return on my money, but I haven't gotten it back yet.

However, it's impossible to owe somebody money who balances your books. Little by little, I paid myself back and I kept the money in a safe that I hid in the closet of my office. Whenever Lenny decided to pay me back, I'll politely replace the money. I was no thief.

Lenny only stayed a few miles from the club so I decided to drive to his house to personally deliver Bobby's message. I don't know why I felt propelled to get myself so involved in his bullshit but I had a strange feeling something serious was going down and it gave me the chance to get a better idea of who Bobby was.

Before I left the club, I made sure my office door was locked, not that it mattered since Bobby had the key. I tiptoed out the front door, casing the parking lot; it was still empty. I tried to call Lenny again for the twentieth time but still kept getting his voicemail. I pulled out the parking lot and headed towards Beale Street. Lenny owned a loft downtown a few blocks from where I rented a condo. Both our places overlooked the city and at night, the views were spectacular.

When I passed by my building, I saw a black Hummer parked out front. I wasn't sure if it was Bobby or not, but it looked like the same car. I couldn't see through the tinted glass windows, so I kept driving.

When I got to Lenny's place, no one answered his door. That's when the concierge guy told me that Lenny had packed up and left the other night, but Lenny hadn't said anything to me about going out of town. I had a feeling Lenny's disappearance had something to do with Bobby. If something strange was going on with the club, I needed to know. Without Lenny I was out of a job and my future business plans where shot.

On that note, I decided to go back to my office to get my safe. I would hate for my money to get tied up in Lenny's mess. That money was all I had.

Once I got back to the L-Peters club, I saw a small group of men huddled outside the front door and someone had put up a sign that said closed until further notice. I chose not to pul into the parking lot. I didn't want to bring any attention to myself but I had to get inside to recover my safe.

It was going on 7 p.m. and the sun was just starting to set. I parked my car a few blocks away from Lenny's second club, "The L-Review", a strip club and walked towards the club by foot. I wondered what the hell was going on. I had talked to Lenny a few days ago and he sounded fine. Usually, when Lenny got stressed, he whined and pouted like a baby. He never once mentioned anything about Bobby.

I hid behind another building and peeked around the corner at the club. About four guys was standing outside the front door sipping from bottles of liquor that they had stolen from the bar and throwing dice just like they were at a block party. I could hear them laughing all the way from where I was standing. I recognized one of the guys from the day I served Bobby. I noticed him from the way he wore his hair in long dread locks tied behind his head. He was a real asshole but I had a feeling he was Bobby's right hand man. There was no sign of Bobby. They were so preoccupied that they didn't notice when I swept past them and towards the back of the building near the storage room entrance.

We used the room to stack inventory and cleaning supplies. The room was about the size of a four car garage and was full of cases of liquor and a few catering supplies we used during our happy hour buffet. Usually, the storage room was kept pretty neat but not after Bobby's friends got to it. Cases of liquor were torn opened and emptied out.

Because my office was across the hall from the storage room, I figured it would be easy to run in, grab my safe and run out. But, it was actually easier than that because as soon as I slipped through the door, the first thing I noticed was my safe sitting on top of a box.

Tip-toeing across the concrete floor, I listened for any other movements. I didn't hear anything; only the sounds of my muffled breathing and beating heart. The thick metal plated safe was dented. There was a screw driver stuck inside the key hole; it looked like they were having a hard time trying to get it open. They must have tried everything to open it, including throwing it against the concrete a few times like it was a basketball but lucky for me, their attempts didn't work.

Once I felt the coast was clear, I grabbed a garbage bag from one of the shelves and commenced to open the lock with my key. When the safe popped open, I emptied all the cash in the garbage bag. When I finished, I locked it and turned to run out the back door, but I didn't have enough time to get out. I heard the voices of the men coming, so I dove behind a stack of boxes to hide.

A crowd of guys huddled in the storage room. The one with dreads led the way. One of them was so drunk, he staggered and stumbled around. They all started going through different boxes like they were hunting for buried treasure. The drunk one pulled out a bottle of Scotch and eagerly twisted off the cap. They looked like they were having a pretty good time with all the laughing and heckling. You would have thought they were on an all-expense paid vacation and I guess they kind of were.

"Jayson…" The drunk one said to the guy with the dreads and held up another bottle of liquor like he was giving him a peace offering. "What?" he said back to Jayson when he turned up his nose at his drunk friend's selection.

"Man, just find me some beer…and not that cheap shit either. I want something imported," Jayson barked.

His friend shook his head before he started to shuffle through scattered boxes, looking for Jayson's special request.

"And hurry up, Bobby gone be here any minute man. Hey, where is the safe?" Jayson yelled.

"I…I…left it right were you had it," the drunk guy stuttered, pointing in the direction of the safe.

Jayson walked over to it and lifted it up before slamming it back down.

"Damn! Shit won't open for nothing!" Jayson was frustrated.

"I bet you I can get that shit open man," one of the guys in the crew said walking up to Jayson.

He picked up the safe and threw it on the ground so hard it made a startling noise. The men started to laugh as the guy kicked the safe across the floor towards his drunken friend like it was a soccer ball. The drunk friend kicked it towards another guy and they kept going until everybody had a turn to kick the safe. The men must have been bored because they were too easily entertained. So much in fact, they didn't notice Bobby slowly walking in and observing their childlike behavior with a stern eye.

Shaking his head at his buffoonish crew, he looked at them and back at his I-phone a few times before saying anything. Then, he spoke. "Aye!" his voice echoed so loud in the storage room, I heard it at least four times before it stopped.

They almost jumped out of their skins. Jayson more so than any of them. Jayson straightened up his posture like he was the mature one, looking at the other guys, rolling his eyes.

"Come on yall," he said shaking his head like he had nothing to do with all the silliness going on.

The men watched Bobby like he was their lieutenant. Some of them looked frightened. The drunk one tried to hide the half empty bottle of Scotch behind his back while the others stepped away from the boxes like they had never touched them.

"What the hell, man? Yall got some kinda party going on back here or something? Yall dudes decided yall ain't gone work today?" He was stern.

"Nah, Bobby…it ain't like that. We got everything done early so I just let the guys shoot back and have a few," Jayson tried to explain.

Bobby gave Jayson a dismissive nod before saying in a demanding tone, "Where my money?"

"Oh," Jayson almost jumped out of his skin, diving for the safe that was lodged in between a cluster of boxes. "Here you go!" Jayson said proudly.

Bobby looked down at the safe and then back up at Jayson. "I asked for my money, not no damn metal box with a lock on it!" Bobby said harshly. "What the hell I'm gone do with that? You ain't open this shit yet?"

Bobby took a deep breath before sitting on top of the desk we used to count inventory. He propped his legs in a chair, leaned his back against the wall, pulled out his cell phone and started texting. The men watched him quietly, barely moving.

When Bobby looked up, Jayson chimed in quick. "I got my man coming up here, you remember the dude I was telling you about from Reno, Red Mike? The one that took that bank back in Vegas for half a mil. Man, this dude is the truth. He can pick any lock and open any combination. When I told him who he was doing the favor for he agreed to fly down right away. He'll be here soon, man. I promise."

"Red Mike?" Bobby said looking up at the air. "I don't know no Red Mikes? He took a Vegas bank for half a mil?"

"Yeah…man! And a few others,"

"Hmm…is he a member?"

"Yeah, man. Of course! He been a member for a year now."

"He pay his taxes?" Bobby asked setting his attention back on the phone.

"Yeah man…everybody pay they taxes," Jayson answered half laughing, shaking his head. "At least if they smarter than this Lenny dude they do."

"I ain't waiting here no more than half an hour, then I'm gone. I got a plane to catch. If he don't show up today, then yall dudes gone stay here until he do!"

"He gone show man, I promise,"

The other guys were so quiet, I almost forgot they were in the room. Some stood in the corner silently, avoiding any contact with Bobby while a few others took seats on top of some of the boxes waiting for Bobby's next command. The room was starting to get so hot, I couldn't take it anymore. I wanted to run out the door but I wasn't banking on my running skills and feared I'd be hunted down by Bobby's men before I even got out the parking lot. Although I wasn't in plain sight, I still was nervous that one of the men would stray to the back and find me hiding.

About twenty minutes later, Jayson's cell phone rang. Bobby watched Jayson as he answered the phone like he was a part of an unofficial conference call. "It's him now, man. It's Red Mike...see I told you he would come through. He pulling up now, Pooh" Jayson said to one of the men, "go meet him out front and lead him to the back. We'll be out of this town soon man...I promise," Jayson assured Bobby.

Bobby didn't seem thrilled or convinced He gave Jayson an aggravated look. Jayson and the rest of the men looked like they were holding their breath, waiting on Red Mike.

"How you find that shit anyway?" Bobby asked, looking at the safe.

"Let's just say I'm resourceful," Jayson said. "I'd been casing that bitch for bout a year. Got that office lit up with cameras and everything."

Bobby checked his Rolex every other second and just when it looked like his patience was about to run out, in walked Pooh with a high yellow, red-headed average built man who I assumed was Red Mike.

The first thing Red Mike did was greet Bobby with a handshake like he was paying homage to a saint. Bobby barely looked at him and, when Red Mike started talking too much, Bobby shot Jayson a look.

Jayson stepped in, shutting Red Mike up. "Here go the safe, man. We need this done quick. We kind of in a rush." Red Mike grabbed the safe, lifted it into the air and analyzed it from front to back.

"Why is it so dinged up? I hope yall didn't think you were going to get it open by throwing it against the wall," Red Mike said to Jayson with a chuckle.

Jayson shot Bobby a fearful look."Man, just get it open for us so my man can be on his way. He got a plane to catch."

Red Mike looked at Bobby, then back at Jayson before pulling something out his pocket.

"Hold up man," Jayson said, storming towards Red Mike. Red Mike held his hands high in the air like he was surrendering. "Pooh, you pat him down?"

"Yeah, he clear," Pooh said with a brief head nod.

Red Mike didn't move. He kept his hands up until Jayson gave him the okay to continue on. Then, he transformed into a more professional crook, pulling out a small billfold with little needle-like instruments inside. "This one right here will do the trick," he said pulling out a short needle that looked like a hair pen.

"You sure man? That look a little thin?" Jayson asked.

"Trust me. This is my special collection. I made them myself. I know this stuff," Red Mike told Jayson.

A few seconds later, the safe was open. Bobby looked relieved. He leaped off the desk and toward the safe. Jayson tried to lift the lid on the safe but Bobby snatched it out of his hand, slightly shoving him to the side. When he flung open the box and saw it was empty, I could see flames sparkling behind his eyes and so did, Jayson.

Jayson stepped back and yelled, "What the hell!" like he'd been duped. "Man something ain't right? I know it was money in that box," he defended himself.

"How the hell you know that? You got special abilities to see through metal!"

"Come on, Bobby," Jayson said in a pleading tone. "I've been casing the brod. She been putting cash in there."

"You sure about that?"

"Yes, I'm sure. I...I don't understand," Jayson stuttered. "I even shook the box and I heard shit moving around. It don't make sense!" Jayson was dumbfounded.

"Where the hell is the money, then?" Bobby demanded, getting closer to Jayson.

At that point, I decided to come out of hiding. I don't know what moved me to do it. Maybe it was the heat or the weary feeling of being stuck without an exit plan. They were going to find me no matter what. I stepped out from behind the boxes, holding my bag of money in one hand and matches and a small tube of lighter fluid I grabbed from one of the shelves in the other. The matches and fluid were my only means of protection. If I had too, in order to protect myself, I would burn the money; holding it as ransom was my only way out.

"If you really want to know where the money is...," I announced myself boldly catching them all off guard. They all jumped like they seen a ghost. Everybody except Bobby. Jayson was so startled he stepped back and almost tripped over the empty safe. He immediately regained his composure, looking back at Bobby hopping he didn't notice how spooked he was but by the way Bobby was scouring at him, he did. I stood my ground, clutching on to the bag of money like it was my life. I kept my eye fixed on Bobby. "Maybe you should consult with its rightful, owner." I continued.

"I knew something was wrong! This bitch is shady as hell and need to be handled!" Jayson yelled in rage. Jayson started charging towards me like a bull. Before I had a chance to duck, he grabbed the back of my neck and attempted to push me to the ground, but before he could make his move, Bobby grabbed him and pushed him to the ground so hard, his body bounced off the concrete.

"What the hell is your problem?" Bobby yelled before shooting me a quick look. He seemed concerned.

"Man, I was just doing my job," Jayson said getting back up from the ground, smoothing down his pants. He was so embarrassed he barely made eye contact with me.

"Everybody get the fuck out and close the door behind you! Wait for me outside." Bobby dictated.

Everyone scattered from the room like roaches under the light. They closed the door behind them and then we were alone. The power behind his eyes was intimidating as he stared at me with a look I couldn't read.

"Is that my money in that bag?" Bobby asked.

"No," I replied, gripping the bag tighter. I still had the matches and fluid in my hand. I struck a match.

Bobby smirked. "What you doing with that?"

"I don't know yet...that depends on you."

"Me," Bobby said, stabbing himself in the chest with his finger. I nodded my head. Leaning back on his left leg, Bobby looked at me like he was trying to read my mind. After a deep breath he said, "I need my money," holding out his hand like he was tired of playing games.

"So do I," I answered back, slowly stepping away from him. He followed me with the same slow steps. "This money is mine! And, I'm not gone let you take it. Are you gone let me walk out of here with it?" Bobby shook his head no. "So, I guess you can call your boy back in here to attack me!"

"Ain't nobody here gone touch you!" Bobby assured me quickly.

I was taken aback by the sudden bass in his voice and the anger. With the protective look he was giving me, I almost jumped in his arms like he was my knight in shining armor. Was Bobby really concerned about me? Where was this coming from?

"Lenny owes me a lot of money. I loaned it to him a few years ago and its pay up time. You say that this money is yours but if you swiped it from him, you really swiped it from me.

"Lenny did all that shady shit behind my back. I was smart enough to keep the cash that I worked hard to make and I'm not going to let you take it."

"You know the saying finders keepers, losers weepers." Bobby said to me, half smiling. He started to walk in circles around me. He looked me up and down, checking me out like I was an item for sale.

"You've heard the saying, If I can't have you, nobody can," I asked him. He smiled back at me like I was amusing him. "Well, that's the kind of relationship I have with my money. If I can't have it," I struck another match and waved the flame over the garbage bag, "nobody can."

Bobby continued to walk in circles around me like I was his prey. I turned my body, following him. The stern look on his face softened and I no longer felt threatened.

"Well...we got a problem here? How we gone resolve it?"

I shrugged my shoulders.

"Well...I'm not letting you leave with the money" Bobby informed me in a matter-of-fact tone.

"Okay, then I won't leave with the money," I said, turning over the garbage bag and emptying the contents on to the ground.

Bobby looked down at the money and then back up at me. He looked at me like he was calling my bluff but I wasn't bluffing. I was going to burn that money and to prove it I started to douse it with lighter fluid. Bobby didn't budge. He just watched me like I was putting on a show.

"You're really gone make me do this?" I asked, preparing to light the match.

"I'm not making you do a thing. You can just leave it right here if you want to," Bobby said sarcastically.

I shook my head at him before striking another match. I kissed the inside of my hand, pointed it towards Bobby's face but blew the kiss downward in the direction of the money. Then, I dropped the match. Flames started to swarm around the bills.

Shocked, Bobby looked at me with wide eyes and a weird grin.

I started to back away from him slowly but he followed me.

"What are you gone do to me? There ain't no law against burning your own property." I took slow steps backward.

The flame started to get taller.

"Law? Whose law you talking about, girl? Where I'm from, I am the law."

"Really? You're the law? Where do you have jurisdiction? Hood County?"

Bobby's face softened as he laughed a bit, genuinely amused by my wit.

I continued to walk backward until I hit a brick wall. Then, I was nose to nose with Bobby. Barricading me in with his perfectly shaped arms, I couldn't move and I really didn't want to. I was so close to him, I could feel the warmth of his lips. I had to control myself from plastering my mouth against his. I extended my breast a bit, dusting my nipples against his chest, creating an electrifying friction between us.

Bobby leaned in to me and whispered loud, "You got a smart ass mouth."

"I know…it gets straight A's," I quipped, inducing another smile from him. "So, what are you going to do with me?" I asked boldly, leaning even closer to him. "Are you going to shoot me?"

"Shoot you with what?" Bobby said pressing his body closer into mine. "I'm not armed."

In a sick way, I kind of found the whole thing to be romantic. We had a flame going behind us and were alone in a dimly lit room.

We watched each other in silence. Finally, I had Bobby's attention but I didn't know what to do with it.

Saved by the bell, Jayson burst through the door after smelling the smoke trail from underneath the threshold.

"Something on fire. Bobby!" he stormed in the room like he was a special rescue agent. Turning around, Bobby addressed Jayson with a threatening look like he was interrupting a private moment.

Jayson didn't say anything else; he knew he'd made a mistake bursting in the way he did. He turned around and walked out the door but while Bobby was intimidating Jayson with mean looks, I had a chance to slip away and I took it.

I was able to duck and free myself from the cage Bobby had me trapped in with his arms. I ran straight for the door that led to the back of the parking lot. I was running so fast, I didn't notice I was almost five blocks away from the L-Bar. I ran straight past my car, forgetting all about it in the heat of the moment. I stepped into a dark alley to catch my breath.

It was okay when Bobby was a fantasy but now that reality was starting to set in, I didn't think I could deal. I was in love with a sexy, dangerous stranger and out of ten grand. Shit!

3

"Another shot of Jager," I told the bartender through a huff. He turned around to fix my drink but I stopped him. "Two shots," I corrected myself.

I was about five blocks from the L-Bar at another bar, ironically called Insanity. I had to clear my mind. I'd been hiding out and nursing shots of Jager for two hours now. Too much was happening, too quickly. I didn't know what the hell I was going to do without any money or a job.

I had left Detroit and came to Memphis for a change but I wasn't expecting all of this, or Bobby. I could still smell his cologne lingering on my dress. He was so close to me, I could feel his heart beat. When the bartender brought my shots, I took one of them half way down and rubbed my eyes. Why did I run? I guess there was nothing else for me to do. Maybe he was going to kill me for burning that money. Or maybe not. I took the rest of the shot down and then started to wonder if I ruined my chances of ever seeing him again. Then I felt crazy for even thinking it. The man could be a threat to me, sexy or not.

I wasn't the type that believed in love at first sight. It was a ridiculous and a childish notion. But, now I understand it. It does exist and the feeling is surreal. There was something within me that connected with Bobby and it was deeper than lust. I sighed heavy and reached for my second shot while plotting my next move. I definitely wasn't going home. I figured I'd hide out in this bar for a few hours before checking myself into hotel.

I swallowed the last shot whole. My head started to spin but it wasn't the Jager. It was my mixed emotions. Whatever type of business Bobby was in, it was serious and obviously off the books. He had to be somebody important. I could tell by the way he carried himself. His men treated him like a king. I wondered if I could ever be his queen. It was annoying thinking about Bobby more than my money but I couldn't help it. For some reason, nothing else mattered.

Looking down at my watch, I figured enough time had passed for it to be safe for me to walk back to my car. I paid the bartender from the last bit of loose cash I had in my pocket and walked out the door. Now, I had no more than 70 bucks; it was just enough for a one night stay in a hotel. After that, I was up shit's creek.

I walked down the crowded streets. Luckily for me, I was able to blend in with the crowd of partygoers. But, I wasn't so sure I didn't want to be found. All I could think about was how I got my ass caught up in some shit this messy and dangerous. Just a few days ago, I was striking through days on my calendar, exciting myself for being closer to my goal of owning my own club. Now, I'm running for my life and having crazy fantasies about a man who wants no more from me than to kill me; I think.

I spotted my Black BMW on the opposite side of the street. It passed right by me. I knew it was my car because the back bumper had a dent in it from when I ran into a pole while trying to park. Whoever was driving my car must have noticed me too because it slowed down, before reversing and making a sharp u-turn. Before I had a chance to run, someone grabbed me from behind, pushing me toward the on-coming car. When I turned, I saw Jayson.

"Get your hands off of me" I screamed.

I trusted Bobby but I didn't trust him.

"Shut up, bitch! You got somewhere to be and I'm kind enough to give your ass curbside service," Jayson grunted.

The car pulled up to the curb. Jayson swung the door open and threw me inside. He switched places with Pooh who had been in the driver's seat.

I tried to open the door from the inside but the child lock was on. Jayson sped off like he'd just robbed a bank. Cars honked and cursed at us as Jayson cut them off on the road. He responded to their ranting by shooting them his middle finger and pressing down on the horn. Giving me evil stares from the rear view mirror, Jayson was surprisingly quiet. They both were.

"Where in the hell are you taking me?" I demanded to know but Jayson just ignored me like I wasn't even talking. "Look you moron; tell me where the hell you're taking me!" I said while pounding and kicking the driver's seat.

I could tell I was pissing him off by the way he was biting his bottom lip but he still didn't say a word. I kicked the seat a second time. His head jerked like my kick had given him whiplash. That's when he spun around with his hand raised in the air, but Pooh grabbed it.

"What you doing man?" Pooh warned.

Jayson yanked his arm away from Pooh, cutting me an exasperated look.

I gave Jayson my middle finger and continued to taunt him. "You hit the ground pretty hard tonight? Did it hurt?"

Jayson's brown skin turned pale and I could see the tension start to build up in his shoulders as his chest swelled with the anger he couldn't dispel.

"I didn't know a big sack of shit could bounce so perfectly," I said through a laugh.

Pooh chuckled.

That's when Jayson boxed him in the shoulder. "Shut the fuck up man!" he warned him.

Pooh wiped the smirk off his face while straightening up his posture. Jayson put an end to the taunting by turning up the stereo, blocking out my insults.

Sitting in the backseat, I was more anxious than scared and I even felt safe. I knew Bobby wasn't trying to hurt me. If it was okay for Jayson to hit me, he would have done so already. It was killing Jayson that he couldn't put his pathetic hands on me and I got comfort in knowing that Bobby had given that order.

About half an hour into the ride, Jayson's phone rang. He swerved into the next lane, turned the volume down and talked like he had a lump in his throat. "We...will be there soon, man. Everything is good."

A few minutes later, we pulled off the highway onto some back road. It looked like we were driving deep into the middle of nowhere. The road wasn't paved; the car bounced up and down as it crushed the rocks and gravel beneath it. We passed fields full of cows, horses and hay. With the exception of the farm animals, there wasn't any sign of real life around us.

The tires kicked up dirt, creating a huge blinding brown fog of dust all around the car. I could barely see through the window but there was nothing much to see anyway. Just plain open fields of grass and dirt. We finally got to a tiny wooden house that sat in the center of a huge space of land. Bobby's Hummer was parked in front. A few miles from the house I saw a small plane parked in the open field.

We pulled up in front of the house. Jayson opened my door and gently escorted me out the car like everything was all good between us. I let him pretend because I was too distracted by the idea of seeing Bobby again. My heart was pumping so fast I'm sure I was burning calories just by standing there. Composing myself, I took long deep breaths until my nerves started to die down. Then, I followed Jayson up the lopsided steps. The other men stayed behind, standing outside of the car like they were waiting on an order.

When we got inside, Jayson barely stepped a foot inside the house. He opened the door and nudged me inside. The inside of the house was empty. The walls were open and not divided off into sub-rooms. The only furniture was a round wood table; on top of the table was a black duffle bag. A folding chair was behind the table.

I heard heavy footsteps that I knew belonged to Bobby coming down a short dark hallway. My legs trembled as I waited for his sexy physique to step into the light and when he did, my heart melted just as if I were seeing him for the first time.

Bobby stared back at me without saying a word. He watched me with his big eyes looking me up and down like he was inspecting me for damages. Taking a seat in the chair behind the table, Bobby pushed the duffle bag to the side so he could get a better view of me. He propped his legs up on the table and leaned back in the chair, continuing to silently stare at me while scratching the bottom of his chin.

"So, you steal my money then my car," I used my fingers to count, "and now you kidnap me, bringing me all the way out in the middle of nowhere and all you can do is stare at me?"

He smiled at me, nodding his head. "Yeah…I like this view."

"Enjoy it while you can."

He chuckled like what I said was cute. Every time Bobby flashed me a smile, revealing that single dimple sitting in the center of his chin, my panties got wet.

"So what are we going to do? Waste time staring at each other or are you going to tell me what you want?" I said it like I was in control and Bobby seemed to like it.

I flashed Bobby an anxious smile that I could no longer conceal. I think I knew what he wanted. I just had to hear him ask for it. I walked over to the table to get closer to Bobby. I traced my hands on top of the duffle bag like I was rubbing Bobby's chest, keeping my eyes on his. "You going somewhere?" I asked softly.

"Yeah…any minute now," Bobby said pointing his finger over his shoulder towards the small plane.

"Well…what are you waiting for? Me to give you some kind of going away party," I joked.

Bobby didn't laugh. "No."

He stood up.

"What do you need then?" I asked flirtatiously.

"Just you," Bobby finally confessed.

My heart raced with excitement and my demeanor softened up so much I felt like mush. He wanted me and apparently was going through major measures to get me. I guess he didn't know he didn't have to do any of that to pull me. I was game from the first day I saw him.

"Me?" I asked bashfully, pointing at my chest while hardly making eye contact with him.

I didn't want him to see how weak I was for him but that was hard to hide.

Bobby came from behind the table and stood in front of me, staring down at me like I was some kind of rare flower he was ready to pick and put in a fancy vase. He nodded, grabbed the duffle bag and threw it at my feet before lowering to unzip it. There were neatly stacked bills inside. I was wowed to see all that money but tried my best not to look at it too hard. I didn't want Bobby getting the impression that the money was more interesting than him because it wasn't.

"I'm about to head out on this plane and the reason I brought you hear was to offer you this," he said scooting the bag closer to me with his foot. "I'm sure it's more than the money you burnt."

"You giving me a loan?" I said a little disappointed. I wanted more.

"No... no loan. I'm just replacing what you lost," he told me. He got up and stood in front of me.

"Why? You don't strike me as a guy that does anything for free."

"You right," Bobby said with an aggressive head nod, "I don't do shit for free but I'm gone make an exception for you," he said, grabbing one of my locks and twirling it around his masculine finger. I leaned into his touch. "And this ain't no money for me. Hell, I wash my windows with this," he said kicking the bag with his foot like it was nothing. "The money is yours if you want it but I got a little proposition for you."

My heart raced with anticipation. What could Bobby be offering me? He studied my face like he was trying to detect what I was thinking. Then he asked me. "You can take the money and go or you can roll with me?"

I didn't answer right away because I wanted to be sure I was hearing right. "Where are we going?"

"To infinity and beyond," he winked at me.

"Seriously, though? I don't have any clothes and what about my car?"

Bobby gave me a serious look. "Your car will be fine and I'm gone get you all new stuff. You rolling with me or not?"

"You sure you want me to leave with you?" I needed to be sure.

"Look," Bobby said sternly, "I mean what I say and I only say it once. So what you gone do?"

Leaning over to zip back up the bag, Bobby threw it back over the table like it weighed nothing. I watched the money and then Bobby again. I knew he wasn't going to ask me twice and I wasn't going to be a fool and let him. Besides, I needed a change of atmosphere and I had no family connections. My mother died of a heart attack the year before I moved to Memphis and my father had been MIA since my birth. I had no other family. There was no reason for me not to go and I never turned down the opportunity to have a good time. I had a feeling that hanging with Bobby was going to be an adventure.

"I'm gonna roll with you," I said, like I just won the grand prize. Bobby smiled back at me, nodding his head in agreement.

I had a strange feeling I wasn't going to return to Memphis or my life as I knew it.

4

When the plane landed, Bobby whispered in my ear, *welcome to Miami*. My eyes lit up with excitement. I loved everything about the beach; being near the water and feeling grains of sand in between my toes was my nirvana. And, to experience it all with Bobby, was going to make it even better.

The city was beautiful. It had a modern appeal without sacrificing its natural beauty. The massive blue ocean, sea breeze, palm tree laced streets and sky scraping buildings was like Manhattan meets Hawaii. I loved it. The plane landed at a stop much like the one we were at earlier; a small concrete house sitting in the middle of nowhere. A black Hummer was waiting for us in the driveway. It looked just like the one from Memphis but I knew it couldn't be. The driver opened the door for us and Bobby handed him the duffle bag of money. He placed the money in the back-seat of the car before pulling off.

The sun was going to rise in a few hours I wanted to get somewhere quick so I could shower and spruce up a bit. Bobby said we were going to be staying at a beach house that was so close to the ocean that it was practically in the water, but it wasn't going to be ready for another two days. Feeling the Miami heat swoop under my dress and wrap itself around my body, I was ready to cool down in the ocean with Bobby.

We checked into a hotel.

The hotel wasn't any hotel but a penthouse that had a breathtaking view which showcased the entire city and the surrounding ocean. I was wowed.

Bobby smiled at me "You like?"

I nodded my head. The place was so chic I didn't care to see the beach house. I took a shower and wrapped myself in a satin bathrobe that was hanging in the bathroom. On our way up to the room, I picked up a few tropical colored sarong dresses from the lobby hotel. That way, I wouldn't feel so fashionably destitute. They really weren't my style but were sure to hug my hips and ass. Besides, other than the clothes I arrived in, they were all I had until the new clothes I ordered online, while on the plane, came in. Bobby handed me his Black card and told me to knock myself out.

When I came out the bathroom, Bobby was looking under the mattress, examining closets and casing the entire penthouse as if we weren't alone. I thought what he was doing was weird but I didn't say anything. The sun was just starting to rise. It shone brightly through the windows. Bobby pushed a button and drapes fell over the windows, blocking off the light just as if it was midnight. I spread out on the California king sized mattress. The penthouse was open and there was only one bed. I assumed Bobby was going to join me but, instead, he pulled out the couch bed and made himself comfortable.

"What are you doing?" I asked sheepishly.

"Getting a few hours rest," he grunted under his breath. "When we get up, we'll have a late breakfast or an early lunch," Bobby said without turning around to face me.

"You don't have to sleep there you know," I added.

"I know," he told me in a matter of fact tone.

I respected Bobby for placing his boundaries. I didn't want our whole adventure together to make me feel like an overpriced prostitute or glorified groupie but that didn't stop me from wanting him.

———

We slept through breakfast so decided to have a late lunch. We ended up at some upscale restaurant not too far from the hotel with a name too fancy for me to pronounce. We sat at a tabled covered in white linen with a small candle on top of it. There were two white roses wrapped in purple tissue paper lying across the table. I lifted the flowers like they were precious and fragile, sniffing in the sweet scent; I wanted to keep them alive forever. Smiling at Bobby with my eyes, I thanked him with a bashful smile.

"They're beautiful."

"I saw them and they reminded me of you in that white dress." Bobby stared at me like I was eye candy. When I leaned in closer to him, he pulled at one of my locks, gently sweeping it back over my shoulder.

"You like this?" I asked referring to my hair. "Some men can't dig it"

"I ain't like everybody else," he released my lock and sat back. "I can dig it. It makes you look exotic."

The wine waiter arrived and I ordered a glass of Chardonnay, but Bobby ordered water.

"No wine? You don't want to relax?"

"I am relaxed. I just don't need my head spinning right now. How I'm gone look out for you with double vision. What if I have to knock a dude out and I miss and punch in the wrong direction?"

"Are you always this…physical?" I asked sarcastically.

"I can be. I can be a lot of things."

He looked at me for a second before doing a quick scope of every corner of the restaurant, lingering in some areas longer than others. He gave me a sexy half smile, tilting his head to the side and staring at me like I was ambiguous piece of artwork. Bashful, I looked away from his gaze.

"Why did you send for me?" I blurted out.

"Because you got my attention is all and ain't too many chicks that can do that. Most females are all the same just with different hair weave and outfits; they just carbon copies. They talk the same talk, walk the same walk, but I'm attracted to realness. Spunk, attitude, sexiness all that shit you got."

"So what are we doing? I mean…"

Bobby cut me off. "Let's just chill for now and not get so technical. Right now, we having fun and enjoying each other's company. Cool?"

"Cool," I repeated and took a sip of my wine.

———

The beach house was ready and I was so excited to see it but wasn't excited to see that Jayson had arrived in Miami and was going to be our new driver. He gave me a snide look out of the corner of his eyes, but I just ignored him. At this point, he was irrelevant.

The house was fabulous. It had curb appeal. Huge palm trees lined the driveway, blocking out the rays of the hot sun and the grass was so green, it looked fake. The house was contemporary. White stucco peeked out behind huge museum-like windows. Other houses were miles away. It was like we had the ocean all to ourselves. The master bedroom had a view of the ocean. The concrete deck housed a trendy swimming pool that flowed onto the concrete pavement just like the ocean did on the sand and alongside the deck was an oversized Jacuzzi. It was romantic.

Not too long after we arrived, it started to pour down raining. A strong wind gushed, sending large waves crashing to shore. It was beautiful but it killed our day.

"They said it was supposed to be some kind of tornado watch today," Jayson said to Bobby while looking out the kitchen window.

"Oh, yeah, I guess we got to stay in."

I was fine with that but I wanted Jayson the hell up out the house.

"I guess I'm stuck, too," Jayson said, making eye contact with me for the first time that day. He knew I wanted him gone, but he seemed to look forward to being the third wheel.

Bobby told Jayson, "There is an extra room in the back. When the storm clears up, you got work to do."

He gestured for me to follow him with a wave of his hand. We ended up in the master bedroom. "I'll give you this room. I think you'll be more comfortable here," he said.

I rubbed Bobby's chest with my hand. "What about you? I think you'll be comfortable here too."

"Yeah," Bobby said scratching the top of his head, "too comfortable." He walked out of the room smiling to himself.

I didn't let him off that easy. I grabbed his hand, leading him back inside the room. "I can't sleep in here alone. I'm afraid of the dark," I said smiling, "I won't bite…I won't even touch you."

"Hmm," was all Bobby said before turning back around, stomping back down the hall and calling for Jayson.

It rained all day. I fell asleep in the master bedroom for a few hours and when I woke up, Bobby was yelling at Jayson about getting a chef to the house.

Jayson transformed that anger to somebody on the other end of the phone.

When I saw Bobby, he was hunched over the refrigerator like he was starving and clueless.

"What's going on?" I said wiping the sleep from my eyes.

"Everything is cool," Bobby replied calmly.

"Man…it's raining pretty bad. They say most of the roads are closed. Ain't nobody coming out here to cook for us. They can't," Jayson said like it was the end of the world.

"What the hell man! I thought you handled everything like I told you!" Bobby slammed the refrigerator door. "Damn!" he said rubbing his head like it hurt. Quickly composing himself, Bobby turned to me giving me an even look. "I'll figure something out."

"I know you will," I told him, lifting his spirits.

Bobby walked from behind the granite countertop and snatched the phone out of Jayson's hand. "Aye, this Bobby B! What the hell I'm gone eat?" "What the fuck that storm got to do with my dinner? You telling me you not reliable?"

While he was on the phone threatening a chef to risk his life to feed us, I walked over to the refrigerator to see if it had anything inside that I could work with. I was surprised that there was so much food; Sirloin steak, chicken breast, fresh caught Salmon. There was enough food for us to eat like Kings all week.

"Um…Bobby," I said humbly, "I'm sorry to interrupt you but…" he lowered the phone, waiting to hear my response, "there is plenty of food here."

"Yeah but who gone cook it?" Jayson asked snidely.

I walked up to Bobby, took the phone out of his hand and threw it back to Jayson. "I got this," I said to him smiling but he looked back at me like I was crazy.

"What you mean? You gone cook?" he asked like he had no faith in my skills.

As much as I enjoyed cooking, I had never cooked for a man before. Bobby was going to be my first and, although I knew I could burn, I was nervous. I could tell by the way he ordered his food at the restaurant that he was a picky eater.

"Yeah," I told him.

I heard Jayson let out a loud sarcastic sigh. Bobby stared back at me and then back at Jayson like he didn't know what to think.

"I guess it won't hurt. Got to eat," Bobby grunted. "Just try not to burn the place down," he told me half joking, half serious.

Jayson rolled his eyes and walked off with an exaggerated stomp like Bobby was making the wrong choice by allowing me to cook. Bobby watched me cautiously for a few moments while I prepped the food like I had a secret plot to poison him. When he felt comfortable, he left me in the kitchen. I overheard Jayson asking Bobby if he was sure he trusted me with his food. I didn't hear Bobby's response.

I decided to go with the steak. Throwing them on the built- in gas grill, I baked three potatoes, sautéed vegetables and made a fresh garden salad, omitting the tomatoes out of Bobby's. At the last restaurant where we had eaten, he emphasized to the waiter that he didn't want tomatoes in his salad and I took a mental note of it.

The steak came out perfect. It was seasoned to perfection and had the appetizing commercial appeal to it with the black grill lines crossing through it. The baked potatoes were soft and the vegetables wilted to perfection. I had the place smelling like a Ruth Chris steakhouse. Bobby and Jayson came from the back room, following the smell. When Bobby saw me standing in the kitchen, whisking hot pots and steaming pans around, I saw a spark of light twinkle in his eye. That's when I knew I did good. I reluctantly set the table for three. Jayson's rude ass was getting all of this goodness by default. When I fixed his plate, he turned his nose up at my food and pushed it aside.

As soon as Bobby sat down, I started to fix his plate. When I brought Bobby the salad, he immediately started to pick through it with his fork, looking for tomatoes.

"No tomatoes," I told him

He stared down at his plate before biting into the steak that cut like butter. "Hmm," Bobby said nodding, going in for a second bite which was quickly followed by a third.

Bobby cleaned his plate but never told me the food was good or asked for seconds. Jayson sat there, watching Bobby's every bite like he was tasting the food through him. I knew his simple ass was starving and I was happy he was too much of a prick to prove it; he just sipped his water.

When Bobby got done eating, I cleared the table, cleaned the kitchen and put on a pot of tea before joining him in his room which was directly across the hall from the master bedroom.

Jayson retired to his room on the opposite side of the house.

It was still raining out but the storm was starting to die down. Now, I was starting to feel the calm. I stuck my head through the door, tapping on it to get Bobby's attention. Bobby was dressed down in his lounge gear. He was wearing a black fitted tank top with loose grey shorts. He was stretched out across the bed, with both hands used as anchors supporting the back of his head as he stared up at the ceiling like he was in deep thought.

"What's up?" he asked like something was wrong.

"Nothing's wrong…I just wanted to come and hang out with you for a while before I went to bed. Am I disturbing you?" Bobby looked at me like he had to think about the question. Then he shook his head no, lying back down in the same position staring up at the ceiling. I laid next to Bobby, scooting my body close enough to where I was slightly touching his. "This house is so beautiful. Is it yours?" I pried.

"Nah, but it could be if I wanted it to," Bobby replied confidently.

"Using your finders keepers saying," I joked.

"I only go by that saying when I have to," Bobby looked at me like he was schooling me. "If I want this house…I'll just buy it." He informed me in a matter-of-fact way.

"Must be nice…having whatever you want when you want and how you want," I told Bobby, softly stroking his chest.

"Hmm," Bobby said before going silent. I watched Bobby looking up into nowhere and wondered what he was thinking.

"Bobby…" I hesitated. I could tell my questions were annoying him. "I don't even know your last name."

"Badd," Bobby replied quickly.

"Yeah right," I didn't believe him.

"I mean what I say. And, my last name is Badd. B-A-double d. Bobby Badd. What about you? Lera Way?"

He let me know that he knew more about me than I knew about him but I had figured that out already.

"You probably know my social security number, too," I joked, getting another laugh out of him. "Mr. Bobby Badd…" I repeated.

"Kind of got a ring to it huh?" Bobby said proudly.

"It does," I admitted. "So, Mr. Badd, what do you do?"

I had to know. I wasn't used to guys who had a lot of cash not boastfully running their mouths about how they made their money.

"Everything," he answered ambiguously. "And, sometimes nothing at all."

He looked at me and smiled. "You a news reporter or something?" Bobby was sarcastic.

"No," I answered quickly. "I just want to know more about you. I mean…I'm with you and know nothing."

"How do you feel though?" Bobby asked, tilting his head in my direction.

"I feel safe. Happy..." I admitted to him.

"Then that's all you need to know."

I laid my head on top of his chest, listening to Bobby's heart beats; even they seemed full of structure and discipline with their timely thumps. He played around in my locks.

"I won't ask you anymore questions after today, Bobby Badd. If there is anything you need me to know, I guess I'm just going to have to trust that you'll tell me," I said sincerely.

Bobby's eyes lit up as he looked up at me like he was trying to figure me out.

"I'm going to fix you a cup of tea. It'll help you sleep tonight," I said, leaning off the bed but, Bobby pulled me back, gently yanking my arm and causing me to fall beside him. Then, he kissed me. It felt so good, I almost forgot where I was.

When he pulled away from me, my eyes were still closed. I never knew that a simple kiss could be so fulfilling; my insides tingled.

"I don't drink tea...but thanks anyway. Good night." Bobby said to me, leaning back down in the same position I had found him in.

"Good night," I said dazed.

The next day, it took forever to convince Bobby to come out and enjoy the beach with me. The storm had cleared away and the sun was out with a beautiful vengeance. It was the perfect day to lounge around but, Bobby was being an impossible stick-in-the-mud.

"What you got against having fun? You're so uptight. Nobody's here but me and you...I won't tell anybody you laughed, I promise" crossing my fingers, I joked with Bobby.

"I do have fun, just not the way you do."

"You want to get to know me Bobby or you just want to look at me all day?" I asked him seriously.

"I want to get to know you," he said to me with a straight face. "And I want to look at you all day."

"Well... you can do both on the beach. Come see my way of fun. Maybe you'll like it," I said with a shrug. Bobby finally agreed.

Bobby wore a pair of swim trunks that hung so low on his small waist it was like his six pack never ended. I followed the trail of finely printed muscles which started under his chest and led all the way down inside his pants. He showed me his fun, flirty and playful side by the way he dipped me in the water like he was dunking an Oreo into a glass of milk.

I wrapped my legs around his waist and squeezed tight. We stared at each other saying nothing, letting our body language do all the talking. All his guards and whatever emotional shields he armed himself with seemed to melt in the water.

"The sun is kissing you in all the right places," Bobby said referring to my budding sun tan.

"Oh yeah…if only you were the sun" I told him in a sexy tone.

Bobby smiled at me for a split second then moved in even closer to my face and kissed me. This time I had to be the one to pull away and the only reason I did that was because I needed air. I barely took a few breathes before Bobby was pulling me back into him to wrap his warm thick lips around mine for another kiss.

We pulled ourselves out of the ocean and started to partake in more of the same behaviors while lying in the sand. I got a better feel of him. Straddling his lap, I felt Bobby hands caress my neck all the way down to my lower back. He slowly moved his hands up and down, caressing every part of me while engaging in a deep rooted, wet kiss. I felt him swell up underneath me and the swelling didn't seem to stop; he just kept growing. Bobby burst out of his swim trunks and I squeezed my thighs, pressing against his throbbing member firmly, slowly winding my waist from side to side. His eyes got soft, hazy.

Bobby explored my body with his hands. He cupped my breasts, squeezing them gently. Then, he touched the side of my face, lifting his body upright so that I was sitting, bull's-eye on his lap. I wrapped my legs around his back, and squeezed my pelvis tight as he caressed the sides of my face like I was a precious jewel. His breathing got heavy as he turned my chin towards his mouth and kissed me even harder. I felt wetter than the ocean behind us and could no longer hold my peace. Flipping me over like he couldn't take it anymore, Bobby planted his heavy body on top of mine, hooking his arm under my left leg and tilting it above his head. I spread my other leg making even more room for him. He pushed his way inside of me so deep, he hit spots that I never knew where there. With one thrust, Bobby filled in every corner of my inner walls. It felt like my first time again; it was the first time I made love. Not just fucked.

Rocking with Bobby, our rhythms were in sync as he journeyed his way deeper inside me. He kissed me passionate y on my mouth and traced around my stiff nipples with his tongue.

Once Bobby's body started to shudder, I exploded from the inside out and then we both went limp in each other's arms.

Resting our half naked bodies against one another's, we tried to catch our breath under the dimly lit sun. I lay underneath his arm, still tingling inside. Neither one of us had anything to say. I guess our bodies said it all. After that, I didn't have to wonder anymore. I knew I was in love with Bobby and it wasn't going away any time socn, if at all. Bobby kissed me on the cheek sweetly and I never felt more safe and comfortable.

"How do you feel?" he asked me, softly.

"Like Christmas morning," I said through a deep sigh and Bobby giggled.

"Hmm," he said before kissing me a second time on the cheek. "Want to feel like New Years?" Bobby asked me with an enticing grin. Before I could reply, he rolled on top of me and we did all over again. What a stud.

5

Three months went by in the blink of an eye and everything felt adventurous and sexy.

Living with Bobby was exciting. He was so random I never knew what I was in for. Sometimes we would take his private plane and fly to California to have dinner at his favorite wine vineyard. My favorite was when we flew to Vegas. Bobby loved Vegas but he wasn't selfish with our time there. He made sure to add all the things I enjoyed on the agenda like going - to the live shows and to the spa. We ate at sushi restaurant. Getting Bobby to agree to eat sushi was like trying to convince a five year old to eat his vegetables. "I ain't eating no raw fish…unless it's a mermaid like you," he said to me with a wink. Once he tried the sushi, he was surprised that he liked it so much and soon the restaurant became our favorite place; it was nice to start developing things in common.

When we weren't doing anything elaborate, we just stayed at the beach house, watched silly moves and played around in the pool. Everything seemed perfect; almost like it would never end. But, after weeks of bliss, Bobby dropped the bomb on me. He told me he was going back home to Atlanta in a few days and he wasn't taking me with him; our little fling was over.

I felt cheated and very much broken-hearted. Watching him pack his bags was surreal. I just wanted to throw myself in the suitcase with him but, I had my pride.

"So that's it?" I looked at him, trying to control my tears.

"Yep. It was cool though, right?" he tickled me under the chin and smiled.

"The time of my life," I admitted. "Why does it have to be over?"

"All things got to come to an end sometimes, baby." He said without looking at me.

Bobby pulled a t-shirt out of a drawer and started to neatly fold his clothes on top of the bed. I couldn't take it anymore.

"Take me with you," I blurted out.

He stopped folding for a second and looked at me like he was almost considering my request. Then he continued to fold his clothes. He just shook his head no, walking back to the dresser. I blocked him from pulling out another drawer.

"Please," I said gently.

"I can't."

"Why? How can you be so easily done w th me?"

"I told you we was just chilling for a while. I never said this was a per-manent thing."

"But, why can't it be?" I wrapped my arms around his neck. He tried to pull away from me but I only held him tighter. "Please, Bobby. Don't just leave me like this. I have feelings invested. Real feelings. Don't you have feelings for me?"

Bobby broke away from my grip. He cave me a considerate look and sighed before taking my hand and leading it to the bed. We sat down. "I'm gone leave you that money, " he said like he was doing me a favor.

He pissed me off. "I can't be bought! I'm not a whore! Is that what you think of me?" I started to cry.

"No," Bobby said softly, wiping tears from my eyes. "I do have feel-ings for you. You make me laugh. You relax me. Got me doing stuff I never did before. Eating raw fish and watching them silly ass movies," he said smiling. "I mean...I have fun with you, girl."

That's when I seen that look behind his eyes. He really did have feel-ings for me.

"I ain't never been around no chick longer than a month. You special, Lera," I felt elated. "But…" my heart dropped. I didn't want to hear the *but* part. "I ain't in the market for a relationship and I know that's what you want. Right?" He waited for me to respond like he needed to be sure his assumption was correct.

"Yes," I answered quickly.

"My life is way too complicated for all that." He got up.

"It can work, Bobby," I grabbed his hand to stop him from walking away.

"You don't understand," Bobby shook his head. "When you co-sign your life with mine, things gone change and I don't think you ready for that."

"Please, Bobby…." I was getting teary eyed. "Let's give it a chance!"

"What you want!" he was getting frustrated.

I knew it was because he was trying to hide his true feelings. He didn't want to leave me. "You want me to be your boyfriend? I'm nobodies boyfriend. That shit sound corny as hell. *Boyfriend*," he said the word like the concept was childish.

"Then be my husband!" I couldn't believe I said it but the words spilled out of my mouth. I know I must appear desperate and I kind of am. I am just that in love with him. "I'm in love with you Bobby Badd."

Bobby was stunned. I held my breath, waiting for his response. Then I saw that soft look haze over his eyes. The look that told me, he loved me too, but he still didn't respond. He stared at me so hard, I thought I was going to crack into tiny pieces right underneath his feet. I buried my face in my hands, preparing to cry. When I felt the mattress shift, I knew Bobby was sitting beside me. He still said nothing.

Bobby started to kiss me. I thought the first time we kissed was intense but I was wrong, Bobby had more to show me. Then we made love. He made love to me like it was the last time he was going to touch me again. I whispered *I love you* in his ear over and over again so that he knew I meant it. He never told me he loved me back but I felt it in the way he held me. When it was over, Bobby fell asleep in my arms.

I stayed up, staring at the ceiling, deep in thought. I wondered what he meant by his life being too complicated for a relationship. Then I wondered what he thought of my sudden marriage proposal. I assumed Bobby was involved in some kind of risky business and because of that he had to be cautious with the people he brought in his life but still, I didn't understand why he was holding back so much; he knew me and I really did want to marry him.

I got up to use the bathroom and stepped on Bobby's wallet which was lying on the floor. I guess it fell out of his pocket during our heat of passion moment. I picked it up and looked back at Bobby to make sure he was still sleeping. I wasn't a snoopy person but I felt propelled to look inside. So I did. His driver's license picture made me smile; it looked more like hot prison mug shot with the bad ass snarling look he was giving the cameraman. My heart fluttered at how much I really loved this man. When I closed the wallet, a hundred dollar bill slid out. But it wasn't any bill. It was the bill Bobby had given me the first night we met. It was the one I put my name and number on. That was all the, *I love you* I needed. I put the money back in the wallet and slid it in his pants pocket.

———

When Bobby woke up, he seemed refreshed. It was like he literally had to sleep on my marriage request and now that he was awake, he had a response. I was laying beside him, still deep in thought when I felt him roll over and squeeze me from behind. He kissed me on the neck like he was telling me good morning although it was late afternoon. I wanted him to at least acknowledge the conversation we had but he didn't. He just held me like it never happened. I felt humiliated and needed a splash of cold water on my face to feel rejuvenated. I rolled out of bed and walked towards the bathroom. I didn't look back at him.

"Aye…" he called to me and I turned to face him. "Marriage huh?"

I shook my head yes, anticipating what he was going to say next.

"You sure?"

"I mean what I say and I only say it once," I used his catch phrase.

"Hmm…" he said, looking up at the ceiling, then back at me. "I can roll with that. Pack your stuff," he jumped out the bed like he was feeling energized. "We got a plane to catch!"

And just like that, we were engaged.

6

Bobby held my hand on the plane. He traced around my ring finger like he was imagining a wedding band there.

"Lera Way Badd...that kind of got a ring to it, huh?" he asked proudly.

"It does" I said happily. "So you really gone do it, huh?"

"You know I mean what I say," he gave me a reassuring look. "You the only woman in the world that can get me to do some shit like this. You know that?"

"I'm gone be a good wife to you, Bobby. I swear,"

"I dig that, but I got to let you know some things. Just so you can be sure you making the right decision." Bobby went serious on me. "I know you love me but there's a lot to me." He took a deep breath and straightened up his posture.

The look he was giving me was making me nervous. I knew he was about to drop another bomb and it had something to do with his life. I was both curious and nervous about whatever he was going to tell me.

"I told you before, my life is complicated and our marriage is going to be anything but average. My way of life is different than most people, and when we jump that broom, your way of life is going to be different, too."

My voice cracked as I replied, "okay." I was in love with him and to me that meant I was down for whatever he was down for. He could have told me he was an axe murder and nothing would have ever changed; I would still want to marry him. He watched me like he was trying to predict how I was going to react to whatever he was about to tell me.

"Okay…what's up Bobby Badd? Talk to your wife," I added with a sexy smile. When he smiled back at me, the air lightened up a bit. Then, he started to talk and he wasn't lying when he said his life was complicated.

In so many words, Bobby basically told me that his family operated a high profile organized crime sect. His father's father had started an operation during prohibition and it got so big that the Badd name became known by crime lords in every major city.

The Badds were so organized that they didn't have to get their hands dirty. People who did get their hands dirty came to the Badds to wash them clean. Serving as a liaison between the crime world and the real world, the Badds were insurance policies for gangsters. They provided muscle, cash, and connections. They were the go-to people of the crime world. Nobody messed with anybody who had an afflation with a Badd. They pumped so much money in certain cities, they practically owned them. They had their hands in every *dirty* money pot across the country and, to top it all off, the criminals paid them what Bobby called taxes on a monthly basis just to keep a good rapport going between them or what he called, a membership. When they weren't collecting money in taxes, they were giving big loans with inflated interest rates or buying up every piece of property they could. They practically owned Atlanta. Even government officials had secret dealings with the Badds. They knew senators, governors, mayors, police chiefs and other crooked politicians.

They operated out of a place that Bobby called The Badd Ranch. It was their headquarters. A huge private development located somewhere in the outskirts of Atlanta. They had the same kind of Tribal Sovereignty of rules and reign at the Badd Ranch as Native Americans had over their land. They were the law there and could do what they wanted on their land without facing any legal consequences. The place was like a city itself the way Bobby described it. Several acres of developed land housed a casino and even a hospital. I imagined it to be like a modern version of Gotham city. Bobby and his brothers – Brock, Billy and Brip – were heirs to it all.

Bobby's mother and father were dead. I could tell he didn't want to talk much about his parents, especially his mother. He didn't tell me how they died and I didn't ask. Brock was the legal ruler of the estate because of his age. All the brothers worked for the organization; Bobby was in charge of giving financing and collecting debts; that's what he was doing the day I met him at the L-Review. Apparently, Lenny got the financing for all his clubs from the Badds but when he didn't pay up, he put himself in great danger. Brip was like a bounty hunter. He found all the people that tried to hide and, according to Bobby, it was only a matter of time before Brip found Lenny, too. He never told me what Brip did to the people he hunted down and I was too afraid to ask.

When he told me that his second oldest brother, Billy was in jail, I got confused. Something didn't sound right and when I tried to get him to elaborate, he changed the subject. He didn't talk about Billy as much as he did the other two brothers. I left it alone though. I was already hearing more than enough information. He told me that once we got married, things were going to be different for me. For one, I couldn't go anywhere alone. Just like him, I was going to have to travel with my own muscle. Bobby said people were going to know me before I ever knew them; everybody was going to learn my name and remember my face.

I knew our relationship was going to be challenging. Just loving Bobby wasn't enough. There was going to be a lot sacrifices and compromising on my end and I knew I had to be strong to get through it all, but spending a life with Bobby was worth it to me.

"So what you think? You still down for me?" Bobby asked with a raised brow.

What he had told me was so heavy my head swarmed. I knew Bobby was involved in some risky business, but I had no idea he was the face of organized crime. However, I was down for him regardless. I nodded before planting a reassuring kiss on his lips.

"Is that all?" I asked.

"No," he said seriously. "There ain't never an end to this story but for now...I guess that's it." I exhaled. I felt both relived and burdened but I was in it to win it.

We arrived in Atlanta just before the sun was setting. Bobby's place wasn't what I expected. It was an old shoe warehouse that had been renovated and zoned for residential in a trendy part of town. There were no walls dividing the individual rooms except for his bedroom which was located in the loft upstairs. His house was picture poster for a bachelor pad. The walls were painted red with black trim and the kitchen was the size of a broom closet. All of his furniture and home décor were accents of red, black and white. Filling the space of the large and open living room was a black leather sectional and oversized zebra print rug. It wasn't my style at all and wasn't nearly enough space for the two of us. I missed the beach house already.

"So this is home?"

"For now," he told me.

I opened the stainless steel refrigerator and the only thing that was inside was a half empty gallon of water and a protein shake. "Um...Bobby, I can't work with this kitchen," I said to him frowning. "And, who decorated in here? Was it some woman you hired?" I huffed.

"Had I known I was going to meet you, I would have left everything blank," he hugged me from behind. "It's just temporary, baby. Once we get things settled, we can start looking for a house," he kissed the back of my neck.

"Fine, but until then...I'm gone have to make a few changes and the first thing to go is that mattress," I gave him a wicked look, "and I have to get some Clorox so I can wash the sins out of your shower."

"Knock yourself out!" he told me before opening up his wallet and handing me a black credit card. "This is for you. Hold on to it so you can get what you need."

"What's the balance?" I asked naively.

"There is no balance," he winked at me. "I got something for you," Bobby skipped up the steps to his bedroom. He returned with a long, rectangular shaped jewelry box. I knew right away that there was a neck-lace inside. He gave me the box and I slid it open.

It was a platinum necklace with an overwhelming amount of gleaming diamonds encrusted around the emblem which was the letter B; standing for Badd. The sparkling necklace was unique and elegant.

"This is beautiful. How long have you had this?" I wondered if the necklace used to belong to somebody else being that he had had no time to buy it since we got engaged.

"I always had it."

He wrapped the chain around my neck. "A lot of people gone recog-nize this B. Consider it an identity card. Wear it everywhere you go."

I nodded. I traced the diamond linings of the B with my finger. I felt branded, but in a good way. "I won't take it off," I assured him and then planted a stream of thank you kisses on his neck.

Bobby slapped me on my butt. "I got to go," he told me, looking down at his watch. "You straight?" He looked back at me like he was really wondering if I was still okay with everything.

"I'm good," I smiled and toyed with my B-necklace. "But, what am I gone do for transportation? And, I have to register my license in Atlanta."

"What you need a license for? Badd wives don't drive," Bobby said in a matter of fact tone. I didn't know how to feel about what he said. Why couldn't I drive? Bobby studied my face to see if I was bother by what he'd just told me. At the end of the day, who was I to complain about having a private driver. So it rolled of my shoulder. "Pooh will be in town tomorrow. You don't mind him do you?"

"No." As long as it wasn't Jayson driving me around, I was cool.

"I'll be back this evening. Put on something nice. We gone meet my brother Brip and his wife, Taffy, for dinner. If you wanna do a little shop-ping, there's a lot of stores within walking distance. I think you'll like them." He kissed me on the forehead and left.

———

Because it was my first time in Atlanta, I couldn't wait to get out and explore. I always heard good things about the city. I walked up and down the street window shopping. I just wanted to get familiar with the stores before I made any purchases. The area was full of trendy clothing and furniture boutiques. There was also a stream of nail spas, bars and jazzy restaurants. The hustle and bustle of the streets hyped up my energy. It was nice to be somewhere fresh and new.

There was a contemporary furniture store called, *A Different Space*, lodged in between a clothing boutique and a day spa. I liked the window display so I went inside to shop for a few things so that I could make Bobby's place feel like our own.

I picked up everything I thought I wanted. I bought new pillows for the couch, a beige colored rug to replace the zebra print one along with silverware, plates, and cups. I was ready to check out when I saw the California king sized mattress on display.

"How much for the mattress?" I asked the sales clerk, a natural haired, thin black woman.

"$6,000, but we have none left in stock. If you order one today, it'll be here within two weeks," she said to me dryly without looking up. When she did look up, her eyes led straight from mine and down to my necklace. She stared at the B like it was hypnotizing. After taking a deep breath she looked up at me and straightened up her posture like she was addressing royalty. "On second thought…" she tilted her head to the side, looking back at the mattress. "I can sell you the display."

"Can you do that?"

"Of course. There's no problem with that Mrs. Badd," she flashed me a million dollar smile. I grabbed the diamond B and rubbed it in my hands like it was my magic genie. Before I went home, me and my necklace stopped by a few clothing boutiques. I was waited on hand and foot.

———

Bobby came home that evening and barely noticed the changes I had made to the house. He walked through the door with Jayson and was carrying a small bag in one hand and fiddling with his I-phone in the other. Jayson had a small scar under his eye. I wondered if that meant Bobby had a bad day.

"Aye, Lera!" he yelled, assuming I was upstairs but I was standing in the small kitchen, having a glass of red wine. I wanted to calm my nerves before meeting Bobby's brother and his wife.

"I'm right here," I waved at him.

I was dressed to kill, sporting my white pencil skirt and black leather corset top. The B charm of my necklace was resting on my top. When Jayson saw my necklace, he avoided me completely. Bobby looked up at me briefly, nodding his head in approval of my outfit.

"Come holla at me upstairs for a sec," he waved at me to follow.

I followed behind Bobby. When I walked towards Jayson, he made sure to move out of my way quickly. He was so jumpy that it humored me. When he saw my necklace, he already knew what was up; no more back talk for him.

As soon as we got upstairs, Bobby threw his cell phone on top of the new mattress like he was relieving himself from it. He didn't notice the new mattress. He swept his hand across his face, starting from the top of his forehead leading all the way down to his chin. He sighed heavily before rolling the stress kinks out of his neck. I could tell he was switching from work mode into lover's mode.

"You look hot, baby," he kept his eyes fixed on my tight skirt.

"All for you," I said with a twirl.

"Oh, yeah." He grabbed my hips and pulled me into him. He was still holding the small gift bag. "I got something for you too," he bragged and kissed me on the forehead. Bobby held the bag up to my face.

"Is that what I think it is?" I said, reaching for the bag but Bobby didn't let me take it. He playfully snatched it back.

I knew it was my ring.

"Well...let's see," he said before getting down on one knee. He looked over his shoulder to make sure that Jayson wasn't close enough to eaves-drop on our private moment. Then he pulled the ring box out the bag and held it under my nose. It was beautiful. It had the perfect balance of beauty and modesty. Not too flashy or too dull. The big solitaire diamond sparkled and shimmered like the northern lights while smaller diamonds, encrusting the white gold wedding band off-set them.

Bobby looked up at me, smiling with his eyes. He slid the ring on my finger and it fit just right. "Will you marry me?" he officially proposed. His smile was so big, it made me blush; especially the way the single dimple in his chin flexed.

"Yes."

He stood up and kissed me, wrapping one arm around my waist and lifting me off the ground. Everything felt perfect.

———

Jayson drove us to a restaurant called the Strip. It was a ritzy, yet contemporary atmosphere full of affluent Black people. We didn't walk in through the front door entrance. Our waitress met us in the kitchen to lead us to our table which was located on top of the restaurant. I noticed Bobby's brother, Brip, right away. He resembled Bobby a lot but had a honey colored complexion and instead of a dimple in his chin, they were in his cheeks. Brip was attractive with the same no nonsense attitude as Bobby.

Brip slouched down behind the table, aggressively chewing on a straw and searching the restaurant with his eyes like he was looking for something to get into. He had an anxious look in his eye as he drummed the table with his fingers while taking quick sips of his cocktail. A blood stained gauze was wrapped sloppily around his left hand. It looked like it hurt but it didn't seem to be bothering him by the way he was knocking against the wood table.

Bobby told me that Brip was 25 years old. Their age difference showed in Brip's demeanor. As soon as Brip saw Bobby, he literally jumped over the table, howling with excitement. "What's up man?" he greeted Bobby like it had been years since he saw him. "Damn! You finally back home, brother!" he said smiling, revealing his deeply set dimples and the slight gap in between his two front teeth. "It seems like you been on mission for years man…welcome home," he slappec Bobby's shoulder. "Ha," he yelled randomly, with the straw still dangling from his mouth. Brip had a lot of energy. I didn't know if he was on something or if it was just his natural way.

"What happened to your hand man?" Bobby grabbed his brother's hand.

"This shit?" Brip said holding his hand in the air, "it ain't nothing," he punched against the wood table. "I had to crack a skull the other day and didn't feel like using my pistol."

"Lazy ass," Bobby joked and Brip laughed before embracing his brother a second time.

After he pulled away from his brother, he took time out to look me up and down. "Who dis?" he said, smiling at Bobby like I was a piece of meat.

"This is Lera Way," Bobby said my name like it was a prize, possessively wrapping his arm around my shoulders.

"Lera Way?" Brip repeated my name quick, giving me a strange look. "Damn…yeah…uh-huh," he grunted, encircling around me.

"Pretty soon…she gone be called Lera Way-Badd," Bobby informed his brother proudly, holding up my ring hand and dangling it in his face.

"What!" Brip yelled, clapping and cheering like his team just hit a homerun. The straw in his mouth fell to the ground right at my feet. "Hell yeah, Bobby….hell, yeah!" he hugged his brother then lifted me off the ground, swinging me around like I was rag doll. "Welcome to the family sis, welcome!" He looked directly at my ches: and grabbed the B from my necklace, holding it in the air like it was a sacred family heirloom and giving his brother a proud look. "Hell, yeah!" he repeated again, rubbing the top of his head like he was amazed.

"Brip, who the fuck is she?" A voice yelled from behind us.

When I turned around, I saw a petite but slightly curvy woman facing us with her hands on her hips, giving Brip a sassy look and me an evil stare.

"Calm your ass down, Taffy!" Brip said and she pouted. "Get over here," he waved her in closer to us. "This is a celebration," he said with a big smile. "Come on yall, let's sit," Brip climbed back over the table. "Aye," he yelled to our waiter who was down stairs with another customer.

I knew she couldn't hear him but that didn't stop Brip from screaming. "Aye!" he said a second time. He was getting angry. An evil look came into his eyes and he started to breathe heavily like he was attempting to control whatever temper that was about to explode. People looked up at him like he was crazy. He grabbed an cube ice from his drink, and threw it at the waitress, hitting her bull's eye on the top of the head.

The waitress jumped and almost dropped the tray of drinks she was holding. Massaging the top of her head, she looked up and, when she saw the scouring look Brip was giving her, she raced up the stairs. "Shit!" Brip said like he was pissed off that easily. Looking for someone to take his anger out on, he turned to Jayson, acknowledging his presence for the first time.

Jayson was standing behind Bobby and I, looking just as out of place as a third wheel on a bike. "Why the hell he here!" Brip slammed his injured hand against the table so hard, a fork fell to the ground. Jayson looked so frightened, I felt sorry for him. Brip was kind of scary. Bobby and Taffy just ignored his antics like they were use to it.

"Chill out man…he leaving," Bobby tried to calm his brother down. He placed his hand on Brip's shoulder and Brip leaned back.

He continued to give Jayson an intimidating stare.

"What the fuck happened to your face man?" Brip asked, looking at a scar under Jayson's left eye. "You let some nigga hit you?"

Jayson took slow steps back.

"Nah…he just had an accident," Bobby tried to defend him. He knew his brother was a nut.

"Accident? Nobody shouldn't be able to accidently sock yo ass in the eye unless you weak as hell!" Brip was growing angrier by the second. "This is an accident," he snatched a glass of water right out of Taffy's hand and threw it across the table at Jayson. The glass cracked at his feet, missing his head by a few short inches. After that, Jayson turned and all but ran.

Bobby shook his head, smirking a little bit.

Brip laughed so hard, he fell over on top of Taffy. She pushed his weight off of her like he was annoying her. "Get me some more water you psycho!" She slapped the table. "I'm thirsty!"

"You love me?" Brip said randomly and aggressively kissed her on the lips.

Taffy kissed him back for a few moments then pushed him away, elbowing him in the side. Then she looked up at me and Bobby. "What's going on?"

The waitress came in the nick of time. "Get my wife some more water and clean all this shit up! All that broke glass is a hazard...you can't see that?" Brip said like he wasn't the cause of it. "And we need some champagne...we celebrating today. Hurry the hell up, too!" Brip demanded the waitress as Taffy gave her an intimidating stare.

"Brip...I need my water now! I can barely speak my mouth is so dry. You know how I get when my throat is dry," she whined. She was a real drama queen.

"I'm sorry baby. It's coming," he said to her softly, gently kissing her cheek.

Taffy kept her eyes fixed on me, searching every corner of my face like she was comparing me to somebody; maybe she was comparing me to herself.

Taffy was pretty; she had the girl next door look going for herself until she opened her mouth. She wore her hair in a short, jazzy cut where one side was longer than the other and her honey skin tone shimmered like bronze. She was sporting a B necklace like the one I was wearing. You couldn't see my B because it was tucked inside my top.

"Lera...show her what Bobby got you," Brip chuckled.

I exposed the B part of my necklace.

Taffy gasped and held her chest. "OMG!" she yelled, getting up and wrapping her arms around Bobby's neck and then mine. "Are you fucking serious?"

"Hell yeah, he serious." Brip answered.

"Where is that bitch with our champagne? We need to celebrate this, shit!" Taffy snapped her fingers, searching the restaurant for the frightened waitress. "I'm Taffy, Brip's wife of three years," she said holding out her hand, dangling three fingers in the air, bragging. "I'm so excited," she shrilled and clapped her hands. "Welcome to the family, girl," Taffy grabbed my hand and squeezed it. "She's so pretty Bobby…"

"She is," Bobby said, looking at me smiling.

"Thanks," I said shyly.

"I love your hair, too," she looked at my locks and smiled. "I think I'm going to do something different like that to mine," she said, rubbing the back of her head.

"No the hell you ain't," Brip snapped. "Your hair is cool the way it is. You change it too much anyway. Shit! I never who I'm gone come home to with all the different looks you be having."

"It's my damn, hair!" Taffy said defensively.

"Since when?" Brip asked like a tyrant. Taffy rolled her eyes at him and shot him a bird.

Brip chuckled before leaning over and kissing his wife on the cheek like she was the cutest thing in the universe. "Sexy ass." Brip said and Taffy blushed.

"So when is the wedding? OMG….we get to plan a wedding," she shrieked.

"You know how these things go," Bobby said to her and she nodded her head like she understood. "We'll have a date soon enough."

"Brock and Mona know about this?" Brip said with a serious look.

"I'll let them know soon. Hell, the shit just happened the other day," Bobby got annoyed.

"Lera, I'm telling you…it's been a long time coming with this one," she pointed at Bobby. "I was about to give up on him. I thought he was going to be a bachelor forever," Taffy said with a smirk.

"See…had you been minding your own damn business you wouldn't have to be concerned about my brother at all," Brip told Taffy.

She gave him an evil stare before brushing off his comments. "Our family is really close and we gone have a ton of fun, girl!" Taffy shrieked again, grabbing my hands and holding them like we were sorority sisters.

When the waitress came back with the champagne, we toasted to Bobby and I's engagement and celebrated the rest of the night.

been in Atlanta for four weeks and it was starting to feel like home. Bobby was just as busy here as he was in Miami. Every morning it was the same routine. He was up by five and back home by noon to meet me for lunch; then he was gone again until the evening. Now that I understood more about who he was, it eased my mind whenever he left.

As the days went by, Bobby and I got closer. From the time he opened up and revealed his family history, he confided in me more. He complained about his older brother Brock being too secretive all the time but he never elaborated on what secrets were being kept from him. Whenever he mentioned Brock or Brip, I couldn't help but get curious about Billy but Bobby never talked about him and whenever I did mention Billy, he evaded the subject. So, I just left it alone.

We still hadn't set a wedding date. I was ready to make the whole thing official but there was so much formality and tradition when it came to a Badd getting married that I had no say in it all. When he told me that our guest list probably would consist of over 1500 strangers, my head started to spin. All I wanted to do was elope in Vegas; something simple and straight to the point, but Bobby wouldn't have it.

"It don't work like that. There's gone be a lot of people who get offended by us eloping and one of them is my crazy ass brother, Brock and his crazy ass wife, Mona. We got to play by the rules then after that, we can do whatever in the hell we want."

I didn't mind playing by the rules but there was just so many of them. Being in love with Bobby was a structured and organized thing; everything that emotions naturally weren't. Then Bobby started to quiz me on so many *what-if scenarios* that I had nightmares thinking about all the bad shit that could go down. His questions were tiresome and I never seemed to get any of them right.

"What if a nigga put a gun to my head and told you that he was gone kill me if you didn't give him what he wanted. What would you do?"

"Give him what he wanted," I answered honestly.

"No," Bobby said, shaking his head like I was doomed. "You never give them what they ask for. Because guess what?...If a gun is ever at my head...they know they already dead for putting it there so regardless of what you give them, they gone kill me anyway. At least they would if they smart."

I hated when Bobby talked about guns at his head and people shooting him. It spooked me out.

"If they shoot you then they might as well shoot me because I'm gone after that."

"What the hell you mean you gone? Uh-uh...you gone have to take that shit wit stride like a real Badd woman. Once I'm gone, you the only part of me that's gone be left. You got to keep going for me. When you stop going, that's when I really die."

When he saw the horrified expression on my face, he changed his tone. "You ain't got to worry about that though. Can't nobody kill me cause I'm invincible. All this talk is for just in case."

As much as Bobby drilled me with his taunting scenarios, I still wasn't sure what to do if something ever went down. It was all too complicated for me. My common sense didn't play a role in Bobby's *what if scenarios*. It was a science to it all and I couldn't understand the formula. If someone had a gun to Bobby's head, naturally, I'd give them myself to keep them from hurting him but that was the wrong way to think. So, I just crossed my fingers and prayed that I'd never got put in a situation because if I did, I wasn't sure I would do the right thing. But, crossing my fingers and hoping nothing went down wasn't enough because the shit started to hit the fan real quick. I really got a good whiff of how funky the life of a Badd wife could get.

———

We were enjoying a romantic and lazy weekend. We'd just gotten back from an evening walk around the city. We picked up a bottle of merlot on the way home. Now, we were just lounging. Bobby was a closet romantic. He loved when I lit candles, ordered wine and chocolates and fed him while wearing sexy lingerie. The house was lit candles; the shadows of the burning flames bounced off the walls. We were lying on the floor on top of an oversized shag rug. The rug was so thick and plush it almost felt just as soft as our mattress. In the background, the soft and sultry tunes of Sade were humming through the speakers.

As I hand fed Bobby chocolate covered strawberries, he had a special request.

"Why don't you give me one of them famous stress melting massages?" He turned over to lay flat on his stomach, and smiled at me.

I flipped him back over, laying him on his back. "I can do that but this massage is going to have a happy ending," I winked at him, lowering my hands down in between his legs, squeezing his dick. Bobby moaned.

"You got some more of that lavender body oil left?" he asked hopefully.

"Give me a sec," I said, lifting off my knees and going upstairs to the master bathroom where I kept the body oils.

I grabbed the lavender body oil out the lower cabinet and inspected myself in the mirror. I was wearing a red-laced baby doll night gown that pushed out my breasts and accentuated my small waist. I smoothed down my locks so that they fell softly around my shoulders, grabbed the oil and turned to go downstairs. The bedroom was dark so when I saw the reflection of a man's shadow, I thought it was an anxious Bobby meeting me upstairs to pounce on me. But, when the shadow jumped, grabbed me and covered my mouth with his large clammy hand, I knew it wasn't him.

The man had a gun at the side of my head and was whispering something in my ear. But, I was so busy trying to remember what Bobby told me to do in a situation like this, that I didn't hear what he was saying. I tried to take a deep breath but his hand was plastered so tight against my mouth that I felt suffocated. He pushed me back in the bathroom and softly closed the door behind him. He flicked on the light and I got a better glimpse of him. The big brooding man was wearing a ski mask. I wanted to scream and he must have read my mind because he lifted up the gun and gestured for me to be silent.

"What do you want?" I addressed him sternly. Bobby didn't teach me this but I already knew that it was always best to stay calm and keep a straight face when approached by an assailant.

"For starters...you bet not scream or my man downstairs is gone kill that nigga!" he said to me harshly. I almost fainted at the thought of Bobby being caught off guard the way I was.

"I don't have to scream," I warned him.

"Good," he said, yanking me by the arm. He led me downstairs at gun point.

When we got to the top of the stairs, I could see Bobby still stretched out on the rug. I had a notion to scream right then and there, alerting him to what was going down but something told me not to. It would only cause a panic. So, I tip-toed down the steps with the man's chest glued to my back and his gun at my head. I didn't see the other man until I got to the bottom of the stairs. He was ducking down in the kitchen, hiding behind the breakfast bar.

I stepped into the living room and Bobby still didn't notice what was going on. He lay on his back and stared up at the ceiling, waiting on his massage. When we got close enough, I broke my silence but I kept calm. I couldn't let them catch Bobby off guard.

"Um...Bobby," was all I said. The man jabbed the side of my head with the gun but it didn't hurt or at least I couldn't feel it.

He must've heard the tension in my voice because Bobby jumped up right away, ready to fight. Narrowing his eyes, Bobby gave the man a stare so evil even I shuddered. The man pushed me over towards Bobby and he caught me before I hit the ground.

"You okay?" he asked, giving me a secure squeeze.

"Yeah," I said calmly. "There's another one in the kitchen," I whispered. His eyes darted over towards the kitchen before throwing me behind his back, protecting my body with his. The man in the kitchen stepped out, waving a gun in the air and joining his friend. They stood side by side. Bobby didn't seem intimidated. He stared at them like they were roaches and he was Raid.

"Yall dudes lost or something?" Bobby was calm. "There is still time for you to walk out the door before it's too late." He started to crack his knuckles, smiling scornfully at the men.

"Nah, we ain't lost. We just here for the money and then we out." He said, clicking his gun in our direction.

Bobby replied, "there ain't no money here for you." He shook his head like he was confused.

"You sure about that?" The man started to walk closer towards us. Bobby squeezed me tighter.

"I bet she know where the money is," he pointed the gun at me before grabbing me from behind Bobby. "Where the money, bitch? You gone make me put a hole in this nigga head or are you gone tell me?"

His friend put the tip of the gun at the back of Bobby's head. Bobby watched, waiting to see how I was going to respond. I guess he was waiting to see if all his training had paid off. I wasn't sure if it did. I remembered the money I found that Bobby had hidden upstairs in a chest in his closet and I also remembered what he told me about not giving them what they wanted.

"I don't know anything about no money. I don't live here. Look, I barely even know this man. I'm just having a good time."

I looked at Bobby. I think he liked where I was going with my lie; he seemed relieved. Luckily, I had my B necklace soaking in jewelry cleaner upstairs so my lie was more convincing.

"All bitches know where the money is," the man pointed the gun at me.

"I'm telling you I don't know. I'm from Memphis. I met him at the L-Bar where I work and I'm only here for the weekend. Just let me go and y'all can get on with y'all business. I promise I'll go straight to the airport," I squealed.

"Let her go," the other man said. "She probably telling the truth."

"Get the fuck out of here," the man pushed me towards the door.

I gave Bobby a sorrowful look and ran. I was so scared, my legs were shaking. I ran down the street in my robe, barefoot like a mad woman. People gawked at me like I was a circus freak. Cars honked. I ran into one of the boutiques where I got the furniture. The owner was just closing when I burst through the doors, demanding her to lock them and give me the phone. I reached up and pulled the shutters down to cover the front windows.

"Do you want me to call the police?" Her eyes were bulging.

"No!" I screamed. This was a family matter but Brip and Taffy were on a weekend vacation so I called Jayson.

Forcing me to memorize and recite Jayson and Brip's phone numbers was a part of Bobby's drill. Now, I'm happy he did. I pressed the buttons so quick, it was like I sped dialed Jayson. He answered on the first ring.

"Bobby's getting robbed! Get there now!" I screamed before he could say *hello*.

"What the fuck!" he yelled. "Where are you?"

"A Different Space. The furniture store down the street. Now, get there right away!" Jayson hung up the phone before I could get done screaming. I started crying like Bobby was as good as dead.

"I'm calling the police," the clerk said, frightened.

"Don't be stupid," I hissed. "You lock those doors?"

"Yes," she shrilled like she was about to cry. "I don't' want to die," she started to whine.

"Shut the fuck up!" I yelled. "Just sit tight until I say otherwise and if you call the cops you're going to regret it," I gave her a threatening point with my finger. I was surprised at how easily the demands were rolling off my tongue; I guess Bobby rubbed off on me.

I paced back and forth. Thirty minutes passed and I didn't know what was going on. When I heard the ringing of ambulance sirens, my heart dropped thinking they were coming for Bobby's wounded or dead body. I tried calling Jayson again but he didn't answer.

"Somebody's at the back door!" The clerked jumped up.

The door knob was turning. "Shut up," I silenced her, watching the entrance door of the store. Heavy hands started to pound against the door like they were trying to break it down. I couldn't see out front. The store clerk shut the shades, blocking out the view just like I ordered her to do shortly after I arrived.

"You got a security camera?"

"Yeah," she sniffed, rushing to her computer in the back office. I followed behind her.

The banging on the door got louder. I locked the office door. The clerk helped me block the door with a file cabinet to further secure it. The knocking on the front door turned into forceful kicks.

"I can't get killed." She waved her hands in the air and nervously pulled on her hair. She was freaking out.

"Pull yourself together and turn on the camera." I needed to see who was out front.

She sat down behind a desk and started to type. She was able to pull up the view of the front of the store. That's when I saw Bobby and Jayson standing out front. Jayson looked like he was trying to pick the lock while Bobby pounded and kicked against the door.

"Quick, help me move this," I pushed at the file cabinet we had blocking the door.

"No! Who is that?" She shook her head uncontrollably.

"Get your ass up and help me."

She jumped up, scooting the desk away from the door.

By the time I ran out the office, Jayson had picked the lock and Bobby was running towards me. I lept into his arms. I tried to control myself from crying because I didn't want Bobby to think I couldn't handle it but I was terrified and I really couldn't handle it.

"Shhh..." Bobby tried to calm me. He kissed the top of my head. "It's over now. We straight...okay...we straignt," he kissed me again and repeated, "it's over, Lera.

But, for some reason, I wasn't convinced.

8

Bobby held his hand out. "Where my damn keys, girl?"

It was the fifth time he had asked me the question. But, I continued to ignore him. I shrugged my shoulders. When Bobby tried to leave to go to work the next morning, I didn't want to be alone, so I hid his keys.

"Stop playing with me, girl. I got money to make."

"Take the day off with me."

"For what?"

"I'm scared," I admitted.

I was still in a panic over what happened. I felt traumatized but it was what I signed up for when I agreed to marry Bobby. I wished I could go back to not knowing all the things he told me, but there was no going back. Even after being held at gunpoint, I still couldn't imagine my life without Bobby. I tortured myself with thoughts of what if. What if I was alone? Or what if I did the wrong thing and got us both killed? I was starting to feel exhausted. I just wanted to be his wife but it wasn't that simple. Nothing was.

"I don't want to be here alone. What if they come back when you're gone? Then what am I going to do? Or do you even care!" I folded my arms and pouted.

He sighed deeply and rubbed the back of his neck, acting like he didn't understand why I was freaking out. In his mind, it really was over.

"I told you they ain't coming back and I mean what I say."

"Well what happened to them? Did you give them the money in the closet?"

"Hell no," Bobby looked at me like I was crazy. "Never give them shit they ask for! I thought I told you that." He answered my question only telling me what he wanted me to know. But that wasn't enough for me. I wanted to know what happened to the men. Obviously, Bobby came out without as much as a scratch but I didn't know if I could say the same about them. It would give me peace of mind to know for sure if they were dead or alive. Or at least I think.

Bobby gave me an exasperated look before pushing past me. He tore the house down, looking for the keys. Bobby grunted as he knocked over the dresser, emptied drawers and tried to lift the mattress with me on top of it. I jumped off the bed. He wasn't even close to finding the keys I had stuffed in my bra. Sweat popped out around his temples and eased down the sides of his face. Bobby looked like he was ready to throw me out the window but he still treated me delicately.

After fifteen minutes, Bobby finally gave up and called Jayson to come and get him. "I hope you know how much you're fucking my day up." He rolled his eyes at me and I gave him a sorrowful look. I wasn't trying to ruin his day; I was trying to conserve mine. Bobby wasn't being sympathetic at all. Ten minutes later, Jayson honked for Bobby to come down and I attempted to barricade myself in front of the door, stretching my arms out so that he couldn't pass. "You still at it?" He was annoyed. He sighed before pushing an aggressive kiss on my forehead and forcefully lifting me off the ground and tossing me on the couch like I weighed nothing.

"Don't leave me!" I sobbed. "Please!"

"I got men all over this parking lot and Pooh coming up in about an hour. You'll be fine until I get back. Just chill out, Lera," he shook his head at me. "Get out the house today. Do some shopping or something. You'll feel better. The shit is over...let it be!" he said and slammed the door behind him.

———

About twenty minutes after Bobby left, Pooh was knocking on the door and I was already dressed in my workout gear, ready to leave. I wasn't staying in this house. I need to relieve some stress so I decided to walk to the neighborhood gym. On the way there, I passed the furniture store that I ran into frantically last night. When the store clerk saw me, her eyes widened with fear, like she was hoping I wouldn't come inside. She kept her eyes fixed on me as I passed by. Bobby had given her a wad of cash which should have helped. But, I guess you really can't buy peace of mind.

Having Pooh by my side made me feel a little more comfortable but nothing could replace the security I got from being around Bobby. I was wearing my B necklace but I hid the B inside my shirt; I was too afraid that I was going to be spotted by one of the masked men that held us up. Pooh escorted me to the gym and waited outside until I finished. My kickboxing class helped take the edge off a little bit, but images of the gun at Bobby's head still tormented me. So, I hit the treadmill for thirty minutes, trying to sweat off scary thoughts. Sweat rolled off my forehead and dripped into my eyes, mixing in with my eyeliner; it burned. The more images I had about the gunmen, the faster I ran. When I was more tired than terrified, I decided to call it a day and leave the gym.

After I left, I walked a few blocks up to a bar. It was barely noon but I was in desperate need of some immediate relaxation.

"Wait here," I told Pooh, stopping him from following me inside the bar. I wanted to be alone. He didn't complain; he just sat down on the curb, following my orders like a good soldier.

I walked into the bar, searching every corner of the small, dimly lit space. Now, I understood why Bobby was so cautious everywhere he went. I wondered if he ever enjoyed himself at all. I didn't know how the men looked but that didn't stop me from giving every male patron in the bar a wary look. I took a seat in the back in plain sight of the door, positioned where no one could catch me off guard.

The bar was considerably full for it only being noon. I guess I wasn't the only person that had fears or other worries to drown. All the barstools were occupied. Most of the booth seats were occupied by a single person, hunched over a glass and rubbing the stress lines out of their foreheads. When the waiter asked me what I wanted, I told him to get me something strong and he did just that. He brought me double shot of Bacardi. Holding my nose, I swallowed the shot in one gulp. Before the waiter left my side, I ordered another drink. The burning sensation in my chest kind of killed my anxiety but it was only short lived. After swallowing down my second shot, I was starting to feel relaxed.

Every time someone walked through the door, I looked them up and down, accusing them in my mind. I was really paranoid. I was just about to sip my third shot when three young black guys walked through the door. They looked college aged but I had a feeling they weren't college students. I wouldn't have watched them so closely, but they had my attention when they neglected the other free seats in the front and came straight towards the back where I was, taking a seat one booth ahead of mine. I watched them like a hawk although they barely noticed me.

Aside from the uniform sounds of chattering and the clanking of glass, the bar was pretty quiet. There was no music playing and the sounds of peoples voices were a little above a whisper. But, because I was extra in tune to everything and only one booth away from the young guys sitting in front of me, I practically heard everything they were saying and what I couldn't hear physically, I read on their lips.

At first, it was a bunch of idle young boy talk. Listening to their silly conversations helped take my mind off of things a little. They talked about hitting a few clubs and all the girls they slept with for the week. I attempted to take a second sip of my third shot but couldn't. I was starting to feel dizzy and nauseous from drinking on an empty stomach. I pushed the Bacardi to the side and tried to rub the daze out of my eyes. Then, I could have sworn I heard one of them mention the Badd name. At first, I thought I was so paranoid that it turned to hallucinations but after tuning in closer, I wasn't wrong.

"Yall didn't hear about that? I promise you...them Badds are going down. Every great empire got to fall at some point and now is their time. There is going to be a fucking war and them dudes they up against ain't leaving none of them standing. They even gone kill they dogs," the young guy said.

"Man, you sick," one of the other guys said. "They can't be defeated!"

"I promise you it's the truth. My brother work for the other niggas. He been trying to get at them since one of the brothers pistol whipped him a few years back. It ain't like this shit ain't planned. It's been in planning for years and believe it or not one of their own is in on it. That's gone make it that much more easy," he tried to convince his friends who were still looking at him like he was crazy but he had my attention. "An inside job is the only way to go with those niggas. Otherwise, it's suicide."

After hearing that, I sunk down in my chair, trying to conceal myself as much as I could. Checking to be sure that my B necklace was not in plain sight, I got up and walked past them to leave. I wondered if what the young boy was saying had something to do with last night. How else could anybody get so close to Bobby unless they had help? If what he was alleging was true, that meant Bobby could still be in trouble and so could I.

As soon as I got outside, I spotted Pooh across the street, talking on the cell phone and walking around in circles. I liked Pooh but I didn't trust anybody. I ran down the street in the opposite direction so that he couldn't see me.

I tried to call Bobby a few times but the phone went straight to voicemail. That made me even more concerned. All the running raised my body temperature, increasing my intoxication level. By the time I got back to the house, my head was spinning. Stopping in the parking lot, I leaned over to take deep breaths and tried to control myself from vomiting on my tennis shoes. Fanning my face, trying to create some cool wind against the hot dry air, I pulled out my phone one last time to call Bobby but he still didn't answer. I debated whether or not to leave Bobby a message, revealing what I overheard in the bar, but I decided against it.

Bobby's Hummer was parked out front but I knew he wasn't home. I wasn't ready to be inside the house alone; especially after what I heard. I went to walk past the car when I noticed something that I didn't notice before. The rear door to Bobby's Hummer was cracked open. I still had

Bobby's keys in my bra. I stared back at the car, growing curious about the half-opened door. Hesitantly, I took slow steps towards the car. I figured the least I could do was close the door; it was the back door to his trunk. It was weird that it was open. But, I was such a nervous wreck when I left the house this morning, the car could have been on fire and I wouldn't have noticed.

I walked up to the Hummer and tried to slam the door shut, but it wouldn't close. I applied more force but still it didn't close; something kept propping it back open. I opened the trunk door to make adjustments, but I couldn't fix what was preventing the door from closing. I didn't want to touch it. There was a dead body, wrapped in a white sheet, thrown in the back of Bobby's Hummer like garbage. A stiff and ashy black arm was dangling from the sheet, preventing the trunk from closing.

I screamed. When I realized the attention I was bringing to myself, I stuffed my fist in my mouth, blocking the horrified shrieks. I turned to run away but when I looked back, I realized I would be leaving the body exposed. I had to go back and fix it. A dead body in the back of his trunk could have put Bobby in more trouble than his Badd name could get him out of.

Closing my eyes tight, I touched the dead man's arm; his body felt stiff and rubber like. I pushed it as far back as I could but it was useless. The only way I could fix the problem would be to break the arm but I couldn't bring myself to do it. I got squeamish and gagged. Taking a deep breath, I tried one last time and pushed the arm towards the inside of the car but that only made things worse. The body looked like it was about to roll out of the car. "Shit!" I said out loud, holding my body against the trunk door, trying to keep it from falling out.

I pulled my cell phone out of my pocket and tried to call, Bobby. Of course, he didn't answer the phone but I left him a message. Not wanting to reveal too much over the phone, I begged him to come home, hoping that he'd hear the distress in my voice and get here right away. I hinted to him that it was a matter of life and death.

I tried to appear as normal as possible but there was no normal way to look when you were trying to keep a dead body from falling out of a car. I was so paranoid; I was hallucinating incriminating looks from people that didn't exist. I felt like an accessory to murder.

I wondered if this body belonged to one of the gunmen from last night. Bobby told me that I didn't have to worry about the guys who robbed us coming back, now I was starting understand why. But, why in the hell would he leave the body in his trunk? I didn't know how I felt about Bobby having something to do with killing someone. I know I would have been foolish to assume that the lifestyle Bobby lived didn't involve crimes like murder but still, I just didn't want to believe it even if I was trying to conceal the evidence.

A little over 15 minutes later, my knees were so weak, I felt like I was going to fall. Tears began to cloud my vision; I tried my best to control them. I didn't need to bring any attention to myself. Bobby hadn't called me back, yet.

I wiped my eyes and looked up to case the street for witnesses and cops. Nobody was paying me any attention but I saw Pooh jogging down the street, looking around like he'd lost his puppy. He spotted me with my back anchored against the car and jogged my way.

"Get the fuck back, Pooh," I demanded, still standing in place.

Pooh took a few steps back, holding his hands up like he was dealing with a mental patient. "Lera? What's going?" he gave me a cautious look.

"Don't come near me!" I warned him. "Take your ass home and leave me."

"Why don't ya just tell me what's going on, girl? Maybe I can help you out?"

"Where's Bobby?" I gave him a suspicious look.

"You know I don't know that. I'm supposed to be looking after you. You running off can really get me in trouble." Pooh watched me closely. "Just come here," he held out his hand, "let's go in the house."

Pooh started to take short steps towards me and I screamed. That's when I saw the hood of Jayson's Escalade, dip into the parking lot. When Bobby jumped out the car I was relieved.

"What's going on?" Bobby looked at Pooh, demanding answers for my erratic behavior.

"Get rid of them Bobby. Jayson too!" I squealed.

Bobby looked at Pooh then back at Jayson.

"I don't know man...she been acting weird all day. She ran off and I found her like this," Pooh explained himself, trembling under Bobby's presence.

Bobby gave me a strange look before coming towards me. When he got close enough, I wrapped my arms around his neck, squeezing him like he was lucky to be alive. He tried to pull me away from the trunk; I yanked my body back in position. "Don't!" I yelled.

"What's going on, Lera?" Bobby seemed concerned.

"There's a dead body in this trunk" I whispered to him and threw his keys at him. He caught the keys with one hand, stepped away from me, and then turned to Jayson and Pooh. He ordered them to go inside the house.

Once they left, I let everything out. "I tried to call you," I said like I was breaking down. My legs were trembling.

"How long you been standing here?" Bobby was getting upset.

"I don't know," I shrugged, "15...20 minutes."

Bobby wiped the sweat from my forehead before kissing me on the cheek. "Calm down, baby. It's gone be alright. I'm gone fix this...okay" he said to me, lifting my chin up so that I made eye contact with him.

Bobby called Jayson on his cell phone, telling them to come back down. He had them switch places with me before escorting my trembling body back in the house.

"What you do that for, Lera?" Bobby asked me once we got inside.

"Do what?" I was confused.

"Put yourself so close to that body. You know what would have happened to you if the police came?"

"What!" I screamed and punched his chest. "You would have gone to jail! I stayed so you wouldn't go to jail you ingrate!" Your sloppy ass left a body in your car right in front of your house! You put me in this situation," I stabbed him in the chest with my finger. "What was I supposed to do? Let you get arrested? Lose you?" I spoke so fast all my words ran together like one sentence.

"Calm down. I'm gone run you a bath so you can relax."

"Who was that Bobby? Is it one of the guys from last night?"

"Lera…I don't' know the person in the trunk of my car," he answered cleverly.

Bobby walked upstairs. A few minutes later, he returned. "Come on." He waved me off the couch. "I got your bath ready."

When I got up, I must have moved too fast because all the blood seemed to rush to the front of my head and caused me to fall back down. Bobby rushed to my side, cupping my face in his hands. I was drunk.

"You okay," he tried to get me to look at him. "Damn, girl. What you been drinking?" he smelled the liquor on my breath.

"I had a little something after you left this morning."

"You can't be drinking like this every time some shit go down. I can't have no weak ass alcoholic wife," Bobby said to me harshly.

I slapped his hands away from my face and stood up.

"I got held at gun point and stumbled across a dead fucking body… so the hell what if I had a few drinks! I'm traumatized and you don't seem to give a damn!"

"I told you everything so none of this shit should surprise you. That's why I asked you if you was sure you can handle all this but now I don't know," Bobby shook his head.

"You couldn't have prepared me for this shit, Bobby! And you know it."

"You right. Some things I can't verbalize; you just have to see for yourself. Now that you got a good look, you need to make your decision again. I'm going out to clean up this mess…when I get back, I want an answer. You either with me or you not!" Bobby started to walk towards the front door.

"But, I love you."

"That don't mean shit!" he said before slamming the door.

9

I was lounging on the couch in my cozy but sexy Victoria Secret sweats. The bath Bobby ran for me sobered me up and, after I ate a small fruit salad, I felt like my mind was clear enough to think about what he said. I wasn't going anywhere but that didn't make any of this easier. Taffy was married to Brip and as crazy as he was, her life had to be wilder than mine and she seemed to have it all together. If they could do it, then Bobby and I could too.

I was deep in thought when I heard someone bang on the front door like the police. Instantly, I thought about the masked men but assuming that robbers wouldn't knock, I calmed down and looked through the peep hole. Two men dressed in suits were standing outside with serious looks on their faces. One of the men was a short balding black guy and the other a tall, athletic built white guy.

"What do you want?" I said in a heavy voice.

"We're looking for Lera Way?" The white guy said with authority.

"Who is we?" That's when the black guy held his police badge against peep hole. I gasped and opened the door.

———

The officers introduced themselves as homicide detectives. They didn't put me in handcuffs but held my forearm tight and escorted me to the back seat of a black Ford Explorer. I kept my cool the best I could. They said they were taking me in for questioning and after that, I would be free to go.

On the way to the station, I saw Bobby's Hummer parked on the side of the road with the driver's door open like he'd fled the scene. Other men in suits, just like them, swarmed around it. One of the detectives watched me through the rear view mirror as we passed by. I tried my best to act like I didn't notice anything. I'd already made up my mind that I wasn't going to tell them a thing and I really didn't have anything to tell; I didn't know what the hell was going on.

I'd never been arrested before, but what the detectives called the station looked more like a POW camp to me. When we pulled up to an old, abandoned building, I started to get even more nervous.

"What's going on? This doesn't look like a police station." I complained.

"Well… it is. When we get done questioning you, you can leave."

"What do you have to question me about?"

"You'll know everything soon," the white guy grunted.

After we parked, the black detective yanked me out of the car with a little more force than necessary. I almost fell on the pavement. "Come on," he barked at me. "And I hope you ain't planning on giving me any trouble. I know how you Badd wives can get." He said the name *Badd* like it left a sour taste in his mouth but I didn't blame him because it was starting to leave a sour taste in my mouth as well. I followed him inside the empty building.

The big empty space was damp and reeked of mildew. Cobwebs covered the concrete block walls and the building would have been completely dark if it wasn't for the sunlight shining through a cracked window. I followed the officers down a long, narrow hallway that branched off into shorter hallways. Every so many feet, there was a steel doors that lead to small rooms. They pushed me inside one of the rooms that was lit up with a bright fluorescent light. The room was empty with the exception of a crooked round wooden table and three crates underneath used as chairs. "Sit down," one of the detectives ordered me.

"I need to talk to my lawyer first! I haven't been read my rights and as far as I know, I haven't been charged with anything!"

"You'll talk to your lawyer when I say you can talk to him," the white man said facing me. "Now sit," he pointed to the dusty crate.

Hesitantly, I took a seat on the crate and blocked my eyes from the blinding light shining directly in my face; the light was hot and it induced beads of sweat to fall down my face. The officers took seats at the other end of the table, facing me. For a while, they didn't talk. They just stared at me, barely blinking. I watched enough cop movies to know they were only trying to intimidate me. I stared back at them, not saying a word. One of the detectives looked at his watch.

"You guys brought me here to stare at me?" I swallowed and tried to keep a straight face.

"Not really...you don't have nothing to tell us?" The black detective asked calmly.

"Nothing to tell but everything to ask," I shot back snidely. "Why the hell am I here?"

"You know why?" the white detective said.

"Um...no," I said sarcastically, "But maybe you can let me know why you think I do."

The detectives looked at one another, smirking like I was amusing them. "I guess you wanna get straight to the point huh?"

"Yeah...this lighting does nothing for my complexion," I said smugly and slapped the light out of my face.

"Okay," the white guy said, slamming his fist against the table so hard, it almost toppled over. Startled, I jumped and took a deep breath. "Who put the body in the trunk?"

I literally had to put my hands under my chin to keep my face straight. I gave him a confused look. "Body? Trunk? What the hell are you talking about?"

"Oh, you know what we talking about."

"I don't know what the fuck you're talking about but if you don't let me call my lawyer, I'm going to sue the shit out of you!"

"Ha," the detective slapped his hands against the table like he was amused. "Sue us?" he was condescending. "Baby, you gone have to do that behind bars" he said with an evil smirk.

The sweat was flowing down my cheeks like tears; maybe they were tears. I was so nervous I couldn't tell the difference. The thought of rotting in jail took my sacrifice for loving Bobby to a whole other level. I felt stuck but I wasn't going out without a fight.

"I'm not saying another word."

That's when the black detective leaned up from the stool and stood over me.

"Look, it ain't you we want. It's Bobby. All you got to do is tell us the truth and you're free to go."

"I don't know any Bobby," I lied.

"Don't be stupid, Lera," the white detective warned me. I didn't know how he knew my name and I didn't ask. He stood over me too. "You can go to jail for a long time. Is Bobby worth that to you?"

"I don't know any Bobby," I repeated again. I sniffed hard and swallowed down the thick lump that was starting to swell in my throat.

"A man is dead and an eyewitness saw you next to the car. It's over Lera…" he slammed his hand against the table and I jumped again. "You love him that much! You gone go to jail for life for this, nigga? Would he do that for you?"

That was a good question but now wasn't the time for me to try and figure out the answer. I had to stay focused. I kept my eyes fixed on the cracked, concrete floor. I saw spiders walking in and out of the slits in the concrete. I wished I could switch places with the spiders and slip away from the integrating officers.

"I guess that's the Badd way. You get stuck and they go free. They some real smart men. Let me tell you something," the black guy leaned in so close to my face, his nose was practically touching mine. I smelled his sour breath, "other places they may have free reign but not here! Not in my town. Your man is going down and that necklace ain't gone be able to save you!" He snatched the chain off of my neck and threw it across the room. "No Badd is above the law and I'm going to see to that!" he screamed.

"Look, Lera," The white guy chimed in like the good, friendly cop. His voice was calm. "We gone give you some t me to think about this. But, just remember…you can be implicated as accessory to murder. This ain't a snatch and grab robbery…its murder! And, that's serious shit," he said before walking away.

They left me in the room alone. I kept my eyes fixed on the floor. I felt like I was trapped in a dungeon and my only way out would be to give up Bobby but that wasn't an option for me. When I told Bobby I loved him, I meant what I said.

The small room was stuffy and humid. I could barely breathe. With the hot light shining on my face, I started to feel faint and I really was in need of some water. I got up to stretch my legs. I had to think my way out of this situation. Out of all the things Bobby and I went through, he never told me what to do if I got interrogated by the police. I paced back and forth. I couldn't help but wonder where Bobby was or if he was already in custody. If he was, I knew he was handling the situation wisely but I wasn't sure I could.

After what seemed like hours, the detectives returned. As soon as the door cracked open, I tried to escape but ran straight into one of the detective's chest. I bounced off of him like I was hitting a rubber wall and fell to the ground. Before I could attempt to run again, one of them yanked me up so quick I saw the top of his head before my feet landed on the ground. "You crazy?" the black guy said to me smugly. "You Badd women are something else. I thought you weren't gone give me no trouble? Huh?" He shook me a little.

Squirming away from his tight grip, I tried to free myself the best I could. I kicked, screamed and did everything but spit to get him to let me go but he only laughed like I was amusing him before shoving me back into the small dungeon-like room.

"I don't know anything," I screamed. "You can't hold me here! You have no right!"

"We're the law…we have the right to do whatever we have to do to get a confession out of a suspect," the detective said to me wearing a sly smirk on his face. "But, it looks like you don't want to cooperate. So, I guess you gone have to sleep here tonight. Maybe if you sleep here, it'll refresh your memory." He turned to the white guy and shared a comical laugh. "Don't worry…you won't be alone. These big ass sewer rats will keep you good company."

"No!" I yelled. "Bobby didn't kill anybody and I'll swear to that under oath. He was with me all day. He never left my sight."

The detectives looked at each other, communicating with their eyes. The white guy nodded at the black guy and he grabbed me by my arm and pushed me out the door. I tried to squirm away from him. "Maybe we need to refresh your memory!"

"Lera…you should have just told the truth," the white cop said, shaking his head like he felt sorry for me.

They walked me a few doors down. We stopped in front of another steel door much like the other room. The black officer pulled out a key from his pocket and threw it to the white cop. Looking at me, shaking his head remorsefully, the white cop asked me one more time, "You sure you don't have nothing to tell?" I shook my head no, taking a deep nervous breath.

"Well…maybe this will help you remember! Open the door," he yelled to the white cop.

He shoved me through the door. When I looked up, I saw a stretcher with a dead body on top. There was a white sheet covering the body just like the one I saw in Bobby's trunk.

"Maybe if you spend a few hours with him…you'll remember. But, don't worry, he won't bite and if he does, then you better call an exorcist." He laughed before slamming the door shut, locking it behind him.

"No!" I screamed. "Please!" I pounded against the door, "let me out! Let me out" I was beyond freaked out. I kept my back turned away from the body but in my mind, I could still see him.

I screamed so hard, I was starting to feel faint. Sliding down the door, I sobbed. "Help me! Somebody please help me."

Curling up in the fetal position, I tried to bury my face in between my legs; it was my only place to hide. I sobbed heavier. I don't know how long I was in the room but I was starting to feel just as dead as the body on the stretcher. I must have dozed off because I didn't notice when the door opened and one of the officers scooped me off the floor. He carried me out of the room.

"You ready to talk now?" the white cop asked, bringing me to my feet. I lost my balance and fell against the wall.

"Give her some water," the other cop said.

The white cop put the bottled water up to my mouth but I didn't drink it; I didn't trust them. "Come on, Lera. I need your good speaking voice for when you give your confession. You ready?"

I nodded yes.

"Let's go," the black cop said. They lead me back to their integration room.

Gently sitting me down on a crate, the white cop practically force fed me water. "Drink the water Lera. You're going to make yourself sick. I wish we didn't have to go through all this." He told me apologetically.

Putting a tape recorder on top of the table, the black cop motioned for the white one to sit down. "You ready?" he asked me calm.

I shook my head yes.

"Good girl!" But I wasn't a good girl, I was a Badd girl and I wasn't giving up Bobby for nobody.

"This is gone be real simple, okay," he said. "I'm just gone ask you one question and all you got to do is give me one simple answer, and we're out of here. You ready?" he said with his finger pointed above the record button.

I shook my head, yes.

Once he pressed the button, he finally introduced himself and his partner. He said my full name, asking me to verify that it was correct. Then, he asked me the same question he'd been asking me all afternoon. *Was Bobby Badd involved in the murder?* They sat at the edge of their seats, waiting for me to respond.

I took a few deep breaths then exhaled slowly. I cleared my throat and leaned in close to the tape recorder and spoke. "Fuck you! I want my lawyer!"

I shot them vindictive looks. I was expecting them to lash out at me like they'd been doing all day but they didn't do anything.

"Okay...I guess we have all we need," the white cop said before pulling me up from the crate.

They escorted me back out the door and I just knew they were going to throw me back in the room with the dead body but instead, they turned towards the opposite direction of the hall. They didn't speak. Their silence was making me even more nervous because I didn't know what else they had up their sleeves. Whatever it was, I'm sure it couldn't have topped locking me in a small room with a dead body. We only walked a few steps down the hall before they stopped in front of another closed door.

"Another dead body?" I sobbed. They didn't answer me. After opening the door, they gently pushed me in the room. When I looked up, I saw Bobby standing underneath a window in hand cuffs.

"Bobby," I ran straight for him, burying my face in his chest. He kissed me on top of the head.

"Calm down..." he told me in a sweet and soothing voice.

"Are you going to jail?" I looked up at him frantic.

"I don't know?"

"I'm not going to let you go to jail, Bobby. I'll tell them I did it." I confessed.

"You gone go to jail for me?" he sound surprised.

"Yes," I said honestly but confused. Did I really love him that much? "I'll probably do less time than you," I said like I had it all figured out.

Then, the sweetest look I'd ever seen covered his face. He pushed his body against mine and kissed me as if he was saying goodbye. "I would never let you do that," he said. "But...you offering means the world to me."

"No, Bobby!" I sobbed.

"Just tell me this?" Bobby was serious. "If I could walk out of here free right now, even after all this shit…do you think you could handle it all? I told you earlier today that I wanted a final answer. So, tell me now."

"I'm with you in or out of jail!" I told him.

He held up his hands, revealing the handcuffs before effortlessly allowing them to slide off his wrist and on to the floor.

"How did you do that?" I was confused but relieved. "Now we can run," I said looking over my shoulder for the cops. I was still frantic.

"I'm a Badd," Bobby said to me in a serous tone. "I don't run away from nothing."

"What about the cops?" I whined.

"Lera…it all was a test," he admitted while giving me a guarded look like he didn't know how I was going to react to his confession.

"What?" I thought I didn't hear him right.

"Don't be mad, Lera," Bobby cupped my face with his hand. "I had to do it. All Badd wives go through the test. It's tradition but it's all over now and you passed my test with flying colors….you my lil straight A student!"

"What do you mean test?"

"I had to know if you was true and how you handle pressure," he stared at me. "I'm sorry, baby. It had to play out this way.

"What about the robbery?"

"That was bullshit," he replied quickly.

"The dead body?"

"More bullshit," he repeated.

"The young guys at the bar talking about the setup?"

"What?" Bobby gave me a strange look.

"The boys at the bar talking about the war somebody got against yall and how everybody affiliated with the Badds is going to die and it being an inside job…"

"When did you hear that?" he stepped back and was giving me a weird look.

"Today at the bar. Was it true?" I started to get frantic again.

Bobby gave me a critical look. He didn't say anything right away.

"Answer me," I was starting to panic.

"It's all bullshit," he said but he didn't sound as convincing as he did earlier.

"So all of it was fake?" I needed to be sure.

Bobby nodded his head.

Relieved, I hugged him but only for a split second. Then, I got pissed off. "Fuck you, Bobby," I yelled, pushing him away from me. The more I shoved him, the closer he got.

"I'm sorry, baby," he whispered, leading a trail of kisses from my forehead to my lips. Bobby pulled my B necklace out of his pocket and wrapped it back around my neck. "I'm gone marry you on January 1st. New Year's Day," he said like our engagement was finally official. That was six months away.

10

When Bobby told me that everything was over, he was only referring to the crazy test he put me through. But, the trying of my patience was still in full effect, especially when he announced that I had to move in with Taffy and Brip for a month and after them, Mona and Brock. It was yet another Badd family tradition.

"When?"

"Tomorrow," he informed me.

"Tomorrow? No, I can't...it's too soon. I'm still shook up. I'm still traumatized, Bobby!"

"After you spend some time with the other two wives, you'll feel better. Taffy been through the same thing."

He tried to make me feel better but it didn't work. I had no desire to move in with Taffy or his crazy brother, Brip.

"What will staying with them prove?"

"It'll give you better insight into what it's like being a Badd," he put his hand on my shoulder. He saw that I was stressing. "If it was up to me, you wouldn't have to go through none of this but it's my brother Brock and his wife Mona who started up all this ritual shit on account of Billy and Dalla," Bobby blurted out by mistake.

"Dalla? Who is that? Is she someone your brother Billy was trying to marry before he got locked up?"

"Look, forget all that," he gave me a dismissive wave. "It's just tradition. Once this passes, we'll have the rest of our lives."

I wanted to know more about Dalla and Billy and what really went down with them, but I knew Bobby wouldn't tell me. I wandered if Dalla was like me; scared and so in love that she ran off. Who really knew what the real deal was when it came to the Badds and all of their tireless traditions.

"This is a good thing. Y'all need to bond. You guys are gone be closer than sisters. Might as well get to know each other and Taffy's cool. She's a little head case but she's cool enough." Bobby said.

Flashing Bobby a phony smile, I kept my fingers crossed. The things we do for love; now, I understood why love was always equated with the word fool.

———

Taffy and Brip just got back from vacation so I assumed she wouldn't be too thrilled about me being in her hair for a month. But as soon as Taffy saw me step out of the car, she greeted me like I was a relative she hadn't seen in years. Brip followed behind her, chewing on a toothpick with an anxious look in his eye.

"I'm so happy you're here," Taffy shrieked. "If you're here, that means you guys finally set a date," she told me and playfully punched Bobby on the shoulder.

"Oh, yeah!" Brip said. "So when's the official date?"

"New Years," I said proudly with a big beaming, bride- to-be smile.

Taffy shrieked and clapped her hands together.

"New Years!" Brip said, disappointed. "You know I always spend the New Year in Vegas." He gave his brother a scornful look then quickly replaced it with a smile. "Fuck it," he waved his hands in the air before leaping into his brother's arms, congratulating him. "Welcome to the team man," he gave his wife an annoying look like Bobby didn't know what he was getting himself into and then smiled playfully at us.

"Take care of my girl," Bobby said staring back at me like he was trusting Brip with his most prized possession.

"Come on man..." Brip whined playfully. "You already know..." he pounded against his chest. "They got to come through me first and I don't break easy!" he said looking back at me as if I had nothing to worry about.

I kissed Bobby good-bye and hesitantly followed behind Taffy and Brip. Brip carried my bags until he got to the concierge and demanded him to take them up. They lived in a Penthouse. The lobby alone was so immaculate I could imagine how their penthouse looked.

Brip left a few minutes after Bobby. Taffy barked orders at her in-house staff to take my bags to the guest room and then she showed me around their place. Brip and Taffy's home was located in the heart of the city but had the charm of a traditional styled home. Thick wood cased columns, two story ceilings and wall to wall expensive white carpet. The place was so spotless; I was scared to walk on the rugs. Everything was white with beige accents. Even her two toy sized dogs. The dogs followed Taffy around the house like they were lovesick for her and she talked to them like they were babies instead of animals. A near life-sized picture of her, Brip and the two dogs hung above the fireplace mantle.

"My house is your house, honey. If you want anything, just let Bruno know," she said referring to her help. "Once you settle in, Brip is going to take us to dinner. I'll give you some time to yourself," she told me after showing me to my room. I was grateful for that because I needed a few minutes to collect myself.

Her guest room was an exact replica of the remainder of the house; all white everything. I was tired and wanted to lie down. When I lay down on the bed, my body started to melt deep into the mattress. The mattress was a water bed. I didn't even know they still made those. As the water bed slightly jilted my body from side to side, I dozed off quickly. About thirty minutes later, Bruno tapped on my door.

"Mrs. Badd requests that you come out to the terrace to join her for tea," he said.

I walked back downstairs and met Taffy on her terrace. She was sitting in front of a linen covered table. It looked just as good as any five diamond restaurant. On top of the table was a bundle of fresh flowers sitting inside of an elegant crystal vase along with a pink and white flowered tea pot and cute matching tea cups. There was a spread of tasty looking sandwiches and a bottle of Rose chilling in a fancy ice bucket.

"All of this for me?" I asked rubbing the sleep out of my eyes.

Taffy's terrace overlooked the city. Her home was lovely and she knew it. "The best for the best," she said, lifting up her B necklace and flashing a million dollar smile.

Taffy literally looked like she scrubbed her body with hundred dollar bills instead of soap. Everything about her appeared to be rich and elegant. She had pearly white teeth and flawlessly smooth skin; she was a well kept woman.

I took a seat in front of her, looking down at the little specks of people below us.

"Don't you just love this view?" she said looking down with me. "I sit out here every morning to eat my breakfast. It makes me feel like I'm flying to be up here." She said proud.

"Your home is beautiful," I told her. It must have been the compliment she was waiting for because she almost seemed relieved.

"Thanks," she said through a sigh. "I really try," she said shaking her head. "I remodel every quarter. I just get bored real fast," she said, blocking the sun from her eyes with her dainty hand. Then, she leaned up and eagerly poured me a cup of hot tea in one of her cute little tea cups. I felt like I was experiencing an adult version of a tea party. "Here you go," she said sliding the tea my way. It was almost 90 degrees outside and hot tea was the last thing on my mind but I didn't want to be rude. I graciously thanked her and commented on how nice her tea set was.

"Girl, I got this when me and Brip were in Paris," she bragged, her eyes widening big from the memory. "I didn't even like tea but everybody out there seems to love it. You should have seen that fool Brip trying to drink from them small cups. He never had hot tea before and drank it instead of sipping it," she giggled, "He burnt the hell out of his tongue. But it served him right for winking at the sleazy French waitress that couldn't take her eyes off my man," she frowned. "He got so upset that he burnt his tongue, he cut a fool up in that little café. He threw his tea cup and mine at the waitress. Then we both had to run out of the restaurant before his dumb ass got us thrown in some foreign prison," she laughed like her husband's poor behavior was cute. "You probably know by now that he likes to throw things," she said shaking her head dismissively. "Anyway girl, I told that fool we are not at home and here they don't give a fuck about you being a Badd. But, you think I could tell him anything?" she said, shooing her hand at me and blowing her tea cool before taking small sips.

Taffy grabbed a plate and started to fork a variety of mini sandwiches and sweet treats on it for me to taste. "This is good," she said, referring to a glazed pastry stuffed with a strawberry cream cheese filling. "We can only have one of these though. Don't forget, you got to get in that white dress," she winked at me. "Have you thought about your colors yet?" she asked me anxiously.

"No, I'm really not in to the whole wedding thing. I'd rather just elope."

Taffy twisted her nose up so far I thought it was going to fall off her face. "What! No wedding?" she said, nibbling on her pastry. "Well, you might as well forget eloping because that ain't gone happen. A Badd wedding is like the fucking presidential inauguration. I had almost three thousand strangers at my wedding and I loved every bit of it too. I felt like a celebrity," Taffy said smiling up at the sky like she was remembering the day she walked down the aisle. "If I didn't marry Brip, that's what I would have been. A movie star," she said like she was day dreaming. "That aisle was like my red carpet. Cameras flashing, people smiling and looking at me like I was the Queen of England. I wish I could do it all over again."

"And the gifts," she slapped the table, "Girl, you ever see the mobster movies when all the guests give the bride and groom money?" I nodded. "Well, it's just like that. We got so much cash that day we couldn't carry it all with us when we left for our honeymoon. We had to leave it all at the ranch. Hell, it was so much money, Brip wrapped a hundred dollar bill around his cigarette and smoked it," Taffy laughed.

Taffy started to rub the back of her neck, smoothing down the edges of her jazzy cut. She wiped the sweat from the bridge of her nose before pulling out the frosty bottle of Rose. "It's too damn hot for this tea. Let's pop this bottle," she said, toying with cork. I could tell she wasn't used to opening her own champagne by the way she was dabbing at the cork. After a few failed attempts, Taffy's face went tense.

"Bruno!" she yelled at the top of her lungs. He came flying out like he was on standby. "Open this shit! Damn, I almost chipped my nail," she said like she was mad at him. Seeing how easily her temper was provoked helped me understood what she saw in Brip and vise versa.

Once the bottle was open, she snatched it out of his hand when he attempted to pour her a glass. "Leave," she said to him like she was talking to one of the dogs. He skipped out the patio like it was on fire. Then, she turned to me and flashed me a sweet smile like I just didn't witness her poor behavior.

"So, are there kids in you and Brip's future?" I asked, trying to make small chat; I felt awkward.

"No," she said sorrowful, shaking her head. "That's one thing being a Badd or this necklace can't help me with. I had four miscarriages. I just can't have babies," she said with a sad shrug. "I guess I'm cursed."

"I'm sorry," I said quickly.

Giving me a dismissive wave, she didn't accept my apology. "Girl, whatever! It is what it is. Brip loves me regardless. At first, I had a real hard time dealing with it. Remember that bad earthquake in Haiti?" She asked me and I nodded "Well, my maternal instincts really went out for all those orphan kids. I felt so bad for those poor babies without mamas that I suggested to Brip we adopt one, but girl, he liked to cut a fool. I guess I should have known better though. Brip ain't raising no child that ain't no pure Badd.

Hell, I could imagine what Mona would say if I brought home a baby that wasn't of pure Badd blood. Hell, Brock just might put a hit out on us both," Taffy told me like she was half serious and half joking. Then she went silent for a while. After a few moments, she said "I just got my dogs and I've never been a dog person but I'm really shocked at how fulfilled I am by having them. They fill that maternal void," she scooped up one of her dogs and kissed it on the nose.

"Does Mona and Brock have kids?" I pried, hopping to get a better insight into who they were. After all, they were my final destination before I could marry Bobby.

With both brows raised, Taffy gave me an amused look. "Do they? Ha!" She clapped her hands. "A whole army of them…literally," she said before laughing. She gently put the dog back on the ground. "They've been married for years. She's the only one of us that met Mama Badd. I wish I'd met Mama Badd but she died the year I met Brip. He told me I reminded him of his mom, that's why he feel in love with me." she smiled.

Bobby had told me the same thing. Unless they had different mothers, I didn't see how we both could remind them of their mother, considering we were two totally different personalities.

"I got to meet Papa Badd though. He's kind of unforgettable, God rest his soul."

Bobby didn't talk much about his mom or dad. I was happy I was able to get better insight of them through Taffy.

"He died of a heart attack last year. I'm sure you already know that though."

I nodded. Bobby told me that much but he didn't tell me how his mother died and I didn't feel propelled to ask.

Dusting off the loose white fur her dog left on her designer shirt, she poured herself another glass of champagne. "Brip is so glad you're here. He even agreed to take us shopping before dinner. I can't believe that. He hates shopping," she told me like I was supposed to be excited.

"Really," I mustered up an anxious voice.

"He's the most family oriented out the bunch," she bragged. "Well…I take that back. That's Brock. He's the most family oriented; in a crazy, stalker kind of way," she whispered the end part like someone could hear us.

"So, did you have to go through the test too?" I switched gears.

"Of course," she said like it was nothing.

"I'm still kind of freaked out."

"Yeah…so am I and that was three years ago," she said with wide eyes. "That crazy motherfucker had me in a body bag, stuffed in the trunk, hog-tied and gagged," she said, shaking away the awful memory. "But, that's just how it goes. I got Brip at the end." She said it like she won the grand prize. "I love him so much. I'm the only one that can tame that fool," she laughed. "Well…kind of tame him. He even listens to me more than Brock and Mona. Before Brip met me, he was like a wild wolf running the streets terrorizing everybody who passed him. I calm his nerves. He says I balance him."

"Has anything like that happened to you since?" I was referring to the test.

"No," she said to me like I was silly. "Can't nobody touch us, girl. All that shit is formality brought upon by Brock and Mona!" She spit out their names like they left a bitter taste in her mouth. At that moment, it was at the tip of my tongue to mention Billy but something told me to wait. So I mentioned Dalla instead.

"What about Dalla? Did she not make the cut?"

"What!" Taffy widened her eyes at me. "Who told you about Dalla?"

"Oh, Bobby mentioned her and I was just wondering what happened."

"Well what did he say?" She looked serious.

"Nothing. I mean I don't remember. Who was she?"

Taffy hesitated for a moment. She looked me straight in the eyes like she was trying to read me. I don't know why she was acting so paranoid.

"She's Billy's wife. Billy married her a year before Brip married me," was all she said.

I left it alone.

Taffy pushed her champagne to the side and started to squirm in her seat like she was uncomfortable. Her mood totally changed.

"So, I don't have to worry about getting attacked?" I asked to break the ice.

She relaxed a bit and a few seconds later was back to her bubbly self. "Girl…please. There ain't nothing in the world like being a Badd wife. We got more protection than the president. It's like we own the world. Our husbands are handsome, powerful and filthy rich," she bragged. "And, at the end of the day, they so into this whole family thing that we don't have to worry about them leaving us for another woman. We in it to the end girl," she said, holding up her hand for me to clap.

"But," she paused. Her face dropped. "The hardest part about being a Badd is cutting all the ties we had before us. We live a private, segregated life and sometimes that can get lonely; that's why I'm happy I have you," she smiled at me. "I didn't have many friends before Brip. My closest ties were with my mother and my older brother, Tony. He and Brip just couldn't get along and he didn't fit in so…" she dropped her head shamefully. Then she shook away the bad memory and pepped back up. "But, mama is so happy! She loves it all. I don't get to see her much but she is so proud of me. Brip set her up in a nice place in Vegas right near all her favorite casinos. She drives a Benz and gets a hefty allowance each month although she finds some kind of way to run through it before the month ends. But, Brip doesn't care…he just makes the deposits as I request them. The last time I seen her, she told me I made her proud."

"I don't have any ties," I said.

"Good for you. Your transition should be easy." Taffy took a small bite of a tea sandwich, chewed it down to nothing before swallowing it like it was a thick piece of meat. "I better not eat any more. I gained three pounds this year," she said like she was disgusted with herself.

"Has Bobby been engaged before?" I asked, trying to get the low down on Bobby's life before me.

She gave me an amused look. "Are you serious? "No way. I thought Bobby was going to die a bachelor. You must really got something special down there…" she pointed to her crotch. "Maybe I can borrow some of that to keep Brip from straying so much," she laughed like what she said didn't bother her.

"Straying?"

"Fucking other women," she said in a matter of fact tone. "They all do it," she told me like it was nothing.

My heart started to sink thinking of Bobby touching another woman.

"I don't care though. Brip comes home to me and kisses only me. That's the one thing we have that's special. The kissing. It's our agreement. Fuck the whores but don't kiss them!" Taffy voice dropped as she looked off into dead space with weary eyes. Then she took a deep breath. "Brip really loves me," she said like she was trying to convince herself. "He's crazy about me."

"I hope I don't have that problem with Bobby. I don't know if I can handle it like you."

"I hate to burst your bubble but, all Badd boys have something on the side but it's just a side dish, we are the entrees," she forced herself to smile.

After hearing her Badd wife confession, I got so tense I had to pour myself another glass of champagne. I didn't take her advice to heart. Bobby and Brip shared the same last name but they were as different as night and day. I dismissed her theory.

11

When Brip came to pick Taffy and me up for dinner, he brought a dozen red roses for each of us. I was surprised because he didn't strike me as the romantic type. As he gave me the roses, he smiled widely. Taffy was just as proud at his kind gesture.

"See...my man is so romantic. Nobody would believe me if I told them that he does stuff like this all the time," she sniffed and patted the roses like they were delicate.

"I hope you don't be telling nobody shit like this," Brip said roughly.

"Shut up, Brip!" Taffy said and snapped her fingers at Bruno, ordering him to place them in one of her crystal vases. "Why the hell you got an attitude anyway?"

"These dudes driving me crazy," Brip started to rub his head, pacing back in forth like he was a ticking time bomb.

I stepped away from him just in case he decided to explode. I didn't want to get caught in the crossfire.

Just like Bobby, Brip had his own crew of minions. The only difference was that Brip's minions seemed to be more terrified of Brip then Bobby's men were of him. Not that Bobby was weaker but Brip was just crazier. His minions were frightened by Taffy, too. When she walked near them, they all scattered like she was plagued.

"What the hell did those ingrates do now?" Taffy threw her hand on her hip and rolled her neck.

"They just fuck things up!" Brip punched a hole in the wall.

"Damn it, Brip…I just fixed that wall. I already told you if you're pissed off, punch one of those fucking assholes, not my wall!"

"I'm sorry, baby," he said, rubbing his hand over the hole like he could fix it. "They just drive me crazy!"

"Bring them in here!" Taffy demanded.

Seconds later, three fidgety men marched in the room with Brip behind them looking like a slave driver. They were silent and kept their eyes glued to the floor. They lined up in front of Taffy like they already knew the procedure. "Which one fucked up your day and in turn part of my evening?" She gave the men evil stares.

"That one," Brip said, pointing to a heavy set guy standing in the middle.

Taffy walked up to him and he closed his eyes tight and flinched. Taffy clutched her small hand into a fist, leaned back on her legs and jabbed him across his chubby cheek. "Ah…" the man hunched over and moaned. Brip whaled with laughter.

"Ha, ha," he leaned over and slapped his knee. "Damn…my baby can throw a punch," he said looking at me with wide eyes.

I gave him an uneasy smile. For Taffy to be as little as she was he was right, she threw a mean jab.

"That's my wife man," Brip said, punching air, causing the other men to jump. "Whoa…" he wailed and punched the guy on the opposite side of the cheek, sending him to the ground. "Ha," he laughed again.

"You feel better now?" Taffy asked meanly.

"Hell, yeah!" Brip yelled, lifting her of the ground and pinning her against the wall to kiss her. "Let's go," he said and slapped her on the butt. "We got some shopping to do."

——

Brip drove the exact style and color Hummer as Bobby; maybe it was a Badd thing. He opened the door for Taffy and I. Taffy sat in the back seat with me. As we pulled off, his group of minions trailed behind us in a black Beamer.

"Girl, you gone love this place. No one knows about it," she raved.

We were supposed to be going to some kind of underground fashion warehouse that had all the designer clothes before they came out. Taffy went on and on about how nice it was.

Brip weaved in and out of traffic, bullying all the other cars with his oversized Hummer. He drove like a madman. He honked his horn, flashed his middle finger and laughed whenever he almost ran someone off the road. I kept my seatbelt on extra tight but Taffy didn't seem to mind. She just let her body jerk back and forth like she was on a roller coaster and held on to the arm grip whenever he made a sharp turn that felt like we were going to flip over. As fast and careless as Brip drove, his men managed to tag behind, staying close to his bumper. I guess they knew better than to fall behind.

"Do they go everywhere with you?" I said, pointing over my shoulder at the men.

"Girl, yes," Taffy said like it annoyed her. "I just ignore them unless I have to intervene like I did a few minutes ago."

"How often is that?" I was curious.

"Too often," she sighed. "One time I broke my finger punching one of them fools. Brip got so pissed, he broke the man's leg," she whispered. "He's a loose cannon but I'm the only one that can keep him from exploding," she said proudly.

Brip turned up the stereo. The music blasted so loud I felt the vibrations in my seat. I couldn't hear myself think. Taffy noticed that I was uncomfortable. She leaned over and slapped Brip across the back of the head. He jumped and gave her a mean look. "Turn that shit down! You're not in this damn car alone!" He turned the volume down. Taking his eyes off the road, he turned toward me to apologize. I accepted his apology quickly, hoping he put his attention back on the road.

"There goes the warehouse over there," Taffy shirked with excitement and pointed over my shoulder at what looked like an abandoned factory. I couldn't imagine a place that housed all the designer fashions Taffy raved about looking so drab.

We were no more than a few blocks from the warehouse when Brip turned the corner and set his attention on a nerdy looking guy, speed walking nervously along the side walk.

"What the hell are you doing, Brip?" Taffy yelled when Brip made a U-turn so sudden, it felt like the car was going to flip over.

The car spun around so fast, I got whiplash. Then he put the car in reverse, speeding backward before slamming his foot on the brake so hard, the tires screeched.

"Brip! What the hell are you doing?" Taffy yelled.

"I got a fish to catch!" Brip said with a smile.

"This was supposed to be family time! Damn...don't you ever get enough of work!" she pouted, folding her arms against her chest.

Brip didn't respond. He continued to watch the man rush down the street. A strange look spread across Brip's face. He leaned up, pulling out a wallet sized photo from his back pocket and stared down at the photo, then back at the man. His face lit up and evil grin stretched so far across his cheeks, the corners of his lips where in his ears. He pushed the picture back in his back pocket.

"What the hell! Is today my lucky day or what?"

"Hell no..." Taffy fussed.

"Damn woman...silence!" he yelled. Taffy sucked her teeth loud and rolled her eyes.

"Ya'll buckle up," Brip warned us. I was already strapped down but Taffy ignored him. "It's about to get ugly over here...Hee Haw!" he yelled out, sounding like a cowboy instigating a dual. He revved up the engine, pressing hard on the gas a few times with his foot still on the break. "He, he," he chuckled and bounced up and down in his seat.

Without further warning, Brip slammed his foot on the gas, speeding in the direction of the man. Swerving his car over the curve and on top of the sidewalk, he blocked the guy's path, causing him to come to an immediate halt. When Brip jumped out, the guy looked horrified. He stared back at Brip with his mouth dangling open like he was looking at the Grim Reaper himself; and to him, I guess that's just who Brip was.

The guy didn't even try to run; it didn't make sense. Brip tackled him down, using more force than necessary, brutally stomping the guy with a heavy foot. He looked like he was enjoying every bit of it. The man curled up into a ball, protecting his face while Brip continued to kick him, looking like he was trying to bust a piñata, heckling insanely.

"Hurry the fuck up, Brip!" Taffy yelled from the window like she wasn't fazed by what was happening.

I tried my best not to look.

A few seconds later, Brip's men pulled up. He pinned the man down with his boot against his back. Cars passing by gave us horrified stares. "Get the cuffs! This dude's under arrest!" Brip yelled. "Hell, yeah!" he screamed again, excited.

One of the men ran back to the car to get the handcuffs. Brip removed his foot from the man's back. One of his men cuffed the guy like they were the law while Brip read the man his own version of the Miranda rights.

"You been charged with treason mutha fucka! Brock is waiting on you at the ranch. You should have known I was gone find you sooner or later."

"Just kill me right now," the man pleaded to Brip.

"Kill you? What you think we are? Murderers?" Brip asked seriously. "Hell, nah. There's an order to all this shit. You going to the ranch for trial. After that, Brock just might kill you. If you lucky," Brip laughed. "First things first my nigga! I feel for you. I really do," Brip said shaking his head at the guy sympathetically. "You in Brock hand's now," he said through a sigh. "Nobody fucks with Brock 'the Rock' Badd...you gone see," he warned him one last time. His men threw him in the trunk of their car.

I couldn't stop my knees from shaking and I'm sure my heart was going to burst out my chest and shoot straight through Brips windshield. I looked over at Taffy and she wasn't fazed by any of this. How could she be so calm? I tried to pretend all this was normal but the beads of sweat popping up on my forehead was a dead give-away. I kept looking out the window, searching the horrified expressions of other's witnessing this crime. After Brip got back in the car, I avoided looking at him.

"What the hell was that about?" Taffy demanded to know.

"Remember that big fish I was telling you about. The one that I couldn't catch?"

"The same dude you been chasing all year?"

Brip nodded his head and Taffy smiled just as big as he did.

"No way!" she slapped Brip on the shoulder. "You found him?"

"Hell, yah!" he screamed. "Brock gone be so happy and now I finally get that big ass bonus he promised me. Damn!" he screamed.

"You getting that bonus *and* the time off, right?" Taffy asked.

"Yeah…just like I told you"

"So, we're leaving the country?" she got so excited she climbed to the front seat so she could be closer to Brip. "We gone take that six month traveling the world?

"We gone do all of that, baby. Shit, I'm just glad the assignments over. That nigga, Brock been down my throat all year about this dude." Taffy leaned over and wrapped her arms around his neck so tight, Brip swerved in and out of lanes.

"Shit, all this excitement got me having to piss. I'm going to the gas station to take a whiz," Brip said pulling into a Texaco.

As soon as Brip got out the car, Taffy climbed back to the back seat with me. "Honey, I'm so sorry you had to witness that. Especially after all you been through. Don't worry…when we get to the restaurant we gone order something cold and bubbly to relax you and when you start shopping, you gone forget all about this shit. The warehouse may not look like shit but it's the bomb! Trust," she patted me on top of the knee. "I have to see shit like this all the time. You lucky Bobby is more of a business man. My husband business is whooping nigga's asses all day" she said prideful. "But, this one guy…Brock sent Brip after him a year ago. He the only man Brip ever took so long to bring in. Usually, Brip find these runways within two months but not this guy. Brock assured Brip a few months ago that if he found this guy, he'd give him a hefty bonus and six months off. That's when Brip promised he'll take me on a tour of the world. We going to Spain, France, and India…" she counted with her fingers. "Everywhere!"

"What did the guy do?"

Taffy shrugged like she wasn't concerning herself with the guy's offense. "Whatever it was it was fucked up enough for Brock to send Brip after him. I don't get into all that. The less I know about who he hunts… the better," she said through a sigh.

A few seconds later, Brip skipped back to the car proudly. "All right ladies. It's time to shop til ya drop."

Brip drove us back a few blocks down the road to the warehouse and we were back on track.

We stayed at the warehouse no more than an hour after the incident. Although the place was every bit of the fabulous Taffy raved it to be, I'd lost my desire to shop; all I could think about was the man Brip tackled and cuffed like a savage.

Brip loaded up the trunk with our things. I sat in the car silently.

"You all right…Lera?" Taffy asked me genuine. She rubbed my back and I felt a little more comfortable. She understood how I felt. "You're just still all wound up because of that stupid…," she whispered close to my ear, covering her mouth "test you had to go through with Bobby. Trust me, it'll get better and I know because I've been there."

Brip hoped back in the car and watched me carefully out the rearview mirror. I didn't want to be rude on account of all the hospitality shown to me by Brip and Taffy so, I forced a smile on my face, pushing the entire incident out of my mind. "I know," I smiled at Taffy. "I really had a good time. Thanks so much Brip," I leaned up, placing my hand on top of his shoulder.

"Don't mention it, sis," he said to me, shaking away my thank you with his head. "I'll do anything for you cause we family." He looked at me through the rear view mirror, smiling with his eyes. "That's the type of family we are. We tight like this," he held up crossed fingers.

"That's right, baby," Taffy agreed, nodding at Brip and me like she finally felt complete.

———

"Where we eating? I feel like that steak place that got that real good crab dip?"

"You mean the one where you fucked the entire staff of sleazy waitress…I don't think so," Taffy said shaking her head, giving Brip a sour look. "On second thought," she leaned in closer to Brip. "Let's go there," Taffy said like she was on a mission.

"Nah…that's okay," Brip said calm.

"I want that crab dip!" She kicked the back of the seat like she was about to pitch a fit. "Now take me there!" she demanded.

"Damn, woman! Alright."

When we entered the restaurant, it seemed like every female waitress got stuck in time when they saw Taffy and Brip; especially, Taffy. They leered at us cautiously as Taffy marched towards a table, seating us just as if she were the hostess herself. She shot the women evil looks as they humbly avoided eye contact with her. Brip just followed behind her like nothing was going on, but Taffy obviously had a motive. She lead us to a table with a reserved card on top of it. She threw the sign on the floor like it was irrelevant.

"Can we sit here?" I asked innocently.

"We can sit wherever we want. Who's going to stop us?" Taffy asked quickly.

The waitresses got uneasy. Huddling in groups, they whispered to one another, watching us out the corner of their eyes. It looked as if they were debating on who was going to be our server. After a few short moments, a woman broke from the crowd and slowly walked in our direction.

"Mrs. Badd," she addressed Taffy with a respectful nod, "Mr. Badd," she said to Brip without looking at him.

"You don't address my husband. Don't even look at him!" she snapped. The waitress nodded at Taffy as she gave her an intimidating stare. "Get us the best and coldest champagne. And I mean cold!" she pounded against the table with her fist, sending the waitress rushing towards the bar. "Brip fucked her too. Can you believe it? That damn girl looks like a gremlin? I mean seriously!" Taffy said to me casually.

Brip looked around the room like Taffy's conversation had nothing to do with him. Anxiously drumming the table with his finger, he rapped a melody under his breath while bobbing his head to his own little tune; he entertained himself, paying no attention to Taffy or her mischievous motives.

"Don't forget to order me that crab dip," Brip said before darting up.

"Where the hell are you going?"

"I got to make a phone call and then take a piss," he whined.

"Are you taking a bathroom break or a fuck break?" Taffy yelled.

Brip didn't respond. He sighed, giving her a dismissive wave. "I'll be back and I want my dip. Get me a Guinness, too. Ice cold," he demanded. Taffy rolled her eyes.

She watched Brip until he disappeared. 'They have good crab dip," she said to me in a sweet voice like she was never upset. "You feeling a little better?"

"I guess," I said with a shrug.

"Good," Taffy said as the waitress returned with our champagne. "Are you our waitress?" she gave the woman an evil stare.

"Yes, mam...I mean Mrs. Badd."

"Hell no...get me Jewels. I want her to serve us and I know the bitch is here cause she ain't got nowhere else to be. Unless she out fucking someone else's husband."

"I'll get Jewels," the waitress told us like she was relieved she had been released from her tortuous assignment.

"Girl, wait until you see this bold bitch!"

"Who is she?" I asked not really wanting to hear her response. I kind of figured who she was already.

"The boldest bitch that ever screwed my husband. This bitch spent two nights with Brip," Taffy gestured with her fingers, "and she got brand new. She started to think that made her wifey. She had the nerve to approach me in public!" Taffy said like that was the ultimate offense. "Telling me about what my man did to her, how she was in love with him and then she told me about all these other bitches in here that he fucked! She even had a threesome with one of the girls in here," Taffy said looking around the room like she was trying to find the girls.

"Brip just comes here for the crab dip but apparently, he leaves with a little more than that sometimes; he can't help it. Women throw themselves at him every day and sometimes he falls into their trap but he only kisses me" she made an excuse for his behavior. "When I told Mona about her approaching me in public, I begged her to let me handle it myself. You don't approach a Badd wife in public; that's a grave offense. Mona handed her over to me and I wore her ass out for a good hour! Hell, talk about a cardio workout. You better watch and learn Lera because these bitches screw our husbands and think they don't have to respect this," She held up her B necklace, "But they wrong."

A few seconds later, a red bone girl with a long auburn colored weave, small waist and huge butt came walking slowly towards the table. She looked like she was walking into a death sentence.

"I'll be your server today," the woman's voice shook.

"Hmm," Taffy said. "I need some ice cold water, with a hint of lemon and *my husband's* favorite…the crab dip appetizer. Lera, you know what you want yet?"

"Just water for now," I said giving the freighted woman an uneasy smile.

"And you better hurry," Taffy said with a bald fist. As soon as she left she turned to me and laughed. "Did you see the scratch on her left cheek. The one that's shaped like a half moon?"

I nodded although I didn't see it; I wasn't looking at her that closely.

"I put that there," she said proud. "Now, when she looks in the mirror, she'll always remember how she fucked up."

Within seconds, the woman returned with a tray of water and the crab dip. She tried to put the glasses and the food down and leave but Taffy wasn't letting her get away that easy. "Um…get back here." Taffy screamed. "Did I say you were dismissed?"

"Can I get you anything else, Mrs. Badd?"

"I don't know. Just stand there a while, I'll think of something."

Looking like a fool, the woman did exactly what Taffy asked. She stood in front of our table with her hands crossed behind her back and her eyes on the floor, waiting for Taffy to summons her. Brip returned to the table with a naïve and hyper look in his eye.

"Where my dip?" he asked Taffy not even acknowledging the girl. I don't even think he recognized her. "Hell, yeah!" he said once he spotted the dip. He devoured it like a savage.

Taffy stared at the girl, making sure she didn't look Brip's way and she didn't. She kept her eyes lowered to the floor. Grabbing her water, Taffy dipped her finger inside and swirled around ice cubes. "This water isn't cold enough," she said to the girl. "See," she told the woman before throwing the water out of the glass on her face. The woman jumped and ran away from the table humiliated; Brip didn't even look up from his dip.

"Weak ass," Taffy said under her breath, shaking her head. "Watch and learn Lera, watch and learn," she told me.

———

After two weeks of living with Taffy and Brip, I started to feel comfortable with them. I was an only child and didn't have many friends back home. It was nice finding both a sister and a friend in Taffy. She was the only person in the world that could understand my relationship with Bobby. Brip still was a little scary but I got used to him; I knew he wouldn't hurt me. I talked to Bobby on the phone all the time. He texted me before I went to sleep to tell me that he loved me. He was out of town on business but promised he'd be back up before I left to stay with Mona and Brock so we could have some time together. I couldn't wait to see him again.

Taffy kept us busy during the day while Brip worked. After we worked out, we spent almost half the day lounging around at a spa. I didn't mind the spa treatments. Getting an hour massage every day and a soothing hot mud bath really eliminated a lot of stress.

One morning, Taffy didn't wake me up like she used to, so I walked to her room to look for her. I tapped on the double doors and waited for

Taffy to reply. It took her a while to answer but through a cracked voice, I heard her tell me to come inside. Taffy and Brip's bedroom looked like something out of a magazine. It reminded me of an adult version of a princess's room, the way the oversized canopy draped sheers around the huge bed. The room was full of light. And of course, everything was white. Taffy looked like she'd been crying. Her eyes were red and puffy. She had a box of tissues in her lap and was dabbing her eyes.

"What's wrong?" I took a seat next to her and placed my hand on her knee.

Taffy sniffed hard, and then to started to sob. She shrugged her shoulders. "I'm just not having a good day."

"I'm sorry," I said, patting her leg. "Tell me what's wrong?" I asked her softly and she started to sob again. "Is Brip okay?"

"Yes," she said blowing her nose. "He's great! Happy and great!" she repeated sarcastically. "And I'm sad," her voice cracked.

"Why?" She wasn't telling me enough.

"Because that's just how shit is sometimes," she looked at me with wide eyes before sniffing hard. After taking a deep breath, she fell back on her pillow, burying her face in the cushion.

"Let's get out the house…maybe some fresh air will make you feel better," I said, pulling her up.

"No…I don't want to," Taffy whined. "I just want to lay here and not get back up," she started to sob again, before throwing the sheets over her head like she was going to sleep the day away.

I pulled them off of her. "Get up Taffy! I'm not going to leave you like this. I'm going to shower and when I get back we're out of here."

"Okay," she said to me before rolling out the bed like a zombie.

About an hour later, Taffy was ready to go. Makeup covered the bags under her eyes and she was dressed flawlessly from head to toe; she really cleaned up well. Taffy was sitting outside on her terrace, sipping a glass of tea. "You were right. I need some fresh air," she said breathing in hard, inhaling the air. "And, I feel like shopping." A strange look appeared on her face.

"Whatever makes you feel better," I told her.

"You're right. I *should* do what makes me feel better. Let's go. I know just the place to shop."

I was surprised when Taffy didn't call a driver. Instead, she took the keys to Brip's silver drop top Benz that he called Bullet, and drove us herself. We went to a trendy area in Atlanta near Ponce De Leon Avenue. It wasn't too far from where Taffy lived. Much like where Bobby lived, it was full of cute clothing boutiques and specialty shops. I was surprised Taffy chose this area to shop because she seemed like the type of girl that only wore the designer labels.

"Is the place we're going to as nice as where Brip took us?" I tried to get Taffy to talk. She was quiet in the car which was totally unlike her. Most of the trip, she stared down at her cell phone. I didn't know what she was looking at and didn't bother to ask.

"Hell, no!" she shot back. "These shitty stores are full of fashions from cheap ass local wannabe designers," she shouted.

"Oh," I said confused about why we were even shopping at a place she thought was beneath her.

"But, you can get whatever you want," she assured me, pepping up her tone. "I know I am," she said before stuffing her cell phone back into her vintage Louis Vuitton clutch.

We parked in front of a cute store called the *Lily Boutique.* Looking at the displays in the window of all the trendy sun dresses and leather strappy sandals, I already was excited but Taffy frowned at the store like she was the fashion police. "This shit is so cheap and tacky! *The Lily Boutique,*" she said under her breath. "There ain't nothing in here that look like a Lily," she complained.

After we walked in the store, Taffy continued her critique by judging everything she looked at with a frown. "What kind of fabric is this?" she said, running her hands across a cute, white strapless dress.

"You don't like it? I think you'll rock this?" I tried to make her feel better, but she shot me a mean look instead.

"*Please,*" she shook her head but grabbed the dress from me anyway, throwing it over her arm like she was going to purchase the item.

Taffy took slow steps, watching every corner of the store. "Tacky," she said shaking her head. Then, she started to go rack by rack, snatching one of each item. Taffy piled up the clothing she thought to be cheap. When she couldn't carry it all, she dropped the pile off at the register. When she saw me with my one item, she got mad. "What are you doing? That's all you want?" I shrugged. "Get one of everything here," she demanded. "Jewelry and purses included, I'm going do the same… okay."

"It's okay Taffy. I don't…"

She cut me off. "You want to help make me feel better?" she asked with her hands on her hip. I nodded, *yes*. "Then just do what I say," she pleaded with me and I did just that.

The counter was so full with our things, the sales clerk had to call the manager for assistance. "Wow. Um…I'm going to have to get my boss out here to help me with this."

"You got one of everything right?" Taffy asked me, looking through my pile of garments that was so high, it looked like a mountain of fabric; her pile was even higher than mine. Some of the clothes toppled over, falling on to the other side of the counter.

"Yes. But a few things they didn't have in my size so…"

"No," she cut me off again, slapping the counter top with her tiny hand. "Just get it anyway. We'll figure out what to do with it all later," Taffy got frustrated. "Maybe we can donate it charity. Bums wear cheap ass clothes anyway!"

"Okay," I said, confused. I went back to the racks and pulled off all the things I left behind and added them to my pile. I knew money didn't matter to Taffy and Brip but with each dress being no less than one hundred dollars, I knew the bill was going to be fat.

The sales clerk returned with the manager who was smiling like it was Christmas. Her eyes lit up seeing all the purchases we were willing to make. After observing her gold plated name tag that read, Lily, I put two and two together and figured she was the owner of the store. Lily looked like a Victoria secret model. She was thin and slightly curvy with flawless skin and big pearly white teeth. I couldn't tell if the long wavy hair that swooped around her shoulder was a good weave or her real hair. What was strange to me was the way Taffy watched the woman like she'd stolen her bike. Taffy looked at her like she wanted to kill her. But, Lily was so fascinated by our purchases, she barely looked at Taffy and didn't notice the evil looks she was getting.

"Wow...I really appreciate your business! I just opened this place and was hoping the sales would pick up. You guys are pretty much buying me out!" She giggled. "To make things easier, I'm going to take these items to the back to tally them up and box them. I'll return with your total" she said through a wide smile.

As soon as she turned her back, Taffy scorned her. "Did you see that bitch's nose? The shit looks like a beak? Ewe!" she said like she was disgusted. "Flossing that cheap ass weave!"

"Well...you giving her enough money today to get herself a nose job," I joked.

"Hmm...you think so?" Taffy asked sarcastically, with an evil smirk.

A few minutes later, Lily returned with balance and the all of our things packed neatly. The sales clerk stacked the boxes on top of each other in a pile so high, we couldn't see her face anymore. "Mam...that will be $17,000. How do you plan do pay for this? Cash or charge?"

"Oh, I'm definitely charging this," Taffy said in a snide, matter of fact tone. "Have your girl start putting my things in the trunk, please." Taffy ordered her and Lily nodded at the sales clerk to go ahead. "Lera...could you help her while I clear the balance up. I don't feel like being here all day."

"Sure," I said and started to grab the boxes to assist the sales clerk.

The clerk grabbed the arm truck and stacked our boxes on top of it, carrying all of our purchases out to the car in one shot. What couldn't fit in the trunk, we stuffed in the backseat. The manual labor of it all was exhausting. When we got back in the store, Taffy was yelling at Lily and waving her fist in the air.

"What's going on, Taffy?"

"I'm fine!" she yelled. "I'm just letting this little bitch know that I'm not giving her a penny!" Taffy knocked a display of faux jewelry off the counter before turning over racks in the store like a mad woman.

"I'm calling the police!" Lily yelled.

"Don't be stupid. You already fucked up enough," Taffy pointed her finger at Lily who was holding the phone in her hand.

"You can't just steal this shit from me! I work too hard!"

"You worked too hard doing what? Sucking on my man's dick?"

On that note, I knew what was going on.

Embarrassed, Lily swallowed hard and lowered the phone. That's when Taffy pulled her B necklace out of her shirt and flashed it in Lily's face. Lily stared back at it frozen and speechless. "Yeah! Don't say another word. This is how I'm paying for this shit!" Taffy taunted her. "Now say something you whore!" Taffy pushed the register off the counter and it crashed at Lily's feet.

"You can't do this," the woman's voice cracked.

"Watch me bitch and learn!"Snatching items off a few racks, Taffy started to scatter clothes all over the floor; she was vandalizing the store.

"I'm calling the cops!" Lily screamed but Taffy continued to wreck the place. She knocked things off shelves, kicked the displays down from the window and threw shoes across the store. She aimed one of the shoes at Lily who ducked.

Taffy walked towards Lily. "This is my warning to you. Stay –the-fuck-away-from-my husband!" she stepped behind the register and jabbed the girl across the cheek so hard, she fell back. "Let's go," she told me before kicking the glass door open. "Trashy, cheap ass bitch!" she yelled over her shoulder.

When we got back in the car, Taffy sped off like a mad woman. She was driving worse than Brip.

"You want me to drive?" I asked calmly with my nails digging into the leather seats.

"No! I'm fine!" she said and started to sob.

"Taffy, pull over!" I urged her. "You're in no position to drive."

"No, I said I'm fine," she told me, swerving over into a lane opposite of traffic, honking viscously at the cars coming in her direction like they were in the wrong.

We were no more than a few miles from the store when I heard sirens chiming in behind us. Taffy was going at least 90 miles per hour in a 35 mile speeding zone and blue flashing lights didn't prompt her to slow down. Instead, she sped up.

"Taffy," I talked to her like she was a mental patient. "You don't think you should pull over? I don't think those cops are going to stop chasing us?"

"Fuck them and that bitch! And Brip!" she sobbed. "Fucking asshole. You know how long I've wanted my own shop! But no, a Badd wife doesn't work." she said wiping away her tears, making room for new ones. "I asked him for a boutique just like that one but no..." she wailed. "He wouldn't have it but he helps that bitch! That ugly bird nosed whore! She doesn't even know what the hell she's doing! I know he gave her the money to start that cheap ass shit! That bastard," she spit out.

Taffy ran a red light, disturbing traffic so much she almost caused two wrecks and the police were still on our trail. I didn't understand why she was reacting so erratically when she told me herself that she didn't care when Brip had sex with other women. She made it seem like it was something she could handle but she was proving me wrong.

"Taffy, you got to slow down. She's not worth us wrecking or getting arrested."

"No one's arresting us!" she said like she was sure. "And, Brip isn't just having sex with this girl! He's having a real affair with her!" she yelled.

I was confused; to me a real affair was having sex with someone that wasn't your spouse but Taffy and Brip had their own set of weird rules.

"He thinks he's so clever, but I stay two steps ahead of him. I have informants out there just like he does. It's been a rumor that he'd been seen out of town with that bitch more than once and that's not like Brip; he hits it, quits it, and comes home to me...his faithful wife! I didn't believe it at first. I needed proof and this morning...I got it." She reached for her purse and pulled out her cell phone. The car continued to swerve in and out of lanes as she fidgeted with the buttons before throwing her phone in my lap. "See," she said. "He's kissing that bitch," she started to breath heavy like she was having a panic attack, "he has his mouth on hers. Brip would never kiss that woman if he didn't have feeling for her!" she started to sob so heavily, I had to take hold of the wheel.

"Taffy, slow down," I told her and she slammed her foot on the brakes so hard, the car did a 360. Luckily, we didn't hit anything or anyone but the cop didn't waste any time, jumping out the car and drawing his gun at us.

"Oh my gosh," I ducked, remembering Bobby and his fake police drill. But now, this was the real thing.

Taffy didn't care about him pointing a gun at us. Annoyed, she wiped the tears from her eyes and rolled down her window. "Get that fucking thing out of my face," she said before holding up her necklace. Right away, the cop put his gun away, holding out his hands like he was sorry. "Are you crazy!" she yelled.

"Oh, Mrs. Badd…you have to be more careful. You were going way too fast."

"Go away," she barked at him and he left. "Brip's going to leave me," she sobbed.

12

Taffy Badd

have to admit, I was a relieved when Bobby came to pick up Lera today. Not that I didn't enjoy her company because I really do like her but I just couldn't save face around her any more. Seeing the way her and Bobby embraced made me remember when me and Brip's love was fresh; new love is the best love. Then reality sets in and you have to make shit up just to convince yourself that nothing's changed or that you didn't make a mistake. I spend most of my days fantasizing about shit that ain't real but hell…it keeps me going.

Had I met Lera a few months earlier, I wouldn't have to fake the funk like it all wasn't bullshit because then I still was convincing myself that I really was living the life. I thought that I was blessed for being a part of a family as affluent and powerful as the Badds. But, to marry one of them is giving up all the power you possess; like your voice, dreams and ambitions. The Badd name is my entire existence and I have no say in anything. The name, the life, the money…it's all bullshit.

I was still street fighting when I first met Brip. He fell in love with me at first sight after seeing me take out his most lucrative fighter. Shortly after that, we were engaged to be married and the timing couldn't have been more perfect because me and mama were really struggling.

Before Brip, my brothers Keno and Tony took good care of us but all that changed when my oldest brother, Keno got himself killed. My other brother Tony survived a bullet in the head but was never the same. Now, he wanders the street, searching for the people he thinks killed Keno.

They made it a business to rob drug dealers but once they got shot, I was forced to do the only thing I knew how to do to make money... fight.

Keno and Tony were heavy into martial arts and boxing. They taught me everything I know. They started training me at five years old and didn't take it easy on me on account of my age or gender either. I got plenty of bloody noses and other bruises but I took it. Keno used to tell me that in order to give a good punch, I had to learn how to take one. They started calling me Scrappy-Bo I got so good at fighting. That was the name I used when I street fought.

Brip gave me and mama a new life. When I first married Brip I didn't think that I was giving up anything; I thought I was gaining more than I was losing but I was wrong. All I wanted to be was his wife and yes, the power and money was just as enticing as my love for him. But now, I'm starting to see things differently. And, Brip gave me these new eyes to look out of once I seen him kissing that Lily bitch!

Brip has always been honest with me. From day one he told me that he was going to fuck around and that it didn't mean anything so I shouldn't take it like anything. He actually had the nerve to compare his fucking random woman like a sport; it was just something he did in his spare time. "I like to play B-ball, gamble in Vegas, and fuck random women! Those are my top three things to do; it ain't no reason for you to be insecure...you can say you're my wife and all them tramps got to say is they spent a few minutes in the back of a Hummer with Brip Badd!"

That's when I came up with the no kissing pact and he assured me that he never kissed the bitches anyway. "These lips ain't never touched no, hoe!" he assured me. He told me I was the first woman he ever kissed and I took that just as if he was telling me that I broke his virginity and in a way, I kind of felt like I did. Or, at least that was my fantasy to make all his fucking around okay. At the end of the day I felt at ease knowing that Brip was saving something special for me. And, I know that's some serious bullshit but it is what it is. With all the freedom I give him I thought he would have at least had the respect to keep his promise to me and never engage in a real relationship with a woman; but, I guess he just doesn't respect me.

Being a Badd wife used to make me feel important, special even. But now, I feel insignificant and used. Every day. I feel myself growing more distant from Brip but he doesn't bother to notice. I pull away whenever he tries to kiss me. I sleep at the edge of the bed instead of in his nook and whenever he tries to fuck me, I complain of random headaches; I don't want to be bothered with Brip and I know whatever he ain't getting from me, he is getting from Lily.

At first I didn't want to believe it when my informant, a male gay social-ite that saw and heard everything even when he wasn't using his own ears or sight, told me about Brip being strung cut over this cheap ass bitch named, Lily.

"I'm telling you chile...it's true I seen it with my own eyes. They be out everywhere and they be tongue tied like two teenagers. You better check that bitch because Miss Thang got a history. She had three married Falcon players and a few ballers. They say she use to work at a strip club and do all kinds of strange thangs that be getting ya'll men off. Brip is sprung honey...and I can prove it to you!" The next week he sent me that picture of Brip and Lily hugged up at some lounge with her tongue down my husband's throat.

Brip little hyper ass don't put no time or energy into something he doesn't care about. The fact that he is hiding this shit scares me. He must really have feelings for this bitch. According to my informant, Brip and Lily have been hooking up for about six months now and Brip hasn't told me a damn thing, yet!

I trusted the picture text but I still needed my own proof. I started following Brip. I followed him for five days before I caught him with Lily. The shit was exhausting but I kept at it anyway. I learned his pattern. They dined out at the same two restaurants, hung out at her shop and he spent a lot of time at her condo in the city which I'm sure he is paying for.

The day I caught them together, was at Lily's cheap ass boutique and they were inside for almost two hours doing Lord knows what. As soon as he walked inside, she wrapped her arms around his neck and put her lips on my husband's mouth before putting a closed sign on the door. The little fucking tramp!

Now, years of resentment is starting to rise and it's so overwhelming sometimes I just want to pack my bags and run, but where would I go? Besides, Brip could find me anywhere regardless of how far I ran. I was a Badd wife for life. There was no divorce. The only way out was death and even then that wasn't guaranteed.

I really need Billy's wife Dalla right now. She's the only one that can tell me how to handle this shit with Brip and Lily. I loved Dalla; she was the big sister I never had. To this day, I don't think I've ever met anyone as genuine as her and I idolized her and Billy's relationship. Billy treated Dalla like a queen. I was thankful that Brip had role models other than Brock and Mona to look to when it came to relationships because the two of them are real freak shows.

If it wasn't for Dalla I don't know if I could have survived Mona. Mona taunted me non- stop with all her silly rituals and Badd wife lessons. I'm not scared of anyone and don't get intimidated easily but Mona and Brock are scary people even for me. Mona is six feet tall and is built like an ox and Brock is so strange, it's eerie being around him. Everything Mona put me through seemed so unnecessary and petty. It was like she just wanted to see me suffer. That's why I told myself that if Bobby every got married, I would show his wife the same kindness that Dalla showed me but with all the drama I got going on, it's going to be hard.

Brip was hurt the day Mona announced that Billy and Dalla had been exiled from the family for stealing. According to Mona, Dalla helped Billy steal over four million dollars from the family safe before they fled. Brock started to speculate that Dalla was a phony all along and was sent by the Lucky family to tear us apart. The entire thing seems like one big Badd scandal especially after what Brip told me about his mother allegedly having an affair with Carlo Lucky and his speculations that came with that. Brock actually believes that Dalla had Billy steal that money so that he could start a war against us. Billy loves his brothers and would never try to stab them in the back and I couldn't imagine Dalla being a fraud. It all sounds likes some paranoid bullshit.

We were told not to speak of Billy again. That's why Lera is under the impression that Billy got arrested but that's all bullshit. No Badd gets arrested. That was a year ago and it's like they've been phased out as if they never existed at all. Mona even removed their pictures from the family wall. Something ain't right, but I got my own damn problems now. I feel for Lera though. She just don't know the drama she's walking into by becoming a Badd wife and I don't have the heart to tell her.

————

Brip and I are having dinner at a steak house. I can't think of a more perfect time to get him to confess all of his dirty little secrets about his whore, Lily.

Brip barely looked at me. He stabbed at the rib-eye like he was trying to kill it again before shoving large chunks in his mouth. When he did look up, he finally noticed my hair. I had gotten bored and instead of playing the scorned wife, I treated myself to a full day at the spa where I highlighted my hair honey blonde.

"When you do that shit to your hair?"

"A month ago," I lied just to get his attention.

He looked at me carefully. "Really? Damn...I guess my heads been in the clouds lately. I'm sorry I didn't notice it before. That shit is hot though."

"So...your head has been in the clouds huh?" I gave him a strange look.

"Yeah... you know I been on the grind trying to find ole dude. I thought that shit was over when I brought the man to Brock but he ain't giving me what we agreed." Brip looked up at me apologetically.

"So you don't get the time off *and* we're not traveling overseas like you promised?" I pouted.

I didn't believe a word he was saying. He had those six months off like Brock promised; he just didn't want to spend it with me.

"Don't get pissed...it ain't my fault," he wiped his mouth with the back of his hand and leaned back in his seat like he was finally full. "I got to get back out there. Apparently, the search is still on. He ain't giving Brock what he asked for so now I got to go find that shit too. I need to find where the man was staying and bring back some paperwork and shit. The shit is getting exhausting," he sighed and looked like he was expecting me to comfort him; I did no such thing. "I don't even know what all this shit is about. It's weird how obsessed Brock is over this guy." Brip's eye trailed off into dead space and then looked back at me seriously. "I don't know why but...I think this has something to do with Billy and Dalla," he confessed.

I ignored him. Brip and I had our own issues and the Badd family drama was of no interest to me at the moment.

"So *me* and *you* aren't going?" I said emphasis the words *me* and *you*, as if he was taking someone else; maybe Lily.

"What you mean?" I finally had his attention.

I slapped the table. "I mean you're not taking me on a trip!"

"Calm down, Taffy," Brip said, rubbing his head like he was getting annoyed. "We gone make that trip, it just ain't gone be as soon as you thought. Come on," he reached over and placed his hand on top of mine. "You know I don't lie to you."

I snatched my hand from underneath his like it was hot. "Do I know that?"

Brip looked back at me like he was trying to read my mind. "What the hell you mean?"

"You didn't understand my question?"

"Hell no!" Brip answered defensively.

"Well...I don't know how to make you understand." I rolled my eyes.

Brip leaned back in his seat and scratched the top of his head like he was confused. The average man would have caught on by now but Brip wasn't average. He was so cocky, he really was under the impression that

I still knew nothing about him and Lily. I trashed that bitch's store and socked her in the jaw a few times, but I knew she wasn't silly enough to let Brip know about my little visit. If anything, that would have distracted Brip so much he probably would've stayed away from her for weeks.

"You ain't pregnant again are you?" he said like he was too drained to deal with it.

"I don't know…"

"Come on…," he exhaled, burying his face in his hands. "I knew something was up with you. Your hormones are off. Taffy we can't keep going through this. I told you that before, baby," he said to me softly.

After my third miscarriage, Brip told me to go on the pill and when I refused, he started wearing condoms when we had sex. He said he didn't want me to have to keep going through the miscarriages. I didn't want him fucking me like he fucked his whores so, I went ahead and started taking the pill. But, I'd been so distracted lately, I hadn't taken them. I knew I wasn't pregnant though.

"I'm the one that goes through it Brip! Not you."

"We both go through it. I was right there with you every time," he stabbed the table with his finger.

"I'm sorry you had to go through all that," I started to get choked up.

"You don't have to be, baby. I told you that you're enough for me." He tried to grab my hand again.

"You lied!" I blurted out. "I'm not enough for you!" Tears rolled down my cheeks.

"Damn," Brip shook his head before joining me on my side of the table. He sat down beside me and wrapped his arm around my shoulder. "I'm lucky I don't have to deal with nine months with you like this. You get too emotional when you pregnant."

"I'm not pregnant, you bastard!" I yelled.

"Then what the hell is wrong with you?"

"Ask that bitch you're fucking!"

"Which bitch?" Brip asked me like he really didn't know who I was talking about. "I ain't been with no random bitches in months."

Not only was Brip kissing this bitch, he was giving up his whores for her too.

"Come on…" he sighed heavily, tilting his head to the side and watching me out the corner of his eye.

I think he was finally getting it.

"I know about Lily," I confessed.

Brip jumped and walked back to his side of the table. He kept his eyes fixed on the ground and his lips were glued shut. Then he stared at the ceiling like he was trying to think his way out of the situation. I pulled out my cell phone and showed him the picture I had of him and Lily kissing.

"Who took this?" he asked angrily.

"I did," I lied. "I seen you guys everywhere, Brip," I pounded against the table with my fist. "I know about the store you fronted for her, the expensive ass condo you putting her up in and how much you enjoy kissing that bitch," my voice cracked and I started to cry.

"It…it ain't like that," Brip said, shaking his head.

"You put your lips on her. You gave her things you won't even give me! You want her to be your new wife?"

"Hell, no. You my one and only wife"

"Then what the fuck, Brip?"

"It's complicated," Brip gave short answers and continued to avoid eye contact with me.

"Brip you're having an affair! With all the other shit I turn my cheek to, it still wasn't enough? You don't respect me and I don't believe you love me."

"Now you going too far with this shit! You my wife. I love you!"

"I ain't never gone be enough for you. Can't give you babies and now…this Lily shit. Maybe I should just leave and let you have her."

"Leave," Brip jumped to his feet. Everybody in the restaurant stopped what they were doing to watch us. "What the hell you mean, leave? You ain't going no damn where and if you do you know I can find your ass." Brip said harsh.

"Stop seeing her then!" I demanded. "Drop that bitch!"

"It ain't that simple."

"Why the fuck not?"

Brip sat back down and started massaging his temples. "Look, don't worry about it. This shit is a phase and it's going to pass."

"If you don't leave her, I'm going to keep myself busy whooping that bitch's ass every chance I get."

"Don't touch her, Taffy," Brip said like he was giving me an order. "Just leave this shit be. It'll pass."

"Fuck you, Brip. That bitch's ass is grass!"

"I said leave her be!" Brip yelled. I never felt threatened by Brip but his harsh tone startled me. I got so upset, I ran out the restaurant.

I was sobbing so hard I felt disoriented. I was hunched over the curb, gagging when he pulled me up. "Calm down, Taffy. This ain't nothing to be dramatic about!"

"You're a liar and a cheat and I'll never trust you again. If I'm a prisoner and I can't leave that's fine with me but you won't touch me again. Not as long as you're with that bitch."

"What you talking about I can't touch you? You my wife!" Brip said like I was his personal property and truthfully I was.

"No, you go play house with that bitch!" I said to him seriously. Brip tried to grab my arm but I jerked away from his touch. "Never again!" I repeated and got in the back seat of the car.

"Get your ass in the front," Brip demanded. "I ain't no damn taxi driver."

I ignored him and put in the ear plugs to my I-phone and covered my teary eyes with shades.

When we got home, I tried to sleep in the guest room but Brip wasn't having it. He kicked down the door, grabbed me and threw me over his shoulder, carrying me back to our bedroom like I was his prisoner. "This ain't no fucking hotel. You my damn wife and in my house you gone sleep in my bed where you belong!" He didn't get away that easy though. I kicked him in the stomach so hard I knocked the breath right out of him.

He looked at me like he wanted to kill me but instead he stormed down-stairs to sleep on the couch.

I got up at four the next morning and Brip was gone. I didn't have to guess where he was. That's when I decided to leave too. I was going to Vegas to pay mama a visit and I wasn't telling Brip shit.

13

As soon as I got off the train, I felt liberated. I traveled by train because I knew it would be harder for Brip to track me. Before I left, I sent the guards on a dummy mission so they wouldn't see me get in the cab with my bags. However, I knew it was only a matter of time before Brip found me and Mama's condo was going to be the first place he looked. That's why I didn't plan on staying with her. I booked a hotel at the next town over. It was a shitty hotel that Brip would never expect me to be at. On the ride up, he texted that he loved me but I didn't respond. I'm sure he thought that was all he had to do to blow this thing over but he was wrong. I turned my cell phone off just in case he tried to call me.

It had been a year since I last saw mama. I called her from the hotel phone and when she heard my voice, she already knew something was wrong.

"Girl, what the hell is going on? I hope you ain't down here having no affair cause if you are you is a fool…but since you here, maybe you can front me a little more cash before my next allowance. I'm straight busted, chile."

An hour later, I was at mama's door. Mama stayed in an upscale condo and everything about her building screamed luxury. There was a doorman, a grand foyer entrance with marbled tile floors and the elevator had red velvet carpet and gold plated walls. Brip and I took good care of mama but it still never seemed like enough for her.

As soon as mama opened her front door, I leaped into her arms and sobbed like a child that just fell of their bike. "Taffy? What's done got into you?" she whined before squeezing me back. Mama was wearing what I called her Wendy Williams wig and pink Juicy Couture sweat suit that made her look years younger than what she was.

"I just need a break, mama," I said and walked through the door. I sat down on her leather couch. When I knocked off my shoes and kicked my feet up, she barked at me.

"Girl, take your feet off my couch. That's Italian leather." She slapped my feet down and I straightened my posture right away. Mama sat down beside me, carefully adjusting her body so that she wouldn't disturb the expensive leather. "Your husband know you here?"

"No, and don't tell him!" I warned her.

"Don't put me in this shit! Taffy you married now and Brip is a good man."

"Brip is a tyrant mama and I'm tired of being his slave!"

"Slave! What slave be dolled up the way you be. Jet setting all over the world, doused in the finest jewels and clothing. Girl, you crazy! You must don't remember the hard times before your brothers made it big. Even Keno couldn't provide for us like Brip do. God rest his soul," mama lowered her head, shaking it from side to side.

"Mama, I don't have an identity anymore."

"So," Mama waved her hand at me like I was talking crazy. "Go back to fighting bitches for small change then and I don't know what I'm gone do," she moaned.

I sighed and walked towards the open balcony door to let the fresh breeze hit against my face. I knew mama wasn't going to tell me what I wanted to hear. She wasn't going to say or do anything to jeopardize her lifestyle.

"Brip is cheating on me, mama!"

Mama grunted, chuckling under her breath. She waved her hand dismissively at me and shook her head like I was naive. "So is everybody else's husband in the world, but *you* want to complain about it. Just give him some more time. He'll grow out of it. Hell, the boy ain't even thirty yet."

I turned my back to mama. "I'm starting to feel like there's nothing left to give."

"I'm telling you the truth! You keep whining and complaining the way you are and you don't have to worry about giving him nothing else cause he gone leave you! Then what we gone do?"

Mama was making this entire thing about her but I knew she would.

"If your husband call me, I'm gone tell him that you here," she pointed to the floor with her index finger, "and to come and get you. Y'all need to work this thing out. This ain't gone be the last problem y'all have and you can't be coming to me for no answers. I don't know nothing about being nobodies wife cause I never been married but I do know marriage is a compromise."

"Brip doesn't compromise a damn thing and this affair he's having is real, mama. It ain't like them sleazy women I was complaining about before. And, if he leaves me for her, we both screwed. You want that?" I tried to put fear in mama and it worked. She jumped off her leather sofa so quick she almost toppled over.

"Did you try threatening the girl?" mama waved her fist in the air.

"I been through all that."

"Well you need to do something else. Here you are all the way in another state and you need to be at home trying to figure out what went wrong between you and your husband. You must be doing something wrong and you need fix it quick! You moping around when another bitch got her hand in your purse!" mama cursed me.

Now that mama realized how Brip's affair affected her, she went on and on, yelling and cursing at me. I got exhausted with her blaming me for everything that was going wrong with my marriage so I decided to leave but not before she beckoned me for more money.

"What are you doing with your money? You don't have bills and we give you more than enough every month."

"Don't be questioning me, chile! I got a life out here and all these white folks in this building be trying to upstage me. Besides, it ain't always for me," mama said, lowering her eyes.

"Who then?" I asked shaking my head.

"I've been helping your brother, Tony out."

"Tony? Where is he?"

"I don't know. He be back and forth between here and Atlanta. The boy ain't doing too good. You know they never got the bullet out of his head and it be giving him all kinds of problems. I wanted to try and get him in one of those institutions for the mentally disabled." Mama said shamefully.

"Is he that bad?"

"He ain't right! You know he still hunting for the men that shot Keno. He act like he don't even remember it was years ago. He been harassing innocent folks on the street, claiming they killed his brother. He broke one man's legs, claiming he shot Keno. The boy is dangerous and after while he gone end up getting his self killed and I can't lose my last son. We got to help him."

I sighed heavily, shaking my head. I didn't want to hear any more bad news. I had too much going on. The last time I saw Tony was years ago. I was having lunch with Brip when he approached me. He gave Brip an evil stare and Brip gave him one back. They didn't like each other right off the bat. Brip still offered him work but Tony declined saying he worked solo, further offending Brip. I figured it would be best to keep the two of them separate, yet another sacrifice I was making on account of being a Badd.

I gave mama the money she was asking for to help Tony plus a little something extra, but I told her it was hush money. If Brip called, she wouldn't tell him a thing about my whereabouts. I knew she was lying when she quickly took the money and dumped it in a small basket on her coffee table.

———

I confined myself to my hotel; I stayed an extra day. I kept my cell phone off and didn't bother checking all the messages I knew Brip left for me. I got a little peace knowing how crazy he was going, searching for me.

Brip hated not being in control. I didn't bother calling mama again either. If I knew Brip like I thought I did, him and his crew had already been to mama's house and were hunting the streets for me.

I tried to imagine my life outside of being a Badd and, even with all the resentment I am feeling, I can't. I felt too connected to it all and I am still madly in love with Brip. Brip is the man of his house; he makes the rules and I follow them. I can't work, I can't drive and, believe it or not I am so damned tired of shopping and redecorating that I don't care if I ever do it again. I am in desperate need of something new. Brip had his women and his Lily but I need something of my own, too. Otherwise, it will be the complete and final end of me and I am too young to die alive. Something has to give.

14

The train ride home seemed shorter. I guess I am dreading going home. I was tempted to stay the entire week just to spite Brip but remembering how crazy he is, I decided to go back home and face the drama while bringing a little bit of my own.

I left all my clothing at the hotel in Vegas. I wasn't going straight home and wanted to travel light. I was planning on having the taxi drive me around aimlessly for a few hours but that was too risky for him. If Brip or one of his men spotted me, I knew that would be the end of him and it didn't make any sense for another innocent person to get hurt on account of Brip's behavior. I was victim enough. I told the driver to drop me off at the nearest exit and ironically, it was the city where Lily's shop was located.

I thought about going inside her shop to raise some more hell but surprisingly, I was so emotionally exhausted I didn't have the energy to do it. So, instead I roamed around a nearby park like a hobo. I was clutching my Badd necklace in my hand like it was some magic charm that could change my circumstance if I beckoned it to.

All my wandering was starting to give me a headache. I sat down on a park bench. I found a little joy in watching the children running around playing. Their carefree spirits almost rubbed off on me. My burdens started to feel lighter. I was almost starting to think happy thoughts again but that was short-lived when I saw Lily and a friend actually pointing my way. They were laughing like I was some charity case. I couldn't believe it. I got up to confront them, with my teeth gnashing so tight together I could have spit sawdust. To my surprise, she was boldly making her way towards me.

"Are you seriously looking me in the eye?" I asked.

She had her hand plastered to her hip and was smirking at me like I just missed the joke. "Aw, you look so sad. You know it really happens to the best of us. There's always somebody out there to take your man and the sad thing is...I didn't even have to try that hard," she told me coldly.

I jumped up to swing at her but she stepped back, missing my fist by a few measly inches. "I wouldn't do that if I were you," she said, waving her finger at me like I was a five year old child.

I was so taken back by what was going on, I was speechless. It was almost like I was having an out-of- body experience. Everyone knew better than to confront a Badd in public with bullshit. The bitch wasn't this bold the last time I saw her. I couldn't help but wonder who or what gave her the false since of courage she suddenly had.

"Do you know who I am?"

"I know who you think you are!" she said boldly. "You may have that necklace, but I got something of my own too." She gave me a taunting look. "Brip told me that if you tried to attack me all I have to do is call him and he'll handle it," she said waving her cell phone in my face. "Oh... and that little mishap in my store the other week." she dusted off her shoulders like what I did was nothing, "didn't faze me one bit. Hell, you actually helped me. Brip paid for everything you took and gave me extra money for the damages, so it all worked out good."

Lily rolled her neck at me before snapping her fingers.

The sound of her snapping fingers snapped me back into reality. I didn't give her the space to duck this time. I swung, punching her in the jaw twice before she even knew what hit her. She fell to the ground screaming and fidgeting with her cell phone. Her friend was so scared she was going to be next that she ran off and left Lily squabbling in the grass like a fish out of water.

Mothers grabbed their children and ran like there was about to be a gun fight. I pulled Lily up by her hair only to knock her down again but this time, my fist landed on her eye. She squealed, shielding her face with her hand. She tried to crawl away but I straddled that bitch, pinning her down to the ground, slapping her across the face so many times my hands started to sting. That's when I heard her saying Brip's name. I thought she was on the phone with him but he was behind me. Brip yanked me up so quick, I was slapping air still thinking I was hitting her face.

"What the fuck you doing!" Brip barked at me like I wasn't his sweet wife.

"I told you she was crazy, Brip. She kicked me in the stomach!" she lied, hunching over. I didn't know why she was lying.

"Take her home," Brip ordered one of his men, pushing me toward them. They jumped away from me. They knew what was up. He dove to the ground to tend to Lily. Lily sobbed an exaggerated cry.

"Brip…she attacked me!" she whined

Brip helped Lily to her feet. "Go home, Lily. I'll catch up with you later," Brip said making me feel less than nothing. That's when I really started to go crazy.

I charged towards both of them but Brip grabbed me. I tried to wiggle my way out of his tight restraint. He wrapped his long arms around me and squeezed like an octopus, squeezing its prey. Spit flew out my mouth and I bit my tongue, I was cursing so fast and loud, I was enraged. The more I squirmed and kicked the looser I felt Brip's grip get and eventually I freed myself and attacked him.

I bent my leg upward then kneed him in the crotch. He fell to the ground in front of everybody. Brip hated being embarrassed and I knew hitting him in public was the ultimate disrespect but I didn't care. After what just happened, that made us even but Brip didn't see it that way. He rolled around on the grass, moaning and holding his crotch. I tried to dive on top of him to finish my attack but he flipped himself up before I could get to him. He slapped me so hard across the face, I passed out.

When I came too, Brip had me restrained in the back seat of his Hummer like I was one of his bounties. My hands were tied to the arm rest with a thick rope and Brip was so mad he looked like the devil. My right cheek was still throbbing from his slap but the part that stung the most was the fact that he actually put his hands on me. Brip had never hit me before.

"Let me go! My wrist hurts!" I sobbed. "I can't believe you hit me, Brip."

"Shut the fuck up!" he yelled. He had never yelled at me that way before. He was talking to me like I was one of his prisoners. This was the first time I didn't feel safe since I'd been with him.

"Are you going to shoot me? You gone dump me in the river and drown me aren't you?" I screamed, trying to free myself from the rope.

Brip gave me a wide-eyed stare before swerving the car three lanes over, bringing it to a screeching halt. He jumped out the front seat, slamming the door so hard the entire car shook He jumped in the back seat like he was about to shank me.

"Don't kill me, Brip. Just let me go!" I screamed, flinching the closer he got to me.

Brip pulled a pocket knife out of his sock and flicked it open. I started to scream for my life, closing my eyes tight and pushing my body as far away from Brip as I could. "Please don't cut me," I begged. I got light headed and felt like I was about to lose consciousness. My head started to wobble around on my neck and my chest was so tight with fear I thought my heart was going to explode. I gasped like I was taking my last breath when Brip cut the rope off my hands and pulled me into his chest to embrace me.

He kissed the top of my head and apologized. "I'm sorry, baby. You really think I would hurt you? Huh? You think I'm capable of killing you?" He turned my chin so that I could face him but tears blurred my vision. "I'll never hurt you, Taffy! Never!"

I tried to pull away from him and he started to sob like a baby. I had never seen Brip crying before.

"I fucked up. I really fucked up man," he started to punch himself on top of the head. "I'm sorry, baby. I'm so sorry," he said before jumping out the car. "I didn't mean to scare you."

Brip continued to punch himself. He paced back and forth, mumbling under his breath. "I fucked up!" he burst out the back window with his fist. Blood stained glass shattered in the seat. He got back in the car and sat on top of the glass. His fist was dripping blood all over the car and me. "Did I do that?" he asked, rubbing the side of my bruised cheek, leaving traces of his blood on my face. "Shit," he said, slapping himself in the face. "I'm sorry, baby. I promise," he said and pulled me into his chest again. I continued to cry but the more he squeezed me and apologized the lighter my sobs got.

———

We didn't go home. I was still in shock from everything that happened and didn't notice we were pulling into the ranch until I heard the guard buzz us in. I didn't feel like being at the ranch. Brock and Mona were the last people I wanted to see.

When Brip married me, he inherited a mansion on the ranch along with a percentage of the Badd estate. I loved the house but hated where it was located. I felt like I was living in Mona's backyard as she came and went from my house to hers on a whim. We had no privacy on the ranch and I had no say in anything. Lera doesn't know how lucky she is because I had to live on the ranch for a whole year after Brip and I got married and it was hell. I felt like I was trapped in a luxurious prison and Brock and Mona were the biggest circus acts I'd ever encountered. Now, we only stay at our mansion during holidays and family events. The best part about going to the ranch during the holidays was spending time with Dalla. She made everything easier for me and Mona didn't bully me too much when she was around. Dalla was the first and last person I ever seen stand up to Mona.

The ranch was like a hidden city. It was located about 50 miles outside Atlanta. Only few knew it existed and it all belonged to the Badds. The land wasn't just open spaces of dirt and dry grass but fully developed. There were paved two lane roads, curbs, sidewalks, new buildings and everything else you would expect to see in an upscale city. It was like a mini Buckhead. Brip and all his brothers grew up on the ranch, living in their own world out in the middle of nowhere. Now that Brock and Mona were the ruling authority over the estate, they were putting their own crazy spin on things. Every time I visited, they were building something new.

"Take me home, Brip!" I demanded. "I want to go home."

Brip turned to me and gave me a wide-eyed look like he was shocked I was talking to him. I didn't talk to him on the way up. "Baby! You talking... you okay?" I heard the concern ring out in his voice. Brip was tough as nails but when it came to me, he went softer than putty. And even with all his tough guy training, he wasn't good at handling stressful situations; he totally flipped out under pressure.

"I want to lie in my bed at home." I moaned.

"You are home," Brip reminded me. "We going to stay at the mansion for a few days and I'm gone have the servants waiting on you hand and foot. Our family is in trouble Taffy and I didn't realize that until today. I'm gone make this right," he tried to assure me and reached his hand back to grab mine but I jerked away from his touch.

"Does Mona know we're coming?" I whined.

"Of course. I called her and Brock both. Maybe we can meet with the family counselor later at the Chapel." Brip said, referring to the two story "church" like building where weddings, funerals and the occasional religious ceremonies took place.

"I don't feel like being bothered, Brip," I said holding my head in my hand. "Tell Mona to give me awhile. I just want to lie down," I moaned. All I wanted to do was sleep. It was the only way for me to temporarily forget about everything.

"I'll let her know to give you a few minutes but she is concerned," Brip said gripping his bloody hand. "Come on, let me get you inside," he opened the car door and scooped me up, cradling me in his arms like I was a baby. He carried me inside the mansion and up the stairs to our master suite.

"Send everybody away," I said after he gently lowered me to the mattress. I buried my aching face deep inside the soft cushions of the pillows. Some of Brip's blood got on my white sheets.

"Whatever you want, baby," Brip said, taking a seat beside me on the bed. He was silent for a while and, although I couldn't see him, I knew he was giving me a teary eyed stare. "I hate to see you like this, Taffy. Tell me what to do?" I didn't respond. Giving him a dismissive wave, I threw up my hand and shooed him away. Brip had done enough. "I'm gone give you time," he said through a cracked voice. "But, I didn't mean for none of this..." he got choked. "I didn't mean to hit you Taffy. I just snapped. You know I can't handle too much drama at once. I go crazy," he said. "When you left me...I thought you weren't coming back. I was flipping out, girl. I mean really losing it." Brip continued to feed me excuses that I wasn't interested in hearing. I just wanted silence. "I'm going to the clinic to stitch up my hand. I'll be back later, baby. Maybe we can talk then." He said before gently rubbing my back. I still didn't respond.

I was relieved that Brip was gone. I waited to hear him crank up his Hummer before I got out of bed. He was starting to sound like a broken record with all his *I love yous* and *I'm sorrys*. I believed him though. But, believing him didn't make the situation any better. His apology and love for me should have been a given and I wasn't so sure that he was sorry enough to give up his relationship with Lily. Brip was spoiled and stubborn. He always got what he wanted but that was soon going to change on my end.

I stumbled into the bathroom, holding my cheek. When I flicked on the light and looked at my reflection in the mirror, I gasped at what I saw. A bright red and navy blue puff sat on my left cheek. I couldn't stand to look at myself. I felt like trash. Dousing my face with cold water, I tried to reduce the swelling. I grabbed a bottle of sleeping pills and swallowed two of them dry. Then I went into the kitchen and grabbed a frozen bag of peas to place on my cheek and lay across my mattress, waiting for the pills to work their magic.

To help speed up the process, I took a tiny shot of vodka and put on my favorite Kenny-G record. His soft, hypnotizing melodies rang out through the speakers, almost inducing my drowsiness before the medication. It was the first time I was able to really relax since I found out about Brip and Lily. Although it was a false sense of relaxation, I took what I could get. After all, I needed to sleep if I was going to have to deal with Mona all week.

——

I slept so hard I felt like I was in a coma. I thought I was having a nightmare when I heard Mona standing over my bed, calling my name like she was yelling at an Army cadet. I felt relaxed when I opened my eyes but when I saw Mona's large body hovering over my mattress looking like a female version of King Kong, my stress returned and was even greater than before. All I wanted to do was down two more pills and fall back to sleep. I would have done anything to get her out of my sight. Even if it was as simple as closing my eyes.

"Time to get up," she said with a husky voice and clapped her hands.

"Up," Mona voice sounded like she had chained smoked cigarettes and drank whisky for years. It all added to her intimating appeal.

The frozen peas I had plastered to the side of my face had completely melted, leaving a small wet puddle on the side of my mattress. I had added to some of that puddle with all the drooling I did. I wiped the side of my face with the edge of my pillowcase and tried to squint the sleep out of my eyes so that I could see Mona better. When I looked at her, standing over my bed like a tyrant, I got amused by her outfit. She had her nerve to be wearing a leopard print cat suit that made her look twice her size.

Mona's body was a tricky thing; she had a masculine build with feminine curves. You really couldn't call her fat because she was as solid as Mount Everest but she defiantly wasn't skinny. She had a big wide donkey-like butt that made her look like a reindeer from behind and she was over

6ft tall with thick, iron-like, legs and hips. And, if she wasn't tall enough already, I never saw her without six inch heels on. If she wasn't so mean, you could see that she really had a pretty face.

"Mona…" I whined, rubbing my head, "I have a headache. Come back in a few hours," I told her although I knew she wouldn't listen.

"No…walk that shit off," she said nudging the bed with her knee. "We got a lot of shit to discuss and the first on this list is why yo lil ass think you so cute that you can leave town without telling nobody. You been around long enough to know the rules and what you did is irresponsible and caused a whole lot of unnecessary drama. Now you got to walk around with your face all fucked up, making us Badd women look sad. You know we can't have that." Mona grunted.

"I had my reasons, Mona."

"You are a Badd wife!" she stomped the floor so hard with her size eleven feet, it felt like the entire room shook. "There ain't never an excuse to leave your husband!"

"I didn't leave, Brip!" I yelled at her but quickly lowered my tone when I saw the wide- eyed look she was giving me. "I just took a break to keep the peace. I was with my mom for a few days."

"I don't care if you was visiting the President of the United States! You leave this state without Brip and it's got to be cleared by me or Brock first." What she really meant to say was it had to be cleared by her nosey ass because she made all the petty Badd wife rules. Brock gave her free reign over us wives, among other things and Mona knew just how to abuse her power.

"Did you know Brip is having an affair and the bitch confronted me in public in broad daylight in front of everybody? She cursed my necklace for crying out loud," I held my necklace up to her.

"She did what!" Mona yelled, looking like a raging bull. If it was one thing Mona didn't tolerate was women trying us in public but not so much because she cared about me but somehow she felt it all made her look bad. Whenever I had problems with Brip in the past, I took my situation to Mona and she handled it. Going to her was always my last resort like the time that sleazy waitress got bold. I told on Brip because I knew he listened to whatever Mona said, because he knew it was coming from his oldest brother, Brock. Mona was Brock's mouth and the finger he used to point orders and sometimes the fist he used enforce those orders.

"Yes, in front of a huge crowd," I instigated, slightly exaggerating on how the thing really went down.

Pushing out the thick red covered lips that were lined with black eye-liner, Mona's nostrils started to flare. She was giving me her angry face or should I say her angrier face cause she always looked upset. "That girl didn't seem that damn crazy to me," Mona told me like she already knew who Lily was. I stared back at her confused, but didn't ask any questions. "If she did that," she stuck her thick finger in the air, "you best believe I'm gone handle that shit," she said with such intensity the veins in her necked popped out. "But, you still wrong, Taffy and we gone talk about it. I'll give you about half an hour," she said looking at the diamond crusted watch on her thick wrist, "then, take the boat across the lake to my house. We having the roads repaved today and I don't want nobody fucking them up." She told me before turning around to leave.

I took the thirty minutes she gave me to down a few more shots of vodka before we had our 'discussion.'

———

Brock and Mona's house was the biggest on the ranch but I guess with all the kids they had, they really needed the extra space. It seemed like they added on to it every year; building more breeding rooms to house all Brock's potential baby mamas. The two of them together were a real freak show.

One of Mona's many servants (that were more like slaves to me because they never had time off or left the ranch for that matter) escorted me to Mona's patio off the kitchen where she was waiting on me. Sitting in front of a spread of fried and greasy foods, Mona was in hog heaven the way she piled her plate up. On one plate she had fried chicken wings, cheese sticks, mini-hamburgers and a wade of potato salad and she ate like that every day. I wished I had the courage to eat the way she did without any guilt or shame but I didn't and I knew that was going to piss her off.

"Sit down," she said to me, sounding like the Godfather or should I say, the Godmother. "Get her a plate," she said to one of her servants.

"I'm not hungry, Mona," I said shaking my head at the servant but he put one in front of me anyway.

Looking up at me like she was annoyed, Mona barked, "What my food ain't good enough for you?"

I sighed, and served myself tiny portions from her heartache buffet just to shut her up. I guess she was pleased because she started chomping down on the food like it was her first and last meal. She chugged down a coke in one gulp before slamming the glass down on the table, gesturing for her servers to refill it. I nibbled around at my food a bit but didn't have much of an appetite. Before I could finish my second bite, Mona was licking grease off her fingers and making a second plate. She let out a loud, vibrating belch. Mona was the least charming woman I knew but Brock still treated her like a queen.

Cutting straight to the chase, Mona got to the real reason why she summoned me to her house.

"So this, Lera girl that Bobby's thinking about marrying, what she like?" Mona didn't look up from her plate.

"She's nice,' I gave her a short response.

She looked up at me with narrowed eyes like she was trying to read my mind. "What the hell that mean? Nice? I don't understand that? Is the bitch anything like Dalla?" she went ahead and asked me directly.

"No," I told her what she wanted to hear but I knew that wasn't enough. Actually, Lera did remind me a lot of Dalla but I wouldn't dare tell Mona that. If I did, the engagement would be off.

"How you know that?" she continued to interrogate me and I shrugged my shoulders. That's when she got pissed and slapped her hand against the table "She been with you for a month and that's all you got. Did you at least try to search her out or were you too busy caught up in your own selfish life? We can't handle another Dalla. What she talked Billy into doing was unthinkable and it liked to killed Brock to have his own flesh and blood betray us."

"How do you know it wasn't Billy's idea?" I asked without thinking. I got so tired of hearing her blame Dalla for everything bad under the sun.

Mona shot me an evil look. "Billy would never do some shit like that on his own accord."

"It doesn't make any sense to me," I shcok my head. "Why and how would Dalla talk him into stealing all that money out the family safe? Besides, how did he pull that off? Nobody can get around this place that easy and..."

"Enough!" Mona yelled. "You worrying about issues that don't concern you. The fact is that lying bitch tried to talk him into a lot of things. Stealing that money was only the first step and they probably coming after the ranch next. Billy is trying to take over Brock's place and he ain't entitled to it. Not as long as my husband is living. Now, we got to watch our backs all night cause we don't know where the hell they at. I didn't send Lera over to stay with you for a month so that y'all could play tea party. I needed your observation. Letting somebody in this family is a very serious thing. You never know the motives people have. Dalla broke this family up and I take blame in that for allowirg her in. I should have seen right through that innocent look!"

"Lera's cool, Mona. She's nothing like Da la. The complete opposite," I told her dryly.

"I guess I'll be the judge of that! She's coming here next week."

I felt sorry for Lera. But, every Badd wife had to go through Mona first.

"What are you planning on doing about Lily?" I changed the subject. Mona didn't respond. She just forked more food in her mouth like I hadn't said anything. "Should I handle it myself?"

"No, leave the girl be. I'll handle it for you."

"But it's my husband and my problem, Mona."

"Brip's been my brother-in - law way longer than you been his wife. I'll handle it! Besides, the shit is more complicated than what you think."

"Why?" Brip told me the same thing. "What the fuck is so complicated about him fucking a disrespectful whore?"

"Cause the girl is pregnant! She ain't no wife and never will be but she still carrying Badd blood in her womb!" Mona told me in a matter of fact way.

My heart dropped and Mona noticed my sour look right away.

"Don't be taking the shit all personal. Everything ain't about you, Taffy. You can't give Brip no kids and he needs a son whether you like it or not. We screened the girl and everything so you ain't got to worry about catching nothing. That chick ain't no fly by night fuck. She's a Badd mother. You think I like women fucking my husband? Well, I don't but that's just the way it is. Brock wants twenty five sons and this pussy ain't pushing out no more than the six I already gave him. A real Badd woman does what she has to do for her man. For some reason, you ain't never learn that but now is a good time cause Brip is going to be a daddy and he happy about it so don't ruin it for him with your drama. And you have my strict orders not to lay a finger on that bitch! You understand me?"

She watched me.

I was speechless and in shock. Brip was going to be a daddy but I wasn't ever going to be a mother. It didn't feel right. My situation had gone from bad to worse and I couldn't hide my resentment any more. I got up and ran out of Mona's house. She didn't bother yelling at me to come back. This whole thing was her idea; that meddling bitch! If I hadn't ran out the house, I would have knocked her ass out. But, I chose to run although I couldn't go far. When I got back to my mansion, I took another sleeping pill.

15

Mona Badd

'm the only wife that takes this shit serious and always have been! Them other bitches think they cute. They got in way too easy. Billy and Brip picked their spouses based on their looks and I bet Bobby is doing the same thing with that Lera, bitch. But, picking a Badd wife don't got nothing to do with looks; it has to do with heart. They can't understand that shit, but I'm gone keep explaining it til they get it.

The other wives don't wear they Badd necklace with the same honor as me. To them, it's about the, power, fame and especially money but it's about more than money; it's about charity. Papa Badd used to always say that money only gave you respect but charity gave both respect and loyalty. Mama use to tell me I wasn't gone be shit and I believed her cause she wasn't shit. But, I proved us both wrong when I became a Badd wife. I don't care about the money. To me, it's about making history; that's the real power. This life we living is a legacy that goes back three generations. It's up to Brock and I to really take this shit to the next level. We ain't get this far to stop. That's why my husband got me running things cause he know I can keep order.

I first met Papa Badd when he started he ping us common folks. The government started cutting off folks' food stamps and welfare checks. Papa Badd developed his own system and kept us fed. He started giving out pre-paid debit cards to people in need with twice as much money. People finally got room to breathe with the extra cash in their pockets. To this day, we still feeding folks and the people love us for it.

Now, I ain't never consider myself no pretty chick but I got heart and Brock seen the beauty in me; especially after I saved Papa Badd's life. One day Brock and Papa Badd was in the projects recruiting and giving out benefits and some crazy dude ran at him with a knife. If it wasn't for my big ass tackling him to the ground and stabbing him with his own knife, I probably wouldn't be a Badd wife to this day. Brock started showing interest in me once Papa Bad gave me a job.

I took Brock for liking one of them dainty ass college chicks like Billy but he wanted me. One day I was screening folks who were applying for benefits. I took my job real serious and didn't let nobody think they could get over on Papa Badd by taking his money and buying crack or other unnecessary things. One bitch came in and thought I was a fool. She was talking bout she was feeding her five kids with the money but the hoe was giving all her money to her pimp. I cut her off right on the spot and her bold ass had the nerve to try and step to me. I hit the bitch so hard she went flying across the room and landed right at Brocks feet; he witnessed the whole thing. Then, he started marching my way, giving me a sexy look. I literally had to turn around to double check that he was coming for me. He looked me up and down, licking them thick lips and said, "you one sexy ass, woman! Hard just where I want you," he pointed to my heart, "and soft where I like you," he patted me on the ass. "I can build with you if you willing?" he held out his hand for me to grab. I left that night with him and when he told his daddy he wanted to marry me, Papa Badd patted him on a back for a choice well made. Now, which one of them bitches can say that? None of them. I was preapproved by Mr. Papa Badd himself and that meant a lot to me; it still does.

Brock and I work too hard to let the other wives and brothers fuck this thing up. We got too much to lose and if we want to keep this thing going, there has to be an order to it all. Whether Billy, Brip and Bobby and all their naïve wives like it or not. It's a sacrifice to live this life but what an honor it is to make. You think Taffy gone make a sacrifice? Hell no. All that little bitch care about is his looking cute in a dress and what the hell good is that gone do for the Badds?

That bitch actually had the nerve to run out of here crying cause her husband bout to have a baby; a pure blooded Badd. That's a blessing no matter who pussy it come from and I know that better than anybody cause my husband got six outside of me and counting. When he told me he wanted twenty five sons to ensure his legacy moves on, I knew it was physically impossible for me to do it so I set up a camp. I started taking applications and screening women to give my husband just what he needs to fulfill his legacy. I know the average wife would think I'm crazy and wouldn't understand all the sacrifices I make but I'm not the average wife, I'm a Badd wife.

What the fuck Brip look like being a Badd without having a heir? Taffy got Brip so sprung, it took him forever to agree with me. When I saw Lily, I knew she would be just the girl to spark his interest. Brip needs a son and I'm gone keep on screening women until somebody gives him one or even two whether Taffy likes it or not. The bitch needs to learn that *this* shit didn't start with her and it ain't gone stop because of her.

With all respect being to the mother of the Badd men, I always thought she was a weak woman. It's no wonder things went down with her and Papa Badd the way they did and Billy followed right in his mama's footsteps by marrying that weak ass Dalla bitch. I knew that bitch couldn't be a true Badd the first day I laid eyes on her prissy ass.

Although they got the same blood in their veins, Brock and Billy are polar opposites. For one thing, Billy was a mama's boy but Brock was just like Papa Badd; they had the same mentality and drive. With Brock being the eldest Badd, he has the responsibility of the entire empire on his shoulders and takes it serious. He's a strong man and don't got no weakness in him. He don't drink or smoke; that's why he always got a sound thinking mind but Billy's ass is just spoiled.

I think he jealous cause Brock was Papa Badd's favorite and next in line to inherit the empire. I couldn't imagine a weak bitch like Dalla filling my shoes. Three generations of hard work would go to shit if her ass had to sit in my seat but no...the bitch had other ideas. She planned to divide us and I believe Brock when he said that bitch was a fraud, working for the other side. Bringing her in so close to us made us vulnerable to our enemies. It ain't no telling who she was working for and what they know about us now. If they ever find her little pissy tale ass, I pray Brock give me five minutes alone with the bitch.

The day Brock told me what happened, I couldn't believe my ears. What they did brought so much shame to our family, we still ain't over it yet and it makes us look weak. Our enemies knew we was four Badds strong but now we down to three and it makes us vulnerable. They must have been planning that scheme for a while. I still don't see how they pulled it off but Billy was one resourceful mutha-fucka and smart as hell; at least when it comes to books. With all that brain power, his ass still made a stupid move that regretfully is going to get him killed.

It ain't just about him stealing money. It's about his plot. Brock say Billy wants his spot and is going to rise up against us all to get it. That's why he took the money. Him and Dalla both probably off in another state somewhere training soldiers as we speak. That's why he got to die. Like I said before, it's an order to this shit. Kill or be killed. Hell, Papa Badd had to kill his brother to protect the empire. It was only his step brother that he reconnected with after spending years apart but I guess that don't make too much of a difference.

His brother was named Lonnie. Lonnie shamed the family by going after the Badd name with a rumor he started. He had the nerve to tell Papa Badd that Mama Badd was fooling around on him with a member of the Lucky family – the only true rival of the Badds. Blood had to be shed. If that shit got out, we probably wouldn't have made it this far. Papa Badd strangled that nigga until he went limp but, just like Brock promised to do for Billy, he gave him a proper burial. He buried him at the family cemetery on the ranch; that was respect in spite of disrespect.

The Lucky family and The Badds been rivals as long as Granddaddy Badd been around but they can't fuck with us and they know it. All that drama took a toll on Mama Badd and she downed a bottle of pills and went to sleep for life; she was too weak of a woman to handle the life but I still respect her for bringing pure Badds into the family. God rest her poor little soul.

Billy was the only one that act like he couldn't get over his mama off-ing herself. He harassed his dad with questions about his mama's death and Lonnie's rumor. He harassed Papa Badd so much he just couldn't take the stress anymore, he had heartache and died. It seemed like Billy would have had some respect to the leave the shit alone. I know Dalla was putting shit in his head, forcing him to drive Papa Badd to an early grave. It was all a part of her plot. At the end of the day, Brock loves his family and all this drama is really taking a toll on him. He don't want to have to kill Billy but he know he got to do it.

I worry about my husband. He just as strong as his daddy but he take things to heart so much I fear that one day I'm gone lose him the same way we lost Papa Badd. Ever since Billy's scheme, Brock has been withdrawn and secretive. He's been moody and gets frustrated with me fast; that ain't like him. He been so tense lately, he ain't even fucked me. Hell, my engine is big and powerful and it needs to be tuned up at least twice a day but Brock has gone totally cold on me. With him being so tense now, I'm tense. I'm really suffering over here but I'll be patient for my man, although I'm one angry bitch when I ain't had no dick.

I'm getting by and keeping myself busy. If I'm not dealing with these eager ass bitches, applying to be breeders for Brock and I, I'm dealing with other Badd business. Bobby's soon-to- be wife, Lera, is staying with us for a month and I'm sure that's gone keep me real busy. I'm gone screen that bitch like my life depends on it and, if I see one sign of betrayal in her, she's out. Bobby said he put her through the test and she passed but I'll be the judge of who she really is. I was leery about Dalla and look what happened. I got good discernment when it comes to disloyal bitches.

I know one thing. I'll be glad when all this shit is over and things are back to normal. If I can help it, this family is going to get back to the way it was before the shit hit the fan. Some kind of way, we gone get over this Billy and Dalla thing. Then, maybe I can finally get a good ole fashion fuck by my man, Brock *'The Rock'* Badd. Then everybody can sleep easy.

16

Taffy Badd

Brip and Mona gave me strict orders not to touch Lily, like she was a sacred queen because she was pregnant with a bastard baby. Maybe if I had had a chance to whoop her ass, this whole thing would have blown over and I would have sucked it all up like a big girl or should I say, Badd wife. But I was going to let them have their way. If they didn't want me to touch her, that was fine. But, that bitch still was going to suffer at my hand some kind of way. So, I came up with the idea to buy her a gift basket but the shit wasn't no peace offering.

I went to my favorite spa and had an elaborate basket full of expensive and exotic smelling lotions, body oils, shampoo and conditioner made. Everything was wrapped up in a pretty bow. All that shit was tainted; you'd be surprised at all the devious shit you can order online. I put a chemical in her lotion and body oils that was guaranteed to make her ass break out in hives and itch for days like she had poison Ivy; or should I say poison Lily. Ha! The best part is the shampoo and conditioner. I put enough shit in there to scalp the bitch. Just one wash and all that whore's hair would be gone with the wind.

Lily has naturally long hair that swirls around her shoulders like her crown and glory. The way she flipped her hair at me in the park, she really thought she had something on me other than my man. I wondered how Brip would treat her with a bald head? It really was going to be hard for her to fuck my husband with all that scratching and itching she was doing and to top it off a head so bald and shiny Brip would be able to see his guilty reflection in it. I felt like a mad scientist the way I was measuring my concoctions and pouring them into the bottles so precisely. When it came to the hair removal liquid, I spared nothing and emptied the entire bottle into the shampoo and conditioner, shaking it up fiercely to make sure everything went in evenly. When I got finished with it all, I had a good laugh. The next time Brip fucked Lily, she wouldn't be quite the same.

My gift basket was ready to send but I needed Brip's signature first and that was going to be easy to get. When he came home, I told him I bought the basket for Lera and needed him to sign the card.

"That's good, baby!" Brip said, rubbing me on the back like he was proud.

"Sign it *with love, from Brip*" I told him.

"What about you?" Brip gave me a dumbfounded look. "This is from us right? As a family?" he said it like he wasn't sure what to call us anymore. I guess he wasn't dumb after all.

"You are us, baby?" I said to him with a sweet voice.

He signed the card the way I wanted and tried to kiss me on the cheek after he finished but I moved away.

"Can I take you out to dinner tonight? We can go to that nice place you like where they have the live show."

"I can't...I already made plans with Lera." It was the truth. To avoid Brip, I called Lera and invited her out for dinner. I hadn't talked to her much since my high speed chase with the police and I just needed some girl time.

"But, I can go with y'all. I can call Bobby and we make the whole thing a double date" he said eagerly.

If he wanted a double date, him, Lily and his bastard child could have gone out. "No, Brip. It's going to be just us Badd girls, tonight."

"Okay, but when you come back home," he patted me on the butt, "we gone have some fun or what?" He grunted like cave man.

"Yep," I said to him coldly. "Just like last night," I reminded him of how fun it *wasn't* for his dick to swim in a pool without water; I can't get wet for him anymore.

Brip actually has the nerve to still try and fuck me like everything is okay. He'd been doing all but throwing rose petals at my feet after we left the ranch last week to let me know he was sorry for hitting me. But what about being sorry for letting Mona talk him into having some slut have his baby? Even through all his apologies he was still too chicken shit to tell me about Lily's pregnancy. I have a feeling he ain't planning on doing it either. *Taffy, I just want us to get back to the way things were*, he often whined. The only way that could happen is if he took the Lily bitch to the clinic.

Brip lowered his eyes to the ground, shaking his head like he didn't know what to say. Taking slow paces away from me, he responded, "cool," before turning to leave.

"Oh, I forgot to tell you," I called to him and he turned around to face me. Brip's eyes widened with anticipation. I guess he thought I was going to tell him I loved him or something because he seemed hopeful. But, that wasn't the case. "Congratulations on your baby! You guys are going to be a beautiful family," I said cold.

Brip looked at me like somebody had just rammed his head into a brick wall. He moved his mouth but nothing came out. After a few moments of awkward silence, Brip left the house without saying a word and I prepared my gift basket for shipping.

——

It was nice being in the company of another Badd that wasn't a crazy, inconsiderate nut case like Brip, Mona and Brock. Lera looked so radiant, she was shining. I could see the feelings of new love beaming behind her eyes and she seemed so happy it was almost contagious but I was way too bitter catch that disease. I was over it.

"Are you okay, Taffy?" Lera asked me with a guarded look. She noticed I wasn't wearing my B-Necklace. I saw her look at my neck a few times like not having the necklace wrapped around it made me look headless.

I hadn't worn my necklace since I left the ranch and it felt liberating. I felt like myself, again.

"Girl, I'm elated," I lied, forcing a smile on my face.

"Good. I was so worried about you the other day"

"I was just having a bad day or should I say B-a-d-d day!" I made it sound like a joke. "You know...they come and go."

"So you and Brip worked it out?" she asked smiling widely.

"Uh-huh," I moaned, avoiding eye contact with her. "Where is that damn waitress...? I need a drink!" I said looking around the room. When I spotted the waitress and motioned her my way, she stopped what she was doing and rushed to me. I guess the B-Necklace was imprinted so deep within me that I didn't really need to wear it. "What you drinking?"

"Just this," she said, holding up her water with a lemon wedge floating in it. "I got to be up early tomorrow. Bobby and I are flying out to Vegas in the morning to spend a few nights before I have to leave again."

"Where you going?"

"I'm going to the ranch to get more acquainted with Brock and Mona," she said like she was nervous.

She had every right to be.

"You need a drink," I warned her. "Trust me!"

Lera looked scared by my comment but I wasn't sugarcoating things anymore. I was going to give her the real deal so she could know all about the shitty mess she was getting herself into.

"Is it that, bad?" Lera leaned in and whispered to me like somebody was listening to us.

"It's all bad. And I mean B-A-D-D," I said seriously.

Lera leaned back, almost falling into a slump. My mood was affecting her but I couldn't help it. I was tired of taking one for the team and always being the person to cheer up a situation. Tonight, I was going to keep it real.

When the waitress got to the table, instead of ordering a bottle of champagne, I ordered a bottle of brandy, two small cups of ice and a side of coke for Lera. I took three shots of the brandy before Lera took two sips from her glass. The brandy went straight to my head and worked like magic. I was pretty much sloppy drunk in less than half an hour. Lera looked like she felt sorry for me but, I felt sorry for her. She had no idea what she was getting herself into.

"Let me tell you something, Lera…you better watch your fucking back at that ranch!" I said, with my head wobbling from side to side. "It's a fucking circus act and though it may be lit up pretty like Disneyland, its fucking hell!"

I poured myself another shot, shaking my head. I'd never been this drunk in my life.

"Taffy, you're really making me nervous," Lera finally admitted.

I shrugged. "The place is fucking haunted" I slammed down my shot glass, spilling the contents on the table. "It's a fucking scary house."

I was talking loudly and people at the next table were watching me out of the corner of their eyes. I turned to one of them and yelled. "Are you looking at me?" They didn't respond. It was a young white couple and the woman had lit cigarette dangling from her mouth.

I got up and walked to their table.

"Taffy…" I heard Lera say to me in a calm voice beaconing me to come back but I ignored her.

"Mind your business, bitch!" I waved my fist in the air, and the woman ducked. Then, I snatched the cigarette from her mouth and sat back down. I had never smoked before but I got used to it quickly. By the third puff, I had it down pat; the cigarette mellowed out the Brandy.

"Maybe I should call, Brip" Lera said, placing a gentle hand on top of mine.

"Fuck Brip and his bastard baby! I hope it dies," I said, striking a wide eyed confused look out of Lera. She didn't dare ask me what I was talking about. I started to laugh and took another drag of the cigarette, slowly blowing the smoke in the air.

"Taffy…" Lera leaned in to me like she wanted to ask me something but hesitated, pushing back in her seat. Waving the smoke I was blowing out of her face, she leaned back in towards me again. "What happened with Billy and Dalla?"

"For one thing, Billy ain't in no damn jail."

I took another shot.

Lera leaned in even closer to me, sitting at the edge of her seat waiting for me to reveal more.

"It was just some stupid ass shit Mona made up for us to tell folks that got curious about why he wasn't around." I flicked the ashes from my cigarette on the floor. "Supposedly, they robbed the Badd safe and fled the country or state or wherever they are. That is some bogus ass bullshit if I ever heard it but I hope it's true. If it is, Billy and Dalla are free. I can't imagine being free from all this shit!" I sighed, dreamily.

"Why would he do that?" Lera asked.

I shrugged my shoulders. "I don't know...maybe he wanted to get away from it all and live a private life! Who knows," I waved my hands in the air. "The ranch is haunted with secrets. Who knows the truth about anything?" I put out my cigarette. "Mama Badd had her own secrets," I said to Lera in an enticing voice, beckoning her to ask me more about the forbidden subject.

I was drunk and bitter but I wasn't dumb. I searched the room before I said another word. The situation that went down between Mama and Papa Badd was so touchy that Brock and Mona would consider it treason just for me talking about it. It was the ultimate shame for them and I was married to Brip for years before he confessed the story to me. When he told me, it was like he was relieving himself of a huge burden and he never mentioned it again. He made me swear on my own life that I wouldn't repeat what he told me to anybody. But, he should know better than anyone that promises can be broken.

I leaned in close to Lera and she leaned in closer to me. After covering my mouth, I whispered what I knew to her. "Rumor has it, Mama Badd really got sick of all Papa Badd's shit," I added my own spin to the story. "So sick of it...she started creeping and not just with any man but Carlo Lucky, the one and only rival of the Badds. Carlo Lucky's family been at it with the Badds since Granddaddy Badd started this shit back in the day. They beef go back three generations and it probably was over some power pulling bullshit." I gestured with my three fingers. "Anyway, they say her and Carlo Lucky started fucking and had been for years. Some even say they were in love. When Papa Badd got wind of the affair, he had Carlo Lucky killed but it was kept silent because they didn't want to ignite a war between the two families. Mama Badd thought he died in a tragic accident like everybody else but years later, somehow the truth came out came out and Mama Badd killed herself due to the grief. That's when Billy got distant."

She was speechless. I felt relieved and somewhat vindicated to tell somebody the Badd's dirty little secrets. Now, I don't feel so heavy and it was only then that I sympathized with Mama Badd because I could understand how things could go that far. I wondered if she resented Papa Badd for the same reasons I'm starting to recent Brip. Maybe Brip was right when he said I reminded him of her but I wondered if I ever had the balls to fuck someone else. Who knew? These days, I was up for anything.

17

Lera Way

When I got home from my dinner with Taffy, Bobby had a hot bubble bath waiting on me.

The bathroom was dimly lit with candles and he was holding a champagne flute with a strawberry dancing inside of it. He gave me the glass and I took a sip before submerging myself in the warm, sudsy water. Then he started to bathe me.

Staying with Brock and Mona made me nervous. I hadn't even met Brock and Mona yet and I already was scared shitless after my dinner with Taffy. The way she described Mona you would have thought she was Satan's wife and Brock seemed like Brip times ten. It was all scary but I knew the quicker I got it over, the quicker me and Bobby could get married.

"Just relax," Bobby told me in a soft voice before he gently stroked my back with a body sponge. He could sense I was nervous about my stay with Brock and Mona. "Tonight is all about you," he gave me a hungry look.

Bobby teased me the way he massaged my inner thighs but instead of moving upward like I was yearning for, he started lathering around my neck and chest. But, his touch was so satisfying it really didn't matter where he touched my body. It all made me hot.

"I'm gone again for another month," I lifted my hands up and touched the side of this cheek.

"Then you back again and we jumping that broom, baby and the rest is history from there." Bobby grabbed my arm, extending it out to lather it with soap. He kissed me on the center of my hand before he lowered it back into the water and grabbed my second hand to do the same thing.

"Taffy gave me an earful about the ranch," I admitted. As soon as I said that, Bobby cut the washing of my second arm short. He gave me a strange look.

"Oh yeah…what she say?" he tried to keep a straight face but I knew he was nervous.

"She was just telling me about how beautiful the place was," I lied and he relaxed a little.

"Yeah…it's cool"

"So why don't you live there?"

Bobby turned up his nose and exhaled hot air. "Cause I do my own damn thing that's why," he said quick.

"She told me that Mona could be a little intense sometimes."

"Well she lied to you," Bobby said, lifting up my leg to massage my feet. "She could be a lot intense all the time!"

I sighed wearily. Bobby saw the nervousness fade over my face. "But, she cool though. Just don't take no shit out of her. Taffy kisses her ass that's why she do her the way she do but you ain't the one to take shit out of nobody. Right?" Bobby nodded his head at me like he was sure that I was touch enough to handle, Mona.

I shrugged. "Maybe in my own environment."

"You wasn't in your own environment when you burnt up my money," he said with a smile, reminding me of how we first met.

"You mean my money?" I joked.

"Hmm," he said, switching and massaging my left foot.

"So, you think she'll like me?" I asked him, referring to Mona.

Bobby shrugged. "No, I don't think she'll like you. Mona's mean as a snake and she don't like nobody so don't take the shit personal. It don't matter if she like you anyway."

"The way Taffy described her she seems like she's the madam of y'all family or something.

"She the madam over at my brother's house. That's his wife. Other than that, she ain't got shit to do with me. But, there is an order and she helps us stick to it and you going there to get a better understanding about my life and to get to know my family. That's all. My brother and his wife got they own way with things but don't let their fucked up shit affect you cause it ain't no reflection of me."

"If you say so," I said, giving Bobby a guarded look. I wanted to get him to open up about Billy and Dalla so he could elaborate a little more about the things Taffy told me over dinner but I couldn't figure out how to push it into our conversation. "So, after the ranch, me and you gone be through with all this formality or do I have to spend a few nights with your brother in jail, too." I tried guide the conversation to where I wanted it. Bobby's expression changed.

"Hmm" was all he said as he lowered my foot back into the water.

He got up and started searching through the bathroom cabinets like he was looking for something. I knew he was trying to avoid the conversation.

"He's the only Badd I haven't met. When does he get out?" I said casually.

"I don't know."

"What? How could you not know? As close as your family is it seems like y'all would be on the countdown waiting for him to come home."

"He ain't never getting out!" Bobby snapped at me.

"Never? So he got life?"

I just want him to tell me the truth. I want to hear everything Taffy told me through his point of view. I knew the secrets he was keeping from me was killing him.

"He ain't get life," Bobby shook his head like I was annoying him with my pestering questions. Now, he was leaning against the sink, looking at me carefully. I didn't care how frustrated he was getting, if I was going to be with him I wanted to know everything.

"Well then he has a release date," I said sarcastically.

"Look, are we gone talk about my brother, who ain't here, or are we gone try and spend some quality time together before we separate again?"

"Bobby, don't get mad. I'm only asking because I feel like I need to know. I'm going through all these measures to be a part of this family and I feel like I should know these things."

"Well, you'll never know everything. I'm just gone tell you that now. Hell, I don't even know it all," Bobby waved his hands in the air like he was getting pissed off.

"Were you guys close?"

"We brothers. What you think?"

"All brothers don't get along. Maybe that's why you don't care about seeing him," I said purposefully.

"What the hell you talking about, Lera?" Bobby raised his brow at me, holding his hands, in the air waiting for me to respond to his rhetorical question.

"I just figured y'all wasn't that close is all. You never talk about him and you just don't seem to care that…"

"Man, shut the hell up!" Bobby yelled at me.

I was so surprised by his sudden outburst, I jumped. My feelings were hurt. He had never spoken to me that way before. I had I really pissed him off. Bobby walked out the bathroom, closing the door behind him. I got out the tub and dried myself off with the towel and wrapped my robe around my naked body before approaching Bobby again. I decided to make peace with him. We only had a few days left with each other before I had to go to the ranch and I didn't want any negative vibes following us to Vegas.

Bobby was laying at the edge of the bed, flat on his back. He looked even sexier when he was pissed off. He was rubbing his face like he was frustrated.

"Bobby," I called his name, but he didn't budge. "Are you mad at me?" I said in the sweetest voice I could muster.

Bobby leaned up and gave me a mean look that softened after a few short seconds. "Nah, I ain't mad. You just shouldn't be making bullshit assumptions about shit you don't know about. I love my brother," Bobby said intensely. "Don't' tell me I don't care about my brother. Don't say that shit again, Lera," his voice was a little softer but still stern.

I nodded my head quick. "I'm sorry, Bobby. That was some stupid shit I said." I started taking slow steps towards him.

"Hmm," he looked up at me like he was accepting my apology. "I ain't mean to snap at you like that. That's my bad and I won't do it again," he said humbly. Then he held out his hand, beckoning me to come towards him. When I got close enough, he pulled me into him and positioned me on his lap.

"It ain't nothing," I said to him before kissing him on his thick bottom lip. I traced my hand around the single dimple that sat deep inside the center of his chin. "This is so sexy," I tried to lighten the air and kissed his chin.

Bobby blushed. "Who knows? Maybe one day you will get to meet Billy but until I know that's possible, I just don't want to think about it, okay?"

I nodded.

"I know he would like you though and my mama…." He smiled big, "she would've absolutely adored you."

What he said meant a lot to me.

"When you get to Brock and Mona's don't mention none of this shit. It's too sensitive of a subject. Understand?" Bobby gave me a serious look.

"I got you" I told him. "Just as long as you don't get arrested, I'm fine."

"First of all my brother ain't in no jail and I ain't never gone be in one either," he blurted out. "He just disappeared. And if I disappear, I hope you'll be smart enough to disappear too. I mean just vanish from all this shit," he said to me like he'd already thought it out.

I sighed. "I hate these conversations. They freak me out."

"They shouldn't. You know that money I got in the closet?" he pointed towards the closet and I nodded, remembering all the cash I'd seen in the chest. "That's my just in case money. Well…our just in case money, now" he corrected himself. "If something happens to me, take that shit and leave. You ain't got to wait for nobody to tell you what to do. If I'm gone, your Badd title is gone. I don't want you stick ng around Brock and Mona. Just leave the city."

"Alright, Bobby…" I whined, cutting him off. Now, I was trying to flip the conversation.

"Lera," he turned my chin so that I was eye to eye with him. "I'm serious."

"I know, Bobby. You mean what you say and you only say it once."

"Well this time I'm gone make an exception and say the shit twice. If something happens to me, I want you to leave. Don't even be at my funeral. You got me?"

"What! Why?" My voice cracked and I was teary eyed.

"Come on, now," Bobby squeezed me tight. "We got to be able to have these conversations without you getting upset."

"I know but…I' just can't conceive living a life without you. I just can't," I repeated.

"Maybe you won't have too," Bobby kissed me on the forehead but I wasn't convinced.

18

Taffy Badd

can't believe I did it. I fucked another man. Surprisingly, I don't feel bad. Now, I understand how Brip can do this kind of shit every night of the week and not feel an inkling of guilt. I was stepping back into my own and, most of all, I felt vindicated and in love again.

His name is Malcolm Lee and he's a powerful artist. Malcolm was definitely a different kind of weather. He was nothing like Brip. He was humble, kind and gentle natured. He wasn't rich, powerful or anything to be feared but even with all that, his presence alone calmed me. I feel a different kind of safety being with Malcolm than I do when I'm with Brip. Being with him made me feel like I was in control of my own destiny again.

I was walking through the West End, a cultured area of Atlanta, trying to practice blending in with normal society. Even in the crowded streets, Malcolm stood out. He had one shoulder leaning against a worn brick wall. He was smoking a cigarette and looking out into the crowd. Maybe watching all the people inspired him. An assortment of paint colors had dried up on his skin, speckling over his arms and forehead, saturating his clothes. He was wearing a white t-shirt with the sleeves cut off and a pair worn and loose fitting jeans. He was barefoot. Malcolm was a handsome man with big hazel eyes that offset the bronze in his complexion. His knotty hair made him look exotic. His element of mystery, triggered my curiosity.

He caught me watching him from across the street and, the moment our eyes met, I felt trapped in his gaze. Flicking out his cigarette, Malcolm smiled at me. Then, he motioned with his fingers for me to come to him and I did. When I got closer to the building, I saw the sign that read *Malcolm Lee's Fine Arts and Studio*.

"You're an artist?" I asked naïvely.

"I don't like to get too caught up with titles but, yes…I create things with paint," he nodded. His voice was deep and calming.

"I've been looking to have a portrait of myself painted," I lied. "Do you do that?"

"Maybe…Maybe not," he said to me calmly. Malcolm turned around to walk into his studio and gestured for me to follow behind him with a wave of his hand.

I walked inside and was surprised. His work was beautiful and it was everywhere. It covered his walls, ceilings and the concrete floors. Being inside his studio was like walking through his mind. "This is really awesome," I complimented him but he shrugged his shoulders like my comments didn't move him.

"It's just what I was made to do," he said humbly.

Malcolm pulled out a rolling stool and took a seat before lighting another cigarette. Then, he started to stare at me, not saying a word. I got so uneasy, I looked away.

"How long have you been doing this?" I traced my hands over a colorful mural he painted against his brick wall of what looked like a sunset shadowing over a rainy cloud.

"Why do you want a portrait of yourself drawn?" Malcolm ignored my question.

"I don't know…it's just something I always wanted to do," I lied.

"You have to know why you want to do things. Especially when it involves something as powerful as art," Malcolm said before taking a long drag from his cigarette. "There's a reason for everything under the sun. That's why it's always shining." He said seriously.

I didn't get him but I definitely dug him. He flicked his cigarette and jumped up like something was on fire before ripping a piece of paper from his canvas and running his hand over it like he was seeing his work before he created it.

A serious look spread across his face and Malcolm started to push furniture around like he was creating a set for a movie. He pushed a black leather lounge chair in the center of the room and draped it with a red velvet blanket but yanked it off a few seconds later, squinting his eyes like he was trying to recreate a scene in his head. He replaced the red velvet blanket with an all-white linen sheet and smiled at me with his eyes like he was satisfied. Then, he pushed his easel and paint in front of it and took a seat on his stool. He stared at the blank canvas, then the chair and back at me while rubbing his chin, mumbling something I couldn't understand under his breath. He clapped his hands so loud, the sudden sound startled me and I jumped.

"Take off your clothes," he said to me causally.

"Huh?"

"Your clothing," he gave me serious look, "take it all off. Leave nothing."

Malcolm jumped up from his stool and started closing his drapes before locking and putting a closed sign on his front door. I stood there debating what to do in my mind. If he really wanted my clothes off, all he had to do was look at me for a few more seconds and I'm sure they would melt off. But, making the conscience decision to take them off was a bit of a struggle for me. I had the strange feeling that being that exposed in front of him, would lead me to the very fate I stepped into.

Malcolm traced his hand over my face like he was reading braille. His flesh smelled like fresh paint and frankincense. He stepped back and watched me with his arms folded, waiting for me to undress.

I put down my purse and started to take off my shoes. The lighter my attire got, the more free I felt and pretty soon I was facing him, completely nude. Rubbing the bottom of his chin, he circled around me, watching me from head to toe like I was his muse.

"I really can see you, now. I think I'm ready," he said to me like he was ready to make love. "Lie back," he pointed to the chair and sat behind his canvas.

Squinting his eyes and biting down on his bottom lip, Malcolm got professional. He studied my body and stroked the canvas with his brush.

He was quiet. Every so often, he would get up and slightly move my head to the left or anchor my body in a different direction. I started to get use to his touch. It was interesting watching him work. He was weird, manic and oh so sexy.

Two hours later, Malcolm Lee finished my painting. I knew he was done because he exhaled like he'd been holding his breath the entire time and lowered his head to the floor, massaging his temples like he had just performed major surgery. I was still in the position he left me in, only moving when I blinked.

"I think I found it," he told me, smiling.

"Found what?"

"All the beauty you've been hiding," he said before flipping the canvas towards me.

Upon seeing the finished result, I gasped and I understood what he meant by finding my hidden beauty. Malcolm caught me in a moment that was so brief and rare, I would have gone the rest of my life and never noticed it no matter how many pictures I took or how long I stared at myself in the mirror.

"How did you do this?"

"It wasn't me," Malcolm said to me seriously, shaking his head, "It was you. You and the gods."

"Thank you," I told him genuinely.

"Don't thank me," he said, shaking his head disapprovingly at me "Thank the stars and the sun and moon…" he told me poetically. He gave me a serious look and I knew it was no way around what happened next.

To this day, I still don't remember who kissed who first but it didn't matter. Malcolm kissed me with such intensity and passion, I saw stars. My body melted against his. His tongue became his paint brush and every part of my body was his canvas. He touched me everywhere, all at one time. He kissed me on my neck and on my ear lobes like I was tender and delicate.

Then he fell on top of me, fitting inside of me like a missing puzzle piece.

I walked out of his studio literally feeling like I was flying and tingling on the inside. I floated all the way home. I had to get rid of the portrait of myself because if Brip found it, the jig would be up. I dumped it in the trash before I went home. I hated throwing the picture away but the memories I had in my mind where just as good. Every part of my body smelled like Malcolm and I didn't want to wash him away but I had to. It wasn't until I got into the shower that I realized the seriousness of what I'd done. My affair with Malcolm was dangerous and at the end of the day, we were up against more than heartache, but death. Because of that, I knew I could never see him again.

———

Just when I thought my week couldn't get any better, Brip came storming in the house scratching and itching like he'd just stepped in a pile of fire ants. When I saw his honey colored complexion patched with tiny little red bumps, I had to turn my face to keep from laughing. That was the confirmation that Lily had received the little package I sent to her.

"What the hell you do, Taffy?" Brip accused me but I played dumb.

"What are you talking about Brip?" I said casual. "You have some kind of allergic reaction or something?"

"You evil girl...evil as hell," he said scratching behind his ear like a dog infested with fleas. I didn't mean for him to get hurt in the crossfire but he deserved it. "What you do to that girl head?" he asked me, disgusted. "I had to rush her to the emergency room. I got clumps of hair all in my damn Hummer and shit. Her scalp was bleeding."

I laughed out loud. "OMG," I said in between giggles. "Without all that hair, that bitch is ugly as hell and you know it."

That's when Brip marched towards me and yanked me up from the couch. "I told you not to touch her," he said shaking me. I pulled away from him, giving him an evil look.

"I didn't touch her!" I was partially honest with him. "I didn't lay one finger on your little whore!"

"Look at my damn face, woman!" he said pointing to his welts and scratching underneath his arms and down near his balls.

"Well…if you lie down with female dogs, you get fleas," I said to him snidely, with a chuckle.

He shook his head at me shamefully one last time before storming back out of the house.

19

Mona Badd

"Am I gone have to force feed you Mr. Badd?" I held an omelet in Brocks face.

He gave me a dismissive wave and continued to stare out the window, waiting for Bobby's car to pull up.

I ain't never seen my man so stressed. He so wound up he won't even eat his breakfast.

I know it's cause of Bobby. Bobby is on his way with his fiancé, Lera. Bobby and Brock hadn't been close ever since that shit went down with Billy and Dalla. He don't come to the ranch as often and they don't talk no more. That hurts Brock. It's been almost three months since Brock even heard from Bobby. Brock had to hear that Bobby was getting married from Brip and Taffy. That made him suspicious and it pissed him off.

After Billy's wife, Brock gets nervous about newcomers. He thinking something weird is going on but I just try to keep the peace by telling him it's all in his head and that he just paranoid. He knows once Bobby marries Lera, he gone have to give him his inheritance money. That's the way Papa Badd set it up. All the Badds get cash, a mansion on the ranch and a percentage of the estate once they married. Brock don't want to give Bobby shit cause he don't trust him. Bobby going to get a big lump sum of money when he marry Lera. Brock thinks that Bobby's marriage to Lera is fake and that he just gone take that money and join forces with Billy and Dalla to try and run us out of here.

I always been cool with Bobby but its hard to read him cause he so damn quiet. That makes him appear to be sneaky but Bobby ain't got no reason stab us in the back. But, then again, neither did Billy. To keep the peace, I tell Brock that shit ain't gone happen again. Bobby and Billy are a lot alike, but I keep reminding Brock that they ain't the same person. Just because Billy fucked up, don't mean Bobby gone do the same thing. If Papa Badd knew all this bullshit was going on between the brothers, he'd roll over in his grave twice. We got to stay strong as a family; otherwise everything is going to hell.

Even though I don't feel like dealing with another whiny ass chick, I'm happy Bobby is bringing the girl cause it'll give Brock something to do other than hang around the prison all day. Ever since Brip brought in that stray, Brock has been spending hours down at the prison, interrogating him. He ain't never spend so much time down there and when he do come up, he be grumpy. I still don't know what that's all about. Usually, I don't get in his business but he gone have to let me in on this shit because it's starting to affect me too. I need to know who the hell that guy is and what the fuck he did that is so bad he has to spend all his time with him. But, I'm just gone hold my peace for now. I don't want to put too much stress on him. With Bobby and Lera coming, he's already under enough pressure. For now, my main concern is getting him to eat. He starting to waste away and I don't think he gone be able to handle me right once he decides to fuck me again. My man needs all his strength to get a big fine woman like me going.

I broke off a piece of the omelet and held it up to his mouth. He slapped the fork out of my hand.

"How long he say they gone be?" Brock yelled. You'd think he was waiting for Santa Clause to come the way he glared out the window.

"They gone be at least another hour; they coming from the city. You know how long it take," I said, closing the curtains. "You need to eat. You need your energy, Mr. Badd."

Brock sighed, grabbing the plate from my hand and picked up the fork from the floor. "You did everything I told you to do?" he asked, taking small bites of the omelet. His posture straightened up and he stuck his chest out the way he does when he staring to feel strong. He was getting his strength back.

"Yes, sir," I said, handing him a glass of orange juice.

When Brock found out they was coming, he told me to set the room Lera was staying in up with video cameras so that he could have 24 hr surveillance of her. He even wanted me to put them in the bathroom. I thought that was low down but I didn't say nothing cause what Mr. Badd says, goes.

"What about that cell phone transmitter? You got that shit hooked up too?"

"Uh-huh," I nodded, placing my hands over his shoulder and massaging out the tight stress knots.

Brock really wasn't playing with this bitch and neither was I.

"So what you think about all this?" Brock looked up at me, placing his hand on top of mine.

I loved that he respected my insight. "I think that you making all the right moves to cover us but I don't think there's nothing weird going on."

Brock pushed his plate away like he'd lost his appetite, again. "I don't know, Mona," he said shaking his head. "I know my brother and I wouldn't have been surprised if he went to the grave single. He know how wealthy he can get by getting married."

"Yeah, baby. That's why Papa Badd did that. To motivate y'all to do the right thing and that's all he's doing. Getting motivated."

"My father also wanted us to stick together," he gritted his teeth. "Sometimes, I feel like I'm the only one that respects my dad. He died building all this shit with his own two hands and these ingrates just want to shit on it. I ain't having anybody disrespect my father's name. I don't give a fuck who they are," Brock got so upset he jumped up and punched the wall.

"And you right, baby but let's not jump to conclusions too fast."

Brock shot me a mean look before shaking his head at me like I didn't understand. "I know them two! Billy and Bobby are sneaky as hell. They both just a damn like. Pussy ass mama's boys! Always have been. That woman ruined them. Good thing me and father took Brip under our wing cause otherwise he'd be the same damn way! That nigga got something planned," he punched the wall again. "I just know it!"

"Why you say that, baby?" I pried but he didn't answer.

He plopped back down in his seat and went into meditation mode. That's when he stared off into space with his the tips of his fingers clasped together. When he did that, I knew to be quiet. After a few moments of silence, he loosened up a bit before grabbing the plate of pancakes and aggressively stabbing them with a fork before forcing large pieces into his mouth, chewing them like they were nails.

"I just got a strange feeling is all," he said with a mouth full of food. "I've been having that feeling since Billy left and the shit won't go away! That's how I know it's something."

"I think you just overworked. You spend all your time in that prison. What's going on, Brock?" I pried.

"Work," he responded short. "That's always what's going on!"

"I ain't never seen you work so hard. At least not in the prison. Most folks you have down there be in and out in a few days but never weeks. Who is he Brock? What the fuck he do?"

"Why you questioning me so much, Mona?" he looked up at me suspiciously. I was hurt by his evil leer.

"Look, I'm in this with you all the way. I thought we was a team and if we are, you need to fill me in on what the fuck is going on around here," I hissed, folding my arms defensively across my chest. "I know something is up and the shit is deeper than work. I know what you like when you working and you ain't this damn tense. You ain't fucked me, you ain't fuck none of the breeders. What the fuck gives, Brock?!" I stumped my foot.

"In due time, everything will be normal again." Brock said before jumping up so quick, I got startled. "I'm going to the prison. Page me when my brother gets here and I mean right away. Otherwise, I don't want to be disturbed!" he stomped out the room.

———

A few hours went by and Bobby finally pulled up with his fiancé. They were an hour late. After I paged Brock to let them know they finally arrived, I watched them through the window for a little while, studying their movements and looking for anything suspicious.

Bobby whispered something in the girl's ear before escorting her toward my front door like he was walking her down the aisle. If it wasn't for those dreads in her hair to give her a little edge, she would be just as dainty as Taffy. I hadn't even met the girl yet but I could already tell that she thought she was cute. She was another spoiled bitch I was going to have to put in her place.

I opened the door before Bobby knocked. "You finally decided to make it home, huh? What's it's been....almost three, four months now?" I said to Bobby but kept my eyes fixed on Lera. She looked nervous. She held on to Bobby's arm like he was her bodyguard. "Come in," I waved them inside.

A few minutes after they got inside, the phone rang and it was Brock. He wanted Bobby to meet him at chapel in the counseling room. When I told Bobby his brother wanted to see him, he looked like he got annoyed. He really had his damn nerve with his ungrateful self.

"I don't got much time, Mona. Y'all keeping me busy with work."

"Well...he'll only be a minute. Your brother misses you."

"Cool," he said shaking his head. "But, 'm gone wait until, Lera get settled first."

"I can handle that!"

"I'm sure you can but I'm still gone wait anyway," he said stern.

I didn't have time to fight with Bobby so I just ignored his rude ass. "Follow me," I led them to my sitting room.

We sat down and that girl still didn't say one word to me. I didn't even know the bitch could talk until Bobby turned and asked her was she okay and she said yeah. Why wouldn't she be okay? Bobby was starting to piss me off and he hadn't even been here two seconds. He was reminding me so much of how Billy got on with Dalla; petting and pampering the bitch like she was some kind of china doll.

"What's your name?" I asked her.

"Lera," Bobby answered for her.

"Nigga, I wasn't talking to you. She can't talk? Is she mute?"

"I'm sorry…I'm Lera," she said all proper like, holding out her hand for me to shake. I didn't touch that bitch; she looked embarrassed. Bobby whispered something in her ear and she perked up a bit before nodding her head at him. I was liking her less and less by the second.

"So, Bobby tell you about the family?"

"She here ain't she?" Bobby jumped in again. I shot him an evil look.

"Her being here don't mean shit if she ain't got the heart for it."

"Bobby explained things to me but I'm here to learn more," she said like she was trying to be smart.

"Oh you gone learn some things before you leave the ranch alright; we both will. Before you leave here, we gone know for sure if you got what it takes to be a Badd wife."

"Well…my mind is pretty much made up when it comes to that," she finally looked me in the eye.

But, what she said didn't mean a damn thing to me. Bobby started grinning but I kept a straight face. She had a lot to prove to me.

"How soon are you looking to get married? You know we got to have enough time to plan these things proper."

"January first. I figured that should be enough time for y'all to plan the big shindig."

"New Years?" I repeated quick. It seemed too fast. That was less than five months away. I knew when Brock heard that, he was going to be even more paranoid because Billy married Dalla so fast. But then again, Brip married Taffy quicker than I could blink. "Y'all sure yall don't won't to wait a while?"

"We know what we doing. Just like you and Brock knew what ya'll were doing before y'all tied the knot." Bobby said to me snide.

"Well, I hope you do. Especially her," I pointed to Lera. "This shit ain't for everybody but I suspect you already know that," I hinted to Bobby about Dalla. Bobby gave me a guarded look, turning his nose up to me like I'd just farted or something.

"So, you met Brip and Taffy?" I asked her just to get her talking a little more.

"Yes," she said through a cracked voice. The bitch was acting like I was Freddy Cougar or something but I wasn't mad cause at least she had enough sense to fear me. Taffy must have told her some real fucked up shit about me. The little spoiled bitch.

Bobby wrapped his arm around Lera even tighter and whispered something else in her ear. He was starting to piss me off with all that damn whispering like I wasn't in the room. He looked up and snapped at one of my servers and asked them to bring Lera some ice water with lemon; fancy bitch.

"Well, excuse me!" I got pissed off. I was the woman of my house not him. "I could do that if you take your ass down there to meet your brother. I got all kinds of stuff planned for me and Lera today. So...you need to get the fuck on," I shooed him away with my hand.

Bobby looked at Lera one last time before kissing her on the cheek and getting up. "Go on now! Mr. Badd had been waiting on yall all morning."

"Call me if you need me," he said to her like he was her lifeline; she nodded and Bobby finally left.

"We got a busy day," I stood in front of her. The bitch was so scared she could barely look at me straight. Maybe she wasn't like Dalla after all cause that bitch was bold. "First I'm gone take you on a tour of the ranch, then we gone have lunch to discuss some things. Let me show you to your room" I snapped my fingers and she jumped up quick. At least she can follow orders fast; I'm still watching this bitch though.

20

Lera Way

After Mona showed me to my room, I felt an eerie feeling come over me.

The ranch seemed just as busy as any major city. There was so much going on. Random cars came and went like the wind. I tried to relax but it was hard. After I had been alone for about twenty minutes, Mona walked into the room without knocking. I guess I couldn't complain being that it was her house.

"You settled yet?" she said hard, giving me a weird look. I don't know what it was with this woman and her hard looks. I nodded. "Good, we got a lot to do today so don't drag your feet. I'm a very busy woman and I don't like my time wasted," she snapped her finger and I jumped, scrambling in her direction.

I knew Mona had children but I couldn't tell a child lived here by how quiet and well kept the house was. "Keep up," she said to me when I was lagging behind too far. We walked down the long spiral staircase, and for the first time, I noticed a huge picture hanging in the foyer. It was a painting of a man and a woman. The woman had eyes just like Bobby and dimples like Brip. I assumed it was his mother. I couldn't take my eyes off the picture; her eyes looked haunted. They looked fearful and sad like she was holding a secret she could no longer keep. The man looked like a tyrant, a black version of Hitler. He had this scouring grimace on his face and a darkness behind his eyes that made him look scary. I almost ran into the wall staring at the portrait.

When we got outside, there was a golf cart waiting on us. "Come on," Mona demanded like she was driving a slave. "This estate is huge and there ain't no way we can see it all in one day but I'm gone try my best. I want you to get an idea of how things are run out here. But first, I'm gone pull around back and show you something that's all me and my husband. By showing you a part of our lives, you can understand just how committed I am to building this legacy. Hopefully, you'll learn something," she said before pulling off so fast, I almost fell out the cart.

I held on tight as Mona flew down the hill so fast I thought the little golf cart was going to topple over sending us in the lake behind their house. She slammed on the brakes once we got to the bottom of the hill and I had to press my feet hard against the floor to keep my balance steady. Before we got out the car, she faced me and gave me a serious look. "My husband and I live in the original house; it's the house that Bobby and his brothers grew up in. It changed over the years and is a whole lot bigger than what it used to be nevertheless, its run the same way. The house is three and half stories and over fifteen thousand square feet and we added on three attachments to the back. All of the attachments are used as living quarters for staff and the women that are willing to help build our legacy." Mona got out the cart and I followed behind her.

She warned me, "Now, my husband and I are private people and I ain't gone show you everything but I will show you the living quarters. After I show you what I show you today, you will have no reason to be back here."

The attachments were designed just as elaborate as the house and if she hadn't told me she added them, I would have never known they weren't apart of the regular house. Altogether, there were four attachments. In one of them, I saw some of the staff, dressed in uniform, walking in and out; I assumed it's where they lived. We entered a second area at the far end of the house. When we got closer, I saw a pregnant woman sitting outside, smoking a cigarette. When the woman saw Mona, she jumped up, throwing the cigarette over her shoulder and pushing a piece of gum in her mouth.

Mona charged at the woman and slapped her so hard across the face that she lost her balance. "Bitch, I see your ass. What the fuck I tell your ass about smoking those damn things while you got my man's blood inside you! You crazy or something?"

"Mona, this is the first one I had since I got pregnant. I swear…those bitches just be stressing me out is all!" The woman whined, holding up her hands defensively at Mona.

"Lisa, you ain't here for those bitches. Do I need to show you your contract?" The woman shook her head. "Let me catch you again and your ass is off the ranch. You understand me?" She waved her finger in Lisa's face and Lisa jumped like Mona was pointing a knife at her.

"Yes, mam?" she assured Mona then walked away rubbing the side of her face.

"These dumb bitches gone send me to the grave before my time," Mona grunted under her breath. "Come on!" she yelled at me.

The living quarters were set up like a rooming house. There were two more pregnant girls sitting on the couch watching TV and eating snacks. Four other girls, who weren't pregnant or at least didn't look it, were in the kitchen chatting amongst each other. When they saw Mona, everybody stopped what they were doing and got serious. Mona eyeballed each of the girls individually before looking around the room like she was searching for something. She turned over pillows, looked under magazines and then opened the fridge. "What the hell?" she said, pulling out an open can of grape soda. "Whose shit is this?"

"Lisa!" one of the girls from the kitchen screamed. "She out there smoking again, too!" she added, pissing Mona off more.

"That damn bitch," Mona spat out, shaking her head. "Ain't none of ya'll suppose to be drinking no sodas, whether you conceived yet or not. Y'all bitches be forgetting what y'all here for. This ain't no damn day spa. You here for a reason."

"We ain't seen Brock in two weeks and I was trying to explain to this bitch," she pointed at a girl in front of her, "that I was up next because last time…"

"Shut up," Mona raised her hand in the air and the girl got silent, sticking out her lip and pouting like a child. "Mr. Badd has been busy but he gone be around here soon enough to do what he got to do."

The same girl looked at me and turned her nose up. "Is that another girl?" She started whining. "We hardly get enough time with Brock as it is."

That's when I noticed all the girls were giving me mean scowls.

"You talk too damn much, Claudia. You can shut up on your own or I can shut you up!" Mona warned, waving her big fist in the air. "This is a future Badd wife. Address her properly."

Upon Mona's introduction of me, all of the women lowered their eyes and changed the grim expressions on their faces, "follow me," Mona said, walking down the hallway.

The hallway led to seven bedrooms. One of the rooms looked like a exam room. An office was located at the end of the hall. On our way down the hall, Mona stopped to pick up discarded trash like empty water bottles and gum paper wrappers. "This group of bitches are nasty as hell," Mona said shaking her head.

I followed Mona into the office. It was set up professionally. There was a waiting area and mahogany wood coffee tables with magazines on top of them. Mona sat behind a large desk and ordered me to sit down in front of her. On top of the desk was a neat pile of folders and a gold plaque with her name inscribed inside of it. What really caught my attention was the picture of Mona, a man that I assumed to be Brock and a slew of kids, all boys. Underneath the picture was written, *the legacy continues*. Taffy wasn't lying when she said that Brock and Mona were circus freaks. But, I kept a straight face, pretending that everything was normal.

"I just want to let you know that I don't give a fuck about what you think about all this." By the look she was giving me, I could tell she was serious. "I only brought you here to see how committed I am as a wife. Do you ever think you can be this committed to Bobby and the other Badds?"

"I can be just as committed to Bobby but maybe not in the same way," I said with confidence. "If this is your thing…I'm no one to judge."

"See you already wrong. This ain't just my things it's for all the Badds. It's our future."

I nodded my head like she was making sense although she sounded like a crazy person. I thought it best just to agree with everything Mona said.

"And all this you see here, was my idea. I did this for my husband and for the Badds. This shit ain't just about shopping and money, it's about continuation. We the third generation and right here in these living quarters," she stabbed the wood desk with her thick finger, "is the fourth and even fifth generation and hopefully each one will be more powerful than the next. I screen seven women a year and they live here until they conceive and give birth to a healthy baby, boy. I raise them boys just like they my own and they are my own because they come from my man!

All our kids live on the lower level of the mansion. They start training from the time they ready to walk. It's a sacrifice but an easy one. The birth mothers hand over the child and sign the adoption papers, I give them a check and they move on with their lives, happy that they got to fuck Mr. Brock Badd."

"What if they have girls?" I had to know.

"I ain't here to breed Badd girls, just men. If they give birth to a girl, they keep the baby. Brock and I provide for them every month. Trust me, this shit is tedious and takes up a lot of my time but my husband is going to have his heirs."

Mona pushed back in her seat, waiting for me to respond but I had nothing.

"I do love, Bobby," I told her, trying to ease the tension.

"Love don't mean shit!" She darted back up, pounding her fist against the desk. "This shit you getting into is deeper than love. It requires a lot of sacrifices, patience and a heart of stone. You think you got that?" She asked me sarcastically.

"Bobby thinks so," I informed her.

"Well...Bobby been thinking with his dick for a long time now and I hope that this time it don't lead his ass wrong, cause then we all screwed." She leaned back again, folding her thick arms across her chest. "This shit ain't just about you and Bobby. The quicker you learn that, the better. Bobby getting married affects all of us. You do some shady shit to Bobby and we all feel it. We work as one single unit," she held up her index finger, "and unfortunately that means if one of us gets hit, we all feel it."

Mona continued to stare at me like she was trying to read my mind. When she mentioned Billy, I jumped just as if she had read my mind. I couldn't help but to think about him and Dalla and if they were the *mistake* that hurt everybody.

"I suppose by now, you heard about, Billy?"

Swallowing hard, I didn't know if I should answer the question truthfully or not. With a controlled voice, I responded, "Bobby told me he was serving time."

Mona seemed relieved by my response but that didn't stop her from looking at me, narrowing her eyes with curiosity. She didn't respond to what I told her and the expression on her face didn't change. I wondered if I had said the right thing. The silence was so awkward, I started to squirm around in my seat, looking off into the distance just to avoid eye contact with her. I cleared my throat and started twirling one of my locks in between my fingers just to cure my jumpy nerves. "He didn't tell me how Billy got arrested," I added quickly. "But, I know how hard that must be for the family, considering how close you all are." I cleared my throat again.

"You want some water or something?" Mona asked me sarcastically.

"I'm fine," I said through a cracked voice.

She continued to watch me hard. I felt so awkward I didn't know what to do. I shifted my weight around in my seat a few times and was going to nervously clear my throat a third time but stopped myself. Then, I locked eyes with Mona hoping I was proving to her that I wasn't hiding anything about what I knew which really was nothing.

I heard a loud crash coming from the front room and some of the girls were yelling and cursing. "What the hell is going on now?" Mona yelled with a sigh. "Let's go!" she ordered me. I was relieved the disturbance got me out of Mona's flaming hot seat and in the nick of time because sweat was beading up around my temples and it was only a matter of time before it rolled down my cheeks, alerting Mona to how nervous I really was.

Mona ran down the hall like a raging bull, ready to attack and I followed behind her like her fearful sidekick. When we got to the front, Claudia, the same girl that was doing all the talking before, had another girl in a headlock, swinging her all around the kitchen, punching at her side. "What the hell is going on wit you crazy bitches now?" Mona yelled, before getting in on the action.

She pried the girls apart like they were five year olds, holding one in each hand. One of the girls tried to reach around Mona's wide body to punch the other but missed and mistakenly hit Mona in the back, causing her nostrils to flare so wide with anger that I could see her brains. Mona grabbed the girl that hit her, pushing her up against the wall with one hand, holding her by the neck. The girl didn't bother to squirm away from Mona. She stood there idle, waiting for Mona to hit her.

"Are you crazy bitch?" Mona asked before sliding her down the wall and slapping her across the face. Then she turned to Claudia and slapped her too. "Get to y'all rooms!" she yelled at the girls like they were three year olds.

"It ain't my fault," Claudia said, holding her face and clinking her teeth angrily at her opponent. "That bitch talking about Brock said he in love with her," she said pointing to the girl.

On that note, Mona widened her eyes, before storming at the girl, lifting her off her feet and throwing her outside like she was trash.

"The only person Mr. Badd is in love with is me!" Mona stabbed herself in the chest with her finger. "Don't none of you bitches get this shit twisted. Understand?" Mona said to the crowd of fearful women.

They all nodded, humbly.

I stood on the sidelines watching everything from a distance.

"Look, we gone have to reschedule this tour. I got personal business to handle," she pulled me to the side and said. "Just go in the house and relax until dinner. Then, you'll get to meet Mr. Badd," Mona said before charging back towards the bickering women. I was happy to be off the hook; for now.

21

Mona Badd

"Bitch, so you think you in love with my man?" I asked that little whore. I had one hand around her throat and was squeezing her little pencil neck until the heifer turned blue. "Mr. Badd is my husband; you ain't shit but a womb!"

These dumb-assed bitches done fucked up my schedule. My time is limited but, I got to keep my focus on Lera. Brock expects me to screen her but here these tramps go distracting me. Some of the girls come for the money and some come thinking they can take my man but they foolish for thinking that's gone happen. Usually, I screen them good enough to read through their phony asses but with all the stress I've been under, I haven't been my sharp self lately.

I put the little scrawny ass chick down when I started to get a cramp in my hand from squeezing her throat so tight. I wasn't trying to kill her, but I was so stressed out, I could have. Having my hands around her neck was relieving my stress more and more with each squeeze, but I had to let the bitch breathe so I put her down. She fell to the ground, gagging and rubbing her neck.

"She's lying. I told you that, Mona" the dumb-assed bitch said, coughing up spit. "I wouldn't disrespect you. I'm the only one here that's real!" she tried to plead with me. "Please don't put me off the ranch. I need the money! If anybody needs to go its, Lisa," she pointed at her. Lisa gave me a guarded look. "She be smoking, don't be eating the foods on the diet plan and she always wandering around the ranch, going outside the areas you told us to stay away from. She should go."

I am so through with these bitches, all of them can go for all I care. If they ain't fighting over petty shit, they argue over whose next in line to fuck Brock. I'll tell you what, ain't none of these bitches getting a turn to fuck my man before me. If they only knew, Brock don't even know how they look. It's all business with him but these bitches always get it twisted.

Lisa is another story; she smoked cigarettes behind my back and basically did whatever the fuck she wants to do when I ain't looking. I caught her trolling around the ranch like she at Disneyland. I was ready to throw her ass out months ago but she got pregnant. She is seven months pregnant with Brocks 13th son. All I have is three more months to deal with her ass. But this other bitch has to leave today.

"You out today!" I told her.

"Please," she whined, clasping her hands together and begging me like she was praying to God. But, what she didn't know was that I wasn't as merciful as God.

"Let's go," I said, grabbing her by the collar and dragging her out the house like the rag doll she was.

"You fat bitch!" she yelled at me, kicking and screaming like a maniac.

I couldn't believe she had the nerve to be so bold but I was surprised at what she said next. "Your man don't want you. He loves me! I sucked his dick so good, a tear fell from his eye. He ain't thinking about your sloppy ass. I'm gone be the next Mrs. Badd!"

Her going down on Brock is the ultimate no-no.... completely against the rules. I tell all the bitches from jump that this ain't about pleasure but business. There are strict instructions to how they fuck my man. First, there ain't no kissing or any foreplay whatsoever and that ruled out dick sucking. If they needed to get him up, they used their hand, not their mouths.

This bitch was too bold. I cold clocked her across the jaw so hard, my knuckles cracked and she went flying across the lawn before landing inches away from the lake. That bitch was out cold. Lucky for me, the bitch ain't conceived yet.

"Get rid of her," I said, snapping my fingers at one of the area guards.

I was on my way back to the main house when I saw Lisa peeping at me from around the corner. When I spotted her, I gestured for her to come to me. She took her time walking toward me. Giving me a guarded look, she held up her hands like she was surrendering to the war I was about to start.

"I promise that was my first smoke in months and it's my last until after your son is born," she said rubbing her stomach.

The bitch was clever. She knew how to swindle her way out of trouble.

"You know I don't say shit twice," I said pointing at her with an angry finger. "Keep your ass where you belong. Your name ain't Alice and this ain't no Wonderland. How many times I got to remind your simple ass that any place behind this lake is off limits. Understand?"

"It's just that the last time I visited with the doctor, she told me to do some walking. The baby need to drop or something," she told me shaking her head.

"Well, walk your big ass in circles but don't cross that lake," I said pointing off into the distance. "There ain't nothing out there for you to see. If you give me any more shit, then you off the ranch and you gone be leaving here with my foot up your ass and a baby to support on your own. You got that?"

"Yes mam, Mrs. Badd," she said again, giving me a stiff nod and a dry look.

———

Brock wanted me to meet him at the counseling center right away. I don't know what was so important but I got there as soon as I could. He probably wanted to interrogate me about what I thought of Lera but I didn't know what to tell him, yet. She seemed just as simple as the rest of the bitches but the simple bitches are always the hardest ones to read.

Brock was pacing back and forth in circles. He looked even more stressed than he had this morning. I thought him seeing Bobby would ease his mind a little but it seemed to make him worse. I was a strong woman but all this drama was starting to take a toll on me.

"Lock the door!" he demanded me like somebody was after us.

"What's going on now, Brock?" I tried not to sound too annoyed by all this secretive bullshit that was going on but it was hard, nevertheless, I was Brock's rock and I had to be strong for him regardless.

"Where's the girl?" he was referring to Lera.

"She's in the guest suite."

"Did you pick her mouth? Try to fish out what's swimming in her head?"

"Of course," I said, swallowing hard. I couldn't get to Lera the way I really wanted too.

"And…"

"I need more time Brock. It ain't been but a few hours since she got here."

Brock sighed, rubbing the sides of his head.

"Bobby had his nerve to question me about Billy. Then, he said he was thinking about moving up north after he got married."

Brock bit down on his bottom lip. "Something ain't right. Did you talk to the girl about Dalla?"

"She don't know nothing."

"You sure about that, Mona?"

"Of course, Brock." I hated when Brock second guessed me. It made me feel insignificant.

"You ain't been on your damn job, Mona. It's like I'm the only mutha-fucker around here that's been working my ass off."

I respected my husband more than anybody else on the planet but, I wanted to knock his ass out. Say anything to me but don't imply that I'm lazy. My whole life is dedicated to building this shit up with him and he got the gall to say I ain't been on my job, but I held my peace. Brock was like the atomic bomb and when his ass exploded, we all was going to be fucked.

"I've been working hard, Mr. Badd," I said calmly. "You just been overworking yourself to the point where you so tired, you ain't thinking straight."

"I ain't thinking what?" He started to walk towards me with his fist balled. Brock and I had our tiffs in the past but I was no victim and he was no wife beater; I could hang with the best of the men when it came to a fight. But, I was in no mood to be dodging his jabs. "Who ain't thinking right?" he bucked at me but I didn't flinch. I flinched for nobody, not even him.

He raised his hand in the air like he was ready to slap me. When he lowered his hand towards my face, I grabbed him by the wrist, stopping him.

"If you want to get physical with me, you'll pull out your dick and fuck me doggy style. If you can't do that then back the fuck up off me cause you starting to piss me off."

He backed up and sat back down on the couch. "You just paranoid and that shit makes you weak," I said and he nodded his head, agreeing with me.

"Yeah…" he said, rubbing his eyes. "There's only one way to solve this shit," He looked up at me with narrowed eyes. "She got to take a lie detector test."

"Lord," I sighed, shaking my head. That was going too far. I knew Bobby would be so pissed it would cause even more division in the family. But the look Brock was giving me told me that he wasn't backing down. I don't know why he was so freaked out by Lera. I understood being cautious but damn, a lie detector test. "What you think Bobby's gone think about this?"

"Fuck what he think" he jumped up. "My father left me the throne. I'm the final say and what I say goes. If he got a problem with that shit, then he can get the hell on. I got some things I need to know and it don't make sense for me to be guessing when I don't have to. I'm Brock, *The Rock*, Badd and what I say goes!" He punched the palm of his hand like he was preparing for a fight. "Set the shit up!

I nodded. "Yes, Sir Mr. Badd," I said to him like he was my sergeant and I was his cadet; at the end of the day, that's just what I was, a soldier.

22

Lera Way

Mona and Brock are a real Jerry Springer case. I was standing near the lake, looking down at her breeding quarters. I didn't see Mona again after yesterday's fiasco with the women in her breeding house. Today we were taking a full tour around the ranch but after seeing the breeding quarters, I wasn't sure if I wanted to see anything else.

Lisa was at the other end of the lake, smoking a cigarette. When she saw me, she jumped. She gave me a weird look. What she was doing wasn't my business and I wasn't going to offer what I saw to Mona either. I turned my back to her and started to throw little rocks in the lake. That's when I heard her call my name. I turned around and she was coming my way. I couldn't help but wonder how she knew my name. When she confronted me, she tossed the cigarette into the lake. Her mouth opened like she wanted to say something but nothing came out. She kept looking over her shoulder nervously. She pulled out another cigarette from her bra and tried to light it but her hands were trembling too much.

"Do I know you?" I asked her sternly and she shook her head, no.

I tried to turn around to continue minding my business.

"Wait," she whispered like she had a secret to tell me.

There was such a strange look in her eyes, I got spooked but she didn't say anything.

"What is it?" I whispered back. Now I was looking over my shoulder. She walked a few steps toward me, looking both ways like she was crossing the street. She opened her mouth to talk but then we heard a golf cart, which I assumed was being driven by Mona, coming our way.

Lisa ran off. I watched her wobble around the corner until she disappeared.

———

The ranch was a extravagant place but it also was a corrupt playground for criminals and gangsters. From the casino to the hospital, it was like being in a hidden city. Mona showed me everything and gave me the history of every site we visited. It took us two hours to tour the ranch. I was relieved when it was finally over.

Before we pulled up to Mona's mansion, she pointed out the other three houses and showed me the mansion that Bobby and I was supposed to inherit. It was beautiful. It was covered in white brick and was dressed with thick stone columns and huge French style windows. She told me that I wasn't allowed inside until everything was finalized with our marriage, but honestly I didn't care if I ever stepped foot inside the house. I was more curious about Billy and Dalla's house than any of the others. I was staring so hard at the empty, haunted like house, that I noticed Lisa lingering around the back of the house, ducking Mona's golf cart. I made eye contact with her and she gave me another strange look. My curiosity was starting to boil. She had something to tell me and I wanted to know what it was.

After the tour, Mona told me that I had free reign to go anywhere I liked. I needed to keep myself busy before I met Brock for dinner. I wasn't looking forward to it. Being in the company of Mona was already too much to handle and I couldn't imagine being with both of them. Taffy told me that Brock was just as crazy as Mona and I believed her. Anybody who had the guts to marry Mona had to be a raging psychopath.

Allowing my curiosity to get the best of me, I decided to take a stroll around the ranch more specifically, to Billy and Dalla's mansion where I had seen Lisa lurking. I was behind Billy and Dalla's house when I spotted

Lisa again. She was walking towards me like we had a planned meeting; she seemed to be waiting on me. I started walking towards her just as quick as she was walking towards me. Lisa still was paranoid, looking over her shoulder every few seconds and I didn't blame her but this time, I wasn't letting her get away without telling me what she had to say.

We faced each other. For a few seconds, she gave me strange stares, creating an awkward silence that I eventually broke.

"What do you want with me?" I asked.

"This has nothing to do with me and what I want."

"What do you mean?"

"I just have a message for you, well for Bobby really."

"Oh, you know my man?" I got defensive.

"Look, I don't have time to waste," she looked over her shoulder again.

I did the same thing.

"Bobby's in danger and if you stick around here…you will be too."

"What?" I felt a lump in my chest.

"Just shut up and listen." She tried to put her hand over my mouth but I backed away from her touch. "Tell Bobby his mother didn't kill herself. Billy was right…she was murdered and I have the *real* autopsy to prove it," she pulled a folded envelope out of her bra and handed it to me.

I didn't grab it. I was too stunned by what she was telling me.

"Take it!"

I grabbed the envelope and stuffed in my bra. My heart was beating so fast, I thought it was going to stop.

"The one Brock has on record is a fake. He did it. Brock really killed her."

She waited for my reaction but I was speechless.

"If you smart, you'll keep this shit away from Mona and Brock. They'll kill you if they find out you have it and if you are really smart, you'll leave this place for good."

"I don't even know you? How do I know this ain't some bullshit? I ain't telling Bobby this shit!"

"You do what you want. I don't give a fuck. I'm out of here after today. My job is done. She's been watching you two from day one, you know."

"Who's been watching us?"

"Dalla," she said and pulled a chain out her pocket and handed it to me.

"Dalla?" I repeated.

I looked down at the necklace and it was just like my 'B' necklace except on the back was the small inscription, Dalla Badd.

"Give this to Bobby when you tell him. It'll help him believe you."

"I don't understand."

"Yeah, you don't know the half of it. If I was you, I'd leave all this shit behind me. Bobby, too. I mean he's a good fuck but is the dick worth death?"

"Excuse me," I hissed.

"Now is not the time to have a catfight," she gave me a sarcastic look. She turned to leave but stopped. "Shit, I almost forgot. She wants you to tell Taffy something too. She said to tell her that Brip killed her brother Keno. And that she sorry and she still loves her like a sister."

"Where is Dalla?"

"I don't know? That bitch is everywhere and if you want my opinion, off the record..." she paused and I anticipated her response, "don't trust her either."

She crept away from Billy and Dalla's house.

"Wait," I chased behind her, but she ran off.

None of it made sense to me. Why would Brock kill his own mother? And, I didn't know if I should believe that Dalla had been watching me. For what?

I love Bobby, but after everything I just heard, maybe I should leave the city. I don't feel safe. Bobby should leave too but I know there was no way I could convince him to leave with me and if I complained too much, he might think I'm weak or that I can't handle the life but honestly, I don't think I can. On the other hand, this could be one of their bullshit tests. I started to get paranoid. If it was a test, then I had a choice to make. The obvious thing to do is tell Brock and Mona everything but if it wasn't true, I was treading on dangerous water. I don't know what to believe.

———

Later that evening, I was still on edge but I had to straighten up my act because I had to meet Mona and Brock for dinner. Every step I took was guarded and I felt guilty for something but had no idea why. I feared that Brock and Mona would know something was up based off my weird behavior alone.

By the time one of the house staff escorted me to the dining room, Brock and Mona where already seated at the large, rectangular shaped table. The table was set up like I was about to dine with royalty. It reminded me of one of those tables you would see in knight movies and just like in the movies Brock, the King, sat at the head of the table with Mona at his right hand side. As soon as I stepped foot inside the dining area, Brock stood up like a solider, giving me such a grimacing stare that sweat dropped down my back. Mona followed his lead and stood up too, giving me the same evil-like stare. They weren't very friendly people. He kept a serious face and didn't take his snake like eyes off me, not even to blink. I walked towards them.

Brock was one scary looking guy. He wore tall black leather combat boots and army fatigue pants with a black wife beater tightly clutching against his thick chest. His arms protruded with muscles so thick it looked like they were going to burst out of his skin. His hair was cut into a rebellious Mohawk, shaved completely bald on both sides and colored the same platinum blonde as Mona's hair with a matching goatee. He had a thick scar that started underneath his eye and curved all the way down to the tip of his chin. Tattoos covered his arms. Across his neck was a tattoo that read, *Badd 4 Life*. It was hard for me to look at him for too long without trembling. I tried my best not to seem too freaked.

"Hello, Brock. I'm Lera," My voice cracked. I held out my hand for him to shake, forcing an uneasy smile on my face. My hand trembled as I waited for Brock to shake it but he never did. He looked at me like I was holding a sack of shit.

Brock nodded at me then sat back down; Mona followed his lead.

"Sit down," she demanded.

Swallowing hard, I tried to calm my nerves by taking slow and controlled, breaths but it wasn't working. And, it didn't help that Brock was still staring me down so hard.

"It's nice to finally meet you," I squeaked. Brock leaned over and whispered something in Mona's ear. Then she addressed me like she was his voice box.

"Mr. Badd wants to know how you're settling in at the Ranch?"

"I love it," I blurted out quick. "I mean, fine." I tried to keep my composure, taking another deep breath. Then, he leaned over and whispered something else to Mona and she addressed me again.

"Mr. Badd wants to know why you want to be a Badd wife?"

I thought before I answered the question. Brock was watching me even harder this time, waiting for my response. I didn't know the right way or the wrong way to answer the question so I just stuck to complete honesty. "Because I'm hopelessly in love with Bobby," I confessed and Mona rolled her eyes at me like I was too simple for her to deal with. Brock didn't budge; he just kept on watching me.

Brock's posture was so perfect it was like he had a metal rod in his spine. Clasping his hands together tightly, he rested his chin on the tip of his ashy knuckles. When the server put food on his plate, he didn't look down at it. He kept his eyes fixed on me. Mona finally stopped staring at me, setting her full attention to the prime rib on her plate.

"Brock, you gone eat?" Mona said to him in the softest tone I ever heard her use. Brock ignored her.

Whispering something in Mona's ear a third time, I was really starting to believe that he couldn't speak. "He wants to know how y'all met?" Mona asked, cutting her meat.

"I was working at the L-Bar and he came in," I kept it short.

"Where is that?" Brock finally spoke to me, causing me to jump. His tone was crude and his voice was raspy; he sounded like he had a frog stuck in his throat.

"Memphis," I said, barely making eye contact with him.

Brock turned and looked at Mona and she nodded as if to say he could trust what I was telling him. "Do you know why I have this scar on my face?" he traced the thick welt with his finger. I shook my head no. "Because I put it there myself. I was proving something to the world. Letting them know that I was the only hand that could harm me." Pushing his plate aside, Brock leaned back in his chair.

I didn't know how to respond to what he was telling me or what it meant. I just shook my head at him, smiling nervously. I tried to push some food down my throat but swallowing it was hard; it felt like it was going to come back up.

"No one can touch me," Brocks eyes widened, "Not even my own blood," he said, causing Mona to shoot him a cautious look, indicating to me that she thought he was going too far.

"Brock, eat some food," Mona stabbed a piece of meat with her fork and held it up to his mouth and he took a bite without looking down at the fork. He chewed hard and slow, still gazing in my direction like I'd committed a crime.

"I really do love your brother, Brock," I blurted out. "And I would never do anything to hurt him or his family. I'm in this thing whole hearted. I promise," I told him innocently

"It takes more than love to be a Badd," Mona said with a mouth full of food. "I told you that shit before."

"Whatever else it takes, I can learn. Bobby is my everything and I'll do what it takes to be with him. It's why I'm here," I said, finally making consistent eye contact with Brock.

Mona tried to fork more food in his mouth but he slapped her hand away so hard, the fork flew across the room. She barked at the servant to get her another fork, giving Brock a look of contempt out the corner of her eye. For some reason, what I was saying to him seemed to piss him off even more. There was no pleasing this man. It was like he hated me.

"Well, I'll know for sure if all you say is true, tomorrow," Brock said, and slammed his fist against the table. Then, he jumped up so quick, I flinched like he was about to hit me. He marched out the dining room like he was on his way to war. I wondered what was going to happen tomorrow.

23

was so taunted by Brock's evil stares, I could barely get a full night's sleep without waking up every few hours, sweating. Having Dalla's necklace in my possession didn't make things better for me either. I still didn't know if this is a test or not.

It was still early and the ranch hadn't got busy yet. I walked around aimlessly trying to blow off steam, fear and frustration. I skipped breakfast, having a few shots of Vodka at the casino instead. My head was swarming. I hadn't talked to Bobby since I got here. I just figured he thought I was okay. I was going to let him think that until I couldn't take it anymore. Although after Lisa's confession, and last night's dinner with Brock and Mona, I felt like I was already at that point.

By the time I left the casino, I was drunk. I was heading back to my guest suite to lie down when I saw Mona speeding my way in the golf cart. *Shit!* Does the woman every rest?

"Girl, I've been searching all over for yo ll ass. I thought I told you we had a schedule to keep," she grunted at me, angrily. "Get in the cart," she demanded but I didn't budge.

Sweat rolled down the sides of my face. All I could think about was Lisa telling me to leave the ranch and Brock insinuating that something was going to happen today; the liquor didn't help my nerves either. It made them worse. I was paranoid as hell.

"What the hell is wrong with you girl? You nard of hearing or somethin'? Get yo ass in the cart….I ain't got all day," Mona started to get pissed.

I slowly took two steps away from the cart. I was just about to take off running when something told me to be cool. Besides, if I ran, I knew I would be hunted down like a dog and it would make them even more suspicious of me and that was the last thing I needed.

"I'm not feeling well, today."

"Drinking at the casino during this hour, it's no wonder," she said like she was keeping tabs on me. "You gone have to suck it up. Mr. Badd got some business to handle and he needs you."

"Me?" I asked suspicious, stabbing myself in the chest with my finger. At the mere mention of Brock's name, my mind went back to what he said last night.

"Yes…you!" Mona said giving me an angry glare. "Get in the cart?"

Hesitantly, I got inside.

"You one weird ass chick," Mona grunted, shaking her head before pulling off.

I tortured myself with horrible fantasies about what Brock could have wanted with me and Mona didn't tell me a thing. Maybe she knew he was going to kill me, just like he did his mom; if the shit was even true. When Mona turned in the direction of the prison, I got so nervous I almost jumped out of the cart. Was he going to hold me hostage?

"Where are we going?" I squirmed in my seat.

"The prison," Mona said, offering no other explanation.

"Why? I thought that was off limits to me?"

"Well…Brock is making an exception today."

"I don't want to go!" I started to breathe so heavily, I thought I was going to hyperventilate.

"You really don't have a choice. This is Badd business and if you can't handle it, you don't need to marry Bobby!" Mona yelled at me. My breathing got heavier and by the time we pulled up to the door of the dungeon like prison, I felt so dizzy my vision blurred.

"No!" I sighed, holding up my head.

"What the hell is wrong with you, girl!" Mona wasn't sensitive to my panic. When she got out the cart, my body shifted and fell to the ground; I fainted.

I woke up to Mona fanning me with one hand and slapping me across the face with the other. "Brock…she's up but I still think we need to take her to the clinic."

"No…we got business to handle. Prop her up."

Mona lifted me from the ground. "Drink this, girl," Mona said, pouring water from a bottle down my throat.

My vision cleared up and I was able to see that I was inside the prison. It was dark and drab and reminded me of the phony jail Bobby hauled me to during my fake arrest, but I had a feeling this wasn't a test. "What's going on?" I said through an exhausted voice.

"You had so much liquor you passed out," Mona said judgmentally. "Badd women don't drink like lushes."

"Why am I here?" I stumbled to my feet.

"I got to put you through a test," Brock huffed at me, narrowing his eyes evilly. "If you gone be in this family, there are some things I need to know first."

"What kind of test?"

"A lie detector test," he revealed.

"Bobby didn't tell me anything about a lie detector test!" I yelled.

"So," Brock said like that didn't faze him. "I'm the head of this estate and if Bobby wants things to work out the way I think he does, he wouldn't mind."

"I already passed Bobby's test. How much more do I have to go through?" I yelled, rubbing my throbbing temples.

"As much as we say!" Mona chimed in, hovering over me like King Kong, with her thick arms folded across her chest. "And watch your tone when you're talking to Mr. Badd," she warned me.

"This is too much," I whined. I felt like I was about to faint again.

"See what she said…she can't handle this shit. I knew it. Call Bobby and tell him the wedding is off," Mona said to Brock like I'd finally said what she'd been waiting to hear all along.

"Shut up," Brock told Mona. "You either take the test or pack your shit and get the fuck up off the Ranch. You say you love my brother? Then prove it," Brock looked at me with anticipation heavy in his eyes.

Mona huffed, rolling her eyes at me.

Brock turned to me and asked. "What you gone do?"

I didn't know what to say. One thing I didn't want to do was lose Bobby. So, I agreed to take the test.

"Follow me," he said, leading me deeper in the eerie quarters of his dark dungeon. Mona followed behind us but Brock stopped her.

"Not you," he yelled, stopping her in her tracks.

"What?" Mona was offended and embarrassed.

"You heard me, Mona. Don't piss me off. Go tend to my kids or something!" he yelled at her with a clutched fist. She hissed at him before turning around, storming out the prison.

I followed behind Brock; I felt like I was walking through a haunted house. The place was eerie. We turned down a long hallway and just like in a real prison, we walked down the aisles of steel barred rooms. "Shut the fuck up! Pussy ass nigga!" Brock said to one of his badly beaten and whining prisoners. After seeing all of Brocks prisoners, beaten and locked away, I was really starting to wonder if loving Bobby and being a Badd was worth it. I tried my best to block out the faint whimpers of grown mean crying and pleading. I just needed to get through this lie detector test and afterwards, I was calling Bobby to come and get me. I don't give a fuck how weak it made me look to leave the Ranch early. I can't handle this shit anymore. I seen too much.

Brock led me into a room that was set up with a ton of technical equipment. He sat me down in a chair in front of a huge machine that I assumed was a lie detector test. Strapping me in, he gave me a vindicated look. He looked excited to be administrating this test but meanwhile, I was nervous as hell. I'd already started to sweat bullets. I didn't know much about lie detector test but I knew my sweating wouldn't put me in a positive light.

"You ready?" Brock asked and I told my first, unofficial lie when I shook my head yes. "Don't take this thing personal. It's strictly business, you know?" he said in a softer voice. I shrugged my shoulders and wiped the sweat from brow. "Let's do this," he clapped his hands excited before taking a seat behind the machine.

"I'm nervous," I blurted out before his finger touched one of the switches. Brock looked up at me like he didn't care. "I just don't want that to affect my results."

"This thing can find the truth even through the worst of nerves," he said to me with an evil smirk.

After fidgeting around with buttons and switches on the machine, Brock covered his ears with headphones then gave me a serious look.

"What's your full name?"

"Lera Way," I said through a huff. My heart was pounding. The first question was simple but, the next question, Brock didn't waste any time. He went straight for the gold.

"Have you ever met Dalla Badd before?" I shook my head no and he snapped at me, giving me an eager look. "Answer the question so that we can hear you," he said referring to himself and the lie detector.

"No," I said nervously. He looked down at the machine then back up at me. His stare was so evil, I didn't know if I passed or not although I knew I never met Dalla before.

"Prior to meeting Bobby, did you have any connections with anybody Dalla knew?"'

"No," I answered again. Brock looked down at the machine and rolled his eyes. He looked like he was getting angry at what it was revealing to him. I guess he didn't want the truth after all.

"Are you and Bobby planning on setting me up?"

"What?" I said, surprised he asked such an outright bold question.

"Answer the damn question!" he hit the table so hard, it seemed to leap off the ground.

"No!" I whined.

"Did Bobby hire you to pose as he fiancé so that he can inherit his money and build up an army against me?"

"No." I hoped not.

"Have you ever been affiliated with Ace Lucky or anybody in his family?"

"No," I answered quickly. I had no idea who he was talking about.

"You sure about that?" he asked me looking down at the machine. I replied, yes. "Has Bobby ever mentioned anything about my father or mother's death?"

"No," I answered immediately. Bobby never mentioned his dad and barely spoke of his mother. "Never," I added dwelling on what Lisa told me.

"How did my father die?" he asked me.

"I don't know!" I lied.

"Yes you do!" he said looking down at the machine again. Brock was getting upset.

"A heart attack," I confessed under the pressure.

"Who in the hell told you that?"

"Mona," I lied.

"Who?"

"I don't remember," I lied again.

"Did Bobby do it?" he asked me in a low voice.

"Did he do what?"

"Did he have anything to do with my father's death!" he yelled.

"What? No! I don't know" Sweat was now pouring down my face like a salty waterfall. This shit was getting too crazy and complicated for me. First Lisa accused Brock of killing his mother and now Brock is accusing Bobby of killing his father. What the hell type of family is this?

"Did Bobby aid Billy in any way when he killed my father?"

Brock was so close to my nose, it felt like his hot breath was going to melt my face off. I pursed my lips to respond to his outrageous question but before the words could come out, Mona came bursting through the door. Brock turned his head so quick to see who was interrupting him, I heard his neck crack. "What the hell! Didn't I tell you not to bother us!" Brock snatched off his headphones and I took a deep, relieving breath. I never was so glad to see Mona.

"This is important," she said, holding up what looked like a fake pregnant belly; I knew who it belonged to. She threw it to Brock and he caught it with one hand.

"What the hell is this?"

"Lisa," she said anxious. "The bitch wasn't pregnant. One of the boys found this out by the shooting range. She was a mole, Brock!"

Brock ran out the prison and Mona rushed behind him. They left me in the room alone and still strapped up to the lie detector. At first, I sat there for about five minutes too scared to move, then I came to my senses and finally freed myself. Now, I know Lisa's confession wasn't a test. The shit she told me was real and I had to let Bobby know everything and get the hell off this ranch. I called Bobby to come and get me.

I hid out in the casino until he got to the ranch.

24

Bobby escorted me back to Mona and Brock's mansion so that I could get the rest of my things. I didn't tell him everything right away but I did tell him about Brock taking me to the prison for a lie detector test and that pissed him off.

As soon as we pulled up, they both were standing at the front door like prison guards. Mona had her hands on her wide hips and Brock had his arms folded against his chest and his legs spread apart like he was standing guard. They didn't faze Bobby. He jumped out his Hummer and ran straight for Brock like he was going to attack him. Mona jumped in between them, guarding Brock's body with hers.

"Hold on, now! This shit ain't about to go down like this. Y'all brothers," Mona yelled, giving me evil looks out the corner of her eye.

"Let him do what he got to do. He a man and that's his woman," Brock pointed at me, pushing Mona aside.

"What the hell is your problem man?" Brock shrugged smiling evil at the both of us. He acted like he had no idea what was going on.

"It's nice to see you too, brother."

"Why the hell you got my fiancé in your torture chamber taking a lie detector test? If there's anything you want to know about me," Bobby stabbed himself in the chest, "You ask me! Keep my woman out of your madness!" Bobby stepped even closer to Brock. Now, they were nose to nose; both of them clutching their fist ready to strike.

"My house, my rules," he said to Bobby snidely, biting down hard on his bottom lip. "Besides, a lie detector test is the only way I can get the real truth around here. I'm tired of all the lies and I ain't gone have no lies damaging this family no more than it already has! I did that shit for you!" he waved his hands angrily in the air.

"I don't need you doing me no favors, Brock. Billy was smart as shit for getting the hell out of here," Bobby let the truth slip.

Mona shot me a wide eyed look and Brock looked like he'd just been punched in the stomach.

"I'm gone marry this woman," Bobby grabbed me and pulled me into his side, "Then you gone give me my money and we getting the hell out of here too!" Bobby yelled.

Mona's eyes widened and she gasped. "See what you did! See how you driving two brothers away. She's just like Dalla Brock...I told you!" Mona waved her finger in my face and Bobby slapped her hand away. That's when Brock grabbed Bobby by the collar and they started to wrestle around the front porch. Both Mona and I screamed for them to stop. Neither one of them struck each other though. They just tossed each other around like two teenage boys wrestling. Mona was able to pull Brock away from Bobby and he dusted off his clothes, looking at Brock with clenched teeth and narrowed eyes.

"I'm done with you man!" Bobby pointed at Brock.

"Lord...why is this happening!" Mona screamed like she was about to cry. "Our family is falling apart. After all these years...it's falling apart. Do something, Brock!" she slapped him across the shoulder.

Grabbing my hand, Bobby pushed past Brock and Mona and led me inside the house to get my things. "Wait Bobby," I heard Brock call out as we started up the steps, but Bobby didn't turn around.

When we got to the guest suite, I started to throw my things inside my bags quickly. I made sure that I still had Dalla's necklace. I was going to give it to Bobby along with the envelope once we got back to the city. I didn't want to initiate another fight. Mona came upstairs, tapping on the door more humble than I ever seen her. Her face was flooded with con-cern and her eyes drooped heavy like she was carrying an ocean of tears. I didn't know she could get emotional. "Bobby, can I talk to you please?" she asked in a soft tone.

"Nah, Mona. Y'all done went too far this time. I can't have my wife around this shit."

"We didn't hurt her," she said like I wasn't even in the room. "Ask her," she pointed her finger at me.

"No! I'm done with this shit, Mona and this thing today ain't the first straw and you know it. Brock is too damn arrogant and cocky. He doesn't listen or give a shit about nothing else but this household. I'm tired of it. If he wants this empire that bad, he can have the shit!"

"Come on now…Brock is just under a lot of pressure. Your father and grandfather done worked too hard to let all this shit fall apart and just when it's getting real good. Please…Brock loves all of y'all like he love his own skin. He don't mean bad. I swear it!"

"Loves me? Huh…" Bobby huffed sarcastically. "He don't even trust me. If he wanted a lie detector test, he should have come to me. Not her. Lera's innocent in all this and I love her just like you love, Brock. Because of that, we should be giving the same respect as you two. If you don't respect my wife, you don't respect me."

"She ain't your wife yet, Bobby!" Mona shot back.

"She will be in a few weeks. We moving up the wedding!" Bobby turned to me and said. Mona and I both gasped at the same time.

"Why so soon, Bobby?" Mona chocked over her words. "That's not even enough time to plan things."

"Well, it's gone have to be. I ain't wasting no more time. I need to move on with my life. All I want from y'all is what my father left me. The rest of the shit, you can keep."

"Please, Bobby. I'm gone talk to Brock. I knew that test wasn't right but Brock been acting weird lately. He not listening to me either. He needs you now more than ever. Please don't leave the family. We already lost one Badd; we can't afford to lose you!"

"Hmm…"Bobby said before grabbing my bags. He ignored Mona's plea.

We left the ranch.

When we exited the gates of the ranch, I finally felt like I could breathe; I was free at last. Bobby's phone was to ringing off the hook. He sent all the calls straight to voicemail. After five calls in a row, Bobby finally turned off his phone and threw it in the glove compartment.

I could tell he was still upset by the way his jaw was clutched together, and the single dimple in his chin twitched. A stress vein bulged from the side of his neck and he looked out on to the road angrily. I didn't want to add fuel to an already blazing flame by telling him everything that went down but I had to. After thirty minutes of silence, I couldn't help but to wonder if he was upset with me.

"Bobby, you okay?" I asked, putting my hand on his leg.

"Why you ain't call me?" he blurted out. "I told you to call me if shit got too weird. You didn't find it weird to be sitting through a lie detector test?"

"Yeah…but, I thought a lot of shit was weird. I was just trying to follow orders to prove my loyalty to you."

"How does answering his questions make you loyal to me?"

"I don't know…" I wailed.

"What the fuck he ask you anyway?"

"Some weird shit. A lot of weird, shit," I was setting myself up to reveal everything to him.

"Like what?" Bobby looked at me with a serious eye.

I sighed. "Crazy questions about you, Billy, Dalla and your father."

"What?" he said, pushing his foot on the break, slowing down.

"He asked me did you help Billy kill your father. Did I know a man named Ace Lucky and did I know Dalla prior to meeting you and all types of shit."

"Hold up, Let me pull over," Bobby saic, speeding off the next exit and pulling over at a truck stop. He parked the car and looked at me. "Now say it again."

I told him everything I could remember about the lie detector test. Bobby got so upset, he jumped out the car and slammed the door. He walked off shaking his head. I hated seeing him that upset but I had more to tell him. It was best that I got it all out in the open, now. I had the envelope in my bra and I leaned over toward the back seat and pulled Dalla's necklace out of my bag. By the time Bobby returned to the car, I was ready to tell him the rest of my story.

Before he cranked the car back up, I dropped the necklace in his lap. Right away, he looked at my neck, assuming that I was giving him my necklace but when he saw that I was still wearing mine he looked confused. "Where did you get this?" Bobby looked down at the necklace then back at me. I flipped over the B part of the chain so he could see Dalla's name inscribed in it. "How did you get this?" his eyes narrowed so tight, they looked like slits.

"Some girl on the ranch named, Lisa. If that was her name."

"What? I don't get it," he said holding the necklace up to the sun light to see if it was legit. Then he looked at me like he didn't believe me.

"You don't trust me?" I said hurt but I didn't blame him. Shit was so fucked up I didn't know what to believe myself.

Bobby shook his head and straightened up the weird look on his face. "Of course I do. You only the person in this world I trust right now but this shit is strange. How could anybody have this?" he dangled the necklace in the air.

I told Bobby everything Lisa told me. When I finished talking, Bobby looked like he aged right before my eyes. His broad shoulders fell into a slump and his head looked heavy on his head. I pulled the envelope out my bra and handed it to Bobby. He didn't bother to open it because he already knew what it was.

"We got to go!" Bobby said sharp. "I'm gone take you back to Miami for a while."

"What! No...I want to stay with you," I whined but he ignored me. He didn't speak a single word until we got back to the city. I never seen him so wound up. He drove with one hand on the staring wheel and the other anxiously massaging the bottom of his chin, deep in thought.

I didn't tell him about Dalla's message to Taffy. It didn't make sense to. At the right time, I would relay the message to Taffy. She deserved to know the truth.

25

Mona Badd

S hit is finally hitting the fan and its blowing the funky smell all over the ranch and according to Brock, it's all my fault.

That bitch, Lisa, really had me fooled. She was complaining about morning sickness and everything. I didn't know any different. Maybe I should have known when she claimed to be pregnant after only spending one night with Brock but hell; I thought it all was a blessing. The quicker I get them in and out, the better it is for me.

"How could you allow that bitch to be here all these months and never know she's pregnant. Do you know how much of our shit she probably had access to? I want all the breeders out of here today, pregnant or not!" Brock demanded and I agreed. He paced back and forth around our bedroom with both hands on top of his head. He was a nervous wreck and I hated seeing him fall apart the way he was.

"I didn't know Brock. You know that."

"NO I DON'T KNOW THAT!" Brock screamed. "I put you in charge and you fuck up like this," Brock hissed at me. He was so angry he was foaming at the mouth. "Who is the doctor that's been checking her. I want her here now!"

"Oh…uh…she quit last week," I hated to tell him that but honestly them doctors quit every other week sometimes because they can't handle the Badd way so that wasn't a red flag for me. "Find that doctor and that lying bitch! Get Brip out here right now! I want his ass hunting for them all day and night! He don't need to rest until he find them!" Brock stumped his foot so hard, I heard his knee pop.

"Yes, Sir Mr. Badd," I told him calm. "I'm sorry, Brock."

"Mona..." he held up his hand, "I don't need to hear that shit right now. What the fuck!" he kicked the wall so hard he had to snatch his boot out the hole he created. "Shit!" he yelled, turning over our breakfast table.

Brock started to go on a destructive rampage, flipping our mattress off the bed frame and knocking down all the stuff I had on top of our dresser. I wanted to tell him to calm the fuck down especially when he went after my things but he was freaking out so bad I wasn't crazy enough to approach him. He finally exhausted himself, sliding down the wall and hitting the ground to rest in a heavy slump. Cursing under his breath, he slapped himself across the face a few times before pounding the back of his head against the wall. I thought he was going to give himself a concussion.

"It's all falling apart, Mona," he said, holding out his hand for me to grab. I rushed to him taking his hand and squeezed it tight before kissing it like he was the Pope.

"No it ain't. The shit ain't done yet! It just started and we gone get through all of this. You hear me," I kissed his hand again. I tried to pull him up but he resisted.

"What about Bobby?" his voice cracked. "He gone leave here and I don't trust that shit!"

"Bobby ain't going nowhere. He just upset. You know how stubborn he can get when he upset. Let the boy be. Him and his weak ass fiancé."

"No more weak links, Mona. No more," Brock said, rising to his feet. Then he gave me the weirdest look I ever seen him muster. "My father had a solution for weak links," he mumbled to himself, pacing back and forth. "I'm gone get me one too! This shit ain't going down like this. I'm the eldest Badd," he pounded against his chest, regaining his strength.

"That's right baby. The one true Badd," I encouraged him.

"The one true Badd," he repeated.

I massaged his shoulders. The man was so tense he felt like he had rocks under his skin.

"What about the tapes?" Brock asked me like he was just remembering the cameras we had stationed all over the ranch.

"I'm gone go over them. Every last one of them two and three times if I have to and I'm gone take good notes, too. Trust me baby, I want miss a beat."

"Go over the recordings in the guest room, too. I want to know what the Lera girl been up too."

"Yes, sir," I said but I was hesitant. I thought Lera was weak but I didn't think she was a big threat. I didn't want Brock focusing so much on her because that would only cause more problems between him and Bobby. I told myself I was gone to keep this family together no matter what and that's what I plan on doing.

"I ain't trusting nobody right now but you!" Brock told me and I felt relieved to know he still had trust for me although he blamed me for everything. That didn't matter though. If blaming me made him feel better, then I'll take the blame.

"Don't worry, baby. I got you. You and Bobby will be back talking good once we start planning the wedding in a few weeks." I let it slip. I hadn't told Brock about Bobby pushing up the wedding because I knew it would only make him more paranoid.

Jerking away from my massage, Brock turned and faced me. He looked at me like I was keeping secrets from him. "What you mean in a few weeks? He ain't getting married until January. That's months from now."

I shook my head. "He told me that he was getting married at the end of the month," I said regretful.

"That's too damn soon," Brock yelled.

"I know but that's just what he wants to do..." I said shrugging my shoulders. "It's okay. Maybe the festivities of the wedding will bring some light over all this gloom around here. Take our minds of things for a little while."

"What the hell I wanna take my mind off shit for? Especially now! If I take my mind off all this shit for one second, everything falls apart. What the hell you talking about woman?" he snarled at me before kicking over our nightstand. "Bobby and that lil bitch of his is up to something," he punched another wall.

"No they ain't Brock! Just..." I didn't have nothing else to say. Nothing was calming him down so I gave up. Hell, I could have used some calming with all the drama I've been going through ately but Brock didn't seem to notice my stress.

"You know what...that's cool," Brock said in a calm voice, pacing back in forth like he had a plan. "He wanna get married quick, let him do it but that nigga ain't getting a dime of our Badd money. That's all this marriage shit is about. He wants that money! He probably planning something"

"What would Bobby be planning, Brock?"

Brock didn't respond. He just paced around the room in circles, scratching the back of his head, deep in thought.

"Do what you think is best, baby," I gave in to keep the peace. "You never steered us wrong," I assured him that I was still playing on his team.

"Yeah," Brock snarled. He shook his head, exciting himself with his plan.

I started to pick up the mess Brock made around the room while he paced back and forth, mumbling shit under his breath. I wasn't listening to him anymore; I was too tired and had too much to do. I had to clear my mind before I sent the breeders packing and monitored the videos from seven months back.

"What you doing?" Brock asked me in a seductive voice.

"I'm trying to straighten up all this mess Mr. Badd. I want you to be able to relax and I know you can't do that with all this shit lying around everywhere."

"What would I do without you, Mona" he told me humble.

"You don't even have to waist your brain cells thinking about that because you always gone have me, Mr. Badd. I'm yours for life and even after that," I turned and told him.

I continued to pick up the mess of shattered glass and tossed pillows. I bent over to pick up a bottle of perfume he threw on the floor when he cleared my vanity with one sweep of his arm, when I felt him grab my hips and push himself into my ass. It had been so long since Brock touched me in that way, at first I thought I was just fantasizing. But, when I felt the stiffness of his hard, throbbing member, I knew it was real.

"Let the staff do this shit," he said, as I leaned up.

"Yes, Sir Mr. Badd." I was so anxious for his touch, I was trembling.

"Come here," he said, roughly grabbing the waistband of my pants and pulling me in closer to him. "With your big sexy ass!" he slapped me on the butt so hard I knew I would feel it for weeks but that was a good thing because there was no telling when Brock was going to touch me again and the sting of that slap gave me something to remember. "Don't no woman on this planet move me the way you do" he said pocking me in the stomach with his big dick. I wanted Brock so bad that I was practically drooling.

Pushing me on the mattress that was turned over on the floor, he unlaced his belt. Following his lead, I pulled off my pants so fast it was like they never was on. His dick was bulging so big and thick, I saw the veins pulsating from it. I licked my lips as he lowered his body into mine. Brock kissed me hard. He snatched off my panties, throwing them over his shoulder before spreading my thick thighs and jamming his dick so deep inside of me, I came right away but lucky for me, he didn't. He pushed up against me forcefully; my titties slapped against the bottom of my chin. Brock wasn't playing around. He pounded against me like he was releasing all of his frustrations. Brock fucked me so hard and long, my eyes rolled back in my head and I came over and over again until he finally flopped down on top of me, exhausted and relaxed. Brock had given me just what I needed to get through the week.

26

"Is this about that Lisa bitch?" One of the breeders asked. "I knew something was up with her …now she done ruined it for all of us.

I had to deal with these bitches. I don't feel like hearing all their complaining. They pissed cause they got to go. I'm gone give them they checks and the ones that are already pregnant, I'm gone pick up the baby once they deliver.

"Ya'll gone know everything when you get to the prison and if you know what's good for you, you won't pester my husband about contracts and having to leave before your time. When y'all was fucking him, that was one thing but he ain't nice as me and if you do that shit, he gone get pissed and you bound to never to leave this place," I gave the girls a serious look, "know what I mean!" They all seemed to nod at the same time. "Just answer what's asked and give whatever information you know about her. Anything will help."

Brock wants to question some the girls himself before they leave the ranch. He wanted to see if any of them knew anything about Lisa and to make sure they ain't rats themselves so after they pack, they all going to the prison. Whatever they tell him, will help Brip find Lisa.

"I might know that bitch from back in the day. Do I get a bonus for that?" one of the greedy bitches asked.

"Yeah…you get to walk out of here alive!" I barked. "Now get packed and don't take shit you ain't come here with." I warned them before leaving.

I called Brip on my way to the breeding quarters and gave him the same orders Brock gave me. He didn't sound too happy to hear from me but I didn't give a damn. He told me he was coming right away. One thing I can say about Brip is that next to Brock, he's the best Badd soldier we got. He's obedient, hard as a rock and trustworthy. I wish I could say that about Bobby and Billy but that just don't apply to them. They always been different.

By the time I got back up to the main house, Brip was pulling into the driveway. The way that boy drives always drove me crazy; especially when his ass fucks up my shrubbery. I waved him in the house from the front door. Before he got inside, I had one of the servants bring him a cold beer. I wanted to calm his nerves. I couldn't take any more whining and complaining. I could tell Brip was pissed off just by the way his footsteps sounded as he marched to my sitting room. I hopped Brock really knew just how much shit I had to deal with. Brip walked into the room, shaking his head at me before leaning over and kissing me on the cheek.

"I know," I said before he could complain, "But this is real Badd business."

"I'm already working nonstop. I thought all this shit was going to slow down once I brought ole boy in. He promised me six months vacation and now I got to work even harder! Hell, Mona! I ain't a machine you know? I mean I'm made of steel," he pounded against his chest, "But I ain't no fucking robot," Brip shook his head anxiously.

"Take this," I said, sliding him the beer. He didn't waste any time chugging it down like it was water. He emptied the bottle in two long sips before letting out a loud echoing belch. He took a deep breath and rubbed the top of his head.

Brip had red blotches all over his skin. He scratched at his neck and behind his ears. Lily told me what Taffy did but I got more important things to deal with.

"Taffy and me ain't in a good place right now. I was gone ask for time off. You know…to take care of house business," Brip looked up at me like he was expecting sympathy.

"I talked to Taffy the other day. She seemed fine."

"Yeah she seem that way but something ain't right. I just know it. The girl is acting different. She being too nice; she acting phony…something's up and I need to tend to my wife before I lose her."

"She leave you and she'll be doing us all a favor. I'll have you another wife in no time!" I said flirting with the idea of Taffy leaving and replacing her for Brip but Brip got pissed off.

"I don't want no new wife no more than you want a new husband, Mona!" Brip jumped to his feet.

"Calm down," I said, waving him back to his seat. "I was just messing with you. That girl will be fine. She always is."

"That's the thing. I just keep waiting for the old Taffy to show up but," Brip started shaking his head before lowering it towards the floor like it was heavy on his neck, "Something's' off," he said under his breath like he was talking more to himself than me. "She must be real pissed off about this Lily thing. You know how bad Taffy wanted to have my baby? That shit hurt me to see her trying so hard and keep losing them. Then I go let you talk me into this dumb shit. Now look!" Brip waved his hands in the air, looking at me with accusation behind his eyes. "I didn't need no baby. Taffy was enough for me!" he complained.

"It was the right thing whether she pissed off or not. You need a heir and I didn't make you stick your dick up in that girl pussy and I sure didn't make you keep it there neither. Nobody asked you to be playing house wit the bitch. That's all on you! Brock be in and out of the pussy without no fucking pillow talk but your dumb ass setting up camp with that bitch and thinking Taffy ain't gone be pissed. Shit!"

"I know," Brip said through an exhausted voice, "I'm done with Lily; shit I been through with her. But still…I need time off to make it right with my wife!"

"And that will come but for now, shit is going down and we need you in full armor!"

"Can somebody tell me what the hell is going on around here? Brock can't keep silent forever. What the hell, Mona!"

"I don't know but whatever it is, it's some serious shit. We had a mole on the ranch for seven months now!"

"What," Brip jumped up. "But...how...what?"

"It was one of the breeders," I said shamefully like the shit really was my fault.

"Who sent her? What she want?"

I shrugged. "We don't know yet but I got a feeling Brock know what's going on. He's on it. You ain't the only one that's been working hard. Brock's been in that prison day and night for months now. Something is up and when's he's ready, I know he'll call a meeting and tell us everything but for now we just need to trust him and do what he tells us."

Brip sighed, slumping back down in the chair. He rubbed his head like it was throbbing before picking up his empty beer bottle, sprinkling the last drop on his tongue. "Does this shit have anything to do with Billy and Dalla?" he asked me in a low voice.

"I don't know but whatever it is...it's big."

———

After Brip left, I went through Lisa and the doctor's file a million times but didn't find nothing strange. Like most of the doctors on the ranch, she wasn't board certified so it's not like I could track her down and Lisa was no different.

I searched every tape from the time that bitch came on the ranch. I thought I never would get finished watching all those damn tapes but I told myself I wasn't coming up for air until I got through them all. I watched the screen so long and hard, my eyes hurt and I got such a cramp in my neck it felt like somebody had stabbed me with a knife. I figured if Brock could be doing his part in the prison I can be doing my part up here. Besides, maybe if I found something, Brock would reward me with the same treatment he gave me earlier. After this day, Lord knows I need it again.

I was starting to lose hope that I would find anything until I got to the last few days of footage. That's when I saw her with Lera behind Billy and

Dalla's house. They were talking for a while. I can't believe they planned a secret meeting right under my nose. Lisa handed her an envelope and something else. When I zoomed in closer I couldn't believe what I saw. A Badd necklace and I knew just who it belonged to. My whole body went numb. Brock was right. Lera can't be trusted. Something was up. I had to let him know what I saw right way. I ran straight to the prison to tell him.

27

Taffy Badd

"What the hell you been doing? I thought you been volunteering at an orphanage, not Habitat for Humanity. You look like a Mexican laborer right about now," Brip said, grabbing my arm and looking me up and down. I pulled away from him. I didn't want him to smell the sex on my body.

I left Malcolm's place in such a rush, I forgot how I must have looked with dried up paint all over my skin, wrinkled clothes and matted hair. I'd been rolling around in paint, naked with Malcolm all morning. He wanted to see what kind of art our bodies made together. Usually, I got home before Brip, giving me time to shower and clean up. But making love to Malcolm left me exhausted. I fell asleep on his chest right in the center of his concrete floor. When I woke up, I saw I had five missed calls from Brip. Now, I had some explaining to do.

"We were teaching the kids to paint and…"

"Paint? You taught them using paper or your body?"

Planning my day around sneaking to visit Malcolm was like rocket science but somehow I managed. Brip was still walking on eggshells around me and, because of that, he was giving me my space so whenever one of the guards tried to follow me, I threatened them and they backed away. I had Brip convinced that I was praying for our relationship at a Catholic Church downtown and when I wasn't doing that, I told him I was volunteering at an orphanage. I don't know how much longer I will be under this grace period, allowing my bullshit excuses to make sense.

"They are seven-year- olds, Brip. Things can get a little messy," I snapped. "You'll learn that once you and Lily have your baby," I told him sarcastically. Whenever I had a hard time explaining my whereabouts, I mentioned Lily and the baby and it worked like a charm every time; Brip would back away.

Brip lowered his eyes sympathetically. "I...I brought you these flowers," he said holding up a bouquet of red roses. "You like them?" he asked hopefully.

Along with the roses was a candlelight dinner. I was so exhausted, all I wanted to do was take a shower and sleep but I had to put on an act for Brip. I didn't know what I was doing with Malcolm Lee but I didn't want it to stop. If Brip found out, he would make an example of Malcolm and that would make me a murderer. What I was doing was foolish and dangerous but, for the first time in years, I felt validated as an individual and not as a group.

"They're beautiful," I smiled at Brip like all was forgiven, at least for the time being. "You did all this for me, huh?" I said in the sweetest voice I could muster.

"Of course." Brip grabbed my hand to lead me to the table but I jumped away from him like I was diseased. He gave me a weird look.

"I need to shower first. I feel too yucky," I told him and walked away. "I'll be down in less than ten minutes." Brip didn't respond. I ran up the stairs to shower.

I showered in record time, hoping that Brip didn't come up and try to join me. When I returned to the table, I caught Brip staring off into space with his hand resting under his chin like he was in a daze. He didn't even notice me until I tapped him on the shoulder. He gave me a weird look that made me wonder what he was thinking about.

I pretended not to notice his mood change.

"I'm so hungry," I said randomly.

"I just wanted to let you know how sorry I am about all of this, baby." Brip blurted out like he'd been waiting all day to tell me he was sorry. Brip apologized to me every morning and at night before we went to sleep. He said I'm sorry so much, I got numb to it.

"I know," I said, looking down at the food. I couldn't look at Brip because I would feel too guilty. I knew he really was sorry and that made what I was doing with Malcolm scandalous and I wasn't ready to accept that yet.

Brip grabbed my hand and squeezed it. "I can't take this no more, Taffy. You don't even look at me the same anymore." Brip sounded hopeless. I pulled my hand away from his touch and poured myself a glass of champagne.

"I need time, Brip," I gave him a serious look and it was the truth. I need more time to work things out in my head. I had to find myself again and somehow doing that involved fucking Malcolm on a regular.

"I've been giving you time. I let you go down to that church and that orphanage and I don't bother you none. I been allowing the guards to give you privacy. Letting you drive by yourself so you can have some *you* time," he said like my recent independence was a favor from him, "I'm trying to give you what you need but are we going to be able to get past this?"

I didn't know what to say. Guilt was starting to overwhelm me so much, I felt tears welt behind my eyes.

"I hope so," I told him genuinely.

"I don't even see Lily no more," he confessed. "I been threw with her for weeks now."

I kind of figured that. He made an effort to come home at the same time every day and he checked in with me throughout the day. That told me that he wasn't spending time with her like before.

"Oh, yeah?" I said, taking a long sip of champagne. "What about when she has that bastard of yours? Then what?"

"I already made up my mind; I'm giving all that up. You my wife and you come first. I don't know that child but I know you and I love you, Taffy."

I was speechless. Him giving up Lily wasn't too much of a surprise to me but giving up a relationship with his illegitimate child was a shocker. I knew how Badds where when it came to their offspring and the fact that Brip would give it all up for me really meant a lot.

"Mona ain't gone like that."

"Fuck, Mona. She ain't got nothing to co with what goes on in my house."

I sighed heavily and looked up and saw the desperation behind Brip's eyes. I knew then that he didn't want to lose me. "I can't let you turn your back on your child. He's innocent."

"I got to do what I got to do. I want you happy again, baby. I love you girl. You my backbone. I've been so weak without you. I'll never fuck up like that again. As a matter of fact, I'm done with all the other bitches too. Fucking around with all them tramps don't make sense when I got you. I'm sick of it. I'm ready start over fresh, Taffy."

Every word that came out of Brip's mouth surprised me more than the next. Giving up a bald Lily was one thing but all the other women too. That really took me by surprise. I didn't know how to respond. I could barely look at him. Brip got up and came around the table and kneeled down beside me. "Please forgive me, baby" he grabbed my hand it kissed it like it was gold. "Please," he begged me.

I got so overwhelmed with guilt, I jumpec up and ran. I locked myself in my bedroom and expected Brip to follow behind me but, he never did. He slept on the couch that night and I cried myself to sleep.

28

I don't know if I'm paranoid or not but I feel like I'm being followed. I'm on my home from Malcolm's house. I always park my car a few miles away from Malcolm's place just in case someone spots me. On my walk back to my car, I just started getting this eerie feeling that someone was watching me. Maybe it was the way my hairs stood up on the back of my neck or the shadow I saw lurking behind me from block to block but I'm nervous as hell. I've been a Badd wife long enough to know the feeling of being followed but then again, I have been into some shady business lately. I could just be paranoid.

Brip taught me just what to do in a situation like this and I followed his instructions closely. Instead of going directly to the car, I detoured. I didn't notice anything suspicious when I turned to case the streets behind me. Just a bunch of strangers getting on with their lives, paying me and my suspicions no mind. I'm tripping. The only person following me is my guilty conscience. Maybe being paranoid wasn't a bad thing. Something had to intervene to stop me from doing what I was doing and I preferred paranoia over Brip's wrath.

I turned back around and headed back in the direction of my car. Strangely enough, I started to think about Mama Badd, Brip's mother. I remember when Dalla told me about the rumors of her sleeping around. Then, it was unfathomable that any Badd woman had the guts to pull off an affair but now, I understood. Badd wife or not, any woman could get sick of the tyrants we had for husbands and apparently that could led you to do crazy shit. The Badd family was full of hidden secrets and I was adding to them all with my affair. By the way Brip's been acting lately, I knew he wasn't strong enough to handle the same shit he put me through. I don't know what he would do if he ever found out I was stepping out on him and hopefully, I wouldn't have to ever find out.

I was a few feet away from my car when someone grabbed me from behind. "Stay calm," a familiar voice said with their hand over my mouth. "I'm gone get in the back seat and you gone get in the car and drive off like ain't nothing wrong. Understand?" I nodded. "Good...don't give me no problems!" He opened the passenger side door. I followed his orders and got in the car at the same time he did.

My heart was racing. My hands shook so bad, the keys jingled for several seconds before I got them steady enough to crank up the car. My captor sat quietly in the back seat and I was too scared to turn around and look at him. Brip purposely put me in a situation like this before we got married but that was a long time ago and I hadn't experienced anything like this since. I was no Mona and didn't know if I had the strength to fight off a man. I didn't know what to do so I just did what he told me. I pulled out the parking lot.

"I'll tell you where to go," he told me in gruff voice. I don't know why the voice sounded so familiar but I couldn't put a face to it. "Go about three miles down and make a right down that alley and don't try nothing stupid like pushing that panic button you got on your dashboard!" he warned me.

He knew about the panic button. Every Badd wife had one. If I pushed the panic button, Brip and all his men would know my location through the GPS and be on their way to save me. I almost forgot about it. That told me this had something to do with Badd business gone wrong; shit!

I got a glimpse of the man from my rear view mirror but couldn't make out his face. He was wearing a black ski mask. I tried to remain calm. Karma had finally caught up to me for what I was doing to Brip and what I'd done to Lily.

"Turn the corner," he yelled, slightly kicking the back of my seat. He was leading me down a dead end road.

"What do you want?" I managed to ask but he didn't respond. I was in no mood to be held as ransom and if it was money he wanted, I would give him the stash Brip had installed in the left rear tire of my car just for situations like this. He really went all out to make sure I was safe.

"This ain't about no money? If I wanted the money, I would've took the money instead of you!" He said angrily. "Keep driving," he nudged the back of my seat again.

If he didn't want money, my mind couldn't imagine the things he could have wanted from me and there was only so much I was willing to give. I pulled down the long narrow alley and continued to drive in the direction of a dumpster before he had me stop a few inches from it. "Turn the car off," he demanded. "Put your hands up and slowly place them on the steering wheel." I didn't know if he had a gun or not but I was following his orders just like he did.

My palms were sweaty and slipped off the steering wheel; I squeezed the wheel tighter. I closed my eyes tight and then reopened them like I was trying to wake myself up from a bad dream, but this was no dream. What was happening to me was real. I felt like I was going to die but my whole life didn't flash before my eyes; instead, I only saw Brip. His smiling face, exaggerated dimples and anxious eyes. If he knew what was going on, he'd risk his life to save me. Would Malcolm do that for me? I'm not sure he would; Malcolm would probably try to say something corny and poetic to him that would surely get us killed. Malcolm and Brip weren't made from the same clay.

"I'm gone open the door now," he said. "Keep your hands on that wheel!" He jumped out the car quickly and snatched my door open before I had time to think of doing anything. Then he yanked me out the car with one hand like I was a rag doll. I started to feel nauseous but then again, I've been feeling sick all week; this made me feel worse. As soon as my feet landed on the ground, I threw up. "Scrappy Bo," he addressed me by the nickname that only few people knew. I gagged one last time but nothing came out. He pulled off his ski mask. It was my brother, Tony. I couldn't believe I didn't recognize his voice sooner. It has been a long time since I had seen or spoken to my brother. I feel so bad about his mental condition that in my mind, I just think of him as dead because he's definitely not the same Tony I remember.

"Tony? What the hell are you doing?" I snapped, wiping the vomit from my lips. My brother looked like a refugee; an escaped prisoner of *street* war.

Tony was wearing army fatigues and black combat boots. The hem of his pants were torn and his shirt was a wrinkled, dirty mess. Surprisingly his beard was well groomed and now he was sporting a shaved head. His body was still in shape which told me he was still working out regularly. The stress lines crisscrossing his weary face and sagging eyes made him look much older than he was.

"I been following you for weeks now," he admitted.

"What? Why?" Last I heard my brother was in Vegas with my mom, getting much needed medical attention. I used to think Tony was lucky to be alive but seeing him like this really made me double think that; he wasn't the same man he used to be and I don't think he ever would be.

"I'm coming to save you the way I couldn't save, Keno," he lowered his head like the idea of Keno's death still stung him.

"Tony, I thought you were in Vegas with mama...getting help so you can be better," I taped the side of his arm.

"Ain't nothing wrong with me. I got all my senses and better than before. I'm tired of folks treating me like I'm crazy!"

"Why are you kidnapping me? You know how scared I was?"

"I wasn't kidnapping. I was just trying to protect you. I knew this would be the only way I can get your attention," he shrugged like what he did was no big deal.

I tried to keep my composure. If it was one thing I knew how to do, it was deal with crazy people and you couldn't talk to them like you were upset.

"Get in the car," I waved him toward the passenger's side door. "I'm taking you home and getting you cleaned up. We can talk there," I rolled my eyes and tried to open my door but Tony slammed it shut.

"We ain't going nowhere! Especially to that house of yours," he hissed. "That's the very place I'm trying to protect you from."

"Tony," I sighed, lowering my head. I felt sorry for my brother and wished I could help him but there was nothing I could do. I knew Tony would do anything for me but Brip couldn't deal with his mental condition and Tony seemed to hate Brip for some reason. "What do I need protecting from?"

"Your husband and his entire murderous family" he spit out the words like they left a sour taste in his mouth.

"Tony…" I dismissed what he said.

"I ain't crazy, Taffy. I ain't," he repeated with bulging eyes. "I got to tell you something," he leaned in close to my shoulder and whispered in my ear. "I don't know how you gone take this shit but I finally did it!" he smiled wide.

I shrugged at him, not knowing what the hell he was talking about.

"I found the dudes that shot Keno!" he clapped his hands with excitement. "I finally did it, I finally found them niggas!" he slammed his fist on top of the hood of my car so loud, I jumped.

Since Keno got killed, Tony made it his life's mission to find the person responsible for murdering him. Even a bullet in the brain didn't slow Tony down. According to mama, he found the person who killed Keno every year and sometimes even twice a year so it really didn't surprise me when told me the news.

"That's good, Tony. Now you can relax a bit," I rubbed the top of his broad shoulder, trying to calm his nerves. His clothes smelled like mildew.

"Not yet, but soon. Right after I kill them mutha-fuckas! Every last one of them gone see my face before they see hell!" he zoned out for few moments. "Then, I'll relax!" he huffed.

I hated hearing my brother talking about killing people because I knew he was insane enough to do it. I feared most that he would end up getting himself killed and that would send mama to early grave no matter how much money Brip and I tried to comfort her with.

"Tony, you sure you don't just want to forgive them?" I said calm.

"What?" he gave me a look like what I just said was unthinkable. "Hell Nah! They all dying. Every last one of them Badds except you of course!" Tony said casually.

"What?" I blurted out confused. "Tony, what the hell did you just say?" my heart raced. "I'm sorry, Scrappy," he tapped the side of my arm apologetically. "But, don't worry...you gone be safe. I'll make sure of it," he said sincerely. "I should have told you earlier but I guess I'll just tell you now. Your husband and his family is the one's responsible for killing Keno."

I couldn't believe what he was saying. Now, I knew for sure he was crazy.

"Tony, do you hear what you're saying?" I said to him slowly. "You're saying you're going to kill my husband!"

"Did you hear what I said?" He huffed. "Your husband shot your brother down like he was a rabid dog."

"Tony...stop this shit! Stop it now!" I screamed.

"I know they did it. I knew I remembered that nigga from somewhere. It's all coming back to me now. I remember everything just like it was yesterday."

"That's not true, Tony!"

"How do you know? You weren't there where you? You was out shopping with mama greedy ass while your husband blew off Kenos' head! Now it's payback time. The shit is really about to get funky."

"Tony if you go after a Badd, that's suicide. No one challenges them; especially one person."

"Who said I was alone?" he smirked and I started to get even more worried. "I know a lot of cats that's been trying to get at them nigga's for years but finally, I ran into the right crowd of nigga's. These nigga's got they own army and shit been brewing between them for centuries."

"Tony, who are you talking about?"

"This cat named Ace Lucky; son of super bad street runner, Carlo Lucky!"

I couldn't do anything but gasp. Tony was crazy but throwing names like Ace Lucky around really made me think he was on to something.

"Tony," I sighed, looking up at him with a plea in my eyes, "Please… please just forget all about this shit. Neither of these people are anybody to be messed with. There only using you to get at the Badds; they didn't kill Keno." My tone was soft.

Tony dismissed my statement. He mumbled something under his breath. "Look, you've been warned. The blood is off my hands but …the shit is about to get ugly. There's a war brewing! Everybody's talking about it and I'm excited to be a soldier in it. Your whole family is going down so prepare for it, Scrappy. I just hope you don't get caught in the crossfire," Tony threw his hands up and shook his head at me before slowly backing away. "Kiss your husband goodnight tonight because you never know…" he held up his hands and smiled evil, "tonight maybe the last time you see him again."

Tony ran off like he was escaping from enemy fire. I didn't know what to do. I loved my brother but helping him was way over my head. Especially, now. If I wasn't in a dilemma before, I really was in one now.

———

When I tried to make love to Brip, he said he had a headache. I guess he learned from the best. I had a feeling this didn't have a thing to do with Lily. Something was up with him. The idea of not being able to see Brip again triggered something in me and I remembered how much I loved him. When he walked through the door later that evening, I wrapped my arms around him and kissed him like I was kissing him for the first and last time. He seemed surprised by my sudden showcase of affection. I hadn't kissed him since I found out about Lily but to my surprise, he pushed me away like he didn't want to be bothered with me.

He interrogated me about the fake Catholic Church I told him I've been visiting. I got out of his questioning when I started to feel so dizzy and fatigue that I threw up. He left me alone after that. This nauseous feeling won't seem to go away and that only can mean one thing; I'm pregnant again. I hope that's not the case because I don't have the energy to deal with it. I already have enough drama in my life and the circumstances of my pregnancy are different now that I'm fucking two men. The baby could just as easily be Malcolm's. I didn't mean to but Malcolm and I had a few slip ups since we've been sleeping together; I should've been more careful. If the fucker had a chance of surviving, I would kill myself with concern but lucky for me, I have no luck in that department. I guess that's one less thing to worry about but there's still so much other shit going on right now.

I had a hard time sleeping. I was haunted by what Tony told me but I couldn't bring myself to tell Brip. I still didn't know how serious Tony was and if I told Brip, he'd take offense to it and react regardless of my brother's mental state. I was torn and scared. I knew Tony was out of his mind but I couldn't help but wonder if what he told me was true. If it was, that would change everything.

I fell asleep early. I had a terrible dream. I dreamed that Tony killed Brip and Brip came back to life to kill Malcolm. I couldn't close my eyes without seeing blood and feeling sorrow. Then, I dreamed about my brother Keno. Brip was laughing, holding gun to his head while Tony pleaded for Keno's life. I tossed and turned all night and when I woke up, Brip was staring at the ceiling in a trance. I feared what was running through his mind. I didn't want to give myself up too easy by assuming his change in behavior was due to my rendezvous with Malcolm. It could've been anything. I got up to use the bathroom. Brip didn't bother to turn his head in my direction.

When I got to the bathroom, I splashed cold water on my face and took deep breaths to combat the feeling of panic. I looked at my reflection in the mirror and it was like a different person was looking back at me. My relationship with Malcolm was changing me. At first I felt liberated but now, I just felt weird. This thing with Malcolm was only supposed to be a one time fling but now, it's turning out to be something different; especially if I was pregnant. I knew I had to let him go. It was time. My family is in trouble I didn't have time to play fairy land with Malcolm anymore. I climbed back in bed. Brip was still looking up at the ceiling. The reflection of the moon light shined off his face, revealing his weariness. I'd never seen Brip look so stressed or sit so still without moving. His erratic behavior was really starting to scare me; Brip was so quite, I couldn't hear him breathing.

I decided that I wasn't going to share the information Tony told me with him. It was too risky for Tony and besides it's a strong possibility that the shit Tony told me was all in his head. But, I still had to know the truth. Just to ease my own conscience. I eased over on my left side to face Brip. He didn't take his eyes off the ceiling. I reached over and touched his chest and he jumped like he'd been touched by a ghost.

"Brip, are you okay?" I dreaded the answer to the question and had such a hard time asking it, I stuttered trying to get it out.

"I'm fine," he said harsh, rolling over, curling up with his back to me.

"I have to ask you a question," he turned back to face me right away. Giving me an incredulous look, he raised his brow anticipating what I had to ask him. I was so shocked by his reaction, I almost forgot what I wanted to ask. He got impatient.

"What the fuck you got to ask me? Hurry up…I got to get some damn sleep!"

"Did you know my brother before you met me?" I blurted out. Brip lowered his brow into a curious scour.

"What?"

"Did you know Tony?"

"How the fuck would I know yo crazy ass brother? I don't fool with dudes like that."

"I was just curious. You deal with so many people…how you know if you ever ran into him before or not?"

"Cause I don't forget a damn face that's why. Why you asking me this shit at this hour?"

"I don't know…." I couldn't tell him the truth.

"Let me ask you something since you making this the question asking hour?"

Brip leaned up and turned on the lamp. Not the only did the light blind me, it revealed the hidden terror on my face. My heartbeat was so loud, I couldn't hear myself think. I feared what he was going to ask me and wasn't sure I could lie to him. He was looking at me like I was a stranger. He stared at me for several minutes but, he didn't ask me anything. He just shook his head before turning off the lamp. "Fuck it," he mumbled under his breath and pulled the covers back over his head. Brip didn't want to ask me a question that he really didn't want to know the answer too. I got off the hook easy. Now I know for sure, I'm done with Malcolm and Tony's bullshit theory. It's time for me to get my head back in the game of being a Badd wife; I miss the way me and Brip where and I want it back.

———

Mona called me early this morning and told me that I had to be at the ranch so I can help her plan Bobby and Lera's wedding events. I can't believe they moved up their wedding date. Good for them. I also couldn't believe how cordial Mona was being towards me. That bitch actually asked me how I was doing and waited for me to respond. What the hell has gotten into her? Whatever it is, I think this wedding is going to be good for the whole family. It'll help take our minds off things; especially me and Brip.

I called Brip as soon as I got off the phone with Mona to tell him the good news but he sent my call straight to voicemail. I called back three times since then and he still didn't answer. I had to be at the ranch within the next few hours and I knew if nothing else would move him to talk to me it would be official Badd business. I assumed he'd be the one to drive me. I was looking forward to the two hour drive. It would give us time to catch up but he didn't pick me up. He had one of his men do it for him. It kind of hurt my feelings but I knew he couldn't hide from me too much longer.

On my way out the house, I saw Tony lurking across the street behind some bushes looking more deranged than the last time I saw him. He was wearing an apple jack hat and huge sunglasses that covered his entire face. When I went to approach him, he, lowered his glasses and saluted me like he was telling me goodbye before darting off behind a building like a stray dog. Tony's behavior was really starting to bother me and I started to reconsider telling Brip about him. I just prayed Brip would have mercy on him. But, just like I knew what Brip was capable of, I knew what Tony was capable of as well. He was dangerous and I had a feeling he was plotting to hurt Brip.

29

As soon as the driver pulled up to my mansion, Mona was standing at my front door holding a clip board. When the driver opened the door for me, I vomited right on his feet. All that bumping motion in the car made me nauseous. Mona rushed to the car like I was having a seizure.

"You sick?" She asked me looking down at my watery yellowish vomit with her nose turned up.

"Uh, yeah...I think I had some bad sushi."

"Damn, girl! You can't be getting sick at a time like this. I need all the help I can get."

"I'll be okay. I took some pills and..."

"You need to go to the clinic. You could have one of them stomach viruses that's been going around and that's the last thing we need to affect these festivities."

"I'm okay"

"No, get back in the car," she said scooting me over with her thick, iron like hip. "Take us to the clinic." She demanded the driver. "You need to get one of them shots just to be sure. None of us can afford to get sick. Let's go!" There was no since arguing with Mona so I just went ahead and agreed to take the shot just to get her off my back.

When we got to the clinic it was crowded with people but we went straight to the back where our doctor, Dr. Burns, saw me in a private room only used by Badds. Mona had called him before we pulled up. He was on her speed dial and always on 24 hour call for us. He was already waiting on us when we walked in the room. Dr. Burns had seen me through all my miscarriages, he knew my body well.

"What's going on?" the old man asked me, looking at me up and down, giving me a visual inspection first.

Before I could answer, Mona answered for me. "She might be getting the flu and she needs one of them shots. We got a lot going on these upcoming weeks and I need her healthy."

The walls in Dr. Burns' examining room were covered with pictures of Mona's children. There were even baby pictures of all four of the Badd brothers, hanging on the walls like trophies. "Alright," let's have a look. Dr. Burns patted the edge of his table, gesturing for me to take a seat. I was so nauseous, I was ready to throw up again but I held it in the best I could not to clue the doctor in on what really was going on with me.

I don't know for sure that I'm pregnant but I've been through this enough times to have an idea. The possibilities of me being pregnant was strong no matter how much I wanted it to go away. Whenever the thought of me giving birth started to cross my mind instead of getting excited, I got scared. Brock made it a Badd rule that all the babies be blood tested within 48hrs of their birth, regardless of how long the marriage was. Mona even had to follow the rule and I couldn't imagine the punishment that would come from me having a baby that wasn't a Badd.

I sat at the edge of the doctor's seat. Mona was standing over us like a watchdog. I wished she would get the fuck out the room and give me and the doctor some privacy but I knew that was only wishful thinking. Dr. Burns reminded me of the grandfather I never had. He talked to me like I was delicate and always smelled like peppermint and Old Spice. He raised his bushy eyebrows and shined a light in my eyes, then scratched his thick salt and pepper beard.

"Just give her the shot. I'm sure it's the flu bug," Mona demanded like she had the education to diagnose me. But, Dr. Burns ignored her. He continued on with his exam.

He touched the sides of my throat with his middle and index finger glued together. His hands felt cold. He pressed down on my abdomen a bit then gave me a suspicious look. "Hmm" was all he said moving his hand from the left side of my stomach to the right, pressing against it some more.

"Let me take some blood first, then if it's needed, I'll give the shot," he looked at Mona. Mona sighed and rolled her eyes. "How long have you been feeling ill, sweetie," he asked me with a smile as he prepared his needle and wiped my forearm with an alcohol swab.

"Just today," I answered quickly rubbing my nose and avoiding eye contact with Mona and the Doctor. I was so nervous, I didn't feel the sting of the needle go in and out of my arm. The doctor dropped the blood filled needle in a bag and sent it through a small chute in the wall. I was already sliding off the table, eager to get out of the clinic. Mona looked just as eager as I was to get on with our busy day. She turned her back and placed her hand on the large brass knob to let us out but I wasn't getting away from Dr. Burns that easy.

"Hold it," he said. When we turned around, he was holding up a small cup. I knew he wanted me to pee in it. Shit, I thought to myself. Mona started to look suspicious and frustrated at the same time. I rubbed the back of my neck, checking my watch like I was out of time.

"Dr. Burns we're so busy today," I waved my hands in the air, still heading for the door.

"This won't take long. I'm going need a urine sample before I can give you the shot. Don't want to go to ahead of myself." Dr. Burns said giving me a telling look.

I looked up at Mona and then back to Dr. Burns. They both were giving me strange looks. I looked down at my watch again, tapping my foot against the linoleum floor like I was in a rush. "Uh…" I tried to get out of it. "I don't have to go right now. I went before I got here." It was my easiest way out or at least I thought.

"Well…I have to leave within the next hour and I won't be available to give any shots until next week," Dr. Burns said looking in Mona's direction. I still was heading for the door when I felt her heavy hand land on my shoulder and spin me around like a spin top.

"I'll get you some water." Mona said, heading out the door in pursuit of the vending machine.

Dr. Burns looked at me like he wanted to say something before Mona got back but I kept looking at the floor. I sat back down on the edge of his table and finally got enough nerve to look him in the eye. I felt like a teenager hiding a pregnancy from my suspecting mother. His arms folded and he looked at me as to say, fess up but instead he just asked me, "You sure it's the flu you got, Taffy Doll?" he called me that from time to time. It made me feel special.

I shrugged my shoulders, looking back at him with the truth written in my eyes. I held out my hand, "Give me the cup." It was no use prolonging this thing. "I think I can go now."

I peed in the cup and my urine and blood work was on its way to the lab by the time Mona came back with a bottle of water.

"Let's go," I said attempting to head for the door.

"You got the shot?" Mona blocked the door with her thick, round body.

"No, I peed in the cup and it's probably gone take a while before my samples come back from the lab. I'll make sure to get it before Dr. Burns leave," I said almost pushing her away from the door in search of the knob. I didn't need her around when Dr. Burns gave me the news but it was too late because he was already back from the lab. That had to be like record timing because he wasn't gone but five minutes before he was back with my results.

"She ain't got no flu" Dr. Burns said like it was no surprise to him.

"Then what is it?" Mona asked curious.

"She just pregnant," the doctor revealed and I tried to look surprised as Mona did. Her chubby bottom jaw jiggled as she stood there with her mouth open for a split second then closed it, regaining her composure. She grabbed the water bottle from my hand, twisting off the cap and taking a long swig. She shook her head like she already knew the outcome.

"I'm gone need for you to make some time to come back in for a checkup young lady," Dr. Burns looked at me through the thick rim of the eyeglasses. I nodded, still trying to avoid eye contact with Mona.

"I knew something was up with you," Mona said half excited, half weary knowing my pregnancy history. "You think you can handle all this shit we got to do in your state?" Mona asked as we headed out the clinic.

I just shrugged my shoulders. I didn't see why I couldn't get past these next few weeks.

"So how long you think you gone be pregnant this time?" She asked me like she was used to the routine.

I rolled my eyes at her rudeness. "Brip really gone need to see a counselor before the year is out. Remind me to schedule a visit for him, will you?" She didn't even turn to look at me.

I tried my best to ignore her comments.

"Two dead babies in less than a year, shit! That type of stuff would even take a toll on Brock and my man solid as they come."

I stopped walking and the door she pushed open almost knocked me down as it flung backwards, hitting me in the head. When Mona realized she was walking and talking alone she turned around and stared at me from the door. I walked through the door quickly.

"What do you mean two dead babies?" I held up my two fingers.

"The one you probably gone lose and his child with Lily which was just a damn waste cause the baby turned out to be a girl anyway," Mona said in a matter of fact tone before squeezing into the golf cart waiting for me to get in.

I rushed up behind her. "Mona, what the hell are you talking about?" I didn't know anything about Lily losing the baby. She had to be no more than four or five months.

"You mean Brip ain't tell you, yet?" She said like she'd put her foot in her mouth. "Shit, it ain't my business to tell." That was bullshit. Mona made everything her business.

"Get your lil pregnant ass in the cart, girl. We got shit to do." She twisted off the cap of the water and downed it until it was finished, squeezing the plastic bottle like it was somebody's throat. I know she was only trying to avoid my questions.

"When did this happen, Mona?"

"A few days ago. That girl was a mess. She in the clinic now, wiping her tears and waiting on her severance check," Mona shouted sarcastically. "I guess I should have just minded my own damn business! Shit, all I was trying to do was help. Hell, Brip act like he seen a ghost when that girl pushed the small, nothing of a baby out her pussy." Mona shook her head. "Let's go!"

"I'll catch up to you later," I said, turning to go back into the clinic before Mona had time to try and stop me. It would be rude not to greet, Lily. After all, she was on my turf and in more than one way!

Lily's baby dying was news to me. I almost felt half sorry for the girl but my envy wouldn't let me take it that far. Her little situation just reminded me of one thing, if something wasn't meant to be then it wasn't meant to be. Brip should have never fucked around with her and that's Karma for your ass but on the other hand, I guess I had a little Karma coming my way, too; I had a feeling this baby wasn't Brip's.

I saw Dr. Burns in the lab. He had his back turned and I was able to slip pass him. I didn't feel like him stopping me and feeding me the doomed speech about the chances of my baby surviving. Besides, I had heard his prognosis speech so much, I knew it by heart. I continued down the hallway. The entire clinic was about the size of an emergency room but the back was reserved for Badds. Two huge, solid wood doors separated our area from the common area. It looked totally different from the public clinic. Instead of linoleum floors and white walls, our side had thick glossy wood floors and deep blue and gray colors on the walls that made it feel like a spa. We got primo service as expected and most of all, privacy.

There was only four rooms in the short hall; one for each family. I recovered in my room more times than I'd like to remember after each miscarriage. It was comfortable there and Mona let me redo the décor, turning my hospital room into a private little retreat that always seemed to get me through my loss. I hoped Mona wasn't bold enough to put Lily in my room. I went through three doors and the last door to open, located at the very end of the hall was the door to me and Brip's room. I knew Lily was inside because a pink balloon was dangling in the air along with other pink *it's a girl* paraphernalia tapped to the door.

I ripped all the *'It's a girl'* decor off the door and relieved the balloon of the last bit of air by popping it with the tip of my B necklace. This bitch really thought she had one up on me having Brip's baby. Hell, so did I but I guess we both was wrong cause now, she ain't got shit but pointless stretch marks and a whole lot of baby clothes she don't need. I burst through the door with my hands full of all her door postings. That bald headed bitch was lying on my bed, wrapped in my down blanket nursing a box of tissues and holding a pink knitted baby blanket tightly against her chest like it was her dead baby.

When Lily saw me, she looked shocked and immediately tried to save face by acting like nothing was fazing her but she was a bad actress. She grabbed her jet black, bob styled wig from the nightstand to cover her patchy, pink head but she was two seconds to late cause I got a good look of the new do I gave her before she covered it with the wig. She sniffed a few times before wiping her tears and straightening her posture out of the depressing shoulder slumped slouch she was in. She bit down on her bottom lip, trying to look me in the eyes with a straight face. I could see her entire body trembling.

"What are you doing here?" She snapped at me.

"I should be asking you that question! You're in my space."

I couldn't stop smirking at her. I dropped all her door posting on the foot of the bed. "This yours?" I asked sarcastically, still smiling at her. On top of her nightstand was an assortment of flowers and cards. I didn't have to read the cards to know what they said because I got the same damn cards every time. A bunch of prepaid sentiments. *Sorry for your loss, get well soon* and some religious with scriptures that had nothing to do with my hurting. I walked over to the nightstand and attempted to pick up one of her cards but she snatched it away.

"Get out!" she pointed her dainty finger towards the door.

"Bitch, you get out! You and your frozen baby. I gave them on of Brip's shoe boxes to bury it in," I laughed. I enjoyed the look of horror that covered Lily's face.

Lily couldn't play tough anymore. She started to cry.

"This room is cursed! I begged them not bring me here to deliver!" she shot back at me and I instantly got the notion to knock the shit out of her; I balled up my fist and waved it at her. She ducked, covering her face with a pillow but I didn't hit her. It didn't make sense kicking a dog while it's already down.

"It doesn't make sense to be upset. Brip didn't want this baby anyway and he damn sure didn't want you. It died because it didn't belong!" I chuckled.

"Oh yeah...what about all the miscarriages you had!" she snapped. I didn't respond. She shocked me with that knowledge. "Yeah, Brip told me everything. Obviously, you can't hang either. Brip wanted this baby alright. He kissed my stomach every night and told me he hadn't been this happy in years!"

I couldn't take it anymore. I came here to play the Queen B but now this bitch was stinging me. I snatched the wig off her head before she could duck and slapped her across the face with it twice before throwing it across the room. She blocked my hits with her hands, screaming violently at the top of her lungs like I was killing her.

"He was lying to you bitch! That's why your ugly ass frozen baby is gone back to hell where it belongs! It should thaw out fine there!"

Lily was so mad she raised her hand at me like she was going to hit me. She came to her senses when I didn't flinch. I was waiting on that bitch. "It don't make sense for you to be angry," I said calmly. "God just made a mistake is all." I walked around the bed. She jumped when I stopped alongside of her but I wasn't going to hit her. "He just made a simple mistake and put the baby in the wrong place but he fixed it" I said rubbing my stomach, hinting to her about my condition. "He put Brip's true baby back where it belongs" I patted my stomach, praying that it really was Brip's baby.

Lily looked like she could burn a hole through my stomach she was eyeing me so hard. Part of her looked envious and the other part looked at me like I was full of shit. She didn't say anything.

"Some things just ain't meant to be. Get well soon," I told her before turning around to leave. I made my point.

When I got to the door, I heard her yell "I'll keep this bed warm for you and my baby is going to do the same thing in morgue for your child. You'll be back soon! Maybe anytime now, any hour, any second. Yeah, I'm going to keep this room nice and warm for you," She laughed. "And you already know I know how to keep your bed warm. Just ask, Brip." I was so pissed I saw red. I went to turn around to attack her but before I could, Mona was coming through the door. She grabbed me by the forearm.

"Damn, girl! I knew you were evil but I didn't know you were this evil! We ain't got time for whatever shit you trying to pull here. We got a wedding to plan! Can't you see she already miserable enough? Leave that bitch be," she said yanking me through the door.

For now, I said under my breath. I walked away without the last word but still feeling vindicated.

30

Mona Badd

"You got quite the appetite," I said, looking at Taffy's plate.

I was surprised as hell when Taffy filled her plate with chicken fingers and other fried foods. We were taking a lunch break from all the wedding planning. I thought now would be the perfect time to fill her in on what's going on around here. Taffy stuffed the chicken in her mouth and almost swallowed it whole, barely chewing it. I dropped six buffalo wings on my plate and covered them with blue cheese sauce before grabbing a handful of the chicken fingers myself before Taffy ate them all.

"It must be the baby," she said, rubbing her stomach like the sucka had a fighting chance.

"You think that baby in your stomach strong enough to give you that kind of appetite?" I didn't mean it the way it came out but hell, who was she kidding. That girl knew that baby wasn't going to make it. They never did.

"Yeah!" Taffy snapped. Still chewing, she held her plate in one hand and her other hand was on her hip, ready to tell me off. "You ain't God, Mona. You know that?"

"Lucky for you!"

"Look, the baby in the morgue" she pointed over her shoulder, "that's your business! But *this* baby is my business. Got that?"

Wow. She was really getting snippy with me. Lucky for her, I didn't have the energy to bring her back down to reality and the bitch was halfway right. What the hell did I care about her and that ghost baby she carrying.

"Whatever! Sit down," I demanded then jumped straight to the point. "I don't trust Lera and neither do Mr. Badd" Taffy stopped chewing. I heard her fork drop on her plate.

"Do you trust anybody other than Brock and yourself?"

"I trust you and Brip," I was honest.

"Yeah right," she sighed like she didn't believe me.

Ever since I told Brock what I saw over the security camera, things got worst with him. He just had to know Lera's connection to Lisa and he didn't trust her for shit now. He was particularly interested in the envelope Lisa gave her. He interrogated me about what was in the envelope like I had the ability to see through paper.

"This is serious, girl! She may be connected to Dalla."

"What!" Taffy jumped up. I had her attention now.

"We found out a few weeks ago that we had a mole on the ranch," she stopped eating again, gasping. "One of the breeders was a damn fake so I started watching the video surveillance and saw Lera with the mole. She got to be a mole herself."

"I don't believe it. Lera's no fake"

"Well believe it!"

"What were they doing?"

"Meeting, plotting....hell I don't know just yet but she gave the girl Dalla's necklace."

"What!" Taffy jumped up again. "But...that doesn't make any sense. What does Dalla have to do with a mole being on the ranch? I mean... if she really did steal all that money like yall say…"

"She did just like we said," I pounded against the table. She was pissing me off.

"Well...her and Billy are probably somewhere living in bliss. Why in the hell would she need a mole here?"

"To try to set us up so they can take over. Her and Billy both. That's why!"

Taffy rolled her eyes at me like she wasn't buying into my theory. "Have you told Bobby any of this?

"He won't return me or Brock's calls and Brip said they both gone off somewhere and he can't reach them. I hadn't heard from them in days until he called giving us a wedding date. They up to something. We all may be in danger." I gave Taffy a serious look. She was staring at me like I just told her puppy died.

"How if Dalla's in trouble?" she said in a low voice. "Maybe that's why Lisa had the necklace."

"I don't give a fuck about that bitch! The only people in trouble is the one's on this ranch. Have you talked to Lera since she left here? Did she tell you anything about Lisa or the necklace?"

"She hasn't been answering my calls either."

"Now, tell me that ain't strange?"

She started to moving things around on her plate like a five year old playing with her food. Her shoulders slumped with disappointment.

"So why are we planning this wedding?"

"Mr. Badd wants to keep things normal. Let them get married. Anything to get them here so he could get to the bottom of things. So, keep your cool and keep this conversation between the two of us. Understand?"

Taffy shrugged, still staring off into blank space like her best friend moved out the neighborhood. "I know you liked that girl and wanted things to work out but at what risk? She poisoning Bobby's mind and I know that Dalla bitch is behind it. We stand to lose everything. Brip in danger too."

"Does he know about this?"

"I told him a little bit but he's so loyal and naïve he don't understand. That's why we need you to talk to him. Tell him everything I told you about the setup."

"What setup? I'm not saying anything unless I'm sure and…"

I stood up, slamming my fist against the table. "Didn't I already tell you everything? What the hell you got to be sure about?" I snapped.

Taffy nodded. "I'll do what I can," she said then left. She rushed out the door like she was late for a meeting. She probably was just going off somewhere to cry with her weak ass. I sighed and rolled my eyes. I was just happy to be alone for a few seconds but that didn't last long. I saw Brock pulling up the driveway. He jumped out the truck like the house was on fire. *Shit*, I don't feel like dealing with him but I guess that don't matter now cause here he come in the house.

31

Brock stomped into the room, wearing his black combat boots, half cut white T and army fatigue bandana tied around his Mohawk. He looked at me like I had answers for him but I had nothing but questions. Brock wasn't telling me everything. If Bobby, Billy and their cunt wives were plotting to set us up, I needed to know why.

"That girl don't know nothing," I said referring to Taffy. "She too simple, Brock. She got her own shit going on with being pregnant and all." I added that just to lighten the air but it didn't work.

"Did you tell her what you saw?" his voice was full of paranoia.

"Yeah. All she did was get scared."

"How you know she ain't in on it?" He shocked me. Taffy was weak but she wasn't no backstabber like Dalla. He was going too far with his accusations and was really starting to piss me off. For all I knew, I might be next person he accused.

"In on what, Brock?" I stood up. He didn't respond. Brock walked over to the buffet, avoiding my question and started looking over the food. "Brock, I asked you a question? I need to know what the fuck is really going around here. Why you so paranoid and who in the hell you got in that dungeon?"

"I told you everything you need to know for now," he said. He picked up a chicken wing and put it close enough to his face to bite it but threw it back down. Then, he turned to face me.

"I need to know more! If you don't start talking, I'm gone start walking" I shifted my weight from one leg to the next, standing my ground.

I didn't plan on going no place but I needed his attention and I got it all right.

He charged at me but I didn't flinch. Not even when he grabbed my shirt collar and pulled me into his chest, hissing at me like a snake. "You leaving me? Huh? Is that what I just heard you say, woman?"

I pushed him off of me. "Nigga! You better get to talking cause I ain't in the mood." He looked at me and down at my clutched fist and saw that I was serious.

Brock paced around in circles, mumbling something under his breath. Then sat down. He sighed heavy, burying his face inside his hands. I walked over to him and placed my hands on top of his shoulders; they felt like stones. I massaged them back to their natural state.

"I got to know what's going on or I'm gone go crazy." I whispered to Brock.

He grabbed a chicken finger off of Taffy's discarded plate and stuffed it in his mouth. I was glad to see him eating. Brock almost never drank but I offered him a cocktail anyway; he needed one and so did I. At first I thought he was going to refuse it but to my surprise, he didn't. I poured us a small glass of Scotch. I extended my glass for a toast. "To getting back on top of things." I said with a smile and he almost smiled back at me before tapping his glass against mine then slowly taking a sip.

I watched him barely sip his cocktail. I took a half a sip of the harsh beverage. I wasn't use to drinking and the Scotch burned my chest in an awful way. But, it was taking the edge off and Brock was more relaxed.

"Let's go to the study" he said and got up. I followed behind him.

I never really used the study. It's where Brock took the male dinner guest whenever it was time for them to stop bullshitting and get to business. It was Papa's Badd old office. He opened the double doors and the smell of Papa Badd's Brandy and Cuban cigars still lingered in the air. The cherry wood paneling on the walls reminded me of a courtroom but then again Papa Badd was the judge and had final say at shit. Brock left everything the way his father left it.

The study was furnished with a long desk, a love seat style leather couch and book shelf full of business books and atlas maps of the city. There was one of those little Crystal springs water fountains you would see at doctors' offices in the corner of the room. I immediately grabbed a cup and helped myself to some cold water. I needed something to soothe my burning chest. Brock took a seat; he looked like the president behind that big desk. It always turned me on to see him sitting there; his power really stood out. I sat down in front of him. I waited for him to start talking. He took his time. Looking around the office, admiring it for what it was.

"This is where it all starts and ends you know. You know how many folks sat right where you sitting as my father sealed deals and created this empire. Making it even stronger than his father before him? Some nights, he wouldn't leave this room at all. He would be in here all day, figuring shit out and when he finally came out…we were on top. I owe him the world for that."

Brock rubbed his hand across the wood desk as if he was channeling his father's energy, trying to conjure up a solution for whatever was caus-ing him so much mental anguish. He leaned back in the cushion of the leather chair, resting his right leg over his knee.

"Presidents, kings, and dictators of the world have an entire nation backing them, supporting them in their quest to create and develop wealth and conquer territories but my father did it all on his own. He had no one. He was strong as hell, Mona and I have to live up to that. I owe him that much. Sometimes I think I'm the only one that appreciates that. Before my dad died, I promised I take this shit to another level. I promised him that I would cut all weak links no matter what."

"And that's just what you done, baby. I know Papa Badd will be proud of you."

"Would he?" Brock said, staring off into blank space. For some rea-son, a chill went down my spine.

"What you mean, baby? You doing it big!"

"Yeah…but the weak links…the weak links are shitting on everything I done. They poison, Mona. One pair of shitty panties funks up the entire laundry basket."

"What you saying, baby?"

"I'm saying my brother Billy was that first pair of shitty panties and now, he done funked up Bobby…weak links are breaking the chain and that's fucking up our business here."

"Brock don't worry yourself so much about what Billy did. We done made that money back three times over since he left."

"This shit ain't about the money. Its deeper than that. Way deeper…"

"Then what is it baby? Tell me…"

My heart was beating with anticipation. Ever since Billy and Dalla fled, I felt like there was something Brock was keeping back from me. I could see it behind his eyes. Whatever it was, it seemed to be eating him alive. Brock took the last swallow of his Scotch, swallowing hard. Leaning in closer to me, he shook his head.

"Billy killed Papa Badd and I got a hard feeling, Bobby had something to do with it too."

All I could do was gasp. I wanted to tell him that he was going crazy and that it was all in his head but the look in his eyes told me otherwise; he was serious.

"He died of a heart attack," I tried to convince myself.

Brock shook his head, giving me a serious look. His eyes were cold. "It wasn't a natural heart attack," Brock grimaced and clutched his fist tightly. "It was induced. You remember how I was after Papa Badd died. I was so messed up in the head that I let Billy handle the funeral, the autopsy… everything," he punched the desk. "I fucked up big time. Right under my own nose…this moth-fucker kills my father!"

"Why would Billy kill his own father? Especially after how hard he took the death of his mother?"

"Because he thought Papa Badd had something to do with Mama Badd's death. He assumed that Papa Badd killed Mama Badd in a jealous rage over all them bullshit rumors about her sleeping around. You remember how he wouldn't let the shit go."

"But, how do you know for sure *he* killed him?"

"Because, a very reliable source told me."

"Who?"

"His own wife, that's who," he gave me an evil stare.

"What? Dalla told you that shit?" I was speechless. "Come on Brock! That's bullshit. Billy wouldn't kill his own father. He may be a lot of things but he never would go that far. Don't you see what this bitch is trying to do? She trying to divide us."

"I believe her," he looked me directly in the eyes then lowered them like he was hiding something. "People can go that far," he swallowed the remaining Scotch then swirled the ice cubes around in the glass with his hand. "The night before I called the family meeting to let all you know about them stealing the money," he continued to look at the floor, "she came to me right here in this study and confessed everything. Billy poisoned Papa Badd. Gave him some lethal ass shit that probably killed him after only one sip of Brandy," he hissed and I almost threw up at the idea of it. "She begged for me not to kill Billy and hoped her coming to me first would help keep him alive." Brock got up and started to pace around the room. He took a deep breath and then looked at me. His eyes where haunted. "I ain't believe her at first, Mona. What the fuck I want to believe some shit like that for but then she dropped a name and I knew it was true."

"What name?"

"Tyler Jones."

Wait a minute," I was thrown back. "Ain't he the one that did the autopsy on Papa Badd? Brock nodded. I remember screening Tyler. We hired him to do all our autopsies. We even paid him to do favors for other people like fake reports. He was very resourceful."

"Yeah and he faked it for Billy."

"Why the hell would he do something like that? He been doing autopsies for us for years and he knows that shit is suicide. He even did Mama Badd's autopsy. That's bullshit, Brock."

"No it ain't!" he stomped his foot and gave me a grimacing stare. "I know for a fact that shit is right up that niggas alley."

"How do you now for a fact, Brock?" I was confused but Brock seemed insistent about it.

"Because he did some grimy ass shit like that before?"

"Of course he has. That's why he's on the payroll but he ain't gone fuck with one of us. He ain't crazy."

"Yes, he is!" He slammed his fist against the table and gave me a wild eyed stare. "He didn't have no problem faking Mama Badd's report for me so what the fuck difference would it make for him to fake my father's report for Billy? If a nigga eat dirt once, he develops an appetite for it."

I gasped, then exhaled. I had to be hearing him wrong. Brock kept his eyes fixed on me. He was waiting for me to say something. He even looked like he was hoping for some kind of reassurance from me but I was speechless.

"Why did you need him to fake Mama Badd's autopsy?" My voice cracked. I looked up at Brock but for some reason, he looked different to me. I couldn't stare at him for too long without getting freaked out by his grim expression.

Brock got up and walked from behind the desk. He kneeled down in front of me and grabbed my hands. I still couldn't look at him. He squeezed my hand but I didn't squeeze back. He buried his face in my lap like he was about to sob but he didn't. I didn't comfort him either.

"I did it for us. Our whole livelihood was at stake and it still is."

"I don't understand? Stop bullshitting and tell me what the fuck is going on. Did you fake your mother's autopsy report on purpose?"

"Yes," he answered quick and jumped to his feet. He folded his arms around his chest and looked down at me arrogantly.

"Why?"

"I just told you why. At the time our future was at stake and I worked too hard to have that jeopardized."

"Why?" I asked again, shaking my head shamefully at him.

"Because my mother was a fucking traitor. Maybe even a mole herself. Not only did she bring shame on my father and the entire Badd name when she fucked Carlo Lucky but she put me in the shit and I'm innocent."

"What are you talking about, Brock? I thought all that was a rumor. Mama Badd would have never fucked around on Papa Badd and with Carlo Lucky of all people."

"She did, Mona. This shit goes so deep that you don't even know the half of it. What she did got uncle Lonnie killed and unfortunately it got her killed too."

"Are you saying she didn't kill herself?"

"No, she did kill herself," Brock said in a matter of fact tone. I couldn't believe it when I saw a smirk curve up at the corner of his lips. "She killed herself the day she decided to sleep with the enemy."

"Who killed her, Brock?" I didn't want to hear him say it but I had to.

"I did," he answered like it was nothing. "It was either kill or be killed and I chose to stay alive," he pounded against his chest.

"But...your mother would never hurt you Brock," I said to him in a careful voice.

"You don't know shit, Mona. Not only was she going to hurt me...but our whole family. We wouldn't be here right now if I hadn't done what I did. She threaten my life and I wasn't going to wait around to call her on her bluff either. I had to do what I did. I just had to."

I didn't know I was crying until a tear dropped off my chin. I knew why I was crying but then again, I really did'nt know why. Brock killing his own mother made our relationship feel different. I thought I knew my husband like the back of my hand but I would have never guessed in a million years he was capable of doing some shit like this. I didn't know what that meant for us. Would he kill me too if he felt like he had to? For the first time ever, I was uncertain about everything I thought we were building on the Badd ranch and of my safety.

"What the fuck you crying for?" Brock asked harshly. He started to walk towards me. When he reached out to console me, I flinched just as if he was trying to kill me. He let out a sarcastic chuckle and took a few steps away from me. "You scared of me now, Mona?" I didn't know what to say. "You think I'm a murderer? Well, I ain't. I told you she killed herself."

"Brock, I love you but..."

"No, buts!" Brock interjected. He kneeled back down at my side. "When I say I did this for my family I mean it."

"Tell me why you killed her! I need to be convinced that it was worth it otherwise this shit is going to be hard to swallow."

"Mona…" he sighed heavily. He didn't want to tell me. "Just trust me…please," he gave me a pleading look. "I locked that shit away so that I can function. I don't want to think about the shit because it drives me mad!" He jumped up again. His hands were waving in the air and, by the look in his eyes, I could tell he was losing it. "You think I wanted to do what I did? You think that shit was easy? It wasn't. I couldn't eat for months but I had to do it. Kill or be killed!" he yelled and gritted his teeth. "I loved my mother but my loyalty goes to my father and it always has. I worship that man. He's everything to me and the shit my mother told me the night she died fucked with me so bad, I almost died myself."

I never seen Brock look so deranged. This shit has been haunting him for years. What he was telling me was heavy but at the end of the day, I loved my man and I trusted all of his instincts. I grabbed him and wrapped my arms around him, giving him the support he needed. He melted into my chest.

"Mona…I'm not evil. I had to do it."

"I know you did," I kissed him on the cheek. It was wet with sweat. "If you ain't ready to tell me why, you don't have to."

Brock seemed relieved. I was a little relieved to. I'd heard enough. He inhaled then exhaled before sweeping his hands over his face. Then he stared off into blank space for a split second. His eyes filled up with sorrow then narrowed evilly. He looked at me. I kept a straight face. Or at least I tried too.

"Everything is fucked." Brock shook his head.

"How?"

"Tyler Jones, Billy, Dalla, Bobby!" he sat back down behind his father's desk. "It's Tyler Jones I got down in the dungeon, you know."

"So he's the one you been integrating. It makes sense now."

Brock nodded. "After using a little physical motivation, I finally got his ass to confess everything. I asked him about Billy killing my father and who he was working with, but he told me that Dalla was his contact for Papa Badd."

"What does that mean? Billy and her both plotted his death?"

Brock looked at me like he didn't know himself. "All I know is that he told me Dalla hired him to fake the report. He ain't say shit about Billy. All this time I've been thinking Billy did it out of rage..." his voice trailed off like he was back to square one again. "I have to be sure, Mona! I have to be sure before..." He paused.

"Before what?" He ignored my question.

"Tyler was a fucking mole. He told me that he been putting in work for Ace Lucky.

"Ace Lucky!" I interrupted. All this time we were being set up and never saw it coming.

"As soon as I hired his ass to fake the report for mama, he ran and gave the real one to Ace for cash. That nigga took that shit and plotted all this shit that's going down now. I hope that money was worth his life," Brock hissed. I wondered if Tyler was still alive. "Ace is behind all this shit! He the one that's been talking in Billy's ear. I killed mama and he used that to convince Billy to kill Papa Badd."

"This is real fucked up Mr. Badd," I couldn't bare too look at Brock. He let this shit get out of hand. He is the real cause of all this but I wouldn't dare tell him that.

"I know, Mona. That's why I need your help," he reached his hand out for me to grab. I grabbed his hand and tried to keep a straight face when I looked at him. "I didn't mean for none of it to go like this. If I knew Tyler would have betrayed me the way he did, I would have never hired him to fake mama's report," Brock admitted but I was hoping to hear him say, he would have never killed his mother in the first place because that's what caused all this shit. Not Ace. "I was hoping to destroy the real report before anybody else got to it. If I was smart, I would've killed Tyler as soon as he handed me the fake report but I trusted him. Now, I'm too late. Ace knows, Dalla knows, Billy knows and I got a feeling it ain't gone be long before Bobby knows too. I can't let this shit get out. I can't! It'll destroy us. The entire ranch is at risk."

Brock was so upset his hands started shaking. Seeing him this way caused chills to shoot up my spine. "I guess after all this time, Ace is ready to avenge his father's death. That nigga probably been plotting the shit for years. I figured the pussy ass nigga would rise up eventually but never like this; this motherfucker playing dirty. He is weakening us, plucking us off one by one before he launch his attack on the ranch." Brock sighed heavy then gave me a desperate look. "I got to find everybody that knows and take them out. Starting with Dalla. She knows too much," he was desperate.

"Why did you let them go if you knew all this? It had to be the reason they took the money." I didn't understand why Brock didn't restrain Billy and Dalla right away.

"They ain't take no damn money. I made that shit up."

"What?" More lies. My stomach felt sick.

"I had to tell y'all that until I figured shit out."

"Well if Billy and Dalla didn't run off, where are they?"

"I don't know where the fuck Dalla is. I made a mistake letting her go but that was before Tyler's confession. I was all fucked up in the head after what she told me about Billy killing my father. I just let her walk."

My heart thumped heavy against my chest with the next question dancing at the tip of my tongue. I didn't want to ask but I had too. "What about Billy? Where is he?" I said carefully but Brock just gave me a weird look.

"We don't need to worry about Billy right now. It's Bobby who I'm concerned about."

"Maybe Bobby don't have nothing to do with this, Brock." I pleaded for Bobby. I didn't want any more Badd blood spilled.

"No..." he shook his head at me. He wasn't trying to hear what I had to say. "He hiding something Mona...I know he is. I got a feeling he already know about it."

"What are we going to do?"

"Fix the weak links."

I knew exactly what he meant and how he was going to get it done. There was no other way around it. I felt tears forming in my eyes but I couldn't let them fall. Brock needed my support. I pushed my tears back and grabbed my husband's hand, giving him a reassuring squeeze and said, "Just let me know what you need me to do."

He smiled at me for the first time in months.

32

Taffy Badd

"Brip?" I called out. I spotted him sitting at the breakfast bar in the kitchen, sipping on a Heineken. He didn't budge when he heard my voice. "Brip…" I said again. I walked up behind him. I hugged him but he flinched like I was diseased.

I left the ranch without informing Mona and I didn't give a fuck about what she thought either. I had to get my house in order; that came first. Before I left the ranch, I had a visit with Dr. Burns. Turns out, I've been pregnant for almost twelve weeks now. I never been pregnant this long before. I didn't notice that I was missing my period. I guess I was too caught up in Brip, Lily and Malcolm to notice the changes. Every time Dr. Burns told me I was pregnant, I was hopeful, no matter what. I refused to believe that my pregnancy would end a few weeks later; although I knew my chances of ever giving birth where slim to none. It was better than being depressed and it kept Brip from falling apart. But, this time was different.

There was a strong possibility that this was Malcolm's baby. My affair with Malcolm was reckless and irresponsible in every sense of the word. We had more than a few slip ups and I didn't care. I was so hurt by how Brip was doing me that I didn't care to try to be careful but I never thought this would happen. The thought never crossed my mind and even then, I knew my history. What difference did it make who baby it was if it wasn't going to live? Getting pregnant was easy for me but giving birth was almost impossible. I guess I was wrong.

Dr. Burns listened to the heartbeat and said the baby had a strong chance to live if I took it easy. That's when I started to panic. Dr. Burns was always honest with me. He was candid about my chances of having a full term pregnancy. He never sugar coated things. He didn't want to give me false hope. Every pregnancy I had before, I yearned to hear the news he gave me. But, things are different now.

This baby was going to survive but if Brip every found out that it wasn't his me and Malcolm both were dead. I didn't have the same grace he did to fuck around and get bitches pregnant with no consequence. I would be judged harshly for this offense. And, Mona. Lord, what would she do to me?

During my ride into the city, I managed to convince myself that this baby was more Brip's than Malcolm's. When Dr. Burns gave me the news, I forced on a happy face and squeezed his neck like it was Christmas morning and he was Santa Clause delivering the gift I've been asking for. Then, I left the ranch in a rush.

It had to be Brip's baby. We been trying for years. It only made sense for it to be his. Right? By the time I walked in the house, I wasn't accepting anything else. This was Brip's, baby.

Brip finally turned to acknowledge me.

"What's up?" he said, still nursing his beer. He turned back around; his voice was cold. I couldn't help but wonder if he was upset about Lily losing the baby. "Ain't you supposed to be at the ranch? What you doing home now?" I could hear the accusation in his voice.

"I came to see you," I wrapped my arms around his neck and buried my face in his back.

"Watch out," he said, jerking away from me.

"Is this about, Lily?" I blurted out. I was getting annoyed by his behavior and if this was about his bastard baby dying, then I had news that might change his mood.

He didn't respond to my question. Instead, he turned around and looked at me like I was crazy. He sucked his teeth, before rolling his eyes.

"Look…things happen for a reason." It was my own way of consoling him. "It wasn't meant to be but all is not lost," I gave him another kiss.

"Oh yeah," he said dryly.

"Yeah"

"Hmm"

"Everything is going to be okay, Brip" I whispered in his ear enduringly.

"I know that," he snapped. He got up from the bar stool and stood over me. That's when I first noticed the lazily wrapped, blood soaked gauze around his right fist.

I reached out and tried to grab his hand but he pulled away from me. "Hard day at work?" I asked uneasy.

"This ain't had shit to do with work, Taffy," he looked at me with contempt.

"Oh," was all I could say. I took a few steps backward.

I stopped seeing Malcolm but something was telling me that my secret was out. I felt sorry for Malcolm but it was what it was. I didn't even bother calling him to break it off, I just stopped coming around. I threw out the prepaid phone I used to call him and I knew he couldn't look me up because I used an alias name, Sarah. He had no idea who I really was. I guess that's why I feel for him. The last time I seen him, he was getting too clingy anyway. He told me that he loved me and actually proposed. He put a fake ring made of aluminum foil that he painted bronze on my finger. In the joy of playing pretend, I accepted his fake proposal. But, the next week, I decided not to see him anymore and my timing couldn't have been more perfect now that Brip is on my trail; at least I think he is.

"I ain't worried about Lily and her baby dying if that's what you think" he confessed. It was weird how he said *her* baby and not *their* baby. "Didn't I tell you that I was done with them?" he squinted at me. I thought it was a rhetorical question but he waited for my response, so I nodded. "I was honest with you. I told you the truth because I knew I fucked up and saw how much I was hurting you."

I just listened without talking; unable to blink, unable to swallow, I feared where this conversation was going.

"I was honest with you, girl!" he stabbed himself in the chest.

"Eventually," I said dryly, defending myself for what was about to come.

"Does it matter when? Honesty doesn't have a time limit. Have you been honest with me?" I didn't respond; I just looked away.

He massaged his hand like it was bothering him.

"Baby, let me get some ice." I ran straight to the freezer. I needed time away to think but it wasn't enough time. I grabbed a bag frozen peas and ran back to him.

"I'm fine," he said as I tried to give him the peas. "This shit don't hurt. It's nothing compared to how some other shit can feel." He looked at me scornfully.

"What happened?" I asked. I don't know why.

Brip chuckled then gently opened and closed his fingers as he admired his wound.

"I was breaking up a fight" he said bluntly. That didn't make sense to me. I knew my husband well enough and he wasn't the type to break up a fight; he instigated them.

"Oh yeah," the weird look Brip was giving made me nervous.

"Yeah…" Brip said, taking another sip of beer and staring off into blank space. "It was fucked up for even me to watch." Brip smiled evil and my body shuddered. He sighed, rubbed the back his head and then looked at his hand again. "That dude really got fucked up."

I felt chills going up my spine. "That nigga didn't have a winning chance. He was pleading for his life. Saying that he was a non-violent person…whatever the fuck that mean?" Brip shrugged then chuckled a bit. "He begged them niggas to stop beating him with that bat. I heard that man's bones crush right in front of me. I heard his legs break, his arms, his fingers….all that shit," Brip gave me another serious look and I swallowed hard. "He begged them to stop, talking about he an artist like that shit made a difference."

My heart stopped. I knew an artist and feared that now, Brip did too. He had found out about Malcolm.

"I felt for him when they went for that fire extinguisher and bashed his face in. Damn…" Brip shook his head. "Before they cracked his face open, he begged them not to kill him. He said he just gotten engaged. He didn't want his fiancé, some bitch name...what was her name?" Brip looked in the air like he was trying to remember the name then he looked over at me like he was expecting me to chime in and I froze. "I think he said her name was Sarah." When he said my alias name, I knew it was true.

"Poor, Sarah. She ain't gone want to see that nigga looking like that if he make it or if somebody ever find the nigga. If he do make it...the way the fire extinguisher crashed into his brains, he probably won't have the sense of a puppy."

I felt my knees get weak. "You think Sarah would want him like that? Huh?" Brip got up and started to walk towards me. I begin to cry silently. I backed away from Brip but he kept coming closer to me. "You think his fiancée, Sarah still gone have feelings for him after today?"

"No...she never loved him!"

"Oh, yeah?" Now Brip was nose to nose with me.

"It wasn't his fault." I sobbed.

I did this to hurt Brip, not Malcolm. He really was innocent. Me breaking his heart was bad enough but his bones and face, I couldn't deal with that; I was to blame for it all. I knew what would happen if Brip ever found out but I was selfish and didn't measure the risks; I just took them. Brip was allowed to fuck around all he wanted and the women didn't have the same harsh consequences that Malcolm faced. It was all my fault. I knew Malcolm's fate but I didn't know mine. Was Brip going to break my bones too?

I didn't know what to do so I went with my first instinct and wrapped my arms around his waist and squeezed tight, begging for both forgiveness and mercy.

"I'm sorry, Brip. I really am. Don't leave me."

"Leave you?" He pulled my arms from around his waist. "What I look like to you Taffy? Huh? "You worried about me leaving you but you already left me, girl. I can't believe you did that shit! That shit killed me when your crazy- ass brother put me on to what you and that artist dude been doing.

Just then I remembered Tony telling me in his own way he was going to kill, Brip. My mind snapped back into reality. Now would be a good time to tell Brip that Tony may be trying to kill him; but, for some reason, I can't.

"What?" I was stunned. I never expected Tony to rat me out, especially as much as he hated, Brip. "When did you see my brother?"

"It don't fucking matter. He gave me the lead, now I'm going to give him this money I promised."

There was no lead. Tony was setting Brip up. He used me as bait. This was a classic Tony hit; mind games.

Brip gave me a strange look. He continued to talk. "He only confirmed what I was trying to ignore. I knew about this weeks ago, Taffy but I was too…" He dropped his head, "…I was too damn sick to even deal with it. It weakened me," his voice dropped.

I'm torn. I love them both. If I tell Brip the truth, I'd lose Tony for sure. But, if I didn't tell Brip, I would be sending him off to be murdered by my brother. I didn't know what to do. I already have enough blood on my hands; I couldn't add my brother's blood, too.

I had to switch gears.

"Brip I'm pregnant," I blurted out before dramatically falling to the ground in a desperate attempt for him not to leave. "Please stay…I can't take too much more of this. I could lose the baby and Dr. Burns say this one really has a chance."

"How do I know that baby is mine?" Brip said cold.

"It is yours. I know for sure!"

"Well, I don't!"

"I promise you!"

"That don't mean shit to me. You been fucking around for weeks and I'm supposed to believe you?"

"He didn't feel me the way you do. I wore a condom," I lied so easily that I believed my own lie. "Come on, Brip. You've been doing it for years."

Brip didn't look up at me. He continued to sip his beer like my good news was no news. I had to walk away.

Everything was falling apart. I came home from the ranch to tell Brip the good news about the baby but everything turned upside down. I never imagined he would denounce our child, tell me he damn near killed Malcolm and had a deal with my brother who wanted him dead. I had to fix this.

After a few more seconds of sobbing, I snapped out of it. I had to tell him about Tony. I love my brother but I can't live without Brip, I just can't.

I walked back to the kitchen. My heart was still racing. Brip was sitting in the foyer with his back anchored against the front door and his face buried in his knees. By the way his chest was heaving in and out, it looked like he was crying but when he looked up, I saw no tears. His gaze was still cold. I couldn't take the way he was staring at me; he watched my like I was a stranger instead of his wife.

"I know you don't want to hear anything I have to say," I held out my hand just in case he tried to interrupt me or jump up to leave, "but I'll make this fast, then I'll pack my shit and disappear."

"Disappear!" Brip jumped up, his voice trembling.

"I'll just leave, Brip."

"No," Brip said to my surprise, rushing towards me. He wrapped his thick arms around me. "You ain't going nowhere." When he kissed me on top of my head, I felt relieved. "You were right. You been having to take this shit from me for years and I never knew it could hurt so much until it happened to me," Brip sighed, "How the fuck you deal with this for so long?"

"Because I love you, no matter what."

"Shit…" Brip said. "I guess I brought this on myself, huh? I know that shit with Lily was crossing the line. I even feel responsible for the baby dying. It wasn't good Karma."

"That's not your fault but we still got blessed anyway," I said, putting his hand on top of my stomach then removing quickly just as if Brip would feel the truth on his hands. "Dr. Burns says he thinks this one is going to make it, Brip. It's going to live if we give it a chance." I tried to distract him.

Brip looked at me like I was just telling him the baby news for the first time. A wide smiled stretched across his face so big, I could see all his teeth. "Oh, yeah" he said caressing my stomach. "This one is going to give us a shot, huh?"

"Yes…I think he will." I grabbed Brip's hand squeezed it.

"Oh, baby I'm sorry," he kissed the top of my head and the kneeled down and kissed my stomach three times. "I'm so sorry…" I pulled him up.

"I'm sorry too, Brip. That shit ain't never going to happen again. I promise. I get disgusted just thinking about it. I was just so upset about Lily and the baby. And, I promise this baby is yours. I'm almost three months. I didn't even know Malcolm existed three months ago," I lied again.

"What!" Brip said happy. He knew the truth now and he also knew that I broke my eight week miscarriage record. "All this time."

"Yeah. He's here to stay if you'll have him."

"Him? How if it's a her?" he winked at me and I shrugged. "After the storm, comes the calm" Brip said caressing my stomach.

I should have felt guilty but this moment felt too right. This had to be a blessing for Brip and I; we've been through so much this was a long time coming. This is Brip's baby and that's all there is too it. I convinced myself one last time.

"You can say that again," I sighed heavy. Relieved that I didn't have to take my affair with Malcolm to the grave and that Brip and I can get over all this shit and be stronger than before. Then I remembered the whole reason I came back downstairs. I had to tell him about Tony.

"Tony is trying to kill you! Don't meet him, it's a setup." I blurted out and then told him everything.

I told him about Tony sickness and his theory on how Keno got killed. Then I begged for him to have mercy on my brother. Brip's face went hard. By the time I was done talking, it surprising y went soft again. He didn't say anything or give me any promises. All he did was kiss me on top of my head again, and pat my stomach.

"I got go." he said. I didn't ask him where he was going. "I'll be back to take you up to the ranch in about an hour or two. Get some rest." He turned to walk out the door but turned back around. "Oh yeah...I didn't touch that nigga, Malcolm, yet. I was just trying to call your bluff and see how truthful your brother was being when he told me about y'all. I know the nigga crazy and I wanted to be sure he was telling the truth before I busted on that man. I did visit him at his little studio though. I interrogated him a little bit and that's when he told me about his fiancée Sarah," he said sarcastically.

Relief flooded over my body so heavy, I almost fainted. That was one less thing I had to worry about. Malcolm was alive and I hopped Brip kept it that way.

"And now..." I asked through a pleading voice. I looked down at Brip's bloody hand. He was massaging it. Then, I begin to wonder if he was lying to me.

"He can continue breathing as long as Sarah never shows back up again. But, I'm still gone fuck him up. Break his leg or his arm or maybe both. Otherwise, it just wouldn't be right." Brip winked at me before walking out the door. At least he wasn't going to kill him.

———

Brip was back in less than the two hours. I didn't know where he went but I trusted him; now more than ever. On our way back to the ranch, I opened up the conversation about Bobby and Lera, telling him what Mona told me. I was relieved when that information pissed him off.

"Both my brother and his wife is crazy as hell! If they don't stop their madness, then they gone be left on they own. I don't want you or my baby around that shit," he gave me a serious look. "Stay out of it. Bobby and his fiancé ain't setting up nothing. Just ignore Mona and Brock. I'm getting sick of it myself. If Bobby leave...I don't blame him. I just might go with him!" Brip informed me and I was surprised and a little excited all though I knew it was just his anger talking.

"After all this shit we been through, I learned that me and you need a lot more privacy. All this Badd business is about to swallow me alive. It's getting too personal and I don't want you caught up in this shit no more."

"What do you mean, Brip?" I asked anxious to hear him say we were leaving the State like Billy and Dalla. But, he never said it. He just shrugged.

"I don't know yet...I don't know."

34

Lera Way-Badd

been on the ranch for two hours and still hadn't seen any sign of Mona or Brock. I was in the event hall looking at the decorations for our wedding reception and watching my back. My eyes moved around the room searching for an emergency exit just in case something dramatic erupted and me and Bobby had to flee the scene but I'm pretty sure things wasn't going down like that. Bobby had a plan and it didn't involve running off the ranch, but driving. Bobby didn't run from anybody.

The Badd family event hall looked like a scene from a Disney movie. The overly dramatic fairy tale décor was so cliché it was borderline adolescent. There were dozens of white flowers all over the floors, tables, chairs; Some even hung from the ceiling. I felt like I was in a fairy godmother's garden. The only flower I could recognize was the roses, the rest were a mystery to me. Luxuries silver, white and pink silk fabrics draped over the tables and laced over the floor.

Everything was bright and dainty; none of it was my style but I didn't care. I didn't want the wedding anyway. I just wanted the man; And, I already had him. A week before we left for the ranch, Bobby and I flew to Vegas and we eloped. I have been Bobby's secret wife for two days now. I was relieved that we still got married despite the recent drama.

We kept our marriage a secret. I had to act as normal as possible. Bobby told me he was marrying me in private because he wanted our day to be special and private. I was just happy to finally be his wife but I still had to endure this big circus wedding.

Our engagement party was at the end of the week. It was going to be at the Casino and the next week was going to be our wedding. I felt better knowing that Bobby would be with me during the week of the engagement party. After that, we were not allowed to see each other until the day of the wedding; more Badd traditions that we were forced to follow. I just needed to get down the aisle, then it all would be over and hopefully we would be far away from everything that was Badd.

––––

Thank goodness Taffy and Brip offered their home to us. We weren't allowed to stay in our mansion until after we got 'married'. I felt safer being with them. They made me feel comfortable. Taffy and Brip were acting like they were on a second honeymoon. They kissed and cuddled on the couch. I guess they were having a good week.

We were getting ready to have dinner at the Casino. Before we left Bobby told me he was going to meet with Brock. I didn't know why they were meeting and I didn't bother to ask. He was gone about 30 minutes. When he came back, he didn't say much and had a stern look on his face. I could tell he was upset. I still didn't ask him any questions. I knew he wouldn't tell me anything anyway. The less I knew the better.

I couldn't wait to get my hands on some alcohol. For some reason, Taffy and Brip didn't have it in the house anymore. So, I was actually excited when we got to the Casino. I couldn't wait to chug down a much needed drink.

We sat in a private room. The Casino was so busy that if somebody blindfolded me before I walked in, I would have thought I was at the Grand MGM in Las Vegas. So many people were on the ranch for our engagement party.

I felt like royalty the way people greeted me and Bobby as we cut through the crowd like butter. The smiles of the strangers were genuine and I almost felt excited. Taffy soaked up the attention too, walking like she was floating on air. I guess all of this wedding business sparked a new kind of romance between her and Brip because the way the two of them were showcasing for the crowd, walking hand in hand, you would have thought they were the lucky couple.

Before we could get to the private dining room, two people had already handed us their own offerings; stacks of money, jewelry and bottles of Cristal that were so frosty, the glass fogged and swirled with cold air. Brip snatched them out of their hands, "Hell, yah! This is how you celebrate," he said holding a bottle in each hand.

We sat behind a Hibachi styled table and an Asian man dressed in all white, stood behind the grill. I didn't have much of an appetite but maybe a few cold glasses of the Cristal would change that. Brip clumsily popped the top to the bottle and poured a waterfall of the champagne onto the Asian chef. The chef didn't seem to mind. All he did was laugh and dab his soaked coat with a towel. He poured everybody a glass except for Taffy and to my surprise, she didn't fuss.

"Aye," he called out to the bartender. "Get my wife a cranberry juice man…"

"No…pineapple juice, Brip. I have a taste for pineapple juice."

"You sure that's your taste?" he winked at Taffy and she blushed, shrugging her shoulders.

Bobby moved over and wrapped his arm around me.

"Let's all toast," Brip said, snatching up his glass so quick, Cristal spilled from the rim of the glass. We all held up our Champagne flutes and Taffy held up her pineapple juice. "To love," he looked at Taffy and smiled, "Peace…and happiness." Our glasses clinked together before we all uniformly took a swallow. I swallowed harder than everybody else.

"Man…I'm so happy for you two," Brip said pouring himself another drink before topping off me and Bobby's glasses. He took a sip, and then held the glass in the air. "This is my shit man.'

"It's the only way to celebrate." Bobby chimed in.

"The Badd way," Brip toasted with Bobby. "I hope you ain't letting the bullshit get to you. I saw you walking out of the main house." Brip's smile faded.

"Some bullshit…" Bobby paused, "I can handle. It's that other shit that gets to me." Bobby looked at Brip. They must have been talking in code because Brip seemed to know just what Bobby meant. He nodded his head in agreement.

"I feel you man. I just hope…I hope y'all have a peaceful life and we don't become strangers. I miss my brother man." He was referring to Billy. "I wish he was here to see this shit. To meet your gorgeous wife. And, balance off all the drama. He was good at that."

"I wish Dalla was here too," Taffy said in a sad tone. "She was like a big sister to me and I know she would love you." Taffy put her hand on top of mine.

"Who knows?" Bobby looked at his champagne. "Maybe we'll see them again. Maybe we all will reunite."

"Hmm.." Brip said, staring off into a distance looking like he was sharing the same secret thought as Bobby. "Will it be happy reunion?"

"For some of us," Bobby said and took a small sip from his glass. He gave Brip a serious stare.

Taffy and I both gave each other uncomfortable half smiles like we were trying to hide something. We both were trying to appear normal. It was what our husbands told us to do. We took another sip of our drinks and looked off into the distance.

35

Finally...the long awaited engagement party was taking place. This meant that me and Bobby were one step closer to hauling ass.

The Casino was full of strangers. They all knew my name. I must have shaken a dozen hands. Everybody smiled at me and congratulated Bobby on his good taste. The women looked at me with envy, sizing me up out the corner of their eyes.

I stayed glued to Bobby's arm most of the time; it was like we were sewed together. Bobby looked sexier than ever. He was suave and ultra-confident in his all nickel colored suit. His blazer fit his body like a second skin and the silk black shirt peeking out underneath his vest really accentuated his muscular chest. He smelled like expensive cologne and was freshly shaven and cut. He looked so good, I wanted to throw him in one of the bathroom stalls and hike up my leg for a few quick seconds but I kept my composure. I looked nice but Bobby has seen me look better. I was wearing a strapless, sequence emerald dress. Bobby said he loved the way the color matched my skin tone. I had my locks fancied into an elegant up do. He kept whispering in my ear how I looked good enough to eat. Hell, I was ready to feed him.

Brock and Mona were so busy soaking up all the attention, greeting business associates and networking with new ones, they didn't stop one time to tell us congratulations or even look in our direction. Mona was wearing a bright red pantsuit that was so form fitting, she might as well have worn spandex. And, as if she wasn't tall enough, she had on six inch heels. I have to admit, she didn't look half bad. The suit she was wearing looked tailored made for her as it toned down her mountainous curves and sucked in her waist a bit. Brock was wearing a black suit. He looked like an edgy funeral director. Some kind of way, he made his combat boots work with what he was wearing. People seemed to greet Brock and Mona more than they did us. They were the true stars of this show but I could care less. Attention was something I didn't like or need from total strangers.

Brip and Taffy coordinated wearing all white with accents of gold. Brip almost could pass as a regular citizen in his white suit jacket, until he opened his mouth and said something brash. Taffy looked like a sexy baby doll in her short and frilly dress and gold stilettos. She was shining from the inside out, soaking up all the attention.

The DJ was playing oldies but goodies. I've heard Bobby listen to several of the songs playing. He played a lot of Curtis Mayfield; Bobby's favorite. When the song "*So in Love*" came on, the DJ rallied the crowd and summons Bobby and I to the dance floor. Bobby grabbed my hand and led me onto the dance floor. As we passed through crowds, I could see people smiling at us with sparks of rekindled love beaming in their eyes. I guess it was something about these engagements that made spectators either crave for love or respect the love that they already had.

Bobby and I swayed from side to side in perfect harmony; we were totally n-sync with the music. Everyone starred at us; after a while, I zoned out and it felt like we were alone. He pulled me in closer to him after every hook. By the end of the song, we were so close, I felt like I was inside of him. "*So…in love,*" Bobby whispered in my ear. His breath felt warm and the bass of his voice tickled my ear drum. He ran his hand down my back and squeezed my waist, still singing in my ear "*So…in love,*" like he was a back-up singer.

He ventured his hands down a little lower, tastefully squeezing my behind and then moving them back up towards my waist. I squeezed his broad shoulders, resting the side of my face on the top of his chest. He kissed the top of my head and I continued to slow grind against him then I lifted my head gently, making eye contact with the man I was *so in love* with and song along too, *"so in love."* My singing brought a bashful smile to his face. I kissed his bottom lip then the tip of his nose before he parted my lips with his tongue. It felt like we were kissing for hours and was so lost in one another we didn't recognize the crowd was clapping and that the sweet melody was finally coming to an end. Curtis Mayfield hummed his last tune but we kept on moving, still hearing the music in our hearts.

We found a private area near the bathroom. Outside of the restroom was a red, leather loveseat. I guess it's where lovers waited on their women while they stood in front of mirrors, powdering their noses. Today, it was a place for me and Bobby to cuddle and dance around the discretion of second base and maybe even third. We kissed our way on to the love seat and he started to run his hand underneath my dress, massage my thighs, driving me crazy.

His warm lips were making their way up my neck, lingering around my collarbone. I raised my chin to give him more room to continue to explore the softness of my skin.

"You a blessing," he said out of nowhere. "And, blessings last forever." Bobby gave me a look so enduring, I felt myself blush. I felt the corners of my eyes water.

"You think of me as a blessing?" I asked shyly.

"Heaven sent," he kissed me on the right side of my neck, then the bottom of my chin. "I knew that from the first time I saw you. You took my breath away and, as much as I tried, I couldn't get you out of my head. I knew then, you were something different cause can't nothing make Bobby Badd weak but girl…" he kissed me on the other side of my neck, ending it with another chin kiss, "you did it to me alright. You made me so weak in the knees, I couldn't walk straight until I had you."

I was speechless. Finally, the tears streamed neatly down the sides of my face. Bobby caught both of my tears with side of his index finger; he kissed me so softly, I cried again.

Another Curtis Mayfield song poured out from the speakers. He sang out the words to *"she don't let nobody,"* a song I knew word for word and it always made me think of Bobby. I jumped up and held out my hand.

"This one's for you, baby," I told Bobby and he blushed so hard, he looked adorable.

"Oh, yeah!" He hopped up quick, smiling from ear to ear.

"*Nobody but you, baby*," I said, repeating the song, adding my own twist. I lead Bobby out to the dance floor, wrapped my arms around his neck and we swirled around the dance floor like we owned it. We kept our eyes on one another was we sang. Bobby swirled me around and I felt like a Queen. I slow grinded against him, pressing my hips against his pelvis. "*Nobody but you, Bobby….Nobody but you.*" I blew Bobby a kiss; we flirted.

Bobby gave me a hungry look before pulling me into his chest and squeezing me. I looked over Bobby's shoulder and spotted Brip and Taffy dancing with the same intensity and, to my surprise a few feet away from them was Brock and Mona. Everybody mouthing the lyrics to each other, possessive and flirty. We all were in our own worlds; If only it could stay that way.

"The next time I see you, all the bullshit will be over," Bobby whispered to me.

"And we'll live happily ever after?" I was sarcastic and hopeful.

"Yes," Bobby said casually. I couldn't tell what his *yes* meant.

"You promise?" I needed to be sure.

"I mean what I say…"

36

The Day of the Wedding...

I woke up confused and with pain in my chest. It felt like somebody placed an anchor on top of me. I even felt restrained. I had a horrible nightmare. It was so bad, I couldn't remember it. I rubbed the sleep out of my eyes and looked around the room. Where in the hell was I?

"Lera," its Taffy's voice. "Sweetie lie back down. Dr. Burns is on his way?"

Doctor Burns? Why do I need to see him?

"What am I doing here?" I finally notice that I'm in the clinic. The pain in my chest kicks back in and so does the feeling of déjà vu. Taffy is looking at me like I'm crazy. She looks like she's been crying. Then, I see it. I see grief behind her eyes.

Somebody died.

"Just lie down," she guides me back to the bed. My head is throbbing.

"Where's Bobby?" I ask hesitantly.

Taffy is just shaking her head at me squinting her eyes real tight like she's trying to control tears from falling. She's biting down on her bottom lip. "Lie back," she gently pushes me down.

"Call Bobby for me! Tell him to get here, now!" Now she's crying hysterically. No wait....that's me. Why am I crying? It's like my heart knows something my mind can't comprehend.

"Honey, Bobby's…" she hesitated. Took a deep breath and tried again. "Bobby's…dead," she says, and starts to sob. Then I remembered it all.

I passed out somewhere in between a devastating scream and a sorrowful moan. He really was dead. The nightmare I had was real.

———

"Where the fuck is Dr. Burns?" I heard Brip yell. His voice woke me up. I wonder how long I was out. However long it was, it wasn't long enough.

"She's up," I heard Taffy say. She ran to the side of the bed and squeezed my hand. It felt good to feel the sincere touch of a person but it didn't change anything. Bobby was still dead.

"What's going on?" My voice cracked. This time, I was looking Brip dead in the eyes. His eyes were red and he looked exhausted and angry.

"Dr. Burns is on his way?"

"Why?" I snatched my hand away from Taffy and tried to get up but they both gently pushed me back down.

"I'm not sick!" I yelled. "Where is Bobby? I want to see him!"

Taffy and Brip looked at each other.

"I'm not sure. He might be at the morgue but Brock probably ain't letting anybody see him yet."

"I want to see my husband!" I demanded.

"Calm down, Lera." Brip whispered. "To me he is your husband and you always gone be a wife no matter what but Brock don't see shit that way."

"No me and Bobby are married!" I confessed.

"Honey, you didn't get married, remember?" Taffy said patting me on the shoulder like she felt sorry for me.

"No!" I yelled and jerked away from her.

"I know it's hard, sweetheart but we gone get through this. All of us. We're here for you." Taffy said softly.

"Bobby and I got married a week ago; we eloped." I leaned up.

"What!" Taffy yelled almost excited but then calmed down once reality hit her.

"You sure?" Brip said, giving me a weird look.

"I have my marriage license in one of my bags at your house. Want me to get it?" I was ready to do anything to prove it to them. I just needed to see Bobby.

"I believe her baby," Taffy said to Brip and he looked back at her like he was trying to decide for himself.

"If that's true…that changes a lot of shit, you know." I knew he meant money.

"I don't want money. I just want to take Bobby and go."

"Take him? Take him where?" Brip yelled.

I shrugged. "Out of here…" I said in a low voice.

"Here is where he belongs. You can't change that!" Brip demanded.

"This family is fucked up!" I yelled to Brip and Taffy gasped.

"Calm down, Lera…you're just upset. You don't want Brock or Mona to hear you talking like this." Taffy warned me.

I started to cry again. "This is so fucked up," I buried my face in my hands.

"I know it is!" Brip agreed with me. His voice was shaky like he was trying to control his emotions. "But, we gone find the mutherfuckers who did this! If I have to work day and night I'm gone find them! Nobody kills a Badd! Nobody!"

"Oh, yeah," I said sarcastic, giving Taffy and Brip evil stares.

"Of course," Brip answered sharp.

"I know who killed, Bobby!"

"What!" Brip shot Taffy a confused look. He went quite.

"Your fucking brother did!" They both gasped. "Brock killed him," I screamed my assumptions like they were facts. "Just like he killed his own mother!" I blurted out. Brock was the only one who had the power to kill, Bobby.

"What the fuck are you saying?" Brip said in one breath. I saw his fist clutch.

Taffy rushed over to Brip and placed her hand on his shoulder to calm him down. "Brip, she's just delusional right now. Give her a break."

"Bitch, I'm not delusional." Taffy gave me a wide eyed stare. "Your mother didn't commit suicide, Brip. She was killed by Brock and Bobby found out about it. Billy didn't just disappear because he stole from the family safe. Something happened! They probably were running for their lives. Wake up, Brip. Your family is made of murderers. First your mother, now Bobby."

"I don't believe you," Brip said to me but I wasn't convinced. He looked haunted by the things I said. "Brock and Mona was right about you…you're a rat!" Brip pointed at me. He didn't want to believe me.

"They're the rats!" I screamed referring to Brock and Mona. "That mole on the ranch was sent by Dalla. She told me everything. Why do you think Bobby pushed up the wedding date?" I paused. I wanted it all to sink in. "He wanted to get us the hell out of here but Brock caught on to what was happening. I know he's responsible for Bobby's death. I just know it."

"Dalla tried to contact you!" Taffy was shocked.

"She's lying, Taffy. Don't believe her…she's a fucking rat!" Brip started marching towards me. He looked like he wanted to take me out. I didn't budge.

Taffy put herself in-between both of us. "Wait, Brip. At least hear her out!"

"What the fuck for? You hear what this bitch is saying? She probably had something to do with Bobby's death. I'm taking her in for treason. Fuck her!" He pushed Taffy aside, grabbed me by the arm and yanked me towards the door.

"Taffy please…don't let them kill me. I'm not lying. Brock's not telling you the truth. He's been hiding shit from you." Taffy was crying and shaking her head like it was nothing she could do. Brip twisted my hands behind my back like he was about to cuff me and pushed me out the room like I was his prisoner. Then I remembered the message Dalla told me to give to, Taffy. Maybe it was my only way out of this.

"Dalla had a message for you too, Taffy." She looked up at me. Brip continued to push me out the door and she followed behind me.

"Wait, Brip!" Taffy screamed.

"Taffy, stay out of this."

"What did she say, Lera?"

"She said she still loves you like a sister and she misses you and she's sorry…"

"Sorry for what?" Taffy was jogging beh nd us.

"For not letting you know that Brip killed your brother, Keno."

"What?" Taffy yelled. She stopped following us.

Brip looked at me like he wanted to kill me. He pushed to the ground and I scraped my forehead against the concrete. "You fucking rat, bitch!"

"Is it true?" Taffy screamed. "Is it true, Brip?" He didn't respond.

"Taffy, we can discuss this later. My brother's fucking dead right now…"

"So is mine and he has been for years. Are you responsible?" she started to sob.

Brip was silent. I watched him humbly walk over to Taffy. When he got close enough to her, Taffy attacked him. She punched against his chest. "Tell me the fucking truth, Brip."

"I didn't even know you then. Shit, your brother was with some thieves. That type of shit happens to thieves! They had to be handled so somebody contracted us out and Brock sent me to solve the problem. That's what I fucking do, Taffy!" He tried to contain her. "It's how we fucking eat!"

"Damn, you! You murderer! You liar," her arms where flying in the air and her legs swinging back and forth. Brip tried his best to restrain her.

"Calm, down. Think about the baby."

"Fuck you and this baby…" she contirued to swing at him. "It ain't fucking yours any!" She blurted out in an angry rage.

Stunned, Brip grabbed Taffy and threw her to the ground. She kicked up at him and he blocked her kicks the best he could. While they were fighting, I escaped.

———

I ran. I had to get off the ranch but without transportation, it was going to be damn near impossible. It was only a matter of time before Brip and an entire army would be after me. I promised Bobby that something ever happened to him, I'd be strong for him. That meant I had to survive. After a few deep breaths, I looked up and noticed Brip's Hummer for the first time. It was parked out front. Without thinking, I ran straight for the driver's door and jumped in. Lucky for me, the keys were still in the ignition. I cranked up the car and the tires screeched as they burned rubber against the asphalt driveway. The car was moving so fast, I almost lost control of it as it swerved off the road and onto the grass. I drove over the curb, smashing shrubbery and plants.

I sped by the mansions. That's when I saw Mona and Brock coming my way on the golf cart. They looked like they were on their way to the clinic. They probably were coming to pick me up and throw me in the dungeon. Mona was driving. They both looked at the Hummer confused, waving their hands trying to stop it. I guess they thought I was Brip. When they saw it was me, Brock jumped out the cart and started chasing behind the car. I zoomed right passed both of them. When I got to the gate, it was closed but I burst right through; my necked snapped back and then forward like a rubber band. I had no time to rub out the pain.

Making a sharp left turn, the Hummer did a 360. I regained control and sped down the road, not slowing down until there were several miles between me and the ranch. The sun was just rising and the roads where clear. That made it easier for me to run red lights. But, when I went straight through a four way stop, I had to slam on my breaks and swerve the away from an oncoming Dodge pick-up truck.

I squeezed the steering wheel but I still couldn't control the car. When I saw myself going towards an oak tree, I knew it was over for me. I was going to run head first into it. I heard a loud popping sound as metal and plastic crushed. Glass shattered everywhere and the last thing I remember seeing was the airbag.

37

Dalla Badd

need to breathe but I can't. Not until I get Billy back. I almost got myself killed when I swerved my truck in front of Brip's Hummer. But that's nothing new. I've been in near death situations since I started this mission.

My plan was to catch him off guard even if it meant crashing to my own death. I thought my timing was perfect when the tracking device Bobby planted in Brip's Hummer showed him coming my way. It was a little earlier than I expected but I was so anxious that I didn't find it weird. I was going to make him crash and then shoot him up with enough drugs to sedate his psychotic ass and then hold him as ransom for Billy. It would be an even exchange but to my surprise, it wasn't Brip in the Hummer. It was Bobby's fiancé, Lera. Shit! Not a complete waste but definitely not the original plan. So I regroup.

The bitch is knocked out in the backseat of the truck. I didn't sedate her. The air bag must have hit her so hard, it put her to sleep. Or maybe she still in such a panic over hearing about Bobby's death that she just fainted. Who knows? Either way it goes, she's with me now and dragging her heavy ass out the car wasn't easy but I just might be able to use her anyway.

Lera is squirming around and moaning in the backseat. She's waking up. I try to clear my head. I have to be careful of what I say to her. She has no reason to trust me but that doesn't change the fact that I need her on my side. I can't do this shit alone anymore. The bitch jumps up like she just remembered she was in danger and starts screaming at the top of her lungs. She's kicking her legs and punching air like she struggling to free herself from restraints but I don't have her tied. I thought about tying her up but she wouldn't trust me that way.

"Calm down," I tell her. I don't turn around to look at her; I just glimpse at her from the rear view mirror. I got to keep my mind on the mission. I need to get to my safe house and then we can have our little chat.

"Who are you?" she moaned.

"Do you think you need to go to the hospital?" I ignore her question when I see her rubbing blood from the side her face and looking disoriented.

"No! Who are you and how did I get here?"

"You can call me the woman who saved your life but for now, just call me Dalla."

Lera jumps up, only to fall back down holding her head, dazed.

I just keep my cool. "Take it easy. I hope you don't have a concussion. We don't have time for that."

"I don't understand."

She was confused and after I get done with her, she would only be more confused.

"What do you want from me? Bobby's dead and it's all because of your little message. I shouldn't have said shit! He would still be alive."

"Nonsense. You might have saved his life."

"Did you just hear what I said, bitch! Bobby's dead and over some bullshit. What the fuck do you want from me?"

"I want to help you and hopefully, you can help me too."

"I'm done with this shit!"

"You may be done with it, but it's far from being done with you. Brock is going to hunt you and hunt you until you give up and turn yourself in; then he'll kill you. You can't hide from them; not like I can. I can help you. I can help Bobby, too." I knew that would get her attention.

She darted forward like I was about to tell her a secret then leaned back with a sigh like she remembered there were no more secrets to tell. "Bobby died this morning," she said so hopelessly, her voice cracked.

"Bobby's not dead. At least not yet." I said quick.

"What?"

Lera leaned forward again. Her shoulders were raised and her chest was full of air. She breathed in deep but never breathed out. She was holding her breath. Her mouth dangled open and her eyes got so wide she looked deranged. Then they started to tear up. She stared at me like she was debating rather or not to believe me. Her heart and mind must have been at war. I'm pretty sure everything in her heart wanted to believe me and believe that Bobby was still alive. But, if she was smart, I'm sure her gut instincts told her not to trust me but in the end, it was her heart that won the battle. Lera exhaled and closed her eyes. When she reopened them, they were full of neatly streaming tears.

"He's alive?" She asked like she just wanted to be sure.

"Yes," I responded quickly.

"Take me to him."

"That's the plan," I said with ease. I finally had her trust. Now, I just got to work on keeping it.

This shit is finally coming to an end. After years of planning and plotting, it's about to be over and I get to see my husband again. That is if he's still alive. I pray he is. Brock knows that I know everything and he's not going to gamble against that with my husband's life. At least I hope he won't. I couldn't live with myself if Brock killed Billy because I had a hand in it; the first hand at that. Killing the man that saved my life, the man that I fell in love with, will be more devastating than the reason that brought me to this past. And, all my hard work would be in vain. But in my defense, there is a good reason for all my Badd intentions.

38

Lera Way-Badd

Bobby's alive. He's alive! My heart can't stop beating. How? I have so many questions that I fear I will never get the answers to and to be honest, I don't really care. I just want to wrap my arms around my husband's neck and hold on tight and never let go. But, I have to keep my cool. Dalla knows I'm weak right now. My instincts are impaired. I haven't taken the time to figure out if I trust her or not. This is a huge gamble but at this point, I have nothing to lose and years of heartache to avoid. I just need to see Bobby, then everything will be okay.

We've been driving for about thirty minutes now. Dalla is supposed to be taking me to her safe house where Bobby is waiting for us. She's not talking. She looks so deep in thought but I can't tell what she's thinking. There is a wall up between us that is bigger than the Great Wall of China. I know I can't break it down. It's too huge but I have to at least poke a few holes in it. There are a few questions I need answered. I climb from the back seat to the front and she jumps like I was about to grab her. She's paranoid but I don't blame her. I hold up my hands, surrendering to her misconceptions about me. She gives me a weird look like she doesn't want me this close to her. I don't know why though. She can see me better in the front seat than she can in the back. Maybe she knows I'm ready to talk.

"I hope you're not about to drill me with a thousand and one questions," she gave me a no nonsense look.

"Not a thousand and one," I told her serious enough to let her know, she was giving me something.

Dalla sighed. "What?"

"What the fuck is going on?" It was short and basically the jest of my curiosity and would sum up all of this madness.

"Honey, I could tell you but it's going to take years and I don't have that kind of time or patience," she said to me curtly, snapping her neck in my direction before rolling her eyes back to focus on the highway.

I had to regroup. So I went in for specifics. "Where is your husband? Where is Billy?"

"Brock has him," she said shortly.

"Why?"

"Because he thinks he killed Papa Badd."

"Did he?" She gave me an antagonizing look and rolled her eyes. She didn't answer my question. So I rephrased it. "Why does he think that?"

"He got an autopsy report that revealed he was poisoned."

"So Brock killed his mother and Billy poisoned his dad. This a real fucked up family."

"Billy didn't poison his dad. He would never do that," she hissed at me.

"Well who did it?"

"Why does that matter?"

"Because me and Bobby are wrapped up in this shit. That's why it matters?"

"Look, I'm going to give you everything in a nutshell but you have to tie the loose ends yourself."

"Okay," I waited eagerly.

"This shit started way before Billy, Bobby or Brock's time. It started with two friends trying to take over the world but they became rivals. The classic origin of enemies," Dalla said sarcastically.

"You talking about Carlo Lucky?"

Dalla just looked at me. She didn't directly answer my question. I assumed that was a *yes*.

"Papa Badd built his empire stronger, bolder and bigger than Carlo Lucky and eventually, Carlo started to resent Papa Badd. He wanted to kill him, damage him and all that revengeful stuff but he couldn't get to him.

He was too big. Too protected. So, he went at it through another angle. His wife," she paused to study my reaction. I heard the story. "Long story short, they started fucking, she fell in love with him and…" she stopped and smiled like what was about to come out of her mouth next amused her. "They had a baby."

At first, what she said didn't click. Then, it hit me. Mama Badd had four sons but one of them wasn't a pure Badd and I had a strange feeling I knew just the one. "Brock," I was stunned.

Dalla shook her head, still smiling. "The day that Mama Badd died was the day that Brock found out he wasn't a pure Badd," Dalla turned to look at me. "Coincidence huh? Not really," she said with a sarcastic chuckle. "After all those years, even after his murder, Mama Badd was still in love with Carlo Lucky. I guess she got tired of hearing her son brag about how he died and boast about killing the rest of the family, who really where his family. So, she told him. She told him the truth and he couldn't handle it. He suffocated her, hired somebody to do a fake autopsy report and thought his secret was dead and gone but it wasn't."

"Somebody else knows? How?"

"I already told you…you have to tie the loose ends yourself. Just know this, Brock will do anything to keep this secret. He already killed his own mother so you can just imagine what else he's capable of. After Papa Badd got poisoned, Brock wasn't just trying to avenge his father's death. He's paranoid. He knows somebody else knows the truth and suspects me and Billy. But, Billy doesn't know anything."

"Well how do you know?"

She just looked at me and shrugged her shoulders. "I just know. If Brock gets exposed for not being a pure Badd, it's over for him and Mona. The empire he lives for will slip right from underneath his feet and go to Billy, the rightful owner. And, Brock is just not ready to accept that he's not a pure Badd. The truth is eating him alive. He'll kill everybody just to ease his mind. Me, you, Taffy, Bobby, and even Brip."

"Does this revelation have anything to do with Carlo Lucky's son, Ace?"

When I said Ace's name, Dalla flinched like she'd been stung by a bee. Dalla kept her eyes on the road, just as if I never said anything. I gathered enough by her reaction to say that it did. But I needed to know what role Bobby played in all this.

"Why did Bobby fake his death? This shit has nothing to do with him."

"It has everything to do with him. Bobby loves Billy and he is not going to see him die like his mother did. He's protecting Brip too. Brock is the enemy now. Bobby knew that if he didn't fake his own death, Brock would have killed him. He think Bobby knows about him not being a Badd, just like he think Billy knows. Well, he didn't know then, but he knows now," she said, vindicated.

"How long have you and Bobby been working together?"

"He found me after you gave him my message."

"So this whole thing was planned? The second wedding and everything?"

"Yes. Bobby put a body in his Hummer and blew it up. What's left of the burnt body is at the Ranch. Brock is going to do an autopsy but it's going to take a while. He's too paranoid. He can't trust anybody to examine the body. It's going to take weeks, maybe even months for him and Mona to screen the right person. By then, hopefully Billy will be free."

I didn't know what to say. So I didn't say anything else.

"How much longer do we have?"

"Not much longer," she looked at me out the corner of her eye. She was trying to see if I believed what she was saying and, for the most part, I did. At least the base of it. I mean, who can make this kind of shit up? I'm no fool though. She's more connected to this than Billy or Bobby knows but I don't give a fuck. When she takes me to Bobby, hopefully I can convince him to leave all this mess behind him. Dalla is just using him to get to Billy. She doesn't care what happens to either one of us.

"So, does that curb your curiosity?"

"For now."

39

Dalla turned on a secluded street.

A long unpaved road stretched out passed the towering trees. We were basically driving through the woods. I started to get nervous because Dalla seemed nervous. She no longer watched me out the corner of her eye and she was eerily quiet. She almost seemed jittery. It was at that moment that my gut instincts kicked in and I decided I didn't trust her, but it was too late.

"Are you sure Bobby's here?" I asked peering out the window trying to see past the thick bushes and overgrown mixture thick grass and weeds. Dalla didn't respond. "Hey, I'm talking to you?" She still ignored me. She kept her eyes fixed on her path. "Where in the fuck are we?" We drove deeper and deeper into the woods. I'm pretty sure that this place wasn't on the map. Where are you taking me?"

The hood of the car dipped as Dalla drove down a bumpy hill. It felt like we were driving through water. Broken tree branches and dirt popped up from the ground and hit against the windshield, fogging our view. Dalla turned the wipers on and I followed an auburn colored leaf as it moved from one side of the windshield to the next, smearing mud. Then I heard a loud clunking sound like we hit a rock and the car came to a stop. We were stuck. "Shit," Dalla hissed and hit the steering wheel. She looked at me carefully like she was reconsidering something. Then she cut off the engine, grabbed the keys and opened the door to get out. I grabbed her by the forearm.

"Where are you going?" I squeezed her arm tight.

"Don't ever put your hands on me," she snapped, jerking away. She looked back at me like she was ready to slap me but had not time. When her feet hit the muddy ground, she cursed under her breath before slamming the door behind her.

I turned to open my door but I couldn't. Some kind of way, she had me locked in the car. I honked the horn. "Hey, let me out of here!" Dalla didn't turn to look at me. She was too busy wiping the mud from her ankles. Her body wobbled from side to side as she struggled to walk through the thick swamp-like bush we were stuck in. She took wide steps away from the car, lifting her feet off the ground like they were made of lead. She almost fell over. I honked repeatedly until she finally turned around, giving me a wicked stare. She winked at me and put her index finger against her full lips, gesturing for me to be quite. Then, she turned and continued to walk away. I watched the back of her head, following the billow of her full reddish brown hair until I couldn't see her anymore. She was gone.

I pulled at the door handles, trying to free myself but it was no use. If I wanted out of this truck, I was going to have to break the window. That fucking bitch! I must have been crazy to trust her. This must have been the perfect set up for her. Playing off my sorrow and vulnerability by luring into me a deserted area, making me the perfect target for whoever was going to pop out the bushes and attack me. Brock? Brip? Shit, it could be anybody. Whoever killed Bobby was ready to kill me.

I jumped in the driver's seat and anchored my back against the driver's side door. Then, I started to kick at the window, hoping it would shatter easily on to the passenger's seat leaving a nice neat hole for me to climb out. But, it didn't. The shit looked easier in the movies. I kicked again, even harder than I did the first time, but the glass wouldn't break. What the fuck? Just when I was about to kick again, I heard the muffling sounds of an engine pulling up behind me. My heart stopped.

I was too afraid to look and see who it was so I cowered away, jumping into the back seat and ducking down immediately. I knew I couldn't hide but it comforted me to try. This was it for me. I was dead. Was it all worth it? I really didn't know. I loved Bobby but was he worth my life? He promised he wouldn't let any harm come to me and I believed him. I heard a car door slam shut.

My heart raced. I started to hyperventilate. Where was Bobby now? I was all alone and too weak to even put up a fight. Whoever was outside waiting to kill me was going to have an easy target because I give up. They pulled at the door handle until it finally swung open. I felt an icy wind swoosh in, slapping me on the face. I shivered for more than one reason. I kept my face buried into the back seat. My knees were on the floor. I closed my eyes tightly, like I was trying to wake up from a horrible dream but I couldn't wake up. This was real.

My breathing got heavier and I felt like was about to pass out but my presumed assailant called my name. "Lera," he said. The voice was deep and flooded with concern and I knew just who it belonged too. It was Bobby. Without giving it a second thought, I darted my head up and spun around only to be face to face with the man I never thought I'd see again.

"Bobby," I said through a gasp. I stared back at him like he wasn't real. Maybe I passed out and was dreaming.

"It's me, baby," he assured me and leaned over reaching his arm towards the back seat, pulling up the lock. He swung open the door and I leaped into his arms. "It's okay, Lera." I squeezed him so tight, I got exhausted. I didn't realize I was sobbing so hard until I started to choke on my own tears. "Baby, calm down. You gone make yourself sick," He held me close. I couldn't calm down.

Bobby pulled me away from him but I fell back onto his chest. My knees were so weak I couldn't stand up. "I'm so sorry, Lera. I'm so sorry." Bobby said remorsefully. "I didn't mean for none of this shit to happen this way." His apology brought me back to life and suddenly I got angry. I found the strength to stand up on my own and looked Bobby directly in the eyes before I punched him so hard in the jaw that my knuckles cracked. He didn't seem stunned. He grabbed his face and waited for me to hit him again and I did. He knew he deserved every bit of what I was giving him.

"How could you put me in this situation? I could have been killed! You don't care! Do you know what I've been through in the last 24 hours! They said you were dead!" I punched against his chest and he didn't try to stop me. "I thought you were dead." I punched and kicked at him until I got exhausted and was about to fall to the ground but Bobby caught me.

He kissed the top of my head, then my forehead and then my cheek. Little by little, his kisses where calming me down. He continued to hold me until my heavy sobs mellowed out into faint whimpers, all the while whispering I'm sorry in my ear and I started to believe him. When the crying stopped and my mind was clear of all the turmoil, I looked at him like I was seeing him for the first time and hugged him again. Then, we kissed with the same passion we did the day we said, *I do.*

Bobby withdrew from the kiss first. "We got to go," he said quickly, looking over his shoulder, casing his surroundings.

"What about Dalla?"

"I'll see her again. She wants my brother back and I'm going to help her get him."

"I don't trust her."

"Neither do I," he gave me a serious look. "Let's go." He put his hand on my shoulder and led me to a raggedy pick-up truck much like the one I just got out of. It definitely wasn't Bobby's style.

"Wait," I pulled away from him. "I need to know what the hell is going on. Dalla told me a lot of shit and…"

Bobby cut me off. He gently placed the tips of his fingers over my mouth. "Lera, I promise, I'm going to tell you everything but not right now. Not here. There ain't going to be no more secrets between us. I promise."

"Were we going? Are you dropping me off somewhere and leaving me again because…"

"No," he cut me off again. "You're staying with me this time. I need you, Lera. You're the only person I trust," he kissed my forehead. "I need your help," he confessed.

"You promise, Bobby?" I pleaded. I couldn't take being dumped off somewhere again.

Bobby gave me a serious look that softened after a moment. He kissed me softly on my lips and responded, "I mean what I say."

To be continued in *Confessions of a Badd Wife.*

Discussion Questions

1. What do you think about Lera's induction into the Badd family?
2. Do you think that Bobby trust, Lera?
3. Do you believe that Bobby had something to do with his father's death?
4. Which Badd wife do you identify with the most and why?
5. Do you think the B necklace is a form of power or control?
6. Would you visit the Badd ranch?
7. If you had to spend a night at the Badd ranch, where would you stay: Brock's dungeon, the breeding house, or Billy and Dalla's vacant mansion?
8. Considering the terms of their marriage, do you think Taffy reacted too harsh once she found out the news about Brip and Lilly?
9. What do you think about the affair between Taffy and Malcolm?
10. Whose baby do you think Taffy is carrying? Brip or Malcom?
11. Which Badd brother do you trust the least: Bobby, Brock, Brip or Billy?
12. Do you feel that Brock and Mona are good leaders of the Badd family?
13. Do you think the Mona is over the top for the breeding house or just devoted to the cause?
14. Do you feel that Brock is capable of killing, Bobby?
15. Do you think Mona lost respect for Brock once she learned the secret about his mother's death?
16. What do you think about Billy and Dalla? Are they a danger to the Badd family or endanger?
17. Why do you think Papa Badd required the Badd brothers to get married before they could get their inheritance?
18. Who is your favorite Badd couple and why?
19. If you could be any Badd wife, who would it be and why?
20. Who do you feel is the most misunderstood Badd wife?
21. What did you think when Lera woke up in the truck with, Dalla?

22. Were you shocked to learn the truth about, Bobby?
23. Would you trust Dalla if you were, Lera?
24. Are you excited about Confessions of a Badd wife?

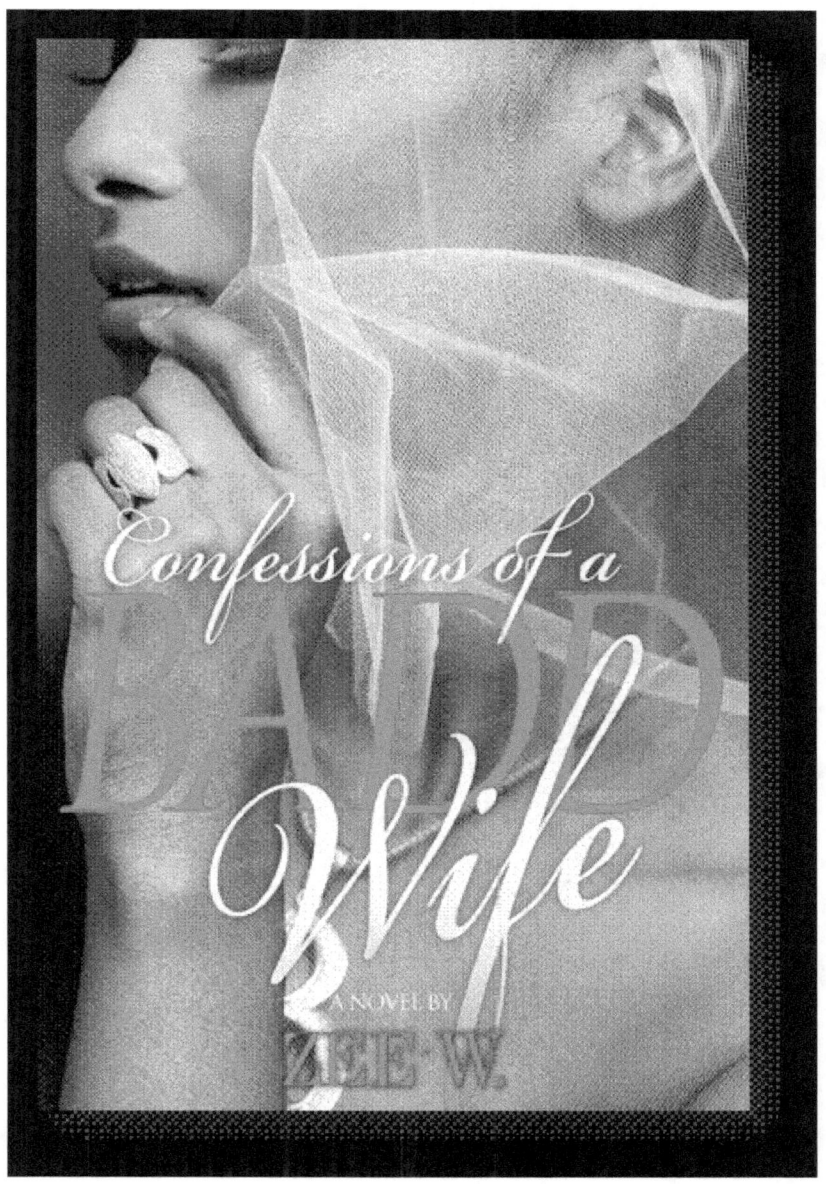

Prologue

Dalla Badd

Badd blood has finally been spilled.

"*Kneel down,*" Ace says to Taffy calmly.

Ace has Taffy sitting on both knees at the edge of his pool. Just before he brought her out, he had one of his men fearfully lead two of his gators into the water. Ace considers the gators to be pets but really, they're killers and he planned on feeding them Taffy tonight. They're swarming in the water in circles; they're anxious and hungry.

Blood is everywhere. It's streaming, pouring and dripping everywhere a body lies. All I can do now is watch it pour from the three bodies that once contained it. I watch the blood change forms. It can go from thin to thick in a matter of seconds. When it's fresh, it's a beautiful bright red but that changes after a while. Then, there's nothing beautiful about it. Especially when it's being coughed up in large clumps or flowing from places you didn't know can bleed. It's no neat mess like the movies either. This is a grotesque sight and I have front row seats to witness all the horror. Ace wanted a blood bath and he got it. It looks like he is finally winning his war against the Badds and he has me to thank for it.

Ace told me he was going to kill me. At first I didn't believe him. I even laughed at the threat. I didn't think he could; it wasn't supposed to be possible. After all, I was a Badd and untouchable to everyone, including him. But, after years of plotting and planning, tonight he's finally going to get what he's been waiting for and then some. When I hear a baby let out a gut wrenching scream sounding as if someone pinched him or he just woke from a horrible nightmare, I know he's going to die too. Ace is sick enough to kill a baby. I hear it scream and I want to run to him but I can't. I want to save them all but I can't. What have I done? Lord, what have I done?

I didn't expect it to end this way. When I met with Bobby a few months ago, I was desperate and running out of time. I spent the last year planting moles at the Ranch, spying as much as I could but it was all worthless until Bobby showed up one day with Lera. It was my first break through since I fled the Ranch. Lera was my link to Bobby. And Bobby was my way out of this mess; At least I thought he was.

Bobby was a hard nut to crack. He didn't want to believe me when I told him the truth about how his mother died, but I had the proof to back me up; the real autopsy report revealing that his mother's death wasn't a suicide but a murder. So he had to believe me. Brock, the oldest Badd brother, killed their mother to protect the secret that's keeping him in control of the Badd Ranch. Being a Badd and running the Ranch is Brock's entire existence. He'd do anything to protect his position, including kill his own. If the truth got out, he stood to lose everything.

The secret is that Brock isn't a real Badd but the product of an affair from their only rivals; the Lucky Family now ran by Ace Lucky. When his mother confessed the truth to him, he smothered her to death thinking that the secret would die with her, but he was wrong.

Ace is petting Taffy on top of her head like she's a dog. It's almost as if he has compassion for her trembling body but he doesn't. Taffy doesn't try to fight anymore. She just does what he says. I warned her about trying to resist Ace but at first, she didn't listen. That's why her left eye is swollen shut and she has thick red welts around her cheeks. Taffy endured days of savage beatings and assaults by Ace. But now, she finally believes that he really is going to kill her. She didn't know that Ace was as sadistic as he is. She didn't know that in his house, her Badd necklace wouldn't protect her. It was the only place in this city it wasn't welcome. Taffy has been a Badd so long that she really did believe that she was invincible. Everybody did but tonight Ace Lucky is going to prove them all wrong.

Ace motions with his hand and one of his men throws him a thick rope and he kneels down on one knee behind Taffy and starts to tie her hands behind her back. Taffy begins to sob. "Don't cry," Ace says softly to her. "You're about to be a part of history." He kisses her on the cheek and ties another knot in the rope; Taffy squinches.

My plan for Bobby was to help me free Billy. Thanks to my informants, I knew exactly where he was. In Brocks dungeon at the Ranch and the last I heard, he was still alive. I told Bobby the truth about his mother to get him on my side. I told him that Billy would be next if he didn't do something. I really caught his attention then. Brock had Bobby and the others thinking that me and Billy stole from the family safe and fled but that wasn't true.

The night Billy and I supposedly stole from the family safe and fled, I planted a bug in Brock's ear and it's still driving him mad to this day. I took Brock's dirt and used it against him. I told him that Billy killed their father to vindicate his mother's death. Brock was so focused on finding Billy that he left me right where I stood. It's how I got away; just as I planned. As strange as it sounds, I lied to protect us both. At the time, I figured Billy was safer with Brock than he was with Ace who had a bounty on his head. If Ace got to him first, he would've killed him right away but Brock needed him alive. At least long enough to find me.

Brock's not like Ace. He's no murderer but he is a killer. He killed his own mother, but considered her a causality of war. I knew he wouldn't be easy for him to kill Billy so fast. He had to be sure that I wasn't lying first and that meant he was going to take a lot of time investigating and contemplating, just as he's been doing. I spent the entire year sending Brock on dummy missions just to delay Billy's death. He's been searching for the bootleg doctor that did the autopsy report and the one forged the fake one. I've really kept myself busy sending Brock one fake lead after another. Including fake leads of my whereabouts.

Brock wants me dead more than he does Billy. I know too much and during his investigations, I'm sure he linked me to a lot of other shit that made him even more nervous. But, without Billy, Brock knew he would never find me. That's one reason Billy is still alive. Once Brock found me, he planned on killing us both and then his secret would be dead forever. Or at least that's what he thought.

I knew Bobby would do anything to get Billy back. He loved his brother. He even loved Brock but he had to do what was right. Bobby had one hell of a conscience. I know that because I played off every bit of it to get to where I was going. That's when I came up with the plan for him to fake his death. I figured he could move around better presumed dead than alive. I was surprised when he agreed with me. He thought it was a great idea and it was.

On all the days to do it, he chose his wedding day. It was perfect timing. If there was anything real about Bobby it was his love for Lera. No one would've expected him to do anything fishy on the day he was to say I do to Lera and receive his inheritance check; we pulled it off but now everything has back fired.

Ace pulls a red bandana out of his jacket pocket and places it over Taffy's eyes to blindfold her. Before Ace covers her eyes, Taffy gives me a horrified look but there's nothing I can do. Out of everybody, I feel like I owe her the most but I'm helpless. Taffy trusted me once. Even loved me but that's all over now. Taffy bites down hard on her bottom lip and takes a brave deep breath and sucks up her last tear. The girl is tough. Ace is so amused by her bravery, he chuckles. Then he gets mad. He wants her to plead for her life. He wants her to beg him but Taffy isn't going to give him the pleasure.

Ace yanks her up to her feet and shakes her a bit. He whispers something in her ear that causes Taffy to shudder then screams, "lights, camera….action," sporting an evil smirk. Within in a matter of minutes, I hear a loud thump and bright light's beam out in every direction from the ceiling. Then, out walks three men with cameras. Ace plans on broadcasting Taffy's death live so that everybody connected to the Badd's can see. He wants to ruin their reputation and take most of their clients in the process. If the tape of Taffy's death gets out, The Badds will be considered weak and their reputation ruined. It looks like the set of a movie but unfortunately, it's all real. I hear the baby crying again and it gets even realer. I have to do something but I'm helpless. I'm all plotted out; there's nothing left in me.

My initial plot was just to free Billy but that evolved over time. Once Billy was free, I didn't care what happened to the rest of them. I was going to reunite my family and flee. But all of that has changed. I'm too involved now. It would have all worked out if Bobby would have just trusted me a little more. He started to ask too many damn questions. Questions I didn't preplan answers for. At that point I'd lied so much, I didn't know fact from fiction. I evaded his questions the best I could but they just kept coming. He integrated me about his father's death, his mother's death, who I really was and how I knew so much about his family? I told him the same stories over and over again but that wasn't enough for him. Bobby was trying to find loop holes. He was too suspicious and he had good reason to be. It was obvious what was going on though; somebody was talking in his ear and turning him against me by telling him things I didn't need him to know and in turn, fucking up my plan. I needed Bobby just as much as he needed me but he didn't trust me the way I trusted him. That complicated things and in the end, led to the disaster I'm witnessing now.

What can I do to stop this or at least celay time before the others get here? If they come at all. Ace is pushing Taffy closer and closer to the edge of the pool. The gators are getting anxious, gliding around the pool, lurking at Taffy with their heads just above water. They can smell the fear on her. I hear Ace ask Taffy if she's ready to die. He has his hand placed firm on her shoulders like he's ready to shove her in the pool at any moment. Taffy responds to him. She screams, "fuck you," not what Ace was expecting to here. He's stunned by her reaction and offended. Ace hates being disrespected, especially by women.

At this point, I know it's over. When Ace placed his boot on her back to push her in the pool with the gators, I close my eyes and pray. There's nothing else I can do.

Author Zee. W
authorzee.w@gmail.com

www.ingramcontent.com/pod-product-compliance
Lightning Source LLC
Chambersburg PA
CBHW070224260626
47160CB00002B/678